The Apartment:
The Complete Affair

Amanda Black

full fathom five

(digital)

Full Fathom Five digital is an imprint of Full Fathom Five, LLC

For information visit Full Fathom Five Digital, a division of Full Fathom Five, LLC at www.fullfathomfive.com
Cover design by Lisa Waldo

ISBN 978-1-63370-079-6

First edition

The author published an earlier, not-for-prift, serialized version of this story online.

Table of Contents

The Apartment

Book One

For Mom
Who wanted this for me even more than I did
and who I will miss every single day

1

"No, Dad, I really don't feel like having deer steaks again tonight. Why don't you just throw them in the freezer? I'll cook them this weekend."

The pretty brunette rolled her eyes, tired of having the same conversation at least once a week. Her father hunted anything for which he could get a license, which meant that their deep freezer was stocked to overflowing with every form of wild game imaginable.

She tapped her pen impatiently on her desk, glancing furtively around her workstation as she listened to the voice on the other end of the phone. She hated drawing attention to herself, and getting caught arguing about dinner with her father while at work always embarrassed her. Just then a loud beep sounded, and she was happy to see that the front desk was paging her.

"Hold on a sec, Dad—other line." She left him rambling on about the shelf life of venison and quickly switched lines, hoping for an excuse to get off the phone. "Yes?"

"You have a chart up, Lily," a female voice replied in a short, clipped tone.

"Thanks, Kim. I'll be right there."

"Don't be too long. You know how much Dr. Wilde hates for this family to wait." A loud click signaled that Kim, the consistently rude receptionist, had already hung up, leaving Lily frowning down at the phone. *That's why I said I'd be right there.*

Remembering that her father was still on hold, she sighed loudly before pressing the flashing button. "Listen, Dad, I need to go. I've got a patient. I'm going to the gym after work, so I'll figure out something else to make when I get home. I should be there no later than six." She set the receiver back in its cradle before he could interrupt her again. Lily loved her father very much, but there were times when he worked her last nerve.

She made her way quickly from the nurses' station to the front office, wondering who'd gotten Kim's panties in a twist. There were only a few families in town that Dr. Wilde ever cared about having to wait, so Lily could never resist trying to guess who it might be this time. Was it the judge's wife? The mayor's sister?

She sincerely hoped not. Every time the mayor's sister was there she had to listen to a whole new round of excuses for why she needed another STD test and free samples of Plan B. Normally Lily would find that responsible, but she knew that it wouldn't be as necessary if the mayor's sister didn't also continually refuse her offers of free condoms.

When she reached the different racks where the charts were stacked in order of doctor and appointment time, Lily saw the bright red sticker on the corner of the chart—the unmistakable code in the office for VIP. Needing two hands to lift the thick chart, Lily flipped it open to reveal whose ass she was supposed to start kissing: *Maggie Foster.*

Much better than the mayor's sister!

Maggie Foster was something of a local celebrity, even if the trashy romance paperbacks she wrote made the elderly people in town shake their heads in disapproval. She hadn't quite become a household name yet, but she had already sold enough books to make a living. Lily had bought all four of them as soon as they'd hit the bookstore and devoured them immediately upon arriving home. The girl wrote *excellent* smut.

However, that's not what put that little red sticker on her chart.

Maggie had achieved red sticker status more than twelve years earlier, on the day she married Richard Foster's son. Richard Foster had the largest family practice in all of Mercer County, and since she was always on the lookout for more referrals, Dr. Natalie Wilde never missed an opportunity to brown nose.

Lily propped open the door to the waiting room with her hip, searching until her eyes landed on a strikingly beautiful raven-haired woman who was talking quietly with her head bent toward someone seated next to her.

"Maggie?" The woman in question stopped and looked up, smiling brightly. She stood eagerly, motioning for the other woman beside her to follow.

"That was fast!" she exclaimed once the door closed behind them. "How have you been, Lily?"

"Oh, you know…same old, same old." It never failed to amaze her that someone as well-known as Maggie Foster actually remembered her name. Since talking about herself always made her feel awkward, Lily quickly deflected the attention back to the patient. "C'mon, let's get you weighed."

"Ugh, do we have to?" Maggie pretended to pout as she kicked off her shoes and shrugged out of her jacket, then hesitated momentarily before pulling off her sweater and standing on the large scale. As Lily watched the digital readout and noted the result in Maggie's chart, the quiet woman who had been all but forgotten behind them finally spoke up.

"Jeez, Maggie, why don't you take off *all* your clothes? I'm sure you could deduct at least a pound or two for those socks." Her snarky comment was followed by a playful giggle.

"Hey, shut it! I need all the help I can get right now." She turned back to Lily and made a grave face. "Okay, what's the damage?"

Easily adopting Maggie's dry sense of humor, Lily frowned. "Two pounds since last month's visit. If you keep this up we'll need to get a bigger scale."

"I know." Maggie tried to hold her dour expression, but she couldn't keep the radiant smile from breaking out across her face. "Isn't it glorious?"

Lily smiled back, ushering the two women into an exam room. While she checked Maggie's temperature with a digital thermometer in her ear, the other woman sitting off to the side cleared her throat loudly.

"I'm sorry, Lily," Maggie said, finally taking the hint. "This is Emma, my husband's sister. She was kind enough to keep me company today since Eric is out of town until tomorrow."

"I thought football season was over, like…two weeks ago?" While Lily was uncomfortable talking about herself, she was actually quite good at getting others to open up. Besides, she knew that Maggie loved to talk, especially about her husband.

"It was, but the team needs to stay in shape during the off-season, not to mention the other clients he takes on during the rest of the year. He's stuck out in California right now looking at a torn rotator cuff."

Eric Foster was a physical therapist for the Chicago Bears. After a knee injury permanently benched him before his freshman year of college was over, he combined his love of sports and a familial inclination for medicine to find the best of both worlds. He and Maggie were college sweethearts, and they got married about thirty seconds after graduation. After moving around the country for a few years, he was thrilled when he finally landed the position he'd wanted more than anything, always hoping to stay close to his hometown. They lived in Chicago year-round now, but happily made the three-hour drive home to Aledo as often as possible.

As she checked Maggie's blood pressure, Lily turned her attention to the newcomer with the sandy-blond pixie cut. She was pretty and polished, with expensive highlights in her hair and designer clothes that Lily couldn't have afforded with an entire paycheck, but something about the warmth of her smile made Lily feel at ease. She decided to return the favor and finally include her in the conversation.

"So, Emma…I don't remember seeing you in here before. You aren't a patient of Dr. Wilde's? I thought all of the Foster women came here." The town of Aledo, Illinois, was small, and Lily worked at the largest private OB/GYN around. They had also recently added a young gynecologist to the staff, which had nearly doubled their clientele.

It didn't hurt that Dr. Jason Adams—or Jason, as he preferred to be called—was extremely easy on the eyes. The rate of lonely single women scheduling pelvic exams had skyrocketed over the last few months.

"No," Emma replied. "Just my mom and Maggie here. I don't get back to town as often as she does, so I have a doctor in Chicago."

"Emma's husband, Brandon, owns his own construction company in the city and Emma is a freelance interior designer," Maggie explained. "Really, Emma, you only go for your annual exam. There's no reason you can't make it here once a year." Maggie looked back to Lily. "I've been trying to get her to switch for months. Dr. Wilde is worth the trip."

"Well, I'm sure she'd love to hear that," Lily said with a smile and a quick nod. She sat down at the small table and made a few more notes in Maggie's chart. "All right, how have you been feeling?"

"Great!" Maggie answered with a beaming smile. "Really great, actually. Better than I thought I'd be."

"No more morning sickness?"

"No, not for weeks now." Maggie shook her head as she replied, causing her long, silky tresses to fall in shiny, black waves around her shoulders. Lily couldn't help wondering what ungodly-expensive endangered animal placenta it took to keep her hair that lustrous.

"Are you having any trouble with your Lovenox injections?" Lily scribbled on the sheet as she spoke, never looking up from the paper.

"No, that's old hat now. There's still some bruising on my belly once in a while, but I'm getting the hang of it."

"How many weeks is it now?"

"Fourteen," Maggie replied. "I've never made it past ten before," she added in a small whisper. Lily looked up in time to see her wipe a small tear from the corner of her eye. "I'm scared. I've been holding my breath for so long now. I'm afraid to relax and make any plans."

Lily couldn't stop herself from leaning forward and covering Maggie's hand with her own. "I don't blame you for worrying, but fourteen weeks is a very good sign. And this is the first time we've tried the injections. They greatly increase the possibility of a full-term pregnancy for women with your condition."

"It's just so damn frustrating!" She was crying freely now. "It's so hard to keep from getting bitter whenever I see so many women having an easy time of it. Don't even get me started on that fucking show *Teen Mom!*" Lily handed her a tissue and she wiped her eyes. "I can't ever just be happy about it. Every time I conceive I have to wonder how long it will be before my body decides to starve it off."

Lily wrapped her arms around Maggie and hugged her tightly. "I'd tell you to just be positive, but I think if someone told me that, I'd slap them." Maggie laughed through another sob before pulling away and composing herself.

"Thank you. I hate hearing that, too." She wiped her eyes again. "I'm sorry, Lily. My damn hormones are all over the place lately. I cry at the drop of a hat."

"Hey, I'm around pregnant women all day. It's an occupational hazard."

"It doesn't help that we have the added stress of helping my mom plan a huge party," Emma piped up from behind them. "That's why I'm back home for a few days. It's my dad's sixtieth birthday and she wanted to throw him a massive celebration."

"Well, that sounds like fun," Lily said with a smile.

"That's what you'd think," Maggie jumped in, rolling her eyes. "It was supposed to be a nice, respectable dinner at the house. But Barbara kept adding more and more people to the guest list. It's getting absolutely ridiculous!"

"My mom just hates to leave anybody important out," Emma explained. "I can understand that, since my dad has so many colleagues through his practice, but what I don't understand is how delusional she's being about the sheer size of this thing. I begged her to book a hall and hire a caterer when I saw the final head count, but she's determined to do it all at home."

"With *our* help, of course," Maggie chuckled. "We've been up to our elbows in fruit tarts and finger sandwiches and decorating every surface imaginable since dawn."

"That sounds really hectic," Lily sympathized.

"I was actually eager to join Maggie today when she asked me to come with her. We both needed a few hours away from the madness that our house is becoming." Emma looked at Lily and smirked. "How pathetic is it when a trip to the gyno sounds like a vacation?"

"Hey! This is not just some run-of-the-mill Pap smear!" Maggie feigned offense. "This is a baby checkup!"

"Yes, dear."

They both broke out laughing before Emma turned back to Lily and explained. "I promised her I'd play Eric's stand-in today. That is totally how he would blow her off."

Walking toward the door, Lily smiled back at the two women. "All right, I'm all done here, so Dr. Wilde should be in to see you shortly."

"Take care, Lily," Maggie called after her as she left the room.

While she was putting the chart in the slot next to the door, she heard Emma's voice again. "Okay, you were right. She's amazing. Damn, now I guess I have to switch doctors."

"Pay up," she heard Maggie mumble. Lily smiled to herself as she walked back to the nurses' station, wondering what it might have been like to have a sister.

"Hey, Lily, what are you smiling about?" A familiar voice cut through her musings. She looked up to see the friendly face of Becky Daniels staring back at her.

"Oh, I was just thinking about how nice the Fosters are." She glanced up at the rack on the wall and saw that it was quickly filling with more patient charts. "Shit! Becky, would you do me a favor?"

"What do you need?"

"Could you please go find Dr. Wilde? I was just about to, but I really need to start these other patients before we get completely backed up."

"I'd love to, but Jason and Dr. Wilde are off together having another '*long lunch*.'" She actually made the air quotes as she said the words.

"What?" Lily gasped.

"You didn't know they were screwing?"

"Huh?" Lily asked distractedly. "Well no, I didn't, but that's not really surprising. She's always been the town cougar. I knew it wouldn't be long when I saw how much younger he was." Jason was still in his early thirties and looked even younger, while Natalie was a cosmetically enhanced forty-five. "No, what's completely pissing me off right now is that I have a red chart up and she's off somewhere polishing his knob!"

"Shit! Forget the charts. I'll start them. Go page her *right now*. If she gets here and sees that—"

"She's gonna have a massive shit fit," Lily finished.

"Exactly. Now go!" Just then the back door opened and a throaty laugh could be heard down the hall. Becky let out a breath. "Oh, thank God, that's her."

"Thank you again for lunch, Dr. Adams. It was very…enlightening."

Lily walked quickly toward the flirty, purring banter. She rounded the corner just in time to see an attractive platinum blonde lean in and brush something off the shoulder of a rugged man with bright blue eyes. For a moment she thought it looked like a leaf, but then decided that she didn't really have time to care.

Jason saw her coming toward them and wiped the smile off his face, all business once again. "Yes, well, don't mention it, Dr. Wilde. It's just my way of saying…uh, thank you…for helping me get settled in around here."

"Excuse me, Doctor?" Lily interrupted. The woman straightened up quickly and turned around. There was no confusion over who was being spoken to—unlike Jason, Natalie expected to be addressed by her title. According to her, she had worked hard her entire life and paid a fortune to earn that title. Lily didn't mind; she actually preferred the honesty. She would happily take Natalie's blatant pride over Jason's false modesty any day.

"Yes, Lily?" Natalie absentmindedly reached up and smoothed her hair, mentally getting back into gear for work. Lily ignored the small blades of grass that fell to the floor as she did so.

"I just wanted to make sure that you knew there was a red chart up in room four."

"Oh! How long?" She glanced down at her watch, which cost more than Lily made in a year.

"Less than five minutes."

Natalie wasted no time, shoving her coat and purse into Lily's hands. "Be a dear and stick those in my office, would you?"

"Sure thing." When Natalie passed her, Lily noticed a small, green leaf sticking out of the back of her hair. "Hold on," she warned. Knowing that Natalie would be mortified if any patients saw her so disheveled, Lily bit the bullet and plucked the offending leaf from her hair.

Natalie blushed but recovered quickly. "Thanks. We had lunch at the new greenhouse in the park. I must've brushed against a branch." And with that she was gone, off to impress another red sticker.

"Hey, what are you doing tonight?" Becky asked when Lily finally returned to her desk.

"Gym, then home."

"Lily, that's what you do almost every night! You never go out. Why don't you come out with Jared and me later? We're going to grab a few drinks."

"I can't. It's a weeknight. I really need to get home and make dinner. Maybe some other time, though."

But they both knew that there would never be another time. Becky had been asking her for years to hang out, and Lily always had some reason not to.

2

A few hours later, Lily was driving downtown in her massive old car toward the gym. As she watched the now-familiar landmarks go by, she let her mind wander back to Becky's invitation.

It wasn't that Lily didn't like her—Becky was the sweetest person she'd met since she'd moved to town three years ago. However, almost a straight year of having no time to herself while nursing her father, George, back to health after a heart attack combined with being a naturally shy person to begin with had left Lily almost completely antisocial.

The heart attack itself hadn't been so bad. The worst part was that her father had been driving down Main Street at the time and had lost control of his car, swerving into the stupid town clock that stood right in the middle of the intersection. The impact had totaled his Chevy and shattered his hip, resulting in major surgery and months of bed rest.

The funny thing about declining Becky's invitation was that Lily was actually desperate for something different in her life, a change of pace. She wanted to get out and live for once. Her father had eventually healed up and, with the help of a cane, returned to his job as the high school guidance counselor. The problem was that he was so happy to have someone at home helping him with his day-to-day activities that he tended to play up how helpless he was, knowing Lily was a sucker for helping people. It had worked for a while, but she was beginning to get annoyed with him. George got everything he wanted, while Lily disappeared deeper inside herself.

As she pulled into a parking space, she thought about the fact that even though this time of day was precious to her, she didn't really care about going to the gym every day. She wasn't some vapid hardbody who lived to feel the burn, but it provided her with a few short hours of alone time and allowed her to work out her frustrations physically. Actually, there was nothing she loved more than popping in her earbuds and losing herself in the music on her iPod, but whenever she tried to do that at home George would inevitably hunt her down and need her to do something.

Grabbing her bag from the seat next to her, Lily locked the doors and made her way toward the gym. The Aledo Fitness Center was in the middle of a long strip of businesses. To the left of the gym was an accountant's office, its employees already working late to get ready for tax season, and to the right was a place that Lily always liked to walk by: Knight's Dance Studio.

The first time she'd seen it she had laughed, wondering how on earth an old-fashioned dance studio stayed in business in such a small town. Even if everyone who lived in Aledo decided to learn the foxtrot, Lily figured that they would run out of customers within a year. But, somehow, it seemed to be thriving.

From what Lily had heard from her father, Mrs. Knight used to work at the high school office a long time ago, but after she retired, she spent a year remodeling the old dance studio that hadn't been in business since the early 80s. The rumors were that she had been quite the dancer back in her youth, and had cried when she heard about it closing. Now she spent her afternoons teaching little girls how to tap dance and elderly couples how to mambo. She was in heaven.

Passing the storefront, Lily peeked in the window like she did every day, smiling as she watched the current class of seventy-somethings shuffle along. Right before she reached the end of the building, she saw something that made her stop in her tracks. There, smack dab in the middle of the window, was a sign that hadn't been there yesterday.

APARTMENT FOR RENT
SEE INSIDE

She blinked a few times, wondering why she couldn't move her feet. After a full thirty seconds Lily finally forced herself to keep walking, right through the gym door and straight into the locker room.

She changed out of her scrubs quickly, throwing on her capri-length black sport pants and one of her favorite concert tees, a dark blue shirt that said *TOO MANY DICKS ON THE DANCE FLOOR* across the front repeatedly in rainbow letters. Making her way across the cardio room, Lily signed for an open treadmill and popped in her earbuds, scrolling through her playlists until she found the one labeled *Workout Songs*. She adjusted the settings on the treadmill for her target heart rate and incline, and within seconds she was humming along with the music as she ran.

Sadly, the first song wasn't even over before the image of the sign in the window flashed in her mind. Lily shook her head to clear her thoughts and hit the skip button on her iPod, hoping that another tune might distract her more.

She smiled widely and started running faster when the beats of an old hip-hop song started playing, thinking that she had finally managed to focus. She was wrong. By the second verse she was wondering what the rent might be for an apartment downtown and how fast it would go. Decent apartments were hard to come by in a town so small—people kept them until death and then willed them to their family. At least, that's how it felt to Lily. She'd wanted to get the hell out of her father's house for a long time, but she could never find anywhere decent that she could afford.

I wonder if they allow animals, she thought to herself. *Dammit! What's wrong with me? Why can't I concentrate?*

Lily turned off the treadmill, knowing with absolute certainty that if both ODB and Rob Base couldn't get her in the mood to exercise, then nothing would.

She stomped back to the locker room and grabbed her bag, tossing the iPod in before zipping it closed and heading outside to her car. She rarely changed again before going home, and she definitely didn't see the point of it today since she hadn't even broken a sweat. However, she did see the point of her jacket as soon as she stepped outside and was reminded that it was late January.

She opened the passenger door and set her bag on the seat, fishing her jacket out and throwing it on. When she glanced back over her shoulder as she slid her arm into the sleeve, her eyes caught the sign once again.

Deciding that there was no harm in asking about it, Lily slammed the door shut and went inside the dance studio before she lost her nerve. The office just inside the front door was empty, so she walked down the hall until she heard what sounded like Latin music combined with a French accordion. She followed the beat farther down the hall until she found a door that was propped open with a large chalkboard on the floor that read *BALLROOM DANCE TONIGHT, 5 TO 7.*

She stuck her head in the door and peeked around the corner, surprised to find that the elderly dance troupe she'd seen earlier had been replaced by younger couples ranging from their late thirties to their early sixties. They were paired up and dancing in tight formations, arms raised high as the ladies twisted and slithered against the men. Lily was amazed to find it rather erotic. The couples were arranged around the room in a large circle, and standing in the middle was a statuesque woman with unnaturally red hair piled high on her head. She was wielding a large, elegant walking stick that she held with both hands, tapping it on the floor in time with the beat of the music and nodding her head as each couple passed.

"Good…good…watch your frame…" She was smiling until one of the women tripped over her own feet and stumbled. *CRACK!* The end of her stick came crashing down so loudly that it echoed over the music. "People! May I remind you that *you* were the ones who begged me to teach the tango this year? I wanted to stop at the samba. You've shown promise so far, but at the rate you are learning, this is going to take us weeks!" She frowned at each couple, completely ignoring the exotic music in the background as she sighed deeply and continued. "This dance highlights the man's ability to lead, as well as the woman's ability to follow. You've got to give yourself over to the rhythm and the moment. Ladies, you have to let your partners have their way with you on that floor. You have to surrender yourself to your emotions and stop letting your head get in the way. We are talking vertical sex here, people!"

The flustered instructor looked up just then, catching sight of Lily across the room. She held up one finger to her and addressed the couples again. "All right, I'll be back in a moment, class. Keep working at it." She stepped through the circle of dancers and made her way across the floor, first stopping at the stereo to repeat the song. "If this song ends before I'm back, you're going to start the whole thing over again." She turned to Lily. "Come!" she barked, sweeping through the door in a grand exit.

They walked into the hall together, far enough away from the door so they could hear each other. Lily was taken aback by how extremely tall and graceful the woman seemed, as well as how much older she appeared close up. The thick makeup she had slathered on did nothing to hide the deep wrinkles and laugh lines on her face. Rather than being repulsed, Lily was in awe of how much living this woman must have done.

"Sorry about that, dear." She smiled warmly down at her and held out her hand. Lily shook it timidly. "I'm Mrs. Knight. Were you interested in signing up for a class?"

"Uh…no. Actually, I was wondering about the sign in your window. The apartment?"

"Oh! Yes, certainly."

"If it's still available, I was hoping I might be able to schedule a time to look at it."

Mrs. Knight looked at her watch and thought for a moment. "Well, I'm going to be stuck here for a while. If you don't mind viewing it by yourself, I could give you the key and you could take a look at it right now."

"Oh, that would be great!" Lily couldn't keep the enthusiasm out of her voice.

"Well, come with me back to the office for a minute. I'll grab the key for you." They walked together down the hall, making pleasant small talk. Lily enjoyed the steady *click click click* of her walking stick as she tapped it out of habit.

Mrs. Knight motioned for Lily to follow her into the small office, sitting down at a desk against the wall. She opened the center drawer and started rifling through piles of loose papers while Lily let her eyes wander around the cluttered room, landing on the many stacks of CDs in the corner. She had music from all over the world, for every kind of dance you could imagine.

"Where in the—?" Mrs. Knight mumbled to herself. "It was here earlier. What on earth did I do with that key?" She looked back at

Lily as if she had the answer. "Wait a minute—that nice young man."

"Young man?"

"Yes, there was a lovely young man who stopped in to look at it earlier. I forgot I gave him the key. But that was hours ago! I've been so busy that I didn't realize he never brought it back down."

"Should you be concerned?" If Lily ended up taking the apartment she didn't want some psycho out there with a key to her place.

"Oh heavens, no! I'm sure that he just set it down up there and forgot all about it." She glanced down at her watch with a frown. "I really must get back. Why don't I show you the way and you can head up and take a look? If you see the key laying around up there, just be a dear and bring it back down with you. If it's not there, don't worry. I'll get the locks changed if I have to."

"Really, if it's too much trouble right now I can come back."

"Oh, don't be silly! You're here now." She stood to usher Lily into the hall. "You know, I really must get another spare key made. I misplaced my last one after the *incident*." She emphasized the last word dramatically as if Lily was supposed to know what she was talking about.

"Incident?" Lily asked, mainly because she could tell that Mrs. Knight wanted her to.

"Oh yes," she sighed. "I'm afraid the last tenant hadn't been seen for days and he wasn't answering his phone. When he didn't answer the door either, I finally had to use my spare to open it up and it must have gotten lost in all the excitement. Poor thing." She shook her head slowly and made a sign of the cross over her chest.

Lily turned instantly pale. "You mean he died up there?"

"Not quite." She reached out and patted her arm. "But Mr. Douglas had a terrible stroke. When I found him, he was face down on the floor. Nobody knows how long he was there. I tried to hold onto his place for him for as long as possible, but the doctors say he won't be coming home. He's in hospice care now." She looked very sad for a moment. "I used to work with him many years ago. He was a teacher at the school. It just breaks my heart to see someone so intelligent brought low like that. He can't even talk now."

Now it was Lily's turn to pat her on the arm. She couldn't fathom what it would be like to go from being a fully functioning human being one day to being trapped inside your own mind for the rest of your life. Sometimes the human mind terrified her. That was why she could never bring herself to work at a nursing home—the thought of being around so many patients with dementia made her want to cry.

"Well, come on. Let me show you where to go." Mrs. Knight led her all the way down the hallway, past the door to the dance studio, until they reached the rear exit. "Now, you can access the apartment from back here," she said, opening the large door. "There's a parking lot on the other side of the alley behind here that all the tenants along the strip use. Most of the stores have at least one apartment upstairs, but some of them are lived in by the owners." She pointed to another door next to them. "This door here leads upstairs. The apartment key will unlock it if you need it, but most tenants leave this one unlocked for visitors. Now, the room is just up at the top of the stairs. If you have any questions come and find me, okay?"

"Thank you so much, Mrs. Knight. I really appreciate it. I'm sorry to have disturbed your class."

"It's no problem, sweetie. I needed a break from those guys anyway, before I started smacking them with my stick!" They shared a final laugh before parting ways, each one going through a different door.

Lily walked up the dark stairway. At the top was a long, skinny hallway, and at the end of the hall was one lonely door on the left-hand side. Lily took a deep breath and stepped forward, bringing her hand to the knob.

The door pushed wide open as soon as she touched it. *What the hell? He couldn't even bother to shut it completely?*

She walked in slowly, looking from side to side in the empty room. It was dark and gloomy, but that could have been due to the fact that the sun had already begun to set. Lily reached over and flipped the light switch. Nothing. Mrs. Knight had failed to mention that the electricity had been cut off.

Deciding that she needed to make the most of the dwindling sunlight so she could see the room, she wandered around looking for windows. There was a small one above the sink in the kitchen that helped brighten things a bit when she opened the blinds.

Not bad, she thought. *Not good, but not bad.* There was a little bathroom with a shower and what looked to be one bedroom on the other side of the living room.

As she walked farther into the dark apartment, she instantly noticed how warm it was. Slipping her jacket off and dropping it to the floor, she stopped to flip the other light switch on the opposite wall by the bedroom as well, just to make sure. Still nothing. Frustrated, she fumbled her way through the darkness until she found the doorknob leading to what she hoped was the bedroom. Right as she started to turn the handle, it began to spin in her hand. Before she realized what was happening, the door was pulled open swiftly, causing her to stumble forward and land against a very solid chest.

She screamed and jumped backward.

Right on the other side of the door she had just fallen through was a man. He made no move toward her, nor did he even blink at her outburst; he simply stared at her.

"Who the hell are you?" Lily gasped as she stepped back a few more feet, praying that she wasn't about to become the first in a string of brutal rape/slayings to terrorize the Midwest. She was just about to yell at him again when she actually managed to get a good look at him.

He was leaning against the doorjamb, wearing a white dress shirt that was unbuttoned a few times at the collar and what looked like artificially distressed designer jeans. Lily knew there was no way jeans that clean could have so many holes in them. His hair, which was a rich, burnished gold, was sticking out in every direction as if he'd been shoving his hands in it repeatedly. His cheekbones and jawline were so chiseled that it almost hurt to look at them, and his thick growth of stubble only served to enhance their beauty.

Lily moved her eyes up slowly, hovering on the most luscious pair of full, pouty lips she had ever seen in her life. They looked soft and pink, and for some reason she couldn't help but wonder how they would feel against her own, how they might taste. Continuing upward, she took in his long, straight nose before finally landing on a sight that made her breath catch in her throat.

Piercing jade eyes stared back at her, surrounded by longer lashes than any man had the right to possess. They were swollen and red, and it was obvious that he had been crying. She had never felt like more of an intruder than she did in that moment, but she couldn't tear her eyes away.

He looked tragic, and broken, and heartbreakingly beautiful.

Lily suddenly remembered Mrs. Knight mentioning the "lovely young man" who had forgotten to return the key. If this was him, then that had been the understatement of the century.

"I'm sorry," she whispered after managing to find her voice. "I didn't know anyone was still up here. Mrs. Knight said she thought you had left." He said nothing, but continued to stare at her warily. Feeling the need to fill the awkward silence, Lily began rambling. "What do you think of the apartment?" She glanced around the empty room. "It's a bit of a dump, to be honest, but it has potential."

When he still didn't answer, she turned and walked back into the kitchen, hoping to give him a moment to collect himself. It wouldn't stop her mouth, though, which made no sense to her because she spent most of her time avoiding people as much as possible. "These cabinets aren't too bad," she called out, opening and closing doors. "There's not much counter space, though."

She went back into the living room and began critiquing the space, wondering to herself the entire time why she couldn't just shut the hell up. Deep down she knew that it was because she wanted to hear him speak to her. It *was* a little creepy that he wasn't saying anything, and she wanted him to break the tension. If she was being honest with herself, she also wanted to find out if his voice was as beautiful as the rest of him.

Spinning around slowly, she nearly jumped when she turned back to find that he was now standing in the kitchen doorway watching her, as if he'd been following her around like a lost puppy. "Any idea what she's charging for this place?" Lily whispered. "I sort of...forgot to ask." She blushed deeply, once again unable to look away from him. He simply stared back at her, and when he blinked again she saw a fresh set of tears slide down his cheeks.

Knowing that she had seen his tears, he spun around and went back into the kitchen. Worried that she'd somehow embarrassed him, she followed him into the small space. For some reason she was drawn to his open vulnerability. He seemed like a skittish, wounded animal that she felt compelled to help rather than fear.

Lily crossed the room and leaned against the countertop, nervously turning the faucet on and off in the guise of checking the water as she waited for him to speak. When he still didn't respond, she knew that she had to stop beating around the bush.

"Listen, I'm sure you'd love for me to get the hell out of here. Even

if you don't want the place, it's obvious that you need some privacy."
He grimaced in response to her words but maintained eye contact.
"Are you all right?" After what felt like minutes he shook his head
slowly. "It's just that…I would feel terrible if I left here and didn't at
least try to help."

That was Lily; always ready to lend a hand to someone in need.
She tried to smile, but it felt odd under his scrutiny. His gaze was
unsettling to her, but strangely she felt more exposed than afraid. His
eyes didn't look past her or through her; they saw deep inside her. The
feeling of being drawn to him returned even stronger.

After a long pause she took a deep breath and bit the bullet. "Is
there anything I can do for you?"

"Yes," he choked out. Although his voice sounded raw, as if he'd
been screaming, she wasn't surprised to hear the musical perfection
behind it.

"What can I do?"

He moved then, slowly walking toward her like a wildcat stalking
its prey. The closer he got to her, the more she could feel something
growing and tingling, as if an electric current was shooting between
their bodies. He didn't stop until he was right in front of her with
his arms on each side of the countertop, effectively caging her in. It
didn't escape her notice in that moment that he even smelled beautiful. Not once did it ever occur to her to feel scared or to move away;
his presence was so magnetic that she couldn't imagine breaking
the connection.

He looked deep into her eyes for almost a minute, allowing the
electricity to build between them to a breaking point.

"You can let me fuck you," he whispered.

3

Lily stared at the beautiful stranger in disbelief. He was only inches away from her face now and his words were still hanging in the air around them, thick and heavy with suggestion.

You can let me fuck you.

"That's not funny," she whispered. He was so close that her breath fluttered against his skin.

"Do you hear me laughing?" His voice sounded gruff now, as if it almost pained him to talk. He only broke eye contact with her long enough to glance down at her lips quickly. When he looked back up, it was just in time to see a brief flash of fear in her eyes. Immediately, his stance shifted. "Hey, I'm not going to hurt you. I just…just…" His face crumbled and he choked on another sob.

Any traces of fear went out of her mind the instant she saw his jade eyes swimming with tears again. Unable to stop herself, Lily reached out and wrapped her arms around his shoulders. She felt his warm hands touch her hips tentatively before sliding around to the small of her back, eventually crushing her to him.

He buried his face in her neck and began to weep.

"I'm sorry!" he cried. "I just wanted to feel…something—*anything*—again." Lily smoothed her hand over the back of his head in what was meant to be a comforting gesture, but she couldn't help sliding her fingers through his unruly hair and noticing how similar the texture was to silk. In response, his grip around her tightened.

"I've been numb," he breathed against the skin of her neck. "Numb for so fucking long that I don't remember what anything feels like anymore."

"Shh, it's okay. It's gonna be okay." Lily continued stroking his hair as he shook. She had absolutely no idea what to think about the man in her arms. She only knew that she couldn't let go.

As she held him, she could feel the electric current growing even stronger between their bodies. Everywhere they touched felt like it would start humming at any moment, and Lily couldn't help wondering in the back of her mind if her hair might start standing straight up. The man in her arms must have felt it, too, because after a few seconds he grew silent, as if he were also listening for the internal hum between their bodies. She felt his fingers grip her tighter before they eased up, sliding beneath the edge of her shirt.

When his fingertips touched the bare skin at the small of her back and began to make little circles, Lily had to stop herself from crying out in surprised pleasure. His touch was like fire—it left small trails of steam as it moved over her skin. Lily fully expected to find welts in the shape of tiny spiral patterns on her back when she looked at it later.

He slowly ran his nose up the column of her neck, inhaling her scent deeply before stopping with his lips pressed against her ear. "Please." It was barely a whisper.

Lily was very confused about what happened next.

She had turned to face him, intending only to politely refuse and say good-bye. Yet somehow her arms acted on their own accord, pulling his mouth roughly to hers.

She didn't recognize the loud moan in the room as her own.

His lips were strong, but soft to the touch, full of a hunger that surpassed anything she'd ever experienced. He tasted faintly of peppermint and coffee, as well as a deeper hint of spice that was all him.

When he finally opened his mouth to drink her in, Lily saw stars.

Everything unfolded rather quickly after that.

There was a frenzy of kissing, their tongues sliding together easily. His hands were everywhere at once, cupping her and squeezing her, sliding over mounds and dipping into valleys until her body was shaking and screaming for more.

Then the beautiful stranger shifted against her. She felt his hand slide inside her pants as he kissed her, groaning loudly into her mouth when he discovered that she was already swollen and wet. She was surprised herself, as her body rarely responded so quickly, but this man's frantic kisses and tangible need were driving her insane. When his fingers started to move in tiny, concentrated little circles against her, she knew that she would soon be done for. Her eager moans and quick responses must have excited him further because he suddenly grunted roughly and removed his hand, disorienting her for a moment until she realized what he was doing.

Without moving his lips from hers, he hooked his fingers into the waist of her workout pants, pulling both those and her panties down as far as they would go until gravity took over and they dropped to the floor. Lily barely had time to step one foot out of them before she was being lifted onto the kitchen counter..

He fumbled briefly with his button fly, quickly freeing himself and wrapping her legs higher around his waist while guiding himself to her hot center. Lily, completely lost in the sensations that were over-powering her, hadn't opened her eyes once since he had first kissed her, but when she felt him nudging at her entrance her eyes shot open.

Oh God, she thought to herself. *This is really happening!*

And then he slid himself home in one swift thrust.

They both gasped out loud and froze, locking eyes once again. His eyes held the question that his mouth was reluctant to ask. After she had a moment to adjust to his size and the shock of his invasion, Lily nodded quickly and shifted her hips, signaling for him to continue. A slow, wicked smile spread across his delicious lips, and he moved her legs so that they were hanging over his forearms, bracing his hands against the edge of the counter for added leverage. The new position bent her legs back toward her at a different angle, which caused her to feel him even deeper inside her.

Looking into her eyes, he slowly pulled his hips back, almost leaving her, before thrusting forward again so forcefully that her entire body rocked back. Lily's head hit the cabinet as she threw it back and cried out, never having felt anything that deep before. Panting loudly, she grabbed him by his hair again and shoved her hips forward, begging him for more. She had never acted like this before and wasn't sure what had come over her.

He latched onto her mouth again, kissing her so hard that she felt lightheaded. His sweet, hot tongue swirled and twisted against hers as he penetrated her, sliding easily into her welcoming heat. He worked her body like a man possessed: thrusting, grinding, and pounding. He broke their kiss with a loud groan and buried his face against her neck, sucking and biting at her in between breathy snarls and grunts.

Lily was on sensory overload. She could feel the stubble from his chin as it scratched her neck, the slickness of his tongue as it flicked at her skin, the flex of his muscles as he shifted his hips between her legs, the broad tip of his cock as it slid back and forth inside her—and over it all, there was his scent. It was potent and masculine and headier than any cologne she had ever smelled in her life.

Before long, his hips began bucking erratically. He continued pumping into her, sliding a hand between their bodies and expertly rubbing more tight circles around Lily's throbbing clitoris.

"Please," he moaned deeply. "So close…please…come for me." He ended his plea with another deep thrust inside her, causing a surprised Lily to explode around him.

"Holy fuck!" Lily screamed out her pleasure as her body convulsed around his aching shaft.

"Yes!" he gritted through his teeth. "That's it, my lovely…I can feel you gripping me." He kissed her again roughly before pulling back to watch her face as she found her release. Her eyes squeezed shut and she bit her lip, moaning and keening as he ground himself inside her even harder, riding out the waves of her intense orgasm until he followed closely behind with his own.

Rather than separating from her quickly, the breathless man picked Lily up and pulled her into his lap right there on the tile floor. He leaned against the wall and clutched her tightly, like a cherished teddy bear.

"Thank you," he whispered against the shell of her ear.

It was the last thing she heard before falling fast asleep.

When Lily opened her eyes the room had gone completely black.

She leaned forward, blinking to get her bearings, startled to find that a pair of muscled arms tightly held her. When she glanced down and saw that she was also draped across a pair of strong legs, the entire afternoon's events came flooding back to her, almost as quickly as the blood flooded to her cheeks.

With no watch and her phone downstairs in her gym bag, Lily had no idea what time it was. Panicked, she disentangled herself from the sleeping man and felt around for her pants. When she couldn't find her panties, a quick flashback of the sight of them dangling from her ankle and bouncing to the rhythm of his thrusts reminded her that she had never fully stepped out of them before things had gotten…heated.

Dressing quickly, Lily was overcome with an inexplicable need to flee the scene of the crime. She was growing more embarrassed by the second of the memories that were replaying in her mind, and if she didn't get out of there as soon as possible she knew that she would have a hell of a lot of questions to face when she got home—questions that she wouldn't have the answers to.

Tiptoeing to the front door, Lily had made it halfway across the living room when she heard his voice right behind her. "Thank you," he said again quietly.

"Uh, sure." She didn't turn around to look at him, choosing instead to stare at the door. In the back of her mind she wished for the power to turn invisible, hoping it might save her from dying of embarrassment in front of this complete stranger who had somehow managed to learn more about her body in a few minutes than anyone else had bothered to in almost thirty years—including herself.

She took a few more steps away from him, pausing only to find the doorknob. When she finally had it open and was about to step into the hallway, his haunting voice rang out one more time behind her.

"I'm taking the apartment." His hand smoothed over the back of her hair. The touch made her shiver. "Come back and see me—anytime."

Like hell! As soon as Lily finally stepped into the hallway, she began running. She ran down the stairs and out the building, cutting back through the alley to get to her car as fast as possible. As soon as she was inside, she turned the key in the ignition, backing up recklessly before screeching off into traffic. She didn't hear the many cars honking at her in anger as she pulled away, only the voice inside her head that had gotten stuck in a loop.

What have I done? What have I done? What have I done?

According to the clock on her radio, it wasn't even eight o'clock yet, which surprised the hell out of Lily since it felt like midnight. Remembering her phone, she reached over and grabbed it out of her bag, glancing at the display as she weaved through traffic.

Fourteen missed calls. *Shit!*

Just then another call came in, displaying an all-too-familiar number on the screen. Lily hit the SEND button and started talking before the voice on the other end of the phone even had a chance. "I know, I know. I'm sorry I'm so late. I got held up at the gym. I'll be home in just a little bit. I've got to grab something to eat." She hung up and tossed the phone on top of her bag, pulling into a parking spot in front of the first takeout place she saw.

She buried her head in her hands and tried to stop the flood of images that were replaying in her mind. It didn't work. The more she remembered, the more flushed she felt—with embarrassment, but also something more. She had never experienced anything like that in her entire life, and she was disgusted with herself for feeling anything but shame.

I didn't even get his name!

Thirty minutes later, Lily opened the front door to her father's house, her hands full with two large, white boxes. "I'm home," she called out.

"In here!" a voice answered, surrounded by the sounds of who-knew-what sports game in the background. Dropping her gym bag from her shoulder onto the small kitchen table as she walked by, she followed the voice into the living room.

"Sorry I'm so late getting home. I figured it would take too long to cook, so I brought us some pizzas."

Two men sat on the couch watching ESPN. Only one of them bothered to drag his attention away from the screen long enough to look at her.

"What gives, Lil?" he said, standing up to help her with the boxes. "I thought you wanted to eat around seven. I've been waiting here with George for hours."

She rolled her eyes and sighed at him. "Like you wouldn't have been here anyway, Scott."

"Well, true." He smiled brightly, taking the pizzas from her and walking back into the kitchen to set them on the counter.

Scott Walker lived on the far side of town near the fairgrounds in a ramshackle little house with his father, Sam, who had once been very close friends with Lily's father when they were younger. Scott tended to spend most nights either hanging out with Lily or his friends from the small garage where he worked. Many nights he would do both, hanging around long enough for Lily to feed him, then taking off to go drinking with his buddies.

"So what took you so long tonight, anyway? And why did you take so long to answer your phone?" He grabbed some paper plates from the cupboard, very familiar with the layout of the kitchen.

"Well…" Lily stalled, trying to think of what to say. "After I was done with my workout, I noticed a sign in the window at the dance studio."

"Ugh…you didn't sign us up for some dipshit swing dance class, did you?" Scott groaned from behind her at the counter, proceeding to dish out two slices of pizza each onto three plates.

"No, nothing like that. I saw a sign for an apartment that just became available for rent."

"Where, above that shitty old dance hall?"

"It's not shitty!" she said defensively. "I like it. It's sweet to watch all those couples learning something new together."

"Whatever. I think they look like idiots."

"Anyway," Lily sighed, trying to stay on topic. "I went up and had a quick look at it. I forgot my phone in the car or else I would have called to let you know I'd be late."

"What the hell do you want with an apartment? Especially over *that* dump?" He looked at her expectantly.

"Well, I didn't take it, anyway. It was pretty crappy. I just wanted to see what it was like."

"Hey, where the hell is your jacket?" he asked suddenly. "It's fucking cold outside."

"My jacket?" Lily looked down at her bare arms. She'd thrown her jacket on the ground as soon as she'd walked through the door of the apartment. How could she not have noticed she wasn't wearing it when she left?

Shit!

"Uh, I must have forgotten it when I was up there. I…lost track of time and when I realized how late it was I didn't even think to look for it." Quietly to herself, she added, "I suppose I'll just have to go back and get it tomorrow." Her thoughts flashed quickly to the dark room and it's even darker inhabitant.

"I guess I just don't understand why you would even want to look at that place, Lil. Morbid curiosity?"

"Well…I've been keeping an eye out for a while now. I thought it might be nice for us to find someplace new and get settled." Lily sighed again, finally meeting his gaze. "You know…before the wedding."

4

___

At the very same time, on the outskirts of town, a black Audi A6 with a rental sticker on the trunk pulled into the circle drive of an extremely expensive-looking house. The man behind the wheel turned off the engine and, rather than exit the car immediately as he would normally do, sat there in the dark quiet of the interior with nothing but his own thoughts for company.

He was startled when he realized that for the first time in days—perhaps years, if he was being honest with himself—he had stopped his sullen, self-absorbed moping. Instead, he was focused intently on the strange events from earlier that evening, wondering repeatedly if they had actually happened. Unable to stop himself, he sniffed his fingers for confirmation and groaned, wincing at the instant, painful erection her lingering scent caused.

He knew that he needed to go inside eventually and face *them*, the collection of strangers that called themselves his family, but he decided that a few more minutes of happy reflection were more than a bit deserved after the hellish week he'd had. He closed his eyes, thrilled at the notion of being able to see something—*anything*—other than the unpleasant memories that had been haunting him lately.

Now in their place were images of beautiful hazel eyes and full pink lips, and the memory of how she had tasted so fucking sweet. Sighing deeply, he replayed every whimper in his mind, every moan.

He still couldn't believe how she had appeared out of nowhere, like an angel sent to pull him back from the brink of insanity. She had looked just like that to him, with her lovely soft features and her sweet face full of concern. Nobody had given more than two shits about him for years, and here this precious thing gave up her fucking *body* just to make him feel better.

And better he felt. Better was a fucking understatement.

He actually felt alive again.

The moment that angelic creature put her arms around him, he'd felt as if someone had flipped a switch inside his brain. She had turned him on again, and in more ways than one. He had felt pure electric pleasure coursing through him when he touched her satin skin. It had been so long since he'd been able to enjoy simply touching someone.

It disturbed him how easily he had forgotten the concept of joy.

He knew there were emotions much more appropriate for his current situation, but he wasn't about to turn his nose up at the chance to feel good again, even if only for a short while. It was already fading away, but it gave him another feeling he hadn't felt in what seemed like forever: hope. Perhaps if he could feel something as wonderful as pleasure again, everything else wasn't as far out of reach as he'd first thought.

He let his mind wander, and it immediately snapped back to his brunette mystery. She appeared just as shocked as he was by the connection between them, but she clearly felt it, too. It hadn't only been him—he knew it just as surely as he knew that she had never even dreamed of doing anything like that before in her life. And she loved it. He knew by how fast she ran off that her mind might not believe it yet, but her body hadn't lied.

He fondled the old brass key in his pocket, remembering how amazing she felt when he was finally inside her, and how that had paled in comparison to her body squeezing him as she came. She had been so unbelievably tight. He could have spent hours inside that girl and probably would have if she hadn't left.

He could still see her running out the door as if her hair was on fire. He would have laughed about it if it hadn't hurt so much to watch her leave. When he was with her, he felt powerful and wanted, which was certainly a feeling he'd missed over the years.

The only thing clouding his fond memories was the knowledge that he would most likely never see her again. He severely regretted not taking the time to go down on her. With a tongue as sweet as hers and a scent that potent, he just knew that her pussy would taste like ambrosia—sweet, dripping ambrosia—and it was a fucking crime that he hadn't tasted her.

Sucking on his fingers, he tried to find a flavor to match the delicious scent that coated them. There was the faintest hint of something tangy and earthy, but not enough to know for sure. It was only enough to tease him, leaving him rock hard.

Just then a loud knock sounded at his window, causing him to jump in surprise. Turning quickly, he looked up in time to see a large man with light brown hair smiling down at him from outside the car. It was dark out, but it was still easy to see that his smile was enormous. The little bit of his face that wasn't shining with teeth displayed deep dimples and sparkling eyes.

Adjusting himself quickly, he got out of the car, not bothering to lock the door before facing the smiling man. "Jesus Christ, you scared the shit out of me!"

"Hey, sorry, Ethan. I thought you heard me calling you." Embarrassed, Ethan realized that a bomb could have dropped and he probably wouldn't have heard it—not while he was thinking of his lovely afternoon distraction. "Come here," the newcomer said, grabbing him tight in a huge bear hug. "I haven't seen you in fucking forever!"

"I thought you weren't going to get here 'til tomorrow," Ethan replied, grunting his discomfort into the taller man's chest, the familiar awkwardness already setting in.

"I caught the first flight out as soon as I could get away. The shuttle just dropped me off." He gestured to a pile of bags near the front steps of the house. "Jeez, you didn't hear that either?"

"Sorry…guess I'm a bit distracted right now."

"Eh, no big deal. Man, I can't believe how good it is to see you!" he said excitedly. "How the hell long has it been this time, anyway?"

"A while, I guess."

"A while?! Try *years*, asshole!" Although his brother's voice was playful, there was a glimmer of pain in his eyes. "Don't get me wrong, I'm thrilled you're here, Ethan. Just maybe pick up the phone once in a while, huh?"

"Yeah, okay," he replied uncomfortably, wanting to look anywhere but in his brother's eyes.

"So mom said something about you and Rachel breaking up?"

Ethan could feel his jaw ticking with tension as he tried to force himself to reply. "That's…putting it mildly."

"Anything you want to talk about?"

He had to fight the urge to scream this time. "*No.* Not…not right now. Sorry."

"Well, I hope you know that I'm here for you if you ever change your mind."

"Yes, thank you." It was the same generic answer he'd been giving to the same generic platitude that everyone in his family had been offering him for days now, including relatives he barely knew or hadn't seen in almost a decade. It didn't escape him that he'd chosen the worst possible time to return home if he'd had any hopes of laying low. However, Ethan also knew that his brother was different: he didn't believe in bullshit for bullshit's sake.

"I suppose we should go inside, huh? Mom's probably going batshit crazy over all the little details." He clapped Ethan on the back and walked with him to the front door, stopping only to pick up his luggage.

They entered the house together, walking into an immaculate foyer that was larger than most homes in Aledo.

"Mom?" the larger man called out.

"In here!" A lot of noise could be heard from the direction of the kitchen. They walked through the doorway to find a beautiful middle-aged woman up to her elbows in flour. When she looked up at them, a very familiar, very large smile broke out on her face.

"Eric! You made it in early!" Barbara Foster, wife of Dr. Richard Foster, ran around the counter and held out her arms, trying to keep the messiest parts of her away from his shirt.

"Yeah, I came as fast as I could get away." Eric leaned down and hugged her around the torso, still managing to get flour on the front of him and not caring in the slightest. "Look who I found lurking around outside," he added, motioning behind him with a nod of his head.

"Oh, Ethan, there you are! I haven't seen you all day. Where did you run off to this morning after breakfast?"

The man with the messy golden hair shrugged dismissively. "I just needed to get away for a while."

She looked him over for a moment with a mother's knowing eye. "Well, whatever you did, it seems to have helped a bit. You look much more relaxed than you did before. I'm glad." She looked as if she wanted to hug him, too, but wasn't exactly sure how well it would be received.

"Mom, what the hell are you doing in here?" Eric asked, staring at the huge mess on the counter.

"Oh! I'm making the fruit tarts for the party tomorrow."

"Are you planning on feeding an army?"

"Don't be a smart-ass. There are going to be a lot of people here. We have relatives coming from all over the place. I'm just trying to be prepared."

"Okay, whatever you say, crazy lady," he teased, scooping a thick finger into a bowl of lemon curd and licking it clean. "Where's Maggie?"

"Emma kidnapped her and Brandon a while ago to go shopping in the Quad Cities. She said it was a last-minute clothing emergency."

"Heaven forbid," Eric groaned. "And Dad?"

"Your father had a meeting at the hospital that he couldn't get out of. It was scheduled for tomorrow, but the others were nice enough to meet with him tonight, instead. He'll be home as soon as possible."

"Mmm…mmhmm." Eric continued to dip his fingers into different fruit mixtures and taste them, causing their mother to make clucking noises at him and shooing gestures with her arms. He finally laughed and backed away, holding his hands up in surrender.

Ethan stood back and watched the easy interaction between his brother and mother. They looked so natural and comfortable together. He thought he remembered being like that with them once, but it was so long ago that he couldn't swear how much was memory and how much was imagination.

"Well, I'm gonna head up and unpack before Maggie gets back and starts stressing out over my wrinkled shirts," Eric called over his shoulder as he walked toward the stairs. "Hey, how did her doctor's appointment go today?"

"All clear," she yelled back, looking straight at Ethan when her older son left the room. "Darling," she sighed, "are you going to be all right?"

"I'm…managing," he rasped.

"Are you?" Her knowing gaze bore straight into him. "I wish you would talk to us. You don't have to carry this alone. We're all here for you."

"I know that."

Her expression turned sad. "I hope you do."

After an uncomfortable beat of silence, Ethan cleared his throat and made his excuses. "Listen, I think I'm going to lie down. I haven't exactly been sleeping very well the last few nights." He walked toward the stairs, but Barbara followed him.

"Do you need your father to prescribe something? I'm sure he would understand."

"No!" he snapped, a little more sharply than intended. Taking a deep breath, he reminded himself that she had no idea what he had been through. "I'd rather not take anything, if I can avoid it. But thank you." As he turned around and started walking up the steps, something caught his eye that he hadn't noticed earlier.

Bright colors and swooping brushstrokes, with the all-too-familiar, pompously embellished "EJF" splashed across the lower right corner.

"I can't believe you still have this," he whispered, staring at the painting that was mounted on the wall in front of him.

"Of course I do, dear, don't be silly. I love that painting. That was one of your first pieces."

"That reminds me." Ethan turned back to face her. He stuck his hand in his pocket and grasped the worn-out key again, rubbing it absentmindedly, as if it were an old lantern that would somehow make his mystery woman appear. "I'm going to be sticking around for a while. I just rented some studio space here in town—a shitty little apartment. I thought I might try to work a bit."

Her answering smile was radiant. "Ethan, that's wonderful! I think working again will help you through this. It might give you an outlet to channel your emotions. Plus, it will be lovely to have you around." Then she added, almost in a whisper, "I've missed you."

"Well, I just wanted to let you know. There could be times when I'm gone for days at a stretch. If I get absorbed by something, I've been known to crash in the studio. I didn't want you to expect me to be here each night or anything like that."

"Whatever you need to do, sweetheart. You're a grown man—you don't need to check in. I'm just happy that you found something that might help you feel more productive."

On that note, Ethan nodded curtly and turned around again, finally making his way upstairs to his old bedroom. Sometime in the last few years, Barbara had turned it into a guest room, most likely assuming that he'd never even set foot in it again.

Lying down in the oversized bed, Ethan prayed for sleep to find him again. That small bit he had earlier in the apartment with his mystery woman had been the most peaceful sleep he'd had in a long time, not just in the past week. As he lay there in the dark, he let his mind travel again to soft lips and delicious kisses, to delicate fingers stroking his hair. He wanted to hold her again. He wanted to bottle her up and keep her for nights just like that one.

And with that thought, he finally fell asleep.

Frantic kisses...bodies entwined in a heap on the floor...soft moans turning into pleasured cries...beautiful hazel eyes...fading...fading... fading...

Searching...looking everywhere...looking for someone...looking for anything...

Empty...

Empty room...empty drawers...empty bank account...empty...

Nothing but a hastily scribbled note:

"Dear Ethan..."

"NO!" Ethan screamed, sitting straight up in the foreign bed. He was pouring sweat and his heart was pounding in his ears.

Glancing at the clock, he saw that it was just after 3:00 a.m. It was the longest stretch of sleep he'd had yet.

He lay back down in the soaked sheets and cringed. When he tried to close his eyes, the images came back again. Rolling over to his side, he tried to distract himself and calm down.

After another hour passed with no luck, he punched the mattress in frustration.

Fuck you, Rachel. You fucking liar.

5

———

The next morning found Lily sitting at the small desk in her upstairs bedroom. It was still dark outside, just after 6:00 a.m., and she was wrapped in an old, ratty blue robe with a towel around her head. Two large, orange-striped tabby cats twined their way around her ankles, but she hardly noticed them. She was too busy staring off into space.

Her jacket.

She still couldn't believe that in her haste to leave that place, she'd left her jacket behind. Just thinking about it made a fresh wave of panic roll over her.

What the hell have I done? We didn't even use anything! There is no excuse for this. Thank God I get the shot, but who knows what the hell he has?

She put her head in her hands, closing her eyes in frustration. Behind her lids, she saw flashes of vibrant jade eyes and luscious pink lips.

"Dammit!" Lily huffed, slamming her hands down on the desk.

All night she had been haunted with his image. She had sat there between her father and her fiancé, pretending to watch the game, all the while reliving every single touch in her mind. Every kiss. Every thrust.

And goddamn, could that boy move.

Regardless of how sick Lily was with herself over her thoughtless actions, she couldn't convince herself that it hadn't been worth it. Well, perhaps *worth it* was a bit of a stretch. She wasn't quite sure the guilt she was feeling was worth it, and if she ended up with some rare strain of herpe-gono-syphil-AIDS, that probably wouldn't be worth it, either.

Amazing. That would probably be more fitting. *Mind-blowing.* That was certainly the truth. Lily had never felt any amount of pleasure remotely close to that before, and it had happened so fast that her head was still spinning.

She thought back to the uncomfortable moment when Scott had tried to kiss her good night before leaving to hang out with his friends from work. He had given her a friendly hug and leaned down for a quick peck on the lips, and Lily needed to stop herself from jerking her head back out of guilt. She knew it was wrong to let him kiss her where another man's lips had recently been, and she couldn't even bring herself to look him in the eye when he pulled away. But even physically, the kiss itself had just felt *wrong.* His lips were the wrong texture, the wrong shade of pink. They didn't make her knees feel weak as soon as they touched her own. They were cold and dry.

She had never noticed anything off about his kisses before; they had always seemed perfectly adequate. They were never unpleasant, but they had never kept her up at night obsessing about them, either. Lily had been with others before, a couple guys she dated in college while she still lived in Minneapolis, and they had all been fairly similar: adequate, but nothing to write home about. She just assumed that reality was nothing like the steamy encounters she hungrily devoured in books written by people like Maggie Foster.

It wasn't as if she was frigid. She had plenty of good memories with her little "friend" that was tucked away in her nightstand. And when Scott managed to really put some effort in—which didn't happen often because it required him lasting longer than about three minutes—Lily sometimes felt a few warm tingles. She had just never felt comfortable asking him for more, and he had never thought to ask.

The few times he had tried to go down on her had been such awkward, embarrassing fiascoes that she just let him think she didn't have any interest in that. She'd heard people joke that there was no such thing as bad head, but Lily would beg to differ.

She wondered briefly if her beautiful stranger would have more skill in that department. She remembered how strong his tongue had been as it swirled inside her mouth, instantly recalling the taste of him. She shook her head to clear her mind, knowing that it was useless to fantasize about something she would never get to experience. It also made her feel even more guilty when she realized how thoroughly she was comparing Scott to a man whose name she didn't even know.

She thought about her jacket again, deciding that she would simply have to get it back. She needed to get it back in her hands so that she could stop focusing on it. She debated simply leaving it there and forgetting about it, but she really couldn't afford another one right now and Scott would never understand what was so hard about just going back to get it. He didn't know that retrieving her jacket meant possibly running into her stranger again.

Remembering that she only had a half-day of work that day, she figured that she could just pick it up on her way to the gym and have it out of her mind that much sooner. If she was lucky, perhaps Mrs. Knight could even go up and get it for her.

A loud yowling interrupted her thoughts. She looked down to see one of the large cats staring up at her expectantly, while the other one pawed at her foot. She sighed loudly and smiled at the one who was staring at her. "I suppose you're hungry, huh, Wembley?" When she was treated to another loud whine in return, she decided it was time to put her worries aside and finish getting ready for work.

"Okay, just a minute, babies. Mama needs to get dressed." She stood up and waded through the furry bodies, making her way to the small closet. She took the towel off her head and draped it over the doorknob, shaking out her damp hair. Throwing on a pair of scrubs quickly, she brushed out her hair and left it to air dry as she opened the door to the hall. "Come on, tubbies," Lily called behind her to the portly felines who were already following her eagerly. "If you ask me, I think you two have had enough to eat."

As much as Lily liked to tease them, she wouldn't have them any other way. She loved their jiggly fat tummies—they reminded her of how much they'd changed from when she first got them.

Wembley and Boober were brothers from the same litter and had been dumped at the animal shelter where Lily had worked while attending school at the University of Minnesota. There had been six kittens in total, all malnourished, and Wembley and Boober were the frailest of the group, which meant that nobody wanted them. Nobody but Lily. She couldn't stand leaving them there every night when she went home, so one day they came home with her.

Her roommates were a bit cross with her at first, but after watching her try to nurse them back to health, they couldn't resist the adorable kittens. Before long, her roommates were all doing their part to sneak them some extra scraps, hoping to fatten them up—and fatten up they did.

Lily walked into the kitchen and filled their food dishes, jumping out of the way before they knocked her over. She took a package of ground beef out of the freezer and put it in the refrigerator to thaw, planning to make a simple meatloaf when she got home later that night. Pouring herself a bowl of cereal, she sat down at the small table and began to eat, trying her hardest to keep the memories from coming back.

After a few minutes, some loud thumping came from upstairs, quickly followed by the awkward *thump* and drag of George limping down the stairs with his cane. He had recovered enough to return to work, but some cold mornings still left him feeling a little stiff. Distracted by the loud thumping, Wembley and Boober turned away from their now-empty bowls and tore off back up the steps, looking forward to a long day of sleeping on Lily's warm bed.

"Goddammit, Boober!" George yelled as the hefty tabby ran over his foot, causing him to stumble down the last two steps. "Swear to Christ I'm gonna string them up by their tails one day," he grumbled to himself as he joined Lily in the kitchen.

"No you won't," Lily muttered, her mouth full of cereal. "Or else I'll string *you* up," she finished after she swallowed her bite. "Besides, you love those cats. Admit it."

George sat down next to her and looked her in the eye with his most deadpan expression before smiling at her, causing his 70s porn-stache to curl up at the corners. "Yeah, they're all right," he replied. Lily knew just how much they cuddled on his lap whenever she was gone. "So, half-day today?"

"Uh…no, actually," she lied quickly. "They changed a few things around on the schedule. I might end up being there a full day, and then the gym. I'll have to see how it goes." Changing the subject quickly, she added, "I'm gonna make meatloaf when I get home."

Her father looked at her, and Lily felt as if he could see the lie on her face, but he simply shrugged. "Okay, whatever. I'm at work until after five tonight anyway."

Sighing with relief, Lily stood up and kissed him on the head. "I should get going. See you later, Dad." She threw on her coat and grabbed her repacked gym bag, closing the door behind her as she left. On the drive to work she wondered why she had lied so considerably about her schedule. By the time she pulled into the parking lot, she had convinced herself that it was simply to allow her more time to get her jacket back—just in case Mrs. Knight wanted to talk again, she wouldn't feel so rushed.

It was the typical morning in the office: Pap smear, Pap smear, pregnancy test, ultrasound, Pap smear. Lily assisted where she was needed and answered calls from concerned patients. At one point, she and Becky shared a laugh over how obvious the flirting had become between Jason and Natalie, who seemed blind to the fact that people had noticed their little games of grab-ass.

Before long it was noon, and Lily's shift was over. "Let's get this over with," she said to herself as she headed to her car. When she pulled up to her usual parking spot outside the gym, she was disappointed to see a CLOSED sign on the door of the dance studio. She got out and took a closer look, groaning when she saw that Mrs. Knight would not be opening up until 4:00 p.m. today.

That's just great. I didn't want to wait around all day for this. I want it done now.

She huffed off to the gym, not knowing what else to do, and changed quickly into a pair of gray sweats and a brown T-shirt that had the words *BAND MEETING: PRESENT* across the front in white letters. This time she signed in for an elliptical machine, taking her trusty iPod with her and queuing up her favorite workout playlist. Soon she was running to the sound of Scissor Sisters and almost feeling like normal.

She closed her eyes to enjoy the beat and was instantly bombarded with flashbacks from yesterday evening. Only now they had a soundtrack. She could feel his hands grabbing her, his lips kissing her flesh, and his hips bucking to the rhythm of the music.

She opened her eyes again, a warm flush spreading over her face. Her favorite thing was to get lost in a good beat, and she wondered quickly what it might be like to actually have sex with someone to music, since Scott always wanted lights out and said music was too distracting. Once the thought entered her mind she couldn't shake the fantasies of trying it…with *him*.

Dammit, this is getting me nowhere!

She turned off the machine, and for the second time in two days, gave up out of frustration. After leaving the locker room again with her bag, she noticed a rear exit down the hall that was eerily similar to the one at the dance studio. Wondering if it led to the same alley, Lily looked around quickly to make sure no one was watching and slipped out the back.

There it was. The door to the apartment building.

Deciding that she couldn't wait any longer and intending to simply check the door and pray that it was unlocked, Lily quietly went up the stairs. As she got closer to the top, she could hear loud rock music blaring from the other side of the wall.

Shit! She had hoped no one would be there yet.

Lily could tell from the thin streak of light on the ground that the door was cracked open, just like yesterday. Over the music she could hear odd noises that sounded almost like a staple gun punching through the floor. She knew that she should get the hell out of there, but something was drawing her closer. She wanted to peek at him one last time. She wanted to know what he was doing in there to make that noise.

She wanted to see him without being seen.

The song was almost over. It was now or never. She slowly inched forward, holding her breath as she watched her hand getting closer to the door. Just as her fingers came close enough to push it just a little farther open, the song ended and she could hear the sound of footsteps. It startled her so much that she reached forward too fast and her hand bumped the door. A loud creaking sound echoed through the hall.

Lily backed up quickly, intending to run away, when the door was suddenly yanked open. There was her beautiful stranger standing before her, sweaty and out of breath, staring down at her in shock. He was messy and disheveled, wearing a black V-neck T-shirt and dark, paint-splattered jeans. Somewhere in the background Lily could hear a sexy techno song starting to play by one of her favorite bands, Prodigy. She stood there, frozen to the spot, and an insane thought entered her mind: this band's heavy techno beats always made her either want to dance or screw—and this guy didn't look like he was in the mood to dance.

After what felt like minutes, but was probably only seconds, the gorgeous creature's too-perfect lips curved up in another wicked smile, as if he were the inventor of the smirk. He reached out and grabbed her by the shoulders, dragging her into the apartment and slamming the door closed. In a move so fast that she had no idea how it had happened, he had her shoved back against the door and half-drunk with his kisses once again.

His mouth was ravenous, as if he were being presented with his last meal. He kissed her fiercely, sucking and biting at her tongue and lips, frantically trying to cover every inch of her skin at the same time.

Lily wanted to say something, but she couldn't remember what it was. She knew it had to have been something important, but whenever she tried to think long enough to come up with it, he would shift his mouth on her or flick his tongue and she would be lost all over again.

When she realized that he was pulling his lips away, she moaned in protest, until she felt him kissing his way down her bare chest. Somewhere in the middle of all the kissing her shirt and sports bra had been removed, leaving her topless before him, but she honestly hadn't even noticed it happening.

His long, slender fingers gripped her breasts, massaging them roughly before his hot kisses took their place. She threw her head back against the door and almost cried from the pleasure of his mouth suckling her hard. She shoved her hands into his silky hair, grabbing large handfuls and squeezing, feeling him groan against one of her painfully hard nipples. His hot tongue flicked it repeatedly, nipping at it with his teeth before moving even lower.

He dropped to his knees before her, pulling her sweats down in one swift motion, making her step out of them as he stared at her, hypnotized. Lily wanted to squirm under his sharp gaze, not used to having anyone pay such close attention to her below the waist, but he wouldn't let her cover herself. He stopped her self-conscious hands and placed them back on his head, and she instinctively knew to grab onto his hair again. When she did, his eyes rolled back into his head for a moment before they looked up to meet her own heated gaze.

He smiled again, licking his lips, before he reached out and slid his hands between her legs, bending his arms back up around her hips until she was forced to slide forward and sit on his shoulders. She was left balancing there precariously, her back leaning against the door and her hands grabbing onto his hair for leverage.

He buried his face between her legs and inhaled sharply, and before Lily had time to be embarrassed or ask him to stop, he snarled loudly and opened his mouth against her. She felt his hot tongue sweep across her wet sex in broad strokes, and she wasn't able to keep from crying out loud anymore.

"Holy *fuck!*"

Her exclamation only drove him on, making him lick her harder. She could feel every flick, every swirl of his evil, perfect tongue. By the time he latched onto her swollen clit and began suckling her again, she was rounding the corner to insanity.

All the while, the song blared in the background.

Lily began screaming as her orgasm ripped through her like a lightning bolt. She gripped his hair so hard that she was surprised it didn't come out in clumps in her hands, and as she rode out her release she began pulling him into her, grinding herself against his eager mouth.

She tastes so fucking good she tastes so fucking good she tastes so mother fucking good! The words ran through Ethan's mind like a chant. He couldn't get enough of her addictive flavor; never in his life had he experienced anything so unique. She tasted like liquid lust—like heaven and sin combined—and he knew with absolute certainty that he would never be able to stop after only one taste.

When his beautiful brunette mystery finally stopped shuddering against his lips, Ethan let her down gently until he could free his shoulders, and then he was picking her right back up again until her legs were wrapped around his waist. He carried her past the living room, where he was halfway through stretching a new canvas, and into the bedroom, where there was now a lavish king-size sleigh bed with a thick down comforter and soft leather frame pushed up against the far wall. The ornate bed stuck out like a sore thumb in the otherwise bare surroundings. He'd only wanted something he could crash on whenever he ran out of energy, but couldn't resist the opulent size and the silky-soft sheets and blankets. He told himself they might help him with his sleeping problems, but if he was honest with himself, he had picked it out with the hope that his mystery woman would return.

And now that he had her back in his arms, he was going to use it for so much more than sleep.

He knelt on the edge of the bed and leaned over, setting her down like a prized treasure. She looked up at him with heavy-lidded eyes and managed a weak smile, grabbing him by the back of the neck and pulling him down to her. Then she kissed him, passionately, tasting herself on his lips and moaning at how erotic both of their flavors were, combined.

As the kiss grew more and more frantic, Lily noticed that she was writhing completely nude underneath him while he was still totally dressed. She slid her hands down his back until she could grab onto his shirt, pulling and yanking until he was forced to lift his arms and allow her to slip it over his head. His lips were right back on hers as soon as she chucked the offending garment on the floor, and then she set about working on his jeans.

The moment her hands slipped between them and touched his button fly, his own hands were shoving hers out of the way, desperate to comply with her obvious wishes. However, by the time he had pulled his pants open and down his hips to kick them off, the amazing sensation of her naked breasts sliding against his chest was enough to make him pause for a deep breath. He leaned his forehead against hers and sighed, opening his eyes to look at her.

"You came back," he whispered.

And then he entered her.

Both of them gasped as he slowly penetrated her body, sinking deeper, inch by solid inch. Lily somehow heard the music change in the other room and then the loud, thumping beat of another song pounded through the walls. He started moving back and forth, grinding against a place inside Lily that she had never felt stimulated before.

"Oh!" she cried out, and he searched her eyes. He moved again, shifting his hips and rubbing more firmly against the tight bundle of nerves there, watching her face react as her body spasmed around him.

"Is that it?" he groaned, already wanting to explode from the way her inner muscles were gripping him tightly. "Is that your spot, baby?" He shoved into her harder, making sure to drag his thick tip along that place each time he passed it.

Lily was lost: lost in the moment, lost in the grinding beats of the music, lost in his unbelievable scent that was pure sex. When she began rocking into him in time to the song, matching his rhythmic movements, he grunted loudly and rolled over, pulling her on top of him. At first she stayed close to his body, not wanting to move far from his lips, but as he coaxed her back slightly, she felt the deeper angle her position created.

Moaning her surprise, she raised up on her knees, leaning her hands back on his thighs and arching back, riding him roughly. He almost lost it again at the sight of her, firm breasts thrust forward with the most delicious rosy peaks that bounced with her motions. Ethan reached up and gripped her hips, pulling her down onto his shaft harder with each upward thrust, wondering how the hell he was going to keep his sanity while he tempted the fates and fucked a goddess.

She began shaking then, and he could feel her growing wetter around him, dripping down his length. The room was flooded with her scent, thick with arousal. Ethan growled deep in his chest, sitting up quickly to grab her around the shoulders and kiss her succulent nipples, pulling first one, and then the other, into his mouth. When he felt her shuddering grow exponentially, he moved a hand back between their bodies and slid his thumb inside her light dusting of curls, swirling circles around her clitoris as he thrust deeper inside her.

Lily came undone, her tight sheath clamping down on him, her nectar flowing freely. She moaned and screamed her release, never having felt any amount of pleasure like that before in her entire life, even by herself.

Ethan began bucking his hips furiously, finally unable to hold on any longer. He exploded deep inside her, allowing the death grip she had on his erection to milk him dry. He cried out, burying his face in her neck and biting lightly.

When the frenzy had subsided for the both of them, he pulled her with him as he lay back on the mattress, holding her on top of him and loving the feel of her in his arms. After a moment, he rolled her to the side so that he could look down at her. Her eyes were closed, from exhaustion or perhaps embarrassment—he couldn't be sure, because the loveliest blush he had ever seen was spreading from her cheeks down to her chest.

"Look at me," he said softly. He traced the features of her face with his fingertips, rubbing his thumb slowly across her full, pouty lips. He leaned down and kissed her softly before pulling back to look deep into her eyes; warm hazel met smoldering jade. "I had a spare key made today. You're fucking keeping it," he growled. "And we're going to meet here, whenever you want. If I'm not here, let yourself in. I should hopefully be along shortly."

Lily blinked a few times as what he was saying to her sank in. "But when would—how would I know?"

"I'll be here working most days for a while. Take a chance."

"But…don't you even want to know my name?" Lily asked, a slightly bewildered tone in her voice.

"No!" he snapped. "And I'm sure as hell not going to tell you mine." After a moment his tone softened and he continued. "That's for everyone else. There's no place for that here. We're going to meet here and it's going to be real—no pretenses. We're going to say what we want and do as we like." He leaned down to kiss her lips again before pulling away and smiling. "Putting a name on things only gives it limitations and expectations. I just want your body…and your soul. Your true soul that you hide away from the rest of the world, buried behind your name."

Lily stared back at him, dumbfounded by his theories. How nice would it be to get away from the rest of the world for a while? Not to worry about dinner or laundry or waiting on her dad and Scott hand and foot. To only worry about pleasing herself for once. The suggestion was extremely tempting.

When she was finally able to speak, she was surprised that it had nothing to do with what she'd just been imagining. "Um…that's twice now that we didn't use anything."

"I realize it's a bit late, but are you taking anything?"

"Yes, I get the shot. But should I be worried?"

"Well, I can get condoms if you'd like, but as for worrying, there's no need." He looked away for a moment and Lily saw a dark cloud pass over his features. "I haven't been with anyone in over a year, and I've been tested in that time."

"Okay," she whispered, pulling him down to meet her lips again, wanting nothing more than to make that dark cloud disappear from his face. When they came back up for air, they were both panting harshly and the dark cloud was nowhere in sight.

He moved between her legs again and began to enter her slowly, his earlier madness replaced by a lazy, languorous pace. She welcomed him eagerly, already feeling as if he were right where he should be.

Two hours and countless orgasms later, Lily lay sprawled across his toned chest, drifting off to sleep. She was weak and sated beyond belief.

One last conscious thought went through her mind before she surrendered to the heavy pull of slumber.

This had definitely been worth it.

6

___

Ethan woke slowly, feeling rested for the first time in days. His first thought was gratitude for whatever deity had allowed him to nap without nasty memories swimming through his head, but when he felt the warm body that was draped over him, he remembered exactly which goddess was responsible for his relaxed state.

He looked down at her sleeping face, beautiful in its slumber. Her long lashes rested against rosy cheeks that were, amazingly, still flushed, and her full lips parted for the most adorable little breathy snores he had ever heard. At that moment she could have started drooling on him and he would have found it cute.

He still couldn't believe she had actually come back.

He wasn't a fool—he knew that she'd been attempting to retrieve her jacket. He'd hoped when he found it on the floor that morning that it might mean he would see her again—he'd bought the bed and had the key made with that thought running through his head. He also knew that she could have simply called the landlady downstairs and asked her to get the jacket. She didn't have to return to this place, no matter what she had told herself. She had been fishing for a reason to come back. He knew it deep in his bones.

She hadn't been ready to admit what she wanted, even to herself—Ethan could sense that. But he also knew that they would work on it. She seemed to like having her decisions made for her by the way she was happy to let him control everything and take the lead, and he could play that game for a while. Why not? It was a major turn-on for him as well. By the time he was done with her, however, he intended to have her demanding pleasure from him without one shred of modesty or shame.

Having a beautiful woman who was willing to let you control her body completely was hot—to a point. Ethan knew that after a while, it could begin to feel a bit one-sided. His needs would be met, but how would he ever truly know if he was meeting hers? Now, having a woman who could go from submissive to snapping her fingers and barking orders in the bedroom—that was a thing of beauty.

She had certainly tasted like a thing of beauty. Going down on her had been almost perfect. The only thing that would have made it better would be if she had told him to do it. He loved oral sex above almost any other act, but so many women were embarrassed to ask for it. At least, that's what he'd heard. He didn't exactly have a wide range of experience to go by, only Rachel and the fucked up threesomes she would sometimes throw together.

Rachel.

Ethan glanced down at the expensive watch on his wrist—a pretentious birthday gift from Rachel, purchased with his own money and intended to showcase his wealth—and saw that it was getting late. He would need to get moving if he was going to keep his family from being royally pissed at him.

Hating himself for needing to disturb her, Ethan placed his hand on his mystery girl's smooth shoulder, gently shaking her awake. "Hey, beautiful," he whispered against her cheek. Her gorgeous eyes flickered open after a moment and looked up at him, taking a second to focus. "I really hate to cut this short, believe me, but I have somewhere I need to be soon."

She blinked a few more times, processing his words, before looking around the room as if she were only starting to remember where she was. The dark-haired beauty then sat straight up, covering her breasts with her hands when she realized that she was still nude. It was a gesture that Ethan found both adorable and completely pointless, seeing as he had already memorized every inch of her bare skin.

"Uh…no, that's fine," she said quietly. "I actually should have left a while ago. Is it after five?"

"Not yet, but soon."

"In that case, I really need to go."

Ethan enjoyed one last view of her heavenly backside as she jumped up and hurried into the other room, following the trail of clothing. He could tell from her frantic movements that she was about to start panicking again. He reached down to where his jeans lay discarded on the floor and fished the spare key out of the back pocket. Walking up behind her, completely unfazed by his own nudity, he grabbed her arms and turned her around to face him once she had pulled her shirt over her head.

"Listen," he said as soon as she managed to pull her gaze away from his groin and settle it on his face, another telltale blush coloring her cheeks. "I meant what I said earlier. You're taking this fucking key." He reached for her hand and pressed it into her palm, pausing for a moment to make sure that she was paying attention. "And you're coming back."

"Yes," she whispered. "Yes, I'll be back. I'm not sure when…or how often. Weekends will be something of a problem."

"I don't care how, when, or why you come. Only that you do." He looked deep into her beautiful eyes, knowing that the moment she left again he would miss them terribly. Slowly leaning down and bringing his mouth to hers, he kissed her softly. "Good-bye for now."

"Good-bye, stranger." A small smile played on her lips.

As she backed away from him toward the door, he couldn't help but see that she spared one final glance down at his dick. A deep crimson spread across her features when she saw he'd noticed, which caused it to stiffen slightly under her regard. With one last, barely audible squeak under her breath, she shut the door behind her and ran down the stairs.

Glancing down at the offending member in question, Ethan chuckled to himself. He clearly had no control over what that girl did to his body. Walking into the small bathroom and turning on the shower, he eyed the dark garment bag that hung on the back of the door as he stepped under the stream of water. Rinsing off his sweaty frame quickly, he thought to himself that there was no better sweat than post-sex sweat.

When he was finished, he stepped out onto the cold tile floor and cursed himself for forgetting to buy some towels. Praying that he'd air-dry quickly, Ethan brushed out his hair with his fingertips, finally giving it up for a lost cause when it began sticking up at odd angles.

Fuck it.

He turned around to the garment bag, unzipping it slowly to reveal a designer suit that had been tailored to fit. This one was a dark charcoal gray color and one of his favorites. As he tightened his silk tie in the mirror, he acknowledged that the suit he was wearing probably cost more than the average person earned in a month.

We must always keep up appearances, isn't that right, dear?

He threw on his dress coat and made his way down to the Audi, reminding himself as he got inside that he needed to contact the rental company soon about setting up an open-ended contract. He'd originally taken it out for a week, but now he had absolutely no idea how long he might stay. Living the life of a wealthy, eccentric nomad had left him with very few ties to any one place, so the duration of his visit was completely up to him.

As he pulled out of the lot, he turned on the satellite radio, already set to one of his favorite hard rock stations. Whenever he was in the mood to start painting again, his musical preferences tended to lean more toward the aggressive side of the spectrum. Except for earlier that day; for some reason, something had made him get up and switch his iPod over from his *Painting Music* playlist to a new one he'd just made that morning, simply titled *Fuck Songs*. And as if the reason for his playlist inspiration had been summoned by the music alone, she had shown up at his door.

Shaking his head to clear it from the images of luscious pink lips and soft brown hair, he directed his attention to the song currently playing on the radio. Startled to find that it was actually a slow song, Ethan paid closer attention. It was by the band Slipknot, which normally sounded much heavier. He started to recognize the tune, but as it played he realized that he'd never listened to the lyrics. They were full of pain and hurt, loss and regret.

Okay, that's enough of that. Ethan turned off the radio, instantly uncomfortable with how closely the song mirrored his own emotions at the moment. He didn't need to sit in silence for long, though, since he had already arrived at the madhouse formerly known as his parents' home.

There were cars lining both sides of the street. Emma had been right; their mother should have booked a hall. At this rate they were going to be lucky if they the cops weren't called for a violation of some sort of city ordinance.

After finally parking and heading inside, Ethan looked around until he saw some familiar faces milling about the foyer. One of them was a lithe beauty with a dark-blond pixie cut, and when she saw him approaching she smiled widely, excusing herself from the group of people she was talking with. A tall, dark-haired man followed closely behind her, unwilling to release her hand as she walked away.

"I knew you'd make it," she said, standing up on her tiptoes to kiss his cheek.

"Did you really ever doubt me, Emma?"

"Of course not, but Brandon owes me five bucks." She nudged the man at her side, causing him to laugh nervously.

"Hey, I only said that I wouldn't blame him if he didn't make it, not that he wouldn't. This is a whole lot of people to take in at once."

"Oh whatever, you still owe me five bucks." She turned her teasing smile from her husband to Ethan, her face growing more serious in the process. "I'm not going to ask you how you're doing again. But please keep in mind that we're all here for you. Always. You don't even have to talk about it—we can just hang out if you want." Dropping her voice to a whisper, Emma added, "I miss you."

"Come here," Ethan said, holding his arms out. Wrapping her in a tight hug, he leaned over and spoke in her ear. "Listen to me. I may not have been around much over the last few years, but don't ever think I don't remember that you were always the other half of me when we were little."

Emma and Ethan were fraternal twins, but as Ethan loved to remind Emma, he was older by twenty-two minutes. They had been extremely close growing up, going so far as to have their own secret language that pissed off everyone around them, especially Eric. Ethan couldn't help wondering what his life might have been like if they had remained close, rather than growing apart in their teens.

"Thank you," she replied, hugging him even tighter. "But now I've got my own other half, and he makes me happier than I ever could have imagined. It makes me so sad to know that you haven't found yours yet. I'd hoped you had, but..." she trailed off awkwardly.

He bit his tongue and nodded gruffly. "Yes, well...these things happen."

Ethan patted her on the back and shared a few pleasantries with her husband Brandon, who he hadn't gotten to know as well as he felt he should have for someone who was married to his twin. He vaguely remembered seeing Brandon on occasion, when Emma first started bringing him home with her on her breaks from the University of Illinois at Urbana-Champaign, but Ethan had already been too deep into his studies at the Art Institute of Chicago—and well on his way to becoming a first-class pompous asshole—to give a shit about him.

After a few more minutes of idle chitchat, they made their way into the main room, which had been decorated elaborately for the occasion. Nearly all the furniture had been removed until it was a wide-open room, perfect for large masses of people to stand around like cattle and exchange stories about his father.

Making his way across the room, he was stopped numerous times by distant relatives and business associates of his father. The gamut ran from cousins he hadn't seen since his teens who had come all the way from Boston to an over-enthusiastic, ass-kissing OB/GYN who Ethan could have sworn was flirting with him. Over and over again he would pause, shake their hands, listen to the same boring stories and offers to get together sometime, all the while remembering to smile and nod at just the right times. He didn't know any of these people anymore and he had a hard time hiding the fact that he truly didn't care to.

Eventually, he was able to free himself long enough to grab a cup of coffee in the small breakfast nook attached to the kitchen. It was the one area that wasn't swarming with people. He had just sat down and taken a large drink when he heard footsteps entering the room. Glancing up at the door, he was relieved to see a tall, distinguished-looking man approaching him. He was still very fit and attractive for his age—the only telltale signs that he was now sixty were the slight graying at his temples and the laugh lines around his eyes.

Setting down his cup, Ethan stood to greet him. They hugged warmly, and as they pulled away, neither one completely let go of the other. "I thought I might find you in here," the older man said with a smile. But it didn't reach his eyes, which remained sad and full of concern.

"Sorry, I was trying to get over to you, but I just needed a minute. It was getting to be a little too much in there."

"I think that's more than understandable right now." He reached up and stroked his hand over the back of Ethan's head, clearly mastering the urge to ruffle his hair. "Besides, don't worry about us. We'll be here after all of this craziness is over."

"Thanks, Dad."

"Where were you this morning? I was hoping to see you at breakfast, but you had already taken off."

"I was getting my studio set up. I wanted to get away for a while— this place is turning into Grand Central Station."

"Yes, I don't think I've ever seen quite so many presents before in my life," Richard Foster said with a light chuckle. He was a highly respected physician in the small town of Aledo—it seemed as if almost every hospital employee had stopped by the house for a chance to rub noses with the good doctor and bring him a gift. "Your mother meant well by all this, but I think the party got away from her." He was quiet for a moment before adding, "Speaking of your mother, she mentioned that you're thinking of staying on for a while to work. I can't tell you how happy that makes me."

"Well, I'm not sure how long it will be, I just don't feel the need to run off quite yet. And I haven't had this strong of an urge to start paint- ing again in a long time, so I want to take advantage of it while I can."

"That's wonderful. Maybe it's what you need right now to get your head straight."

"What do you mean?" Ethan didn't miss the knowing look that his father gave him.

"Son, we know you're not sleeping well. Your mother and I can hear you screaming at night. You have just been through something that's obviously upsetting you, and you won't talk to anyone about it. Perhaps this urge to work again is a way for your body to release some of the emotions you're bottling up."

"Maybe. I don't know much about that stuff," Ethan shrugged.

"Well, whatever the reason, I'm just thrilled that you'll be in town longer. We've all missed you. I know that you like your privacy and I don't expect to see you at the dinner table every day, but it makes me feel better just knowing that you're close by."

Ethan sighed. An uncomfortable look came over his face. "Dad, I know I've been…distant. I'm sorry I haven't really been around for such a long time."

Richard smiled, patting him lightly on the shoulder. "Don't be silly. I know how it is to be young and in love. Sometimes it can feel like nothing else in the world exists. You and Rachel were quite the glamorous jetsetters, with art shows around the world. Who could blame you for getting wrapped up in that?"

Ethan smiled back, not having the heart to correct his assumptions. Maybe one day he would set him straight, but for the moment he couldn't stomach the idea of seeing the light of respect die in his father's eyes.

"Were you ready to return to the party? I noticed you haven't had the chance to talk to your mother yet."

"You go on ahead. I'll be there in a minute." Ethan picked his rapidly cooling coffee back up and began to sip it, effectively ending the discussion.

"All right. I'll see you in a bit." Richard walked toward the door, stopping when his hand touched the knob. "You know, Ethan," he turned back around. "I know that you weren't expecting to be bombarded by the entire family so soon after your arrival. Normally things aren't quite so crazy around here. Don't get me wrong, I'm thrilled to have you here for the celebration, and I'm so happy you'll be staying for a while, but I can tell you're uncomfortable. I won't ask you to do any more than you think you can handle right now, but please stop holding all of us at arm's length. We just want to know you again."

Ethan watched him leave, grimacing at the now-cold coffee as he swallowed the last of it down. It was almost as hard to digest as the words his father had spoken. Ethan hadn't realized he was being so obvious to everyone, but his father was right. He *hadn't* wanted to see anyone right now, not even Eric or Emma. He wanted to hole up and lock the world away until he figured out how he was going to face them all again. Taking a deep breath, he went back out into the swarm of people, trying to be a little more receptive to all the party guests this time.

Before long it was well after nine o'clock and most of the guests had filtered out. Ethan was left standing with his parents, both of them hugging him close. When they pulled apart, his mother leaned up to kiss his cheek.

"Darling, we're so happy to have you here after so long. It meant so much to us to have you present for your father's birthday. I know it was a little crazy, but I can't thank you enough for staying."

"I was happy to be here," Ethan replied, to which his mother arched an eyebrow in disbelief. "Well, maybe not happy to be at this enormous party that you never should have had at the house," he teased, "but definitely happy to be with you both again."

"Well, that's good. Are you going out for a drink with the boys, sweetheart?" Maggie and Emma had already gone to bed, but Eric and Brandon were refusing to call it a night. They'd announced that they were going to the local bar for a few rounds if Ethan wanted to meet them there.

"I'm not sure yet. It's been a really long day. I don't know if I'm up for it."

"All right. You do whatever you need to do. We're going up to bed." She kissed him one more time before grabbing Richard's hand.

"Good night, son," he added, before turning with his wife and walking to the stairs.

Ethan stood in the empty room for a few minutes, rubbing at his eyes and running his fingers through his hair. It felt so odd to be back in a place filled with so many happy memories. For so long, all he wanted was to be standing right where he was—and now that he was there, he didn't know how to process it. His family had been nothing but welcoming and caring since he'd arrived, which is what he'd thought he needed, yet the closer they tried to get to him the more he backed away. He had wasted so many years separating himself from them for one reason or another. At first it was because he'd foolishly imagined himself above them all. Now it was because he knew that he didn't deserve them.

Just being home again felt awkward and painful. Ethan didn't know how to bridge the gap that he'd created—he only seemed to be making it wider. His family clearly loved him and supported him even after he'd been such an ass for so long, but the thought of actually seeing the disappointment in their eyes once they finally discovered what had become of his life kept him frozen with fear. He didn't want to lose his mother's love and his father's respect now that he was so close to finding his way back into the family again.

"You're a fool if you think that your family would want anything to do with you now."

He flinched at the bitter memory. Had Rachel been right after all?

Ethan wiped at his eyes with the back of his hand. Looking at the family portrait hanging on the wall, he saw his parents, siblings, and younger self grinning down at him from a time when happiness was easily within reach.

"I should have left her years ago," he whispered to the smiling faces. "I'm sorry that this is what it took to finally bring me home."

With that, he turned and left the house, walking quickly to his car to avoid breaking down in plain sight of anyone who happened to be looking out the window.

He got in his car and started driving without any destination in mind, tears running freely down his face. So many emotions were raging through him that he didn't know which was the strongest. He was sad about the ugliness of Rachel's departure, but he felt betrayed and furious about it as well.

While it was true that he'd been miserable over a large part of their partnership, he never wanted things to end this badly. But when he had finally worked up the nerve to tell her how he felt, he'd been surprised to find that she'd beaten him to the punch and already left—taking a large portion of his savings with her.

When Ethan finally parked the car after driving around for over an hour, he realized that he had gone right back to the apartment. As soon as he made his way upstairs, he collapsed face-first onto the bed, completely drained.

He was asleep the moment he smelled his mystery woman's scent on the pillow.

7

———

"Mrowwrr."

"Ugh…" Lily groaned, trying to roll away from the offending noise of Wembley so close to her face, but finding herself trapped. She opened her eyes and looked around. The room was illuminated by the morning light that filtered through the curtains in colored streaks. At some point in the night she must have rolled onto her stomach. Boober was curled up on top of the covers between her legs. She laid her head back down on the pillow for a moment, every ache and sore muscle becoming apparent.

Her body had never been worked so thoroughly in her life.

After returning home, she had spent the entire night trying not to walk funny in front of her father. When George had finally noticed her slight limp, she'd simply played it off as a result of overexerting herself at the gym. She laughed at the memory, deciding that "overexertion" was probably the understatement of the century.

"Mrowwrrr."

"All right, Wembley," Lily sighed. "Let Mama up, babies." She wiggled her legs until Boober moved, allowing her the freedom to get out of the rumpled sheets. Moaning and stretching as she stood, she threw on a robe and went downstairs to feed her cats.

Sitting down at the table with a bowl of cereal, Lily wasn't surprised to find the usual Saturday morning note from her father explaining that he would be gone hunting all day. Rolling her eyes at the thought of even more meat in the freezer, she finished her breakfast and set about finishing her weekend chores.

As she threw in a load of laundry and cleaned the bathroom, she did her best to avoid thinking about the amazing things that had happened to her the day before in that crappy apartment. Lily knew dwelling on it would only drive her crazy, and if she actually intended on repeating her not-so-noble actions, then she would have to learn to cope with the feelings of withdrawal whenever she went back to her less-than-interesting life.

She knew she had been unfaithful and disloyal to Scott. She also knew beyond a shadow of a doubt that this man had made her feel more alive in two days than she had ever felt in her entire life. This was a fleeting affair. She had absolutely no idea how long he would be around and that uncertainty made her want to lock herself away with him in that apartment, soaking up every ounce of passion she could get her hands on until it was time to go back to her bleak reality. There was no doubt in her mind that this would never be more than a fling.

It was a limited-time offer she couldn't ignore. Sort of like whenever the McRib made a reappearance: she would gorge herself stupid on them in fear that each time she ate one it might turn out to be her last.

And this guy tasted way the hell better than a McRib.

Lily knew she would go back. Even she couldn't fool herself that much, and no amount of guilt could keep her away. She reminded herself that she wasn't married yet—this was her last chance for adventure. However, knowing how easily she tended to cling to things, she forced herself to acknowledge that she needed to get a grip early on. He could leave any day and didn't even want to know her name. He was only providing one thing right now, and when he was gone, she would never have it again. She kept telling herself repeatedly to just have a good time while it lasted, and for God's sake, stop thinking about it.

Shaking off her wayward thoughts, Lily dove back into her house-work. She had just folded the last of George's clean shirts when she remembered that she was supposed to spend the afternoon with Scott. She went back into her bedroom and grabbed her cellphone from its charger. After making sure that she hadn't missed any calls while she was vacuuming, Lily quickly pulled up his number and hit the SEND button, waiting as it rang.

And rang.

When it finally went to voicemail, she left him a brief message and jumped in the shower. After she was dressed she tried him again. On her fourth try, he finally answered.

"Mmm…yeah?" he murmured into the phone.

"Jesus, Scott, it's almost eleven. You're still sleeping?" Her tone came off much harsher than she had intended.

"Ugh." His groan echoed through the phone, followed by the rus-tling of sheets. "Sorry, babe," he mumbled around a loud yawn. "I'm still sleeping it off."

"Out late again with Ryan and the guys?"

"Yeah." She could hear him rubbing his hands over his face, trying to wake up. "Card game over at Mark's. What's up?"

"Well, I thought you wanted to hang out today. I was just calling to see what was going on before I went to the grocery store." A week ago they would have been arguing by now—she would have called him all morning and been offended that he had yet again made plans and not followed through with them. But now? Now she had to remind herself that Scott even existed.

If she was being honest with herself, she had been too busy won-dering how soon was too soon to return to the apartment. She had been too worried about how she was going to last all weekend without seeing her beautiful stranger again.

Seeing Scott had become a chore.

Engulfed by a fresh wave of guilt, Lily focused on the conversation again. "Anyway, I was about to go get some stuff to make for dinner. Did you want to come pick me up?"

"Ugh, now?" he groaned again, coughing sharply. "Babe, I'm really fucking hungover here. I could use another hour or two. Besides, the Honda is running for shit right now. I didn't even take it out last night."

"Okay," she sighed.

"Listen. Let me rest a little bit more. You go to the store and come get me when you're done. We'll have a movie night at your place."

"All right, but that won't even take me half an hour. You said you needed some time." Lily could hear him groaning into his pillow, his annoyance becoming more apparent the longer he was kept awake.

"Then go do something else first. How 'bout you go to the gym? You like that, right?"

After a few seconds of silence Lily finally answered. "You know, Scott, I think that's a fine idea."

"M'kay, see you later," he mumbled, already drifting back to sleep. "Love you."

"Yeah." *Click.*

Twenty minutes later, Lily was pulling her car into a parking space in front of the gym. But this time, rather than bothering to stop off at the locker room first, she went straight to the back of the building and out the alley door. Lily had worn her workout clothes straight from home—a pair of black, flared yoga pants and a white T-shirt that said *TEAM BUILDING EXERCISE '99* across the front in dark blue letters. She figured that the pretense of exercising was necessary in case anyone bothered to actually pay attention to her while she was there.

Once she was at the top of the stairs she knocked on the door, not wanting to barge in, and was surprised when there was no response. Lily put her ear to the door, listening for any sounds. Remembering that he'd said *anytime*, she fished her key ring out of her jacket pocket, looking for the newest addition. As she felt the key turn in the lock, an unbelievable thrill ran through her body. It was as if she were unlocking the cage that held her deepest desires in check.

"Hello?" she called out, slowly closing the door. "Stranger?" she said with a smile. Lily walked around the apartment, making sure he wasn't in another room, but came up empty. *Damn.*

She took in the newly treated canvas that stood on an easel in the front room. It was large and completely blank. She wondered what sort of images might end up there. Would it be a realistic still life, or something more abstract?

She noticed an unused palate on a small table off to the side, covered in tubes of oil paint in various colors. Lily was struck with a vision of her beautiful stranger standing there, shirtless in blue jeans, covered in streaks and splatters of paint as he violently attacked the canvas. It was a sight she'd give anything to see in person.

Walking over to a shelf on the opposite wall, she noticed his iPod sitting in its dock. Turning it on, Lily began searching through the playlists, wondering what type of music he preferred. She found one titled *Painting Music* that was full of some great heavy rock songs, but the one labeled *Fuck Songs* really made her take a closer look.

She hit PLAY and was immediately taken back to the previous afternoon. As the familiar techno song played, she couldn't stop herself from looking over at the door, remembering how it had felt when he lifted her against it. He was so strong, so forceful. He knew what he wanted the moment he saw her at the door. And it had been amazing.

Lily walked into the bedroom and sat down on the luxurious bed. It was incredibly gaudy and probably cost more than her car three times over, but Lily couldn't dislike it—it was incredibly comfortable and had been the location of the most amazing sexual experience of her life. She couldn't shake the memories of his hands and his mouth on her body and the music was only making it worse. She lay back against the pillow, closed her eyes, and was hit with an overwhelming wave of his scent. Rolling over and burying her face in the pillow, she inhaled deeply, feeling sudden warmth spread throughout her body and settle between her legs.

What the hell is this man doing to me?

She heard the song switch over and realized that the iPod must be set on shuffle—it wasn't the song she had been expecting. A different sexy beat began to play, causing Lily to groan when she recognized her favorite song by She Wants Revenge.

Jesus Christ! What is it with this guy? It's like his musical taste is directly connected to my vagina.

She rolled over onto her back, letting her hands roam along her body. Between the music, the memories, and his intoxicating scent, Lily was well and truly drunk with lust. By the second verse of the song, her fingers were slipping beneath the lace of her panties and she was wishing that she had brought her little vibrating friend.

She really started getting into it after that, sliding through her slick folds, swirling her fingers around her swollen bundle of nerves. Visions of smoldering jade eyes and perfect pink lips filled her mind. She could see him there above her, making her body sing. Her fingers became his fingers, stroking her more firmly, sinking inside her.

"Oh God," she moaned, her fingers plunging even deeper inside her. She could smell him, she could feel him, and if she concentrated hard enough, she could even hear him. His rich, sultry voice kept replaying over and over in her mind. *Yes…yes…you feel so fucking good…come for me…come for me now!*

"Fuck!" Lily convulsed around her fingers, shaking and moaning. She had never climaxed so intensely by herself, even with her little vibrating friend. Ever since this man had come into her life, every single remotely sexual feeling was magnified by a thousand.

She rested there for a few minutes, collecting herself. When it became apparent that she would not have time to wait for her mystery man any longer, she pouted briefly before deciding to have one last little bit of fun. Taking her pants off, she slid her now thoroughly wet panties down her legs and slipped them off, then pulled her pants back on.

She placed the small scrap of lacy fabric in the middle of the pillow and walked back into the front room, looking for a piece of paper. Spying a brand new sketchbook on the floor by the easel, she ripped out one of the blank pages and grabbed the pencil that was next to it. After scribbling a quick note, she kissed the paper, leaving a very clear lipstick outline, and folded it up. Once it was placed on top of her discarded panties, she smiled to herself.

There was no reason she couldn't let him know what he had missed.

Lily turned off the iPod and locked the door behind her, sad to be returning to her daily grind so soon and without seeing the only person she had hoped to see. After she left, she stopped off at the grocery store and purchased all the ingredients for the pasta dish she wanted to make later, along with some ice cream for dessert.

When she was done there, she directed her car to the far side of town, pulling off the road into the gravel driveway of a small, rundown house. Leaving the engine running, she walked up to the door and knocked, praying that Scott was the one who'd answer. He wasn't.

"Hey there," said a middle-aged man with one side of his face drooping from paralysis. He backed up awkwardly to make room for the door as it swung open. "How's my little Lily?" he slurred through his good side.

"Hey, Sam."

"Haven't seen you 'round for a while. How you likin' my old ride?" He nodded toward the idling Oldsmobile.

"Good, it's good. Scott did a great job fixing it up."

"Yeah, well…I s'pose. Wanna come in?" He backed up a bit more and gestured to the small kitchen behind him.

"Oh no, no. I really can't stay. I'm just here to pick up Scott. Is he up yet?"

"Who knows? I think I heard him moving around in there a while ago." Sam Walker spun around clumsily and slowly made his way into the hallway, yelling, "Scott! Get your ass out here! Your girl is out here waiting on you!"

Lily heard another door open. "Yeah, yeah. Stop shouting. My head is fucking killing me." Loud footsteps echoed as he walked into the kitchen. "Hey, babe. Sorry about the wait," he said as he grabbed a jacket from the back of one of the chairs.

Scott stood before her, well over six feet tall and very muscular. By all accounts he was extremely attractive, beautiful even, and had always seemed to be more than enough for Lily in the past. But now, he was *too* tall…*too* muscular. His deep brown eyes that had always looked so warm to her were now the wrong color. They weren't jade, and they didn't smolder.

"That's okay, I—"

"Scott!" Sam interrupted from behind him. "When you gonna be home?"

Scott rolled his eyes and threw on his coat, heading for the door.

"I don't know. Later." He turned his attention to Lily. "Let's get the hell out of here."

"Well don't forget you need to do the laundry later," Sam called after him as he closed the door. "And bring back another bottle!"

"Jesus Christ," Scott muttered under his breath. When they reached the car he stopped and grabbed Lily's arm before she could walk around to the other side. "Hey, come here." He pulled her into a big hug. "Sorry about that. I didn't hear you pull up, or else I would have been at the door. He misses you, though. It's nice for him to get to see you once in a while."

"Scott, he doesn't even really know me," she said as she broke the hug prematurely, walking around to the driver's side. "I barely remember him from when we were little, and we don't exactly hang out now."

"Well, we could, if you would ever do dinner over here. He would love your cooking, and he's always on his best behavior whenever you're around."

Lily didn't respond to that. She simply pulled out as fast as she could and got back on the main road that headed into town. Sitting around and watching Scott's dad get hammered and yell at him all night was not exactly her idea of relaxing. And if that was what Scott considered to be Sam's best behavior, then she would certainly hate to see anything worse.

Sam had always made Lily nervous and uncomfortable, even when she was a little girl and his face hadn't been disfigured. He'd always seemed to be too hyper, too excitable, too loud and rowdy. She had hated whenever her father would take her over there to play with Scott when they were young so he could hang out and watch the game. Whenever her father asked her why she didn't like Sam, she could never explain it in a way that he understood, so they continued to go there.

It wasn't until Sam's stroke that George, or anybody else in town for that matter, found out about his massive meth addiction. George did what he could to help Sam clean up—he got him into rehab and physical therapy for his stroke, but things were never the same between them again. George couldn't get past the fact that his own little girl had been able to notice that something was off with his best friend when he couldn't, and he felt even worse that he'd continually forced her to hang out with an addict.

Scott had gotten the worst of it, though. He was stuck at home in a house with an angry invalid for a father and a distant ghost of a mother. He was sixteen when she finally took off and left him there to fend for himself. By that point, Sam had turned to a much easier drug of choice: alcohol.

Lily shook off the painful memories of the past, hating how they were making her feel even worse for Scott than she already had been. She turned her focus instead to getting back to her house and cooking him the best guilt-free meal she could manage.

A few awkward hours later, dinner eaten and bowls of ice cream in hand, they both sat down in her living room to watch a movie.

"What did you want to watch tonight? Did you have anything in mind?" Lily asked as she sat down on the couch with one knee bent underneath her.

"Just don't make me watch that fucking *Eagle vs. Shark* movie again, please," he responded, grabbing the remote and flipping through cable channels.

"I wasn't going to…but that *is* my favorite movie. Chances are I might want to watch it again sometime."

"Then watch that shit on your own time, seriously. I can't understand one fucking word they say in that thing. What the hell language are they even speaking?"

"Scott, they're speaking English! They just have New Zealand accents. You get used to it." She was tired of arguing about it, so she decided to just drop it. He wasn't even looking at her anyway; he hadn't taken his eyes off the channel guide since he sat down.

"Whatever, I'll take your word for it," he mumbled. "Ooh! Check it out—*Blade* is just starting. I haven't seen it in years! Is that cool with you?"

"Yeah, sure." She sat back and started eating her ice cream, wondering why Scott was suddenly so much more annoying than he'd ever been before.

Don't take it out on him. It's not his fault you didn't get to cheat on him today, you selfish bitch.

As the movie started, Lily soon realized that it must have been a long time since she had seen it, too. In the opening scene, when all of the vampires drag their unsuspecting victims to some underground rave, they begin dancing and grinding to a rather familiar techno song.

Lily nearly dropped her bowl of ice cream on the floor. She had completely forgotten that song was in the movie, and the moment she heard it she was flooded with images of the most amazing sex she'd ever had. It had been playing on his *Fuck Songs* playlist the last time they were together.

"I know, this is a cool scene, isn't it?" Scott said over his shoulder in response to her gasp. He was perched on the edge of the couch and hunched over his own bowl. Lily sat back again, relieved that he hadn't seen the instant blush that had risen on her face. Suddenly she was worried that she was never again going to be able to put her stranger out of her mind.

Later that night, across town, Ethan was finally getting back to the apartment after spending the day with his parents and siblings at a much smaller, family-only luncheon for his father's birthday. It was a lot easier being around just them than half the town, but he still found himself forcing more than a few smiles and checking his watch to see if it had been long enough to sneak out of there without offending his mother.

He was exhausted. The only thing that got him through the day was the ability to let his mind drift away and focus on his amazing memories from the day before. He would have given anything to have his brunette goddess there at that moment.

Stripping off his suit, he briefly debated starting on his new painting but decided that he was just too tired. He thought that perhaps a nap first might help. Then he could start working whenever he was inevitably woken up with another nightmare.

Crawling onto the empty bed in his boxer briefs, he was surprised to find something resting on his pillow. He leaned over and switched on the cheap lamp he had sitting on the floor. When he rolled back over, he couldn't believe what he saw.

Sitting right in the middle of the pillow was a pair of lacy blue panties, and on top of them was a note. It was simply addressed *Stranger*. When he unfolded it and read what was inside, he nearly cried out from a mixture of frustration and arousal.

Dear Stranger,

I'm sorry I missed you today.
I tried to wait, but don't worry.
I found a way to entertain myself.
Here's a souvenir.

Next to her words was a kiss mark on the paper from her lipstick. She had been there.

Ethan set the note to the side and picked up the panties with a hand he noticed was shaking. Unfolding them, his attention was drawn immediately to the fact that they must have been quite damp earlier today. He would much rather have found them when they were freshly wet as opposed to almost dry, but that fact didn't seem to have any effect on the raging erection he was now sporting.

He was angry he had missed her, but he was so turned on by this bold gesture that his eyes were nearly crossing. Lifting the panties to his face, he inhaled deeply and was gifted with a fresh, potent wave of her heady scent. His cock twitched in approval.

"Fuck!" he groaned into the material. His hand was shaking again as he held it to his face, breathing her in, even going so far as to lick and suck the flimsy scrap of lace. His other hand had already freed himself from his boxers and started working his shaft in harsh, angry strokes.

"God, yessss," he hissed loudly, overcome with visions of her perfect breasts as they bounced in his face, how eagerly she had perched on his shoulders to let him dine on her delicious pussy.

"You taste so fucking good," Ethan whispered, as if she were there and could hear him. "I could smell you all day."

He gripped his erection even harder, swirling his thumb around the tip on the upstroke, imagining it was her tongue. "Yes…please…I want to feel your mouth on me." She hadn't granted him the pleasure of reciprocating the day before, and the only thing he'd been able to think about since then that wasn't a direct memory of their encounter was how it might feel to have her beautiful, plump lips wrapped around his cock.

Smelling her delectable pussy while he stroked himself made it that much easier to imagine having her on top of him, facing away as she took him in her mouth, leaving him to feast on her yet again. He could hear her muffled cries as she moaned around him, letting him thrust between her lips over and over again. "Oh fuck...yes!"

His entire body began to shudder, and he knew that he was close. With a supreme effort, Ethan pulled her panties away from his face and wrapped them around his cock, stroking himself roughly until he was spurting his release all over the fabric.

Despite what he had just done to them, he was unable to let go of her panties, choosing instead to curl up on his side and clutch them to his chest like a beloved stuffed animal.

After that, the room was completely silent except for the quiet thank-you he whispered into his pillow.

He had no nightmares that night.

8

Sunday absolutely sucked.

Lily was a cranky shit the entire day, scowling to herself as she cooked even more stupid fucking deer meat for George, making sure to use his stupid "special" dry rub. She understood hunting as a sport, but kept wondering why the hell they had to actually eat the shit he killed so much. Couldn't he hand it out at the school? Or sell it to a restaurant?

She usually loved Sunday dinner with her father. It was the one day he stayed home and spent time with her, and sometimes Scott would come over and make it feel like a real family dinner. It was the one day she looked forward to, always viewing it as a true day of rest with a lovely dinner to top it off.

That Sunday was no different than any other Sunday, but for some reason everything kept pissing her off. When she watched her father sitting on his lazy ass in front of the TV while she prepared the meat, she realized that it wasn't going to be that much of a day of rest, at least not for her. When he called out for her to bring him another beer while she stood there sweating over a frying pan making his dinner, trying to avoid kicking her cats as they circled around her legs in hopes of renegade food hitting the floor, she almost threw the can at his head.

"Why are you so moody?" George finally asked her when they were sitting at the table. She had slammed the shaker down in front of him after he asked her to pass the pepper.

"I'm not moody!" Lily snapped. She took a deep breath and counted to five, reminding herself that it wasn't fair to take out her frustrations on him. She seemed to be doing that a lot lately. "Sorry. I've just got a bad headache."

He shrugged and kept eating, ending the longest bout of concern he had shown for her in months. It wasn't that George was indifferent to Lily—she just so rarely complained about anything that he had stopped feeling the need to ask.

Monday morning wasn't much better.

Half an hour into Lily's shift, people were going out of their way to steer clear of her. Kim stopped calling back new patient charts after she snapped at her and then hung up on her, and even Becky was tiptoeing around her. When Lily got pissy with Dr. Wilde when she asked her to run some extra tests on the mayor's sister, Becky had seen enough.

"Lily, what the hell is wrong with you today?" she whispered harshly, pulling her aside in the hallway.

"That nasty bitch is here all the time to treat one STD or another. It's like she never learns!"

"Yeah, we all know that. It's like she's never heard of condoms. But it's Natalie's job to treat her, and it's your job to help her do that. You've been biting everybody's head off all morning. What the hell is up your ass today?"

"It's nothing. I just…I guess I don't feel very good today," she hedged.

"Well, that's obvious," Becky replied with a laugh. "Lily, is everything okay? I've never seen you quite this grouchy before, and I remember when you tried to come to work with the flu."

"I'm sorry. I don't know what's wrong with me. It was just sort of a bad weekend." It had been bad simply because she hadn't seen her beautiful stranger. She sighed deeply before adding, "I don't really want to be here right now."

"Well, you only have an hour left. It should go fast."

"An hour? What? What are you talking about?"

"Jeez, Lily, you really are out of it today. Don't you remember? Natalie is going to some medical lecture in Moline this afternoon. She canceled afternoon clinic."

"Oh my God!" Lily reached out and hugged Becky. "That is excellent!"

For the rest of her shift, Lily had a much sunnier disposition.

After speeding off to the gym and rushing through her locker room routine, Lily quickly stashed her gym bag and ran up the back stairway to the apartment. She could hear the loud music blaring as she climbed the steps. It was another heavy rock song. Hearing the confirmation of his presence sent a wave of heat through her body.

That time, she didn't even knock.

She went straight for her key, sliding it into the lock as if she lived there. When she felt the tumblers click open her heart skipped a beat. Opening the door slowly, Lily froze.

She thought she was prepared to see him again. She was wrong.

She was not prepared to find her beautiful stranger just as she'd imagined him: shirtless, jeans hanging low on his hips, his well-toned body splattered with various colors of paint. Since his back was to her and the music was so loud, he hadn't heard the door.

Lily stood mesmerized as he moved his arm back and forth across the canvas in long, rapid strokes. The large brush he wielded was covered in a deep blood-red mixture, and his frantic movements left what almost appeared to be bloody streaks and splatters on the painting. As he shifted to his side, she could see other shapes and figures, one of which looked like an abstract, dangling arm holding a small vial. Although it was still a work in progress, the overall effect was rather violent…and unbelievably powerful.

He looked powerful. And just as she'd suspected, he also looked sexy as hell.

Moving slowly so that she didn't disturb him, Lily made her way to the iPod dock on the shelf. Reaching into her jacket pocket, she pulled out her own older, less expensive model and turned it on, queuing up a specific song. When his current selection began to wind down, she quickly hit the stop button and pulled his iPod out, replacing it with her own.

Startled by the shuffling noises behind him, Ethan turned around so abruptly that he dropped his brush on the floor, leaving a crimson stain on the wood. He was so surprised by her silent entrance that he was struck immobile for a moment, simply staring at her heatedly with that jade smolder that had been haunting Lily for days.

"I hope you don't mind," Lily said timidly from across the room, "but I made my own little playlist." Clicking the iPod into place and hitting the play button, she immediately felt bolder when the grinding beats began filling the room. "Not that I didn't love your list of *Fuck Songs*, but I thought it was time I contributed a little bit."

She watched as his features shifted, becoming aggressive…predatory. Lily could sympathize—she felt the exact same way. Two days away from this man had been too long. She was over being shy and reserved. Now she only wanted to wrestle him to the ground and devour him.

She never once took her eyes from his as she slid her jacket off her shoulders and let it drop to the floor. Walking slowly toward him, she could see his nostrils flaring and his chest rising rapidly. In the back of her mind, Lily couldn't help hoping that his chest wasn't the only thing rising rapidly.

For a moment, Ethan thought he had finally lost his mind and his fantasies were manifesting in front of him. His brunette goddess had been living in his thoughts on a constant loop over the entire weekend, so when she suddenly appeared before him it took him a moment to realize that she was actually there. The instant he locked eyes with her, only one word made any sense to him anymore: *mine*.

The notion confused him because he had never been possessive. Rachel had flirted blatantly with nearly every man she met just to get a rise out of him, but it never made one bit of difference. However, something about this woman made him want to club her over the head and drag her back to his cave and make her his own personal plaything for as long as he wanted. He quickly reminded himself to get a grip. It was just a fuck. She meant nothing to him and he meant nothing to her. She didn't have a name. It wasn't anything more than pleasure.

He watched her saunter toward him, the look in her eye just as heated as his erection. When she was standing directly in front of him she dipped her head a bit, so that she was looking up at him through her lashes. Her slick pink tongue darted out from between her lips, moistening them before she whispered, "Miss me?" A smile tugged at the corners of her perfect mouth.

"*No*," he snapped, suddenly angry that she was right. He couldn't stop staring at her glistening lips, nearly growling when he remembered his fantasy of having them wrapped around him.

"Not even a little bit?" She pouted playfully, reaching out with her fingertips and dragging them up and down his abdomen, feeling along the ridges of his muscles. She circled his navel and made her way back up until she was scratching through the light dusting of hair on his chest. The sensation of her hot fingers on his skin was making him lightheaded.

"No." His tone was lighter now; the swirling patterns she was making on his pecs were rather distracting. He could feel the familiar itch in his own fingers telling him to reach out and grab what was his.

"Well, I missed you," she practically hummed, leaning forward and kissing each of his nipples slowly, gently. The chasteness of the kisses somehow made the action even more erotic, causing Ethan to grit his teeth against the moan that wanted to escape. "In fact, let me show you how much."

Lily gripped his hips and dropped to her knees, unable to miss the rather prominent bulge in the front of his jeans. "Mm…seems like someone around here missed me." Bringing her hands up, she cupped him lightly before gripping him more firmly, causing him to hiss through his teeth. Leaning forward, she placed her mouth over the tip of the bulge, kissing it quickly and flicking at the denim with the tip of her tongue.

If Ethan had thought her kissing his nipples was erotic, watching her do that was bound to drive him insane. It also didn't help that he hadn't bothered to put his boxers on that day and he could feel everything much more intensely.

"You're a dirty fucking tease, do you know that?" he growled at her, unable to tear his eyes away from the sight of her small fingers working at the buttons on his fly.

"And why is that, exactly?" She smiled up at him, tugging him closer by his waistband so she could get a better grip on the bottom button. He was tempted to tell her that opening a button fly was much faster if you just pulled it apart quickly—all the buttons would pop open in a row—but he was having too much fun letting her take her time.

"You sneak in here when I'm gone and get me all excited, and then don't even have the decency to come back and finish what you started."

"Aw, poor baby," she cooed, happy that he had missed their time together just as much as she had. She pulled on his jeans until they were sliding down around his hips, unable to bite back a moan when his erection sprang free in front of her.

She had yet to appreciate it so closely. Lily had been able to tell that it was nice, but up close it was truly a thing of beauty. Long and thick, covered with the smooth ridges of multiple veins, it curved upwards toward his stomach proudly and was crowned with the most gorgeous swollen tip that was turning darker under her scrutiny.

Lily reached out and ran her hands up the front of his legs, spreading out her fingers as they moved higher, until her thumbs were brushing against the dark brown hair at his groin.

"You like what you see?" he grunted.

"Like is an understatement." She finally touched him then, wrapping her fingers around the base of his shaft. Leaning closer, she flicked her tongue out, licking at the glistening tip. He was already leaking for her, and she lapped up the drops of moisture that she found there. It tasted both sweet and salty, and was now her new favorite flavor—after the taste of his lips, of course.

Just the sight of his dick that close to her lips was enough to do him in. By the time she licked up his pre-cum, Ethan's thoughts had turned into one long litany of curse words. *Oh fuck...oh fuck...don't fucking come yet...she hasn't even put it in her mouth yet...Jesus Christ, don't fucking come!*

"Oh, I nearly forgot," Lily said, pulling away from him far enough that he actually whimpered. "Did you get my present?"

The image of lacy blue panties flashed in his mind, causing him to growl again. "Yes," he gritted through his teeth.

"And did you like them?"

"*Like* them? I fucked them!"

A wicked smile crept across her lips until she was absolutely beaming.

"Good." And with that, she grabbed him more firmly around his shaft and sucked him deep inside her mouth.

"Fuck!" Ethan threw his head back and groaned loudly, swaying on his feet. Just as he'd suspected, her mouth was pure bliss.

Unable to keep his hands to himself any longer, he plunged them into her dark hair, enjoying the feeling of her head moving up and down underneath his touch. He let his thumbs sweep out across her blushing cheeks, over her silken skin, until they were tracing her luscious pink lips as they slid along his length.

Lily looked back up at him through her lashes again, loving the look of intense pleasure on his face. That was one of her favorite things about doing this—being able to make a man weak in the knees. She had almost forgotten how much it could turn her on when the recipient really got into it.

She pulled all the way back, barely letting him slip out. Holding him steady at the base, she puckered her lips tightly and slowly pushed her mouth over his broad tip. As he penetrated her deeper, she sucked in her cheeks around him, trying to simulate what actual sex might feel like. On the upstroke, she wrapped her tongue around him for added texture, swirling it around the tip before plunging back downwards. The loud moan he let out told her that he seemed to enjoy it.

Trying to ignore how badly she was beginning to throb between her legs, she slid her hands around his firm ass and cupped it tightly, pulling him toward her so that he slid deeper into her mouth. She repeated this action a few more times, hoping that her beautiful stranger would take the hint.

And take it he did.

Ethan grabbed her more firmly by the back of the head for leverage and started slowly thrusting, pulling her face toward him as he shifted his hips into her. He watched as he fucked her mouth, watched as the veins on his cock slid back and forth through her lips, and when she moaned around him his eyes nearly crossed at how good it felt.

When she began pulling him into her mouth even more eagerly, he started to thrust faster. He looked into her heavy-lidded eyes to confirm that it was what she really wanted. She moaned and nodded, the sensation making him cry out. He kept thrusting faster and faster, knowing that he was going to lose it at any moment. It was just too fucking intense. He honestly didn't know how he'd made it so long.

When he noticed her starting to squirm and moan even louder, he quickly realized that something was different. One of her hands was no longer gripping his ass. Glancing down, he saw that she had slid her hand inside the front of her workout pants and was furiously rubbing herself.

That was all he needed to set him off.

"Are you fucking touching yourself?" he panted as he felt himself starting to lose control. She simply nodded again and moaned some more. "Oh God…that's not fucking fair! I want to watch that."

Suddenly all he could think about was her tight, wet pussy and how it felt, how it tasted. "Fuck, I can't take it anymore! Give me your hand!" He reached down and pulled at her arm until she finally took it out of her pants, whimpering at the loss of friction. "Don't worry, I'm gonna take care of you, but I have to fucking taste you when I come. I'm so goddamn close right now!"

He fully expected her to shy away, but instead she groaned loudly and started sucking on him harder than he thought physically possible. "Holy shit!" he cried out, nearly falling down, his legs were shaking so badly. "That's it…yes…just like that."

Lily watched as he pulled her dripping fingers up toward his mouth, bending slightly to reach them. The moment his slick tongue wrapped around them, they both whimpered. She could feel the heat and strength of his mouth as he sucked them clean, and he could taste the divine flavor that had been driving him insane since they'd first met.

Groaning loudly and sending vibrations all the way down her arm, Ethan bucked his hips once, twice, and then erupted in thick spurts down the back of her throat.

Normally Lily was a firm believer in swallowing, but there were times when she had needed to spit before—sometimes the guy was just too damn bitter no matter how much she liked him at the time. But this was the best she'd ever tasted. She swallowed every drop eagerly, hoping it would enhance his climax to feel her mouth working around him to the end.

Once Ethan had calmed down enough to think again, he looked down at his goddess. Her eyes were bright, her cheeks were flushed a lovely shade of pink, and her succulent lips were slightly swollen, making him want to kiss her even more.

"That was incredible," he panted, running his fingers through his hair. "You didn't have to do that, you know…at the end." Rachel hadn't swallowed in years, deciding that it grossed her out, and before that it had only happened a handful of times.

"Don't be silly," she smiled. "Of course I had to. You tasted too fucking good to stop."

Jesus Christ, is this girl for real? he wondered, already feeling his cock beginning to stir again.

Kicking his jeans off the rest of the way, Ethan leaned over and scooped her up. He carried her into the bedroom and tossed her on the bed. "Sweetheart, you've got entirely too much clothing on. If you don't want them ripped off of you in exactly five seconds, I suggest you start stripping."

Lily was only too happy to oblige, pulling her shirt and sports bra over her head before yanking her pants and underwear down and tossing them on the floor. With Scott, she still felt self-conscious to be on display like this, completely nude, but this man had a way of making her feel sexier than she'd ever felt before.

"Now," he said from the doorway, standing over her. "I want you to show me what you were trying to do out there."

"What do you mean?" She knew exactly what he meant, but had never been asked to do that for anyone before. It was hard to imagine that anyone would even want to see that.

"Don't play stupid with me. I want you to lay back and finish what you started out there." His voice turned husky when he spoke again. "Show me how you get yourself off."

Blushing furiously, Lily scooted back until she had room to lie down. "You actually want to watch that?"

"Don't go getting shy on me now. You had no problem doing it out there."

"Yeah, but you weren't watching. I hoped you wouldn't notice."

"There is no way in hell I would have missed that." His voice took on that husky tone again. "That was what drove me over the edge, knowing you were doing that. Now open your legs."

She slowly bent her legs at the knee and parted them, figuring that if he really wanted to see it then who was she to judge. As long as he thought it was sexy, she could find the courage to do just about anything.

"Wider, baby," he whispered as he sank down to his knees for a closer look. After she parted her knees even wider and slid her fingers between the slick, swollen folds, she could hear his breath hitching. "Fuck...you have the most beautiful pussy I have ever seen."

Lily could feel herself growing bolder under his gaze, loving the feel of his eyes on her as she moved. She was still pretty hot from earlier, but this was reaching a whole new level. She was amazed to realize that having him watch her was turning her on even more.

Ethan watched as her fingers slipped over the wet petals of her sex, always coming back to circle around her clitoris. He listened as her breath broke into pants and moans, and it surprised him that even just her breathing patterns were driving him wild.

Wanting to be more involved, but not wanting her to stop, Ethan began running his fingertips up and down her ankles and calves. "Tell me about the first time you ever did this," he whispered against her knee before he kissed her there lightly.

"Why?" she moaned, writhing in front of him as she ground herself against her hand. She couldn't resist reaching up with her other hand and squeezing one of her nipples before moving on to the other one.

"Because I want to know more about you."

"I thought you said no names," she replied, looking at him questioningly.

"I did, but I don't need to know your name to know the things I want to about you. I don't care what you do, where you live, whether you're married with five kids or used to be a nun. None of that matters here." He gripped her calves tighter, making sure that she was paying attention to him. "That's all just window dressing. I want to know the real you, the you that nobody else has ever been allowed to see before."

"Okay. What did you want to know?" She was more than flattered. People she had known her entire life didn't give a crap about her deep dark secrets. They only cared if she went to the right school, got the right grades, and dated the right boys. Who had ever cared about the real her before? Did she even know who the "real her" was?

"Tell me about the first time you ever did this," he repeated. "And don't you dare stop what you're doing."

"Well," she thought back, trying to focus over the growing sensations in her body. "The first time I can remember, I'd found a stack of dirty magazines that belonged to one of my mom's old boyfriends. He had lived with us at the time."

"Did he show them to you? Did he touch you?" Ethan couldn't fight off the wave of protectiveness that attacked him.

"No, no! Nothing like that. I went snooping around one day when they were gone and found them. They were these really old copies of *Playboy* and *Penthouse* from the late seventies and early eighties."

He could remember when he and Eric had been caught sneaking a few peeks at those very magazines when they'd been younger. One of Eric's friends had brought some to the house, and when Barbara had caught them they had both been grounded for two weeks.

"Go on," he prodded, meaning both her story and her actions.

"I remember knowing that it was wrong to look at them, but that excited me even more. The women were so beautiful and natural looking back then, but what really caught my eye were the pictures that showed two people having sex. You never got a really good view of things, but you could tell what was going on."

"Yes, I remember those."

"Well they were my favorite, and as I flipped through the pages and looked at those scenes, I started feeling the strangest throbbing right here," Lily gasped as her fingers kept moving, swirling through her folds. Her orgasm was fast approaching, causing her speech to become erratic as she fought through moans. "And then I…would lay awake at night…and wonder what it felt like…to do what the people in those pictures did…oh God!" She started to tremble, feeling his eyes on every inch of her skin at once.

"Are you going to come?" he asked, his voice sounding thick as honey in her ears.

"Soon," she gasped.

"Finish your story," he commanded. "You would lie awake at night and think about it."

"Yes," she moaned. "Yes…and whenever I thought about it, that same throbbing would happen. So I touched myself…here…and it felt so good." Her body started shaking harder, fighting for its release. "And I found out that…if I touched it long enough…in different ways, I would shake all over…and feel so warm!"

"Now I want you to come for me," he said, never taking his eyes from her frantic finger swirls.

That was all Lily needed to hear, since she had been teetering on the edge already. She began to shudder and moan, throwing her head back and crying out, "Oh fuck!"

"Thank you for sharing that with me," he said calmly when she finished, as if he weren't affected by what he'd just seen. The only thing giving him away was the way that his hands shook where he touched her. He thought for a moment before adding, "Next time, I want to watch you use a toy…and then maybe I can use it on you, too."

Lily would have blushed if she weren't so turned on by the thought of it.

Ethan leaned in closer, his face only inches from where she was spread wide before him. "I want to see what you do with something that's made to fit right *here*." He slid two fingers deep inside her, making her arch her back and moan, her inner muscles gripping him. "Do you like that?"

"Yes," she moaned.

"What do you want right now? Be honest. If you aren't, I'll never learn what you truly like."

"I like what you're doing now. Don't stop that yet."

"What else?" He caught the blush on her cheeks and pressed her further. "Come on, tell me." He worked his fingers deeper inside her, trying to make her focus on her arousal rather than her embarrassment.

"Oh God," she panted. "I really liked...well, actually..." she took a deep breath before continuing. "All right, I fucking loved it when you went down on me the other day."

That was exactly what he was hoping she'd say. "So tell me what you want."

She looked down her naked body until she found him, perched between her legs. Taking a deep breath, she finally blurted it out. "I want you to finger me while you lick my pussy. Is that clear enough?"

"I think that can be arranged," he smiled, barely containing his glee at her request before burying his face between her legs.

"Holy shit!" she screamed at the sudden onslaught, already so sensitive from her recent orgasm.

Ethan lapped at her juices, sucking her clit between his lips while sliding his fingers even deeper, eventually adding a third finger. Flattening his tongue against her, he used thick, broad strokes that he knew would have her coming within seconds.

"Yesss," she hissed through her teeth. "Oh yes...oh fuck! Don't stop!" Lily reached down and grabbed handfuls of his hair, pulling him into her harder while she ground herself against his face. The dual sensations of his fingers inside her and his tongue working her over were the most intense feelings she'd experienced in...well, ever.

In less than a minute she was shaking and convulsing. Ethan could feel her tightening around his fingers, her fluids dripping freely and covering his hand in her moisture. If her loud screams were anything to go by, she'd just had one hell of an orgasm.

His dick was so hard again that it was becoming painful. He leaned back on his knees and looked down at her, his amazing sex goddess. Just seeing her spread out before him was enough to make his erection jump in anticipation. He grabbed it with his dripping hand, spreading her nectar along his length before pumping it a few times to relieve some of the pressure.

Lily sat straight up, her eyes locked on his hand and what it was doing. She was quickly realizing that it truly was exciting to watch.

"Turn over. Get on your hands and knees."

"But I really want to watch you do that," Lily said eagerly, her eyes wide in wonder. His long, slender fingers were gripping his perfect cock and sliding up and down. She couldn't look away.

"Next time, I promise, if you still want to. But I need to be inside you right now. I'm sorry, I can't wait. Turn over." Lily finally complied, getting up on her hands and knees, making sure to arch her back to give him the best view possible.

"Goddamn!" Ethan moaned. "I didn't think it was possible, but you look even sexier like this."

He scooted closer behind her, reaching out to rest his other hand on her hip. Guiding his erection to her dripping opening, Ethan slipped the tip just inside her before moving his hand up to grab her other hip. Now that he had her where he wanted her, he gripped her hips tightly as he slid himself the rest of the way inside.

They both threw their heads back and groaned deeply.

Using her hips for leverage, he began thrusting inside her to the hilt, over and over again. Not wanting to come too quickly, he began to draw out each thrust, shoving deeply and pulling back out with an agonizing slowness.

Lily's eyes were rolling back in her head. Each heavy drag of the tip of his cock inside her sent ripples of perfection through her body. It felt amazing, but there was very little contact this way, and Lily wanted more of him touching her.

Looking back over her shoulder, she caught his eye before panting another request. "Grab my hair."

"What?" he asked, hardly believing what he'd heard.

"I want you to hold me by my hair while you fuck me like this."

Happy to oblige, Ethan gathered her hair at the base of her skull and pulled back, causing Lily to arch her back even more. He held her in place, pounding into her faster, dragging loud grunts and moans from each of them.

Still not happy with the lack of contact, Lily rose up on her knees, leaning her back against his beautiful chest. That felt much better. She could feel his light coating of chest hair as it scratched against her sensitive skin, and his small nipples rubbing against her shoulder blades.

Ethan was shocked at how much he loved the shift in position. Not only did it free up his hands to roam over the front of her body, but the angle created an intense grinding sensation where they were connected. He moved slower inside her, dragging himself against her front wall, making sure to hit that spot inside her that he knew so well.

She laid her head back on his shoulder and enjoyed the feeling of him sliding inside her, moaning loudly when he wrapped his arms around her and began caressing her breasts. Both hands gripped and worked them equally, stopping to squeeze and pinch her tightened peaks between his fingers.

"Yes!" she cried into his neck, lifting her mouth up toward his. Ethan pulled her even closer, planting his mouth on hers hungrily. Their tongues swirled together and fought with each other, neither one truly wanting to win, as long as the war could continue. Lily brought her arm up around his neck, pulling him even closer to her by the back of his head.

They remained like that for some time, practically locked together, connected at so many points it was impossible to count. The slow grinding and thrusting continued, and whenever a certain movement caused them even more pleasure, they would swallow each other's cries, panting into each other's mouths.

Ethan knew that he was getting close, so he slid his right hand down the front of her body and began swirling his fingertips around her swollen clitoris. Lily gasped at the extra stimulation and bucked her hips, causing his fingers to slide down enough so that he could feel where his body was entering hers.

"Oh God," he moaned. "Quick, give me your hand, baby." He reached up and grabbed her arm, bringing it back down to the juncture of her legs. "Here." He covered her hand with his, slipping their fingers between her soft curls and down to where they were connected. "Do you feel that? Do you feel us?" He spread their fingers apart, so that they slid from up around her clit to down around either side of his shaft as it moved deeply in and out of her.

"Oh... Oh yes! Can you feel me touching you there?"

"Fuck yes," he gritted through his teeth. "It feels amazing."

They separated their fingers then, leaving hers to slide around the sides of him while he moved his back up to start rubbing her more firmly. Her fluids were flowing freely down around their fingers, making everything slippery as they moved closer to the edge.

Ethan slid harder against the rough patch of nerves inside her, stroking her clit in time with his thrusts. He could tell the moment she found her release because her entire body shook in his arms and her inner muscles clamped down, constricting around him.

"Fuck!" he yelled. "Yes...come for me, baby. Come all over me!"

She turned her head and screamed into his neck, riding out the most powerful orgasm she'd had to date.

Ethan kept thrusting and stroking her, knowing he was going to finish any second. "Give me your fingers!" Lily moved her hand from between her legs quickly, shoving them into his mouth. He sucked her fingers clean, groaning around them as he exploded inside her.

They napped briefly after that, curled together. When Lily awoke she saw that it was already time for her to head home, whether she wanted to or not.

She rolled away from his beautiful sleeping body, hoping not to disturb him as she got dressed. As much as she preferred him awake, his features looked much more peaceful when he slept, and she had the strangest feeling that he didn't sleep often. When she'd first seen him there, he had dark circles under his eyes.

Pulling her shirt over her head, she heard his quiet voice behind her. "You sure you can't stay any longer?"

"Dammit, I'm sorry," she apologized. "I was trying not to wake you."

"No biggie," he smiled, making her heart skip a beat. Propping himself up on his elbow to look at her, he repeated his question. "So, you gotta run?"

"Yeah, I really do. Why? You're not actually up for another round already, are you?"

He chuckled lightly. "Sweetheart, even I need a little time to recoup after something like that. Although I must admit that you bring out the animal in me. I've never been quite so hungry for someone before."

"I feel the exact same way," she said, flashing a shy smile. "So, if no round two, then why do you ask?"

"Oh…well, it's just really nice sleeping next to you. It would be nice to do for a longer stretch sometime." He actually blushed.

"Oh! Well, I only get so much free time, and we usually use that for…other activities. Though the thought of sleeping in this amazing bed is pretty enticing—"

"Never mind," he interrupted, waving it off. "I just didn't know your availability, so I didn't know if you ever had longer times to be away. It's really nothing."

"The only problem is that I rarely know my availability, either. It's very play it by ear right now. But if any opportunity arises, believe me, I'll be here." After tying her shoes she knelt on the edge of the bed, leaning forward to kiss him good-bye.

"I've been meaning to ask," he said as she pulled away from the warm kiss, "what's up with all the T-shirts?"

"Huh?" She looked down, not remembering what she was wearing. It was one of her favorites, a deep green tee that said *BRUNETTES, NOT FIGHTER JETS* across the front in gold letters. "It's just what I wear to the gym."

"Oh, I figured that. I just wondered why you had so many Flight of the Conchords T-shirts."

Lily gasped. "You've heard of the Conchords?"

"Of course. Why? Hasn't anyone else you know?"

"No! And it's really frustrating! I love them so much—like, to an obsessive degree. I have all the DVDs, all the CDs, and a whole bunch of goofy merchandise, but anyone I try to share them with just looks at me like I'm crazy. Doesn't anybody in Aledo understand dry humor?"

"Well, I don't know about that, but I've always liked them. I like The Mighty Boosh better, though."

"Oh, I love the Boosh, too! Absolutely classic." Lily stood and walked to the door, stopping briefly to call back over her shoulder, "But the Conchords are better!"

Ethan lay back down and laughed a loud, belly-clenching laugh. "Go on, get out of here, crazy lady!" He stopped laughing when he heard the door *click*, but mostly so he could listen to her run down the stairs. It was that much longer that he could be connected to her. When he thought back on the absurdity of the entire conversation, it only caused him to laugh even harder, making his sides hurt and tears run down his cheeks.

Ethan hadn't laughed like that in a very long time.

9

Ethan rested there on the bed for some time after his goddess left. He was wide-awake, but reluctant to leave the place that smelled so heavily of her essence. She was everywhere around him, from the long brown hairs he could see on his pillowcase to the rapidly cooling wet spot he refused to roll away from. He could smell her on his fingers and taste her on his lips.

He licked them both once again for good measure.

After another minute of reminiscing over his lusty afternoon, he realized the music was still playing in the other room. He could hear a lighthearted song about feeling good start up and couldn't help staring up at the cracked ceiling while he listened, smiling at the lyrics.

Good was an understatement. This was the best he'd felt in months. Hell, longer than that. If he really tried to think back to the last time he'd felt this relaxed and sated, he would only draw a blank.

Rachel had certainly tried to keep things exciting, and sometimes she would succeed, but the boredom would always set in faster and faster after each new thrill. Whenever she had seen that look in his eye that hinted he might be wondering if he was really where he wanted to be, she would dangle a new vice in front of him like a carrot to get him back in line. It worked for a while.

The last one had been cocaine.

"Here, baby," she said, holding out the small brown vial in her hand.

"This will make you feel so good. You'll be able to stay up and paint for days and days."

"I don't know that I want that right now," he replied, glancing around his cluttered studio, anywhere but at her eyes and the disappointment he knew would be there. "I was thinking about maybe going back to America soon. I haven't seen my family in a long time."

"Family?" she huffed. "Ethan, I am your family. Those people back there are nothing but dead weight. You agreed with me when I became your manager that you wouldn't let them hold you back." She put her hands on her hips and started tapping her foot—signs that she was prepared to go the distance on this topic.

"But that's just it. I don't think they are trying to hold me back. They have always been supportive." He sighed before adding quietly, "They have only ever wanted me to be happy."

"Happy? Your parents would be fine with you painting motel land-scapes as long as you were happy. They have no clue what it means to be truly great as an artist. Why can't you ever just shut up and trust me? Have I ever steered you wrong? Look how far you've come in such a short time!" She gestured wildly out the window at the beautiful Italian scenery. "Now, you have a show in Venice next month and you are nowhere near ready!"

When she realized her tantrum wasn't making the same impact that it would have about five years earlier, she switched tactics. Giving him her best and most-practiced pout, she walked up to him slowly, running her fingers up and down his chest. "Please Ethan…for me?"

He hated when she pulled that shit, but she also hadn't touched him in weeks—she'd been too busy partying it up at clubs and leaving him home alone to work. She would go through phases with her sexuality, sometimes inviting other women into bed with them for days-long sex fests, only to turn around and be cold and distant for a while, shutting him out completely. Since Ethan still refused to step outside of their relationship for any sort of physical comfort, and it appeared that she might be ending their latest dry spell, his body began to rule his actions.

Rachel knew that she was close to victory as soon as she felt him growing hard against her. "Know what else this stuff is good for?" she smirked, holding out the vial again. She looked up at him and batted her lashes, rubbing herself against the front of him. "Fucking all night long."

"Where did you get this shit anyway?" he asked, his control flagging.

"From Julia, down at the club. Oh, you'll love her, baby. She's got a tight little ass and firm tits." She slid her hand down his abdomen until she was cupping him firmly, making him shudder. "I bet she could do some amazing things to this cock with me. Should I ask her over?"

Ethan reached out slowly and took the vial. "Call her."

That night had led to a nasty addiction that had taken him almost a year to kick.

No, Ethan couldn't remember ever feeling so good.

As he hummed along with the song, it slowly dawned on him that it wasn't a song he had loaded into his iPod. Forcing himself to stand and walk into the front room, he found a classic, scratched up, 30-gig iPod sitting in his dock, while his brand new iPod touch was on the shelf in front of it.

His goddess had forgotten her music.

Reaching out with trembling fingers, he hit the stop button and pulled it free from the dock.

Should I? What if her name is in here somewhere?

He quickly told himself to stop being a pussy and just look inside. What could it hurt? He was just looking to see what kind of music she liked, that's all.

Ethan quickly scrolled through the menu options, searching through the different artists and playlists. Although he told himself that he didn't want to know her name, it didn't stop him from trying to accidentally learn it. After five minutes of digging and hunting, he knew it was a lost cause, but he was still amazed to find how much they had in common when it came to music.

Just as he was about to put it back on the dock to start listening to a playlist titled *Kiwi Genius* that had caught his eye, the shrill ringtone of his cellphone intruded on his peaceful afternoon. He almost let it go to voicemail when he didn't immediately recognize the number, but he noticed that it was a local area code, so he begrudgingly answered.

"Yeah?"

"Ethan? Is that you?"

"Emma? Sorry, I don't have any of your numbers in my phone. What's up?"

"Well, Mom made me promise not to bother you, but I thought you should know that she is making dinner for everyone before we all drive back to Chicago tonight. Since we're all here in town an extra day to visit with you in the first place, it might be a nice idea to make an appearance."

"Sorry, Em. I didn't know you guys were even still in town. I thought you went back yesterday."

"We all stayed over through Monday, jackass! We thought you might need to be with family right now. Little did we know that you would pull a disappearing act after lunch yesterday." His twin sister had always been one of his biggest supporters, but she was also the first one to call him on his bullshit.

"Hey, Em, wait," he called out, knowing by the tone of her voice that she was about to hang up the phone. Sighing deeply, he continued. "Listen…I'm sorry. You have all been great, honestly. I'm just not used to needing to check in with anyone when I'm working. I didn't mean any offense."

"I know you didn't. And I know this whole thing has been a very intense experience for you, but Ethan, we haven't seen you in forever. I know that it can be cathartic to lose yourself in work, especially with what you do, but you're back now and we want to spend some time with you while you're here. I'm always afraid that each time I see you is going to be my last."

He knew she had a point. He had been so exhausted by trying to keep up his prodigal son routine that he had fled the first moment he was able. "No, you're right. I've been a little...distracted. I got so used to handling things by myself that it feels awkward to lean on anybody else."

There was nearly thirty seconds of silence, but to him it felt like hours. Her voice was sad and quiet when she finally replied. "We just want to know you again."

"What time is dinner?" he sighed, shoving his fingers through his messy hair.

"Six o'clock."

"I'll be there." He hung up the phone and looked at the time on his display, noting that he had less than an hour to get there. Glancing down at his naked body, he made the quick decision to forgo a shower and just throw on some clothes. Besides, that way he could smell like her that much longer.

Twenty minutes later he was pulling off the road onto his family's property. As he parked his rental car next to his father's silver Lexus, he turned off the upbeat New Zealand songs playing on his mystery woman's iPod and slipped it inside his jacket pocket to finish snooping through later. Slinging a bag full of dirty laundry over his shoulder,

Ethan walked inside the front door, unsure of what his welcome would be.

He could hear female voices laughing from the kitchen, so he set his bag down at the foot of the stairs and followed the happy sounds until he was quietly standing in the doorway. His mother, Emma, and Maggie were all sitting around the island countertop, talking as they plated various snacks and side dishes.

"Oh, dear, don't worry," Barbara was giggling and patting Maggie's arm. "When I was pregnant with Eric, I threw up all the time. I even threw up all over Richard once when we were…well, you know."

"Mom!" Emma gasped, her laughter cut off abruptly.

Maggie waved her off and Barbara paid her no mind, continuing with her story. "And good lord, let me tell you, when I was pregnant with Emma and Ethan, they gave me twice the gas!" Both women broke into another fit of laughter, leaving poor Emma looking completely horrified.

When Maggie was able to stop laughing, she cleared her throat and spoke, her tone suddenly serious. "Thanks, Barbara. I know so many women can have a hard time of it. I'm just happy for any type of new symptom these days. I think I'd even be happy to get hemorrhoids if it meant that this pregnancy goes full-term."

"Eww, Maggie!"

"Oh, grow up, Emma. You are thirty-two years old. I think you can handle hearing about this stuff," Barbara scolded. She turned back to Maggie, her expression turning to one of concern. "Darling, there is no reason you can't say 'baby' by now, instead of 'pregnancy.'"

"I just can't yet," she whispered. "Not again. It hurts too much when things go bad."

Barbara moved to hug her, and in doing so she noticed the new addition to the room. "Ethan!" she beamed. "I didn't think you'd be here tonight!" She met him halfway across the room as he entered, her arms already around his neck in a fierce hug.

"Of course! You know I can't miss one of your amazing dinners." He held her tightly, looking over her shoulder to mouth the words "*thank you*" to Emma, who smirked back at him in a very *I told you so* sort of way. She had perfected that look.

"Well, you're just in time. We were about to set the table. Why don't you go find your father and the boys and tell them to meet us in the dining room?"

Ethan followed loud whooping noises into the living room, surprised to find Eric and Brandon jumping up and down in the center of the floor, brandishing white controllers that they aimed at the TV.

"Yeah, baby! Suck it!" Eric yelled after swinging his arm in the air toward the screen.

"Ah, shit!" Brandon swore, tossing his controller on the carpet in front of the entertainment center.

"Pay up, d-bag," Eric laughed.

"What the hell are you guys doing in here?" Ethan interrupted his brother's moment of victory.

"Hey, man! Good to see you!" he crossed the room quickly, clapping Ethan on the shoulder. "Brandon here bet me that he could take down my as-of-yet undefeated high score in tennis. Not only was he wrong, but I managed to set a new high score."

"That's…great?" Ethan replied, not having any exposure to game consoles since he decided in middle school that Eric could knock himself out on Super Nintendo all he wanted—he'd rather go to his room and sketch. "Mom wanted me to let you both know that dinner is ready. Where is Dad?"

"I think he's still in his office," Eric called back to him, already halfway to the dining room with a ravenous gleam in his eye, Brandon hot on his heels.

Ethan made his way down the hall, stopping at a closed door that he hadn't knocked on in years. Tapping lightly, he could hear the muffled sounds of a one-sided conversation before his father's voice rang out.

"Come in."

As he walked quietly through the door, Ethan found Richard sitting at his large desk, his hand covering the mouthpiece of his desk phone. His eyes lit up when he saw who it was, and he whispered, "Ethan! Come on in, son. I'll be done with this call momentarily." He spent another minute wrapping up the call from the hospital, leaving Ethan to wander around and look at the many priceless works of art hanging on the walls.

When he spied a particular piece hung in an obvious place of honor, he felt a lump rise in his throat.

"Sorry about that," Richard apologized, coming up to stand beside him. "Ah, I see you've found my favorite." He nodded toward the painting with a smile.

"I...uh," Ethan cleared his throat before speaking again. "I didn't realize you owned this one."

"Of course I do! It cost a pretty penny and I had to pull a lot of strings with the dealers I know to get it over here from Europe, but I knew as soon as I saw your catalog for that show that I had to have it." The pride in his voice was unmistakable.

"Any reason you chose this one specifically?"

"Well," he smiled, "everyone I spoke with tried to go on and on about the 'Duality of Man' and the struggle of 'Adult vs. Child' and blah blah blah," he chuckled. "But I knew exactly what this was the moment I saw it. It's a bit distorted, but there's your favorite rocking horse from when you were a boy," he said, pointing to it, "and there's your stuffed bear, and, if I'm not mistaken, that is the old tire swing that used to hang out back."

Richard patted him lightly on the back before adding, "It's a beautiful piece, but I didn't need anyone to tell me any hidden meaning. To me, this was simply evidence that my son has amazing talent, and that perhaps from time to time he misses us, too."

Ethan blinked a few times, his eyes suddenly stinging. Richard had no idea how right he was.

Father and son walked back into the dining room together, joining the rest of the family who were already seated and waiting at the long table. With Barbara on one end and Richard on the other, the table stretched out to allow six more places, three down each side. Both married couples sat across from each other, leaving two empty places at the end near Richard.

Ethan sat down at his father's left and glanced at the empty chair across from him. Rachel had only sat there a handful of times throughout the entire duration of their relationship—almost ten years total. He found it odd that only now, when that chair was empty once again, did he finally feel as if he were truly back home.

If he was being honest with himself, he had to admit that she had never fit there. He couldn't help wondering if anyone ever would.

As his family ate and talked around him, Ethan realized that he was stroking the iPod he had tucked away inside his pocket, causing the metal to become quite warm. He had to force himself to loosen his grip, knowing that it would look odd to eat his entire meal with one hand in his pocket. Focusing his attention back to the room around him, he picked up snippets of a conversation between Emma and his mother.

"I'm telling you, Mom—you two have got to go eat there with us the next time you visit. They have the most delicious boneless chicken wings. I can't get enough of them whenever we go."

"You mean chicken nuggets?" Brandon interrupted with a smile before Barbara could reply.

Emma groaned and rolled her eyes. "Ugh, not again!" She looked at Barbara apologetically before explaining, "We get into this every single time we go there." Turning her attention back to Brandon, she continued. "They are called boneless chicken wings. It says so right on the menu. Why do you insist on calling them nuggets? You make it sound like we're eating at McDonald's for God's sake!"

Brandon's face broke into a huge grin as he looked around the table, chuckling lightly to himself before answering her. "Baby doll, I don't get this new trend of trying to fancy them up to sound dignified. I've eaten chicken nuggets my whole life, and those are nothing but chicken nuggets. They just cost more."

"Exactly!" Maggie joined in. "I was just saying the same thing to Eric the other day! Everyone is jumping on that bandwagon!"

Laughter broke out at the table, leaving everyone but Emma either wiping their eyes or clutching their stomachs. She simply shook her head and looked mortified, wondering when her family had been replaced by a bunch of hyenas.

Ethan wondered when he'd last laughed with his family like this.

Later that night, Ethan tossed and turned in the large bed upstairs. He'd decided to stay over in his old room for the night because his laundry was only halfway done, but by 3:00 a.m. he was regretting his decision. The simple bed was comfortable but cold, and the room didn't smell right. There wasn't the right scent lingering in the air.

Get a grip, Foster, he thought. *She's just a fuck. An amazing, delicious fuck...but just sex all the same.* Sighing loudly, he threw back the covers and padded across the room to the stack of clothing he'd worn earlier. Fishing through his jacket pocket in the dark, he felt an immediate wave of calm flow over him the moment he had the iPod in his hand again. Digging deeper, he pulled out his ear buds and returned to the bed.

The moment he hit PLAY and the mellow music began, his mind was flooded with images of warm mahogany tresses and soft pink lips.

He was asleep within minutes.

10

The next afternoon, Ethan was back at the apartment and putting the finishing touches on his latest painting when he heard light footsteps in the hall. He had plenty of time to go unlock the door, but it sent a thrill straight to his groin whenever he heard his beautiful stranger willingly using her key in the lock. By the time the final click sounded in the room and he saw the knob starting to turn, he was fully aroused.

Setting his brush down on the table, he turned in time to see her smiling face walk through the door. She was wearing her ever-present workout clothes again—this time it was a red T-shirt that said *RECYCLING: NOT FOREPLAY, BUT VERY IMPORTANT.* However, instead of being empty-handed as usual, she was toting a large gym bag with her that she set down next to the wall as soon as she shut the door.

"Forget something?" he asked. At her confused look, Ethan nodded toward his docking station where he had returned her iPod. It was currently playing her *Sexy Songs* mix, as Ethan had been unable to think of anything but the previous afternoon all day.

"There it is! I was looking for that all night!" She ran over to the shelf and retrieved it, switching it out for his. He noticed that she set it to his *Fuck Songs* mix before walking away, which pleased him to no end. He watched her walk back to her bag and slip her iPod inside before zipping it back up, thoroughly enjoying the view as she bent over.

Walking up behind her, he felt the now familiar tingle in his fingertips that told him to reach out and grab what was his. *His.* There was that possessive feeling again. It made no sense to him at all, but that did nothing to lessen the urge.

Ethan wrapped his long, slender fingers around her hips, causing her to gasp loudly as he pulled her back into him, rubbing her firm bottom against the prominent bulge in his jeans. Lily groaned loudly at the contact, straightening up so that her back was flush against his bare chest. She laid her head back on his shoulder and closed her eyes.

"Mmm…did *you* miss *me* this time?" Reaching her hand around the back of his head, she pulled him down until her face was flush with the side of his long neck. Inhaling his hypnotic scent deeply before flicking the tip of her tongue along his skin, she reveled in the strong saltiness of his flesh. Lily finished with a simple peck on the edge of his jaw before rolling her head to the side in a daze, already high on the feel of him against her.

Ethan held her closer, tightly wrapping his arms around her middle while swaying slightly back and forth where they stood. "Mmhmm," he mumbled as he nuzzled her skin, peppering light kisses along her collarbone and up her neck. "You know, I think I did."

He smiled as he caught her earlobe with his teeth, tugging briefly before sucking it between his lips. Her loud moan caused him to buck his hips forward, creating the most delicious friction between them. Ethan began rubbing himself against her more firmly, shattering any coherent thought she might have been trying to form.

"Can you feel what you do to me?" he whispered in her ear, eliciting the sexiest whimper he'd heard from her yet. "I was hard before you even opened the door."

"And I was wet the moment I saw you," she gasped.

"Oh, really?" Ethan slid his fingers inside the band of her black

Capri pants, beneath the lace of her panties, and through the tightly trimmed curls between her legs. He could feel the moisture collecting there, already making her outer lips slippery to the touch. The jolt of electricity that shot through him at the feel of her was enough to make him hunch forward and bite her shoulder, groaning into her skin.

Lily whimpered again and turned her head back to face him, tugging on his hair, making his perfect lips finally press against her own. She urged him forward, begging silently with her mouth and tongue, until his kiss turned hungry and he devoured her gasps with a growl. Their tongues fought with each other, leaving them both breathless and dizzy with need.

When they finally parted for air, Ethan panted roughly against her lips. "I need you. I need to feel you again." He released her from his tight grip, spinning her around to face him and kissing her again quickly. When he pulled back, he was curious to see a dark blush spreading over her skin.

"What is it?" he asked, knowing instinctively that she was embarrassed about something.

Turning an even deeper shade of red, Lily bit her lip before meeting his eyes. "Well, I…um…" She took a deep breath and laughed at her own nervousness. "Sorry, I thought this would be easier by now."

Ethan reached out and held her hands, looking deep into her eyes. "Hey, listen to me. You have nothing to be embarrassed about with me. We're not here to judge. Can you trust me enough to share this with me?"

Lily nodded quickly, letting out a relieved sigh. "Yes," she whispered.

"Thank you." He leaned forward and kissed the tip of her nose. "All right then, what is it?"

"I brought my toy."

Whatever Ethan might have expected her to say, that was not it.

Based on her reactions yesterday, he didn't think she'd be ready for that one for a while yet. Once his heart rate had slowed enough for him to speak, he was able to choke out two words.

"Get it."

Lily turned around and dug through her gym bag quickly, returning to him on shaky legs.

"Show me," he quietly growled.

She held her hand out, palm up. Laying there for his inspection was a lilac purple vibrator molded in the shape of an erect penis. It even had a broad tip and veins along the length of it. It wasn't quite as large as he was—only about six inches long while he was closer to seven, and it was a bit thinner in girth—but it was certainly a respectable size to work with.

"Bedroom," he said through his teeth, grabbing it from her open palm. It seemed that he was able to say less and less the more excited he became. He held out his hand, motioning her ahead of him.

Lily walked into the room, her beautiful stranger following her and then turning her to face him.

"You're wearing entirely too many clothes again," he whispered, slowly looking her up and down. "Take them off."

Lily blushed again as she began to strip, but this time it was from excitement. She quickly rid herself of her shirt and pants, tossing them off to the side of the room, but she went a little slower with her bra and panties. Making sure that he was watching her every move, she glanced back at him over her shoulder with a smirk as she unclasped her bra. When it joined the rest of her clothes in the pile on the floor, she finally hooked her fingers into her panties and peeled them down her legs, turning away from him to let him watch as she bent over to pull them the rest of the way off.

"Get on the bed," he barked roughly.

Lily settled onto the middle of the mattress, resting back on her elbows as she looked up at him expectantly.

"Fuck," he groaned, slowly taking in her naked body on the midnight blue sheets. "That color looks breathtaking on you."

Emboldened by his words and his hungry eyes, Lily spoke up. "You look so sexy in your jeans and nothing else, but I want you to take them off."

"Oh you do, do you?"

"Yes. I don't want to be the only one naked."

Ethan smiled and slowly began unbuttoning his fly, thoroughly enjoying the admiration in her eyes. He knew that he was an attractive man, but he'd never in his life felt as desired as he did when she looked at him.

When his jeans were pooled around his ankles, he stepped out of them without taking his eyes off of her. "There. Is that better?" he asked, coming forward to kneel on the foot of the bed.

"God, yes," she moaned. "You are so beautiful, sometimes it hurts to look at you."

"Where does it hurt?" he said with a smile, arching his eyebrow.

"You know exactly where," she giggled.

His face suddenly became serious. "I can't believe you actually brought this with you today," he said, holding up the vibrator. "Don't get me wrong, I'm thrilled, but I wasn't sure that you would be ready yet."

"Well, I wanted to watch you again, too. I had no idea that seeing you do that could be so…erotic." Lily bit her lip again, eying his swollen erection, which was currently curving back toward his navel.

"Believe me, beautiful, if you share this with me today, *that* is a definite. It's already getting difficult to keep from stroking it. You look so amazing like this." He looked down at the toy in his hand

and back to her. "God, just thinking about seeing you use this is making me throb."

"Oh!" Lily felt her stomach clench violently, her lust hitting her like a punch in the gut.

"Now," he said, holding the toy up in front of her, "I want you to answer a few questions for me, is that okay?" When she nodded, he continued. "Is this the first toy you've owned?"

"Yes—my only one."

"Do you think it's big? I mean, have you experienced bigger?"

"Not before you," she blushed again.

"Will you show me how you use this? And not just how you think I want you to use it. Pretend I'm not even here if you must." He handed it to her and she took it eagerly, her nerves all but vanished.

Lily lay back on the pillows and turned it on to the lowest setting. She slowly parted her legs, revealing her dripping flesh to his gaze. As she moved it down between her thighs, she watched his face closely for his reaction. She had no intention of pretending that he wasn't there—it was turning her on more than anything she'd ever experienced.

She started out by sliding the vibrator over her slick skin, letting her juices coat it as she enjoyed the feeling of the vibrations against her clitoris. Her stranger was watching its movements with rapt attention, and when she saw him lick his lips she couldn't bite back a moan.

Unable to wait any longer, Lily shifted her hand so that the toy slid down lower, to her entrance. With a slight adjustment she angled it correctly and slowly began to insert it, moaning louder at the feeling of fullness as well as the deep vibrations.

After pushing it all the way in and pulling it nearly all the way out a few times, she heard him hiss violently, almost as if he were in pain. "Fuck!"

When he finally looked up into her questioning eyes, he groaned again. "God…I don't know how long I'm going to be able to handle this." His cock was already weeping and he hadn't even touched it.

"Do you want me to stop?"

"No! Hell no, this is the sexiest thing I've ever seen. Tell me—does it feel good?" His voice was shaking.

"Yes," she whimpered.

"May I help?" he asked, licking his lips again.

"Oh, God, yes!" she cried out.

Ethan leaned forward and replaced her hand with his own. He pulled the toy out gently, looking it over closely before bringing the tip of it back to her glistening folds. "You're so wet," he moaned, sliding it up and down against her, circling her clit again before carefully pushing it back inside her. "God that looks amazing. Does it feel good like this?"

Lily was beyond speech, too busy twisting and moaning on the bed, her only communication grunts and moans. When he suddenly turned up the speed on the vibrator, her hips bucked wildly and she let out a surprised yell. Ethan started thrusting harder and she knew by the involuntary shaking of her body that she wasn't going to last long.

"No…wait," she panted, desperate to break his rhythm.

"What?" he replied, barely able to tear his eyes away from the sight of her body thrusting against his hand.

"You!" Lily gasped. She knew then that she didn't have anything to lose by being honest. "I don't want to finish yet. I want to watch you!"

Ethan didn't need to be asked twice. He grabbed her hand and placed it back on the toy. "Here, you control the speed, all right?" When she nodded, he sat back on his knees and watched her again, but this time his gaze was full of such concentration that she expected him to start drooling at any moment.

"Wait!" she interrupted before he had even touched himself. "I can't see you well enough from this angle. Please, come closer." She was starting to like how it felt to tell him what she wanted.

He scooted around the edge of the bed, stopping when he was kneeling at her left side. He hadn't taken his eyes off her movements, but now Lily could see him as well. She watched as he took a deep breath and gripped himself tightly, shuddering from the contact. At the very first pump of his fist, she started to shake.

"Oh, please don't stop!" she begged him, grinding her hips harder against her vibrator, fucking it in earnest. "I want you to fuck your hand," she panted as she moved more violently.

He groaned loudly and reached over, slipping his hand between her folds, working his fingers around the toy until they were dripping. Moving quickly back to his erection, he smeared her fluids all over his swollen cock for lubrication. That time when he gripped himself, he threw his head back and cried out at the sensation of her moisture.

Lily watched him work himself, squeezing and pulling, much more roughly than she would have imagined he'd like. She could see the beautiful tip turning darker as his hand pumped up and down, his hips thrusting forward.

"Oh God!" Lily moaned. "That's it! Please...I want you to fuck it like you're inside me." She kept moving her gaze back and forth from his face to his pumping fist and his flexing hips. "Because I'm fucking you right now. This is you inside me...it's your cock...it will only ever be you whenever I use it from now on."

Ethan snarled loudly, reaching his free hand over and rubbing her clitoris while her hips bucked against her own hand's movements, penetrating herself deeper with each thrust.

"Come for me," he growled, leaning over her now, pumping his hips forward into his slippery grip. "I'm so fucking close. I want to watch you come for me first!" The desperation in his voice mirrored the feelings that were swelling in Lily's chest.

She began shaking and bucking her hips wildly, tears streaming freely down her face as she found her release.

"Fuck!" he screamed. "You're so fucking beautiful! God, I can't hold it!" He sat back on his knees again, but when he tried to move away from her, she reached out and grabbed his hip, pleading with her eyes for him to stay right where he was.

Ethan cried out at the top of his lungs, his orgasm ripping through him like a freight train. Lily watched his body erupt in thick bursts of fluid, and when she felt the hot liquid land on her chest she surprised them both by letting out a loud cry, her body clenching tightly around the toy that was still sending vibrations through her sensitive body. She hadn't expected the second orgasm so soon, but feeling his come had triggered something primal inside of her.

After handing her one of his old T-shirts to clean up with, Ethan collapsed next to her on the bed, his mind reeling from what they had just shared. Lily discreetly wiped herself off and wrapped the toy up in the shirt until she could wash it later, setting it down beside the bed. Curling into his side, she kissed him sweetly before laying her head on his chest.

"That was amazing," she purred against his skin, loving the feel of his fingers gently stroking her back.

"Will you stay?" he whispered as he kissed her shoulder, not ready to let her go just yet. He would worry about why he felt that way later.

"For as long as I can," she promised quietly, stifling a yawn, not wanting to think about boring dinners and obligations.

As they drifted off to sleep, they both realized that they had never experienced anything so honest and open in their lives.

11

Later that night, after barely dragging herself away from her beautiful stranger, Lily went back to what she had now come to think of as her humdrum life. After a quick jump in the shower before her dad got home, she ran downstairs to finish dinner.

She had prepared a casserole before work—that way, when she got home, she only needed to throw it in the oven to bake. She was cutting corners everywhere she could think of to get the most out of her free time. Cooking had always been a fun, relaxing thing for her to do when she got home at night; it always helped her wind down. But now, she could hardly give a shit if she ever ate again, as long as she could slowly starve with him. If it weren't for her need to keep up appearances, she would tell George to go back to burning his beloved steaks all by himself and not to expect her back for dinner—ever.

While the casserole baked, Lily let her mind wander as she cut up some vegetables for a salad. Unable to stop them, the steamier events of the afternoon replayed themselves in her mind over and over again: the salty taste of his sweaty skin, the look of hunger on his face as he watched her use her toy, the way he threw his head back and bit his lip before exploding all over her chest. She even found herself wishing that she hadn't needed to wash it off so soon. She would have liked to smell like him for as long as possible.

Lily didn't know what to make of that desire. Semen had always been a necessary evil in the past, and one that she was happy to have trapped away in a slimy condom after the deed was done, but there was just something different about her stranger. The thought of using condoms with him made her want to cry. She wanted the most potent, pure essence of him, and she couldn't get enough. She wanted it dripping from everywhere: her pussy, her tits, even her mouth.

What the hell is wrong with me?

She had never been so wanton in her life. She had always enjoyed sex to a point, but had never experienced any true freedom in that department before now. Now, this beautiful man made her body sing out loud with joy—he could play her like a violin. He completely obliterated any traces of shame or bashfulness whenever they were together.

Scooping the chopped vegetables into a large bowl, Lily found her thoughts drifting from her mysterious partner's sexual prowess to the man himself. Where was he from? Did he paint professionally or for fun? How long was he going to be in town? What was he doing for the rest of his life?

What the hell was his name?

She often came back to that one, usually while lying in her bed at night. Nothing she tried to call him seemed to fit—he was just too different from anyone she had ever met before. Whatever his name, she knew it just had to be something unique or uncommon. It would surprise her to find out after all this time that his name was John or Steve.

Setting the bowl down on the table with a loud thud, Lily decided that it was time she got some answers from him. She knew that she'd never get the big questions answered, at least not yet, but he had been enjoying extracting information from her lately, and she wanted in on the fun. She was halfway through creating a mental list of questions to ask him the next time she went to the apartment when her father walked in.

"What are you daydreaming about?" he said from the doorway, startling Lily so much that she jumped.

"Nothing," she replied, fighting back a blush.

"You can't fool me," he smiled. "I know that look. You were off in la-la-land there, weren't you?"

"No!" She couldn't hide her blush this time, so she busied herself with taking the casserole out of the oven. George rarely played around, so she was surprised when he continued with his teasing.

"Come on, you can tell your old man," he smiled. "Were you hearing wedding bells?"

"Huh?" Lily was completely at a loss.

"You two. Did you ever get around to setting a date? I thought you agreed it would be later this fall."

"Oh," she consciously forced herself to stop from rolling her eyes. Scott. He was the last thing on her mind at the moment. "No, we still haven't set it yet. We talked about September, but I'm not sure if I want it that soon."

"Hmm, well better get down to it, Lil. I know you don't want anything fancy, but from what I've heard, it can take months to finalize those plans, even if it's only something small."

"Yeah," she mumbled. "Uh, dinner is ready," she said, eagerly changing the subject.

Just as they were sitting down to their meal, a loud rumbling could be heard outside, followed by the echoes of heavy footsteps climbing the front stairs.

"Knock, knock," a familiar voice called out, opening the door without waiting to be invited.

"Hey, Scott! How's it going?" George said with a smile. "Come for dinner?" He reached over and pulled out another chair at the small table.

"Yeah, if that's okay." He sat down and looked over at Lily. "I tried to call you earlier to see if we were still on for tonight, but your phone kept going straight to voicemail."

"Oh. Sorry about that. I turned it off when I got to the gym. I must have forgotten to turn it back on."

"Well, don't just sit there, Scott, dig in!" George helped himself to a large portion of casserole and the tiniest scoop of salad. Scott followed suit, wolfing down the food while barely taking time to chew it.

Lily sat there watching the two men in her life as she picked at her own food. Only a week ago she had thought they were the most important people in the world to her, even if they were a bit annoying at times. George had his hunting with its never-ending supply of gamey meat, and Scott had his daddy issues and he often ignored her for his drinking buddies, but still, she had cared about them. Hell, she still cared, but there was something growing inside her that was shifting her priorities around.

For once in her life, Lily was putting herself first.

She was getting increasingly irritated with the need to check in or explain where she'd been, and Scott's visits were making her resent him for stealing her free time. Of course, that only made her feel guilty for being selfish, when he hadn't actually done anything. She had to keep reminding herself that it wasn't his fault that she'd rather screw a complete stranger than let him touch her.

Lily watched him more closely while he ate, wondering where it all went wrong. Obviously she could pinpoint one major difference in her life recently, but it didn't change the fact that they had been drifting apart for a while. She realized that her feelings for him had been changing for a long time. Whenever she saw him lately, it was as if she were hanging out with a brother or cousin, and having such a major distraction over the last week had only served to intensify that feeling.

She remembered the first time George had set them up. She had barely been in town for a month nursing him back to health when he started dropping hints. At the time, she could hardly recall the boy she used to play with—though she had no trouble remembering Sam and how wary he made her feel.

"*Do you remember Scott Walker?*" *George asked her after she finished feeding him his lunch. At her blank stare, he prodded further. "You know, Sam's son. You used to play with him when you would visit in the summer.*"

Lily vaguely remembered a young boy with big brown eyes running around after her as they played. "I think so. Maybe. Why? And how is Sam these days?"

"We don't really talk much lately," George hedged, "but that boy is a great kid. I've tried to keep tabs on him over the years since his mom left." He looked around the room quickly—down at the tray of food on his lap, out the window over her shoulder, anywhere but at her directly. He was obviously nervous. "It just seems to me that he could really use a new friend. He's so isolated out there, and I'd really hate for him to fall in with a bad crowd. Lord knows Sam never watches after him." He mumbled so low it was almost to himself, "Unless he needs more booze."

"So what are you saying, you want me to babysit some guy in his late twenties?"

"No, no, nothing like that. He's all grown up and can take care of himself. I just thought it might be nice for him to make a new friend, that's all."

"I don't know, Dad. I just got here. I haven't even really met anyone yet."

"Well, then that's a great reason to get to know him." He looked up at her finally, a slight blush tinting his cheeks. "He'll be here tomorrow to take a look at your car."

"Dad!" she gasped. "You shouldn't interfere like that!"

"What? That old thing needs a tune-up, and he's the best guy to check it out. It used to be his—he completely rebuilt the engine."

After debating for a few minutes, she let out a deep sigh. "All right, fine. Just don't push, okay?"

"Me? Never." He smiled brightly, grabbing one last bite of his sandwich before she cleared the tray.

The next afternoon, Lily had been ready for some young goober of a kid to show up at her front door. She was prepared to play nice, but was totally geared up to let the kid down easy. Therefore, when the knock came at her door, she had been completely unprepared for the tall, dark, sexy man standing in front of her.

He had such an enormous smile that his eyes lit up, making him appear to glow. She had been a goner from that moment on, and George wouldn't stop gloating for days.

He had asked her out that day, after allowing her to ogle him for a good two hours while he worked on her Oldsmobile, shirtless. Lily had never seen such lovely tanned skin before, and his muscles were insane. She eagerly accepted, and in the beginning it was fun. He could make her laugh like nobody she had ever met before and he seemed to genuinely enjoy her company. But when it became physical between them, things never fully clicked, much to Lily's dismay. It wasn't that it was *bad*—it just didn't feel right.

She could sit with him and talk and laugh for hours, but as soon as he would start trying for more, the energy just seemed to fizzle.

It didn't help that they never really had a lot of privacy between his drunk father and her bedridden one, but even the few times when they would find a moment alone it just felt forced. She found him attractive and enjoyed his company, but the second he would kiss her she would start wondering what was wrong with her, what was missing. She had simply chalked it up to her own inexperience and assumed that she was frigid. Even the few men she had been with before had always left her wanting, so that led her to believe that either they were all terrible at it, or she was.

When he actually proposed to her, she thought that she would be an idiot to pass him up. He was a great friend, and wasn't that really the most important thing? From what she had heard, all lust would fade over time, but having a true friend as a companion when the passion fades was the secret to a successful marriage. Plus, George couldn't have been happier.

When she really thought about it, every time she had even slightly questioned to herself whether they were making the right decision by getting married, George was right there telling her how happy she made him by choosing Scott. How much of their relationship had actually been her choice?

And now she was starting to feel as if she just might know what she'd been missing. Her inner voice wouldn't allow her to ignore the new feelings that her beautiful stranger had been stirring inside her.

Be honest, Lily. If he asked you to run away with him tomorrow, you would.

Her inner voice was absolutely right, which scared the living shit out of her. She knew nothing about him, not even his name, but deep down she knew that if he looked her in the eye tomorrow and said he couldn't live without her, she would have to agree. Never mind the fact that they'd barely spoken to each other and had only met a week ago.

It's just sex, Lily! Get over it. Just enjoy it while it lasts, have a good cry when it's over, and go back to your real life. Scott will still be here, and you can learn to make it work.

That was her practical side speaking up. Every day it worked its hardest to trample her emotional side into the dirt. Although she knew it was right, she couldn't help but be shocked at how cool and calculating she was being toward Scott. Yes, she would hate to stir things up for nothing, but she couldn't ignore the fact that stringing him along was wrong.

"Yoo-hoo, Lily?" She blinked a few times and realized that Scott was waving his hand in front of her face. "Where were you just now?"

"She was doing that earlier," George explained as she tried to hide her blush. "I told her that I could practically hear the wedding bells chiming in her brain."

"Oh really?" Scott smiled.

"Yep, I caught her right there, daydreaming in front of the stove. Say, when are you two kids gonna finally set a date?" George was on his second helping of casserole. The salad still sat on his plate untouched.

"Well, it's a funny thing you should mention that," he returned with a big smile. Reaching into his pocket, he turned to face Lily. "Okay, I told you months ago that I was going to do this. I bet you thought I forgot, but I've just been trying to save up some money." He held out his hand to her. Inside it was a small, maroon box.

She stared at it for a moment, not quite sure what was happening.

"Go ahead, silly. Open it up." He held it closer to her, an expectant look on his face.

Everything seemed to happen in slow motion after that. Lily took the small box between her fingers, trying to ignore the sinking feeling of dread as she opened the lid. Inside the satin lining sat a small, delicate diamond ring. It certainly wasn't the biggest diamond she'd ever seen, but she had never cared about that before, and that wasn't why she was unhappy about it.

"Scott…this is too much. You didn't have to do this."

"Oh, hush up," he scolded, grabbing the box around her fingers and taking out the ring. "I told you that one day I would put a diamond on this finger," he said, sliding it into place on her ring finger. "There, that looks much better." He smiled up at her. "Now everyone can see that you're my girl."

"Well it's about damn time, kid," George said, clapping him on the back. Lily was still staring at her hand, dumbfounded, as if she were waiting for the ring to start screaming at her, telling her she was a filthy liar.

"Don't you like it?" Scott's voice was tinged with worry. He had finally bothered to pay attention to the look on her face.

"Of course I do," she said automatically, unable to ignore the driving need to keep everyone happy. "I, uh, just wish you hadn't blown all your money on me."

"Don't worry about that," he dismissed her, pulling her hand close and leaning down to kiss it quickly. "I should have had it when I first asked you. And now that it finally looks official, I feel so much better about setting a date. What do you think of October? Maybe the twentieth?"

"Um…" She looked back and forth from George to Scott and the matching looks of anticipation on their faces. "Yeah, I guess."

"Hot damn, it's a date!" Scott jumped up and pulled her to her feet, hugging her tightly. Her father watched them with a smile, his eyes suspiciously wet.

Lily couldn't wait for the night to be over.

12

—

"Tell me about the first time you ever had sex." Her voice was a quiet whisper in the bedroom, but it was enough to drag him back from the brink of his light slumber.

"Mmm…what?" Ethan had just begun to dream about luscious pink lips and silky brown locks, but the soft voice beside him was much more enticing.

"You heard me," Lily blushed. "Tell me about the first time you ever had sex." She was determined to get him to open up this time and had spent the entire night and all day at work thinking of different things to ask him.

What she hadn't counted on was the dark look that crossed over his features.

"I don't think so."

"Please?" She couldn't keep the pout from her lips as she rolled over and propped herself up on his chest.

He took a deep breath and sighed loudly, looking into the eyes that had filled his every waking thought lately. "Why do you want to know?"

"Well…because. You keep asking me new questions every day. It's getting a little one-sided."

He ran his hand through his hair in frustration before resting it on her bare back, slowly stroking a circular pattern between her shoulder blades. "It's just that it isn't really a fond memory for me."

"Come on," Lily coaxed. "You keep saying that we can tell each other anything here. Don't pussy out on the first thing I ask you."

"You're a sassy little bitch when you want to be, aren't you?"

"Yes," she smiled. "Now spill it. Were you young and impressionable? Was it an older woman who was eager to teach you? I'm dying to know."

Ethan was quiet for so long that Lily thought he wasn't going to reply. She laid her head down on his chest and huffed, only to be surprised by his velvety voice near her ear.

"It was my—" The word "manager" stuck in his throat. She didn't deserve that title any more. "College sweetheart, for lack of a better term. At least, *I* was still in college."

Lily flipped back over and faced him again. "Not until college? *You?*"

"Yeah, almost the end of school, actually. What can I say? I was a late bloomer." His smile was wickedly sexy, but she refused to let him distract her.

"What made you wait so long?"

"Well, I wouldn't say that I was waiting. I was always interested, but I was ungodly shy. I covered up my insecurities by becoming a pretentious snob, and I let people think that nobody was good enough for me."

"Hmm," Lily mused. "I probably would have just assumed you were gay."

"Excuse me?" The instant arch in his eyebrow made her giggle loudly.

"Well, come on, look at you! Any time someone that gorgeous doesn't date in school, it usually means they're hiding a secret longing for other pretty boys."

"And you're an expert on the homosexual community, are you?"

"No, not at all, but it seemed that most of the attractive guys who didn't date at my high school were living loud and proud by the time I ran into them again a few years down the road."

He thought for a moment before chuckling. "Maybe that would

explain why so many guys used to wink at me when nobody was looking."

"Can't say I blame them. I bet you were delicious even then." She leaned down and kissed his chest, flicking her tongue over one of his flat, dusky nipples, causing it to pebble up.

"So, some woman finally got her hooks in you?" she prodded.

Ethan sighed again, stroking her back more firmly. "If you only knew how appropriate that statement really was."

"Bad relationship?"

"To put it mildly," he whispered. His thoughts went back to the first time he had ever seen Rachel, working at Sullivan Galleries for the School of the Art Institute of Chicago. She had been the one to help him organize his first college exhibition. "She was so striking, so glamorous. She was older than me and way more experienced. She intimidated the shit out of me, so of course I went out of my way to avoid her. Well, she must have seen me as a challenge or something, because she hunted me down like prey."

Lily suddenly didn't want to hear any more—not about this particular woman, at least. The thought of anyone else having their way with him was disturbing enough, invoking a jealousy that surprised her, but she could tell that something really bad had occurred in his past. It made her want to hunt down the skank who was responsible and rip her arms off before beating her with them.

"Okay, different question," she smiled, leaning over to kiss his other nipple. "What's your favorite position?"

Happy to be changing topics, Ethan's mood lightened immediately. His smile nearly blinded her with its brightness. "Do I really have to pick just one?"

"Yes."

"Well, that depends," he pondered.

"On what?"

"On what your goals are," he explained. "Are we talking about favorite position for oral, or for actual sex? And there are different favorites for different reasons. One position might be my favorite for how intimate it is, while another one is my favorite for deeper penetration. There are lots of things to consider before making a statement about favorites."

"Oh…my." Lily's eyes were nearly crossing from the instant rush of heat between her legs. "I guess I never really thought about it like that."

"Would you care for a demonstration?" he asked.

"Oh, I think that's a definite yes." She could barely keep the drool off her chin.

"All right, then, get up on your knees for me." Lily complied quickly, looking down at him with a question in her eye. "Now, turn around and face my feet." When she did so, she was happy to notice that he was fully aroused again. "Good girl. Now scoot over here and straddle me, right over my face."

"Really?" she whispered, lifting her leg over him until it was settled on the other side of his head. "Are you sure about this?" She had always wanted to try this position but had been too embarrassed to ask for it in the past.

"Fuck yes," he groaned deeply.

She felt his hands come up to grab her hips and pull her down, lining her up closer to his mouth. She waited for him to either say something or do something, but he lay very still for almost an entire minute. The only sound that could be heard in the room was his heavy breathing that was beginning to sound like panting. She could even feel his warm breath landing on her sensitive skin.

"Is…is there something wrong? Did I do something wrong?" Lily called back behind her.

"No," he said quietly, his voice a hoarse whisper. "Matter of fact, I don't think this could be more perfect. You have the most beautiful, delicious pussy."

"Oh." She blushed, thrilling at his praise.

"Now, let me show you my favorite position for oral," he growled deeply before digging his fingertips into the flesh of her hips and pulling her down roughly against his mouth. The first warm, wet sweep of his tongue along her slick skin made her buck in surprise, but he held her there firmly with his hands, refusing to let her squirm away from him.

"Holy shit!" she screamed, not fully prepared for his onslaught.

At the first taste of her honey on his tongue, he snarled so loudly that it echoed off the walls. He began lapping at her dripping center, losing himself in the act of devouring her. When he felt her juices run down his chin he wanted to cry out in satisfaction.

When Lily was able to gather her wits enough to focus on the task at hand, she reached forward and wrapped her fingers around the thick base of his shaft, amazed at how firm such soft skin could feel. He moaned beneath her at the contact, and the vibrations from his mouth did unspeakable things to her body.

She leaned over and brought his erection closer to her, rubbing the tip of it over her lips back and forth a few times before flicking at it with her tongue. He thrust his hips up in response, seeking out the warm depths of her talented mouth. When she finally parted her lips and sucked him inside, they both moaned at the sensation, which sent even more vibrations coursing through each of them.

The next few minutes were full of noises that wouldn't sound very appealing anywhere outside of the bedroom: slurping, grunting, panting, and moaning. Lily squirmed against him as her release washed over her in waves, the throaty groan that she let loose wrapping itself around his erection and making him see stars.

"Scoot forward," Ethan commanded, smacking her lightly on the ass to get her moving. She reluctantly released him from her mouth and slid farther down his body. As soon as she had cleared his shoulders he put his hands around her waist and lifted her up, setting her down on his lap. Her wet folds were right above him then, sliding along the underside of his cock, which was trapped between their two bodies. "Oh God," he groaned. "You're so fucking wet."

"That's entirely your fault." She would have laughed at how easy he was to tease if she wasn't so busy sliding herself against the length of him, driving them both crazy. He maneuvered his hand between them and positioned himself at her dripping entrance.

"Now...sit down on me. I need to be inside you right now."

Lily flexed her hips and sat up, sinking down on him in one thrust. She arched her back and cried out, amazed by how full she felt.

"This," he panted, "This is one of my favorite positions for deeper penetration. Do you feel the difference?" He thrust up into her more forcefully, loving the way her hungry body pulled and gripped him from the inside.

"Yes!" she gasped, unsure of how long she would be able to keep her sanity. He held onto her hips tightly, pulling her down on him as he pushed up. After a few more thrusts Lily fell forward, bracing herself by her hands on the mattress between his legs.

"Don't tell me you're done already," he growled behind her, his thrusts never stopping. "I need to feel you come on me again, as many times as you can before I can't hold it back anymore." She moaned and started pushing back into him harder. "Yes! You feel so fucking good!"

Lily felt her beautiful stranger's hand sliding back away from her hip, toward where they were connected. She could feel his fingers slipping around between them, rubbing her clit a few times and pulling back again. She wasn't quite sure what he was doing until she felt his wet fingertips circling around her rear entrance.

"Has anyone ever been inside here before?" he asked her, his own moans betraying how excited he was.

"No," she panted, the word barely audible.

"Never? Be honest."

"No, never!"

She felt his fingers applying more pressure as they circled the delicate opening, coaxing it gently until she felt one single fingertip slip inside the tiniest bit.

"Well, we will have to fix that one day. I'm going to claim every single part of you, do you understand?"

"Yes!" she cried out, feeling his finger slide the rest of the way in. He was unbelievably gentle given their awkward positioning and the fact that he was on the brink of his own volcanic orgasm, and the most amazing feeling of dual stimulation sent Lily over the edge. Her entire body clamped down on him, gripping him so tightly he had to bite back a scream.

When her shaking finally stopped he pushed her forward a bit until he could pull out, grabbing her quickly and pulling her down to the mattress. "Lie back...fuck, I'm so close...I need to see you when I come."

He flipped over and crawled on top of her, grabbing her legs and wrapping them high around his waist. He quickly guided himself back to her entrance, sinking back inside her slowly. Her body was so tired, but she welcomed him eagerly, feeling like he belonged deep inside her.

Ethan got up on his knees, arching over her body to kiss her panting mouth. When he pulled away he whispered against her lips. "This is my favorite position for intimacy." He kissed her again. "I want you to keep your eyes open. Look at me, baby."

He slid his hands down her arms and grabbed her by the wrists, bringing them up and pinning them to the mattress beside her head. She opened her hands in invitation, and Ethan wrapped his fingers around hers, holding her hands tightly while he continued to thrust.

She watched him closely, his beautiful face so full of need that she felt choked up with emotion. Suddenly his focus shifted, and she felt his fingers grip her left hand tighter.

"What the fuck is this?" he panted, stopping his movements and turning her hand over to examine it. When Lily realized what he was talking about her eyes went wide and followed his gaze.

The ring. She had totally forgotten that it was still on her hand.

She looked back at him and was startled to find that anger had replaced his look of bliss. "I asked you a question," he said coldly.

"It's just a stupid ring," she whispered, her voice faltering. "It doesn't mean anything to me when we're here."

"Take it off. Right now." He released her hands long enough to let her pull the offending object off and toss it on the floor. "Now look at me." He grabbed her hands again, lacing his fingers between hers once more. "You will never wear that fucking thing in here again, do you understand me?"

"I'm sorry…you said you didn't care," she tried to explain, not understanding why he was reacting so harshly.

"No, I said I didn't want to know. I don't give a shit what goes on outside this room, but I don't want to know about it! Do you see the difference?"

She didn't, really, but if he was okay with pretending the outside world didn't exist, then that was just fine with her. Her happiest moments had been in this room, away from her boring life.

"Answer me!"

Lily closed her eyes and nodded, and he began to move inside her again, this time much more roughly. She wanted to cry at her stupidity, ruining such a beautiful moment by being so forgetful. She was shocked to feel his lips on hers again, kissing her frantically, his hands gripping her fingers even tighter.

"Don't cry," he gasped against her mouth between his kisses. "Please don't cry…" She began kissing him back and he moaned, his hands shaking in hers. "Open your eyes…please…I need to see you."

As soon as their eyes met he started thrusting harder, kissing her again and again.

"I need you to understand," he panted. "When we are here…you are mine. *Mine!*"

Lily started moving faster with him, meeting him thrust for thrust, scared by how turned on his words were making her. Their eyes remained locked on each other, the only interruptions his possessive kisses that she eagerly returned.

"Say it!" he growled. "I need to hear you say the words. You. Are. Mine!"

Her body began to convulse around him as she came again, shaking violently with the power of his forceful thrusts.

"Yours!" she screamed at the top of her lungs. "I'm only yours!"

Ethan cried out with the most triumphant, possessive snarl she had ever heard in her life, before his lips came crashing down on hers roughly and his entire body tensed up. She could feel him then, his seed pumping deep inside of her, as if he was trying to mark her as his own from the inside out.

That sounded perfect to her.

13

Ethan lay there in the dark, staring at the brown stains on the ceiling from the leaky roof. He could hear the weather worsening outside, forming some disgusting mixture of snow and rain that was too offensive to be called sleet. He had been in the same spot for over an hour—since the exact moment his beautiful girl had left.

But she wasn't his girl at all, and he couldn't stop reminding himself of that little fact. She belonged to someone else—someone who had absolutely no taste in rings. It had probably taken him months to save up for that ugly little chip of a diamond.

Ethan knew that it wasn't fair for him to hold such vitriol for someone he had never even met. Aledo was a tiny blue-collar town in the Midwest, and his family made up most of the wealth in the entire population. She probably had no idea what a piece of crap that thing was.

It hadn't suited her at all. He would have chosen something so much more appropriate for her, even with the same budget. Groaning loudly in frustration, he rolled over and shoved his face in the pillow, but that only served to stir her scent around him.

He needed to get a grip. His head had been full of these thoughts ever since he'd seen that fucking craptastic ring on his girl's—on her finger. It had been eating at him to the point of agony, and he didn't know which part was worse: the fact that he now knew for certain that she was taken, or the fact that he cared so much.

He had been overcome with a blinding rage, fueled by a completely ridiculous sense of jealousy. Not directed at her, but at the outside world for daring to intrude on what was his, at the physical evidence that she cared about someone more than she cared about him. *That* thought fucked with him most of all. It made no sense. None.

Ethan didn't do jealous.

Rachel had learned that the hard way. She'd wasted so many years throwing herself at other men, hoping to make him angry enough to fight for her. He never did.

He had told her as soon as he'd noticed her little games that he had no interest in playing along. She wasn't happy about it—Rachel craved the drama—but by then she had already discovered how much money he was worth and what untapped talent he possessed. So she did away with the theatrics for a while and approached him like a business partner.

The business of being a couple.

"Listen Ethan, we are different than these nobodies. We have the potential for something amazing here. With my experience and your family connections, the opportunities for us are endless. You have the ability to become truly great, and with my head for business, I can make that happen."

He looked at her in disbelief. "Rachel, we've been together less than a year. It's been unbelievably hot, don't get me wrong, but I never really got the impression that you were in love with me. I just assumed you would dump me when I graduate."

"How can you say that?" she asked with a well-practiced pout. "Of course I love you! I thought I had shown you just how much." He was surprised that her nose wasn't growing longer as she spoke, but it was nice to hear, regardless. "But darling, I'm not talking about love right now—no matter how much I love you," she added quickly. "I'm talking partnership."

"How can you talk about a relationship like this, as if it were a business transaction?"

"Because I'm smart enough to know that the best relationships are."

Something in her attitude had struck a chord with him. He had never experienced the mopey, clingy neediness that was synonymous with love. His parents were deeply in love, and his siblings had both quickly found the ones for them, but he had never met anyone he simply couldn't be without. Even Rachel, with her open sexuality that kept him coming back for more, was not someone he would say he was attached to. He simply enjoyed fucking her, and she enjoyed having a rich, talented young artist to promote.

He was attached to his art.

How he felt about painting was the closest thing to love he had ever experienced. The way he could lose himself in creating something and give himself over completely to an emotion only to have a tangible piece of it when he was done never failed to amaze him.

So for Rachel to offer him fame and fortune for doing something that he loved so much, and offer to come along for the ride as a pleasant physical release without demanding that he show her the same emotion he did his art, well…it's no surprise how quickly he accepted. He was young and full of himself, and having her around to feed his ego only made him more of a pompous ass.

The arrangement had actually been rather successful for a while. She really did have a good head for business, and once she took over the management side and put his family contacts to good use, they were the hit of Europe within months of arriving. Ethan had access to anything he needed, including Rachel and her myriad amusements, and she had her new, famous phenom's coattails to ride to stardom.

He hadn't realized until it was too late just how dependent he had become on her. She controlled everything, down to the tiniest detail, and whenever he would show the slightest sign of being unhappy she would find a new distraction for him. He had thought she was the best friend he'd ever had, that it must have grown into some form of love, even if not the kind you read about. He thought she had been taking such good care of him, but she turned out to simply be protecting her investments.

He'd known it needed to end when he finally hit bottom. He had been face down on the floor of some random Parisian hotel bathroom, a pool of vomit drying next to him and blood caked around his nose when he woke up after a four-day cocaine bender. The first thought that entered his mind when he finally regained consciousness wasn't "where am I?" or "how did I get here?" It was "what kind of 'partnership' is this?"

He found her in the bedroom, passed out between another young couple in the nude, cocaine residue smeared over every flat surface he could see. Without thinking twice he threw a few things into an overnight bag and walked out, not even leaving her a note.

After checking himself into the nearest rehab center he could find, he spent weeks getting himself cleaned up. He somehow found the strength to quit cold turkey, but the detox and craving that his body went through would still give him nightmares if he thought about it too long.

He missed his home and his family. He couldn't remember the last time he had spoken to any of them. In rehab, he started to believe that everything would get better if he could just jump on a plane and go back, make a fresh start. Surely his family would welcome him home with open arms. It all seemed so clear.

Until Rachel found him there.

He still had no idea how she'd found him; the woman's resources were terrifying. The second she saw him she had started crying and playing up the role of the wounded victim, demanding to know how he could just walk out on her without even a word. When that failed to get the response she wanted, she got angry.

Angry Rachel was almost an art form in itself. She never yelled, she never ranted, but one could physically see the exact moment when she was done being deceitful and ready to be truly cutthroat. Her entire body would go still and her features would freeze, as if she were finally letting the ice in her heart flow through her veins.

She had turned on him then, like a viper, and proceeded to strike at the heart of his insecurities. As if she had been reading his mind, she told him he was a fool if he thought that his family would want anything to do with him now. They would never accept a filthy addict into their home—it would be too humiliating. They had their image to protect. She told him that if he went home now he would become nothing more than a broken down has-been and his family would probably need to move away out of shame.

Looking back at the conversation now, Ethan didn't know who he was angrier with: Rachel for saying such hurtful things, or himself for actually believing them.

After she worked him over until he was ready to curl up into a ball and cry, she reminded him that he still had her. She would always be there for him, unlike his family. She would never run away from him. If he would only come back with her, they could start over. Another town, another show, and before long he would forget that any of this had ever happened.

He went back with her that day.

He made her swear that there would be no more drugs involved, and she promised. She actually managed to keep that promise, but Ethan had no idea how low she was willing to sink. The worst was yet to come.

Hating the memories that were flooding back, Ethan focused on the problem at hand. Why was he suddenly jealous now? He'd been through a nasty rollercoaster of a relationship and the strongest feeling he'd ever felt for her was anger. Why did this small-town nothing of a girl hold any attraction for him at all?

The only thing they knew about each other was that they were compatible sexually. More than compatible. But something about this girl made him want more than sex. He wanted to hold her when she slept and kiss her when she woke. He wanted to ask her more about herself than her sexual history. He actually…cared. And that freaked the shit out of him.

He wasn't ready for this. He didn't want to care; he didn't want it to be real. He didn't want to need her so badly.

He kept telling himself that if he only wanted her body, things wouldn't get serious. He could enjoy her company and feel perfectly fine with letting her go whenever he decided it was time to leave town again. He should be thrilled that she was engaged.

But he wasn't.

Seeing that ring had made her more than a fantasy to him. It reminded him that she had an entire life outside of this shitty room that he had no knowledge of—and that made him angry. The thought of anyone else putting their hands on her delicate skin made his stomach turn. The idea of her gasping and crying out someone else's name in the dark made him feel sick.

Ethan knew deep down that if he was already feeling this attached, he should probably end it now before it only got worse—but that thought made him feel even sicker. He was becoming addicted to her. She was the only thing that could soothe him anymore.

Deciding that it was pointless to spend any more time obsessing over it that night, he buried his face in the pillow again and inhaled deeply. As soon as he breathed her in, he was infused with a warmth that his body was beginning to welcome.

Once again, he was asleep within minutes.

14

By that Saturday afternoon, Lily was already feeling claustrophobic and cranky. Her bedroom walls felt like they were closing in on her and even her cats couldn't cheer her up.

She missed him. The thought of going another whole weekend without him made her want to scream.

That's why, when Scott called her to ask if she wanted to do dinner at his house that night, she actually jumped at the chance. Even a night with Sam Walker's drunken ramblings would be better than sitting around and pouting. When Scott picked her up in his beat-up Honda twenty minutes later, she was waiting impatiently by the door.

"Hey babe," he said with a smile as she jumped in the car. He kissed her on the cheek and backed out of the drive, heading to the store for groceries.

"I thought I'd make spaghetti for dinner. Do you think Sam will like that?"

"Shit, he'll be thrilled to get anything that I didn't make. And you can only eat so many microwave dinners." He winked at her before turning his gaze back to the road. "I gotta be honest, I'm a bit surprised that you agreed to come over so easily. I just thought it was time that you got to know Dad a little better. You know, get more comfortable at my place."

"I know, you're right." She was only half listening to him, looking around at the storefronts as they drove through town.

"I've got some news," he said a few minutes later, breaking the silence.

"Yeah?"

"Yeah. I just found out about it last night, though, so I hope you aren't mad about it."

"Okay, spill it."

"I'm gonna be gone for a few days, maybe a week. Ryan wants me to ride with him to St. Louis to pick up a car that he's buying for his girlfriend. We thought we'd take our time and make a trip out of it, stay over a couple nights here and there. Maybe stop and do stupid touristy shit while we're out, I don't know."

"Wow, that's quite a road trip!" Lily said, her enthusiasm unmistakable.

"So you're not mad?" He looked over at her suspiciously. "I probably won't be back in time for Valentine's Day. I'm sorry."

"Of course I'm not mad, don't be silly. I didn't even remember that Valentine's was coming up so soon. That was nice of Ryan to ask you instead of Mark or Josh."

"Well, he needs Mark to hang back and run the garage, for one, but he did say that he'd rather have me along in case the car needs a tune-up. He thinks I'm the better mechanic."

"That's really great, Scott. I'm proud of you." Lily smiled at him as he pulled into the parking lot. She had forgotten how nice it could be when they were able to just talk, as friends. It happened so rarely nowadays.

They walked inside, Scott insisting on pushing the cart around because "women are terrible drivers"—an ongoing bad joke that he told to make Lily roll her eyes whenever they shopped together. They moved throughout the store, gradually filling the cart for dinner as they talked about their weeks at work. He told her about some lady's flooded carburetor and Lily laughed with him about Jason and Dr. Wilde's not-so-secret affair.

It felt like old times again, which made her sad if she thought about it too hard. She wondered how much was really different between them now and how much was her projecting her own unhappiness on him. Was he really so distant from her now, or did she just imagine the distance to soothe her guilt?

As they loaded up the groceries into the back of his cluttered car, he leaned down and quickly stole a peck on the lips before smiling again and getting into the driver's seat. Lily stood there for a moment, frowning. Still dry and cold. Nothing. She wasn't imagining it—there just wasn't any spark left, if it had ever been there at all.

She suddenly got the strangest feeling that someone was watching her, like a tingle up the back of her neck, but when she looked around the lot for a familiar face she didn't see anyone other than the regular customers going about their business.

"You coming?" Scott's voice carried back to her from the front of the car.

"Yeah," she mumbled, turning around and getting in.

As they drove back through town toward Scott's place, Lily stared out the window, lost in her thoughts. She was startled back to reality at one point when Scott slammed on the brakes, cursing under his breath.

"What's wrong?" she asked, trying to get her breathing under control.

"Sorry, babe. It's just that this fucking Audi won't stop riding my ass." He turned off the road toward the fairgrounds, flipping the bird out the window as the black car sped by. "Yeah, fuck you, too, buddy," he muttered.

They parked in front of the little house and went in with the groceries, not noticing as the Audi made another lap in the opposite direction.

15

"Fucking muscle-bound, white-trash dickhead."

Ethan was sitting on the floor of the main room of the apartment, propped up against the wall. He was staring at a blank canvas that he'd just propped on the easel, trying to visualize his next painting.

But all he could see was her...being kissed by him. It should have made him feel better that she hadn't responded at all, but it only made him feel worse. He couldn't understand why the hell she was even with that guy if that was her reaction to his kisses. Ethan knew for a fact that whenever he kissed her she exploded into flames.

He hadn't meant to follow them.

He had been running a few errands, picking up a few more art supplies, when he decided that it wouldn't kill him to have a few groceries around the place since he was practically living there now. It was only supposed to be a studio, but he felt so much better when he was there lately. He hadn't had any nightmares in days.

He hadn't seen them inside the store at all, but when he was getting ready to pull out of his parking spot something just made him look up directly at them. It was as if his eyes were drawn to her like a magnet.

The big burly idiot had been tossing bags in the car before leaning down to steal a kiss, and it had taken everything inside of Ethan to keep from jumping out of the car and socking him in the jaw. Even though he was seeing through a blood-red rage cloud, he couldn't take his eyes off her face. She looked so sad, so alone.

The next thing he knew, he was driving. It was simply instinct, his body following hers. He hated to think how easily he could have rear-ended them when the Neanderthal had slammed on his brakes; his eyes had been locked on her profile through the back window the entire time. It would have made for an awkward accident report, that's for sure.

He had felt something painful deep in the pit of his stomach when they both went into that tiny little house together. Suddenly the pitiful ring made much more sense. Did they live there together? What was she missing there that kept her coming back to him?

Ethan sighed deeply and threw his head back against the wall in frustration. "Fuck!" he growled. He wondered why he had to pick now to give a shit about something.

In an effort to distract himself, he broke another chunk off the large candy bar that he'd purchased. He sucked the melted chocolate off his long fingers before chewing loudly, regarding the blank canvas again. As a few different images began to filter through his mind, he could hear a familiar light cadence outside in the hallway, slowly climbing the steps.

He stopped mid-chew and stared at the door, not daring to get up. He almost thought his ears were playing tricks on him until the knob began to turn, that amazing sound of the tumblers turning in the lock making his insides melt. The door opened in slow motion before him, revealing the loveliest face he could have ever hoped to see at that moment.

His brunette goddess entered with a smile so bright that her eyes were glowing. She was in her standard gym attire, this time sporting a pair of dark gray pants and a light blue shirt emblazoned with the words *PART-TIME MODEL* in black letters. She shut the door behind her and crossed the room, stopping once she was standing right in front of him and crouching down until she was looking him in the eye.

"Morning, stranger," she whispered, the smile never leaving her face. He couldn't keep from glancing quickly at her fingers. All bare. Good.

"What's got you in such a good mood this morning?" he replied, still feeling sore about yesterday, but already noticing her contagious good mood spreading throughout his senses.

"Well," she sighed, "it's the weekend, and I have found an entire Sunday to be just where I want to be." She leaned forward slowly and brought her mouth to his, kissing him lightly. When she pulled back she flicked her tongue out and licked her lips, tasting the slightest hint of chocolate. "Mmm, you taste rather sweet today."

Lily sat down next to him, propping herself against the wall. She reached over and took the chunk of chocolate from between his fingers, biting off a small piece before sharing another smile with him that he felt all the way down in his groin…after it first left his stomach fluttering in the strangest way. It was a sweet smile that told him she really was happy to have finally found time to be with him.

"So are you just a big Conchords freak, or is it all things New Zealand?" he asked, nodding toward her shirt of the day. He tried to ignore how loud his heart pounded when her eyes lit up.

"Oh, New Zealand, all the way!" she gushed. "I didn't know much about it before I started getting into the Conchords a few years ago, but I just love so much about the culture."

"Have you ever been there?"

"God, no, I could never afford that," she sighed. "But if I could go anywhere…" She didn't need to finish her thought; the wistful look on her face said it all. She blushed a deep red when she noticed he was watching her closely. Taking another quick bite of chocolate, she used it to give her a moment to catch her breath before handing it back to him.

They sat together in silence for a few minutes, their simultaneous chewing the only sound that could be heard.

"So," Lily finally said, gesturing to the canvas. "What exactly are we looking at here?"

"Well, it's supposed to be my next great masterpiece. Right now it's nothing."

"No," she whispered, meeting his eyes again. "Never nothing."

Ethan had no choice after that—he simply had to kiss her. He shifted slightly until their noses were almost touching, inhaling her deeply before bridging the gap and settling his mouth over hers. Rather than the explosion of fire that they were used to, it was a slow burn that spread over them both, radiating throughout their bodies until even their fingers felt like they were glowing.

Neither of them had ever felt anything so sweet.

Somehow he forced himself to break the kiss, resting his forehead against hers and exhaling. "So you have all day?" he whispered, almost afraid to open his eyes and find out he'd misunderstood her.

"Yes." He could feel the warm sweetness of her breath on his lips as she answered him. "Unless you need to work?" her voice faltered. "I'd hate to be a distraction."

"Oh, you're a distraction all right," he groaned, lifting his hand to the back of her head and spearing his fingers through her hair. "To my sanity."

He pulled her mouth back to his and kissed her more roughly, pouring every drop of anger and uncertainty he'd felt over the last few days into it until it grew more and more heated. When she gasped at the onslaught he slipped the tip of his tongue between her soft lips and caressed it against her own.

She responded instantly, moaning into him and running her hands frantically up across his chest and shoulders, desperate for something to grab onto. When she had finally fisted enough material from his tattered T-shirt between her fingers she yanked him toward her.

He followed with a hungry grunt.

Wrapping his other hand around her waist, he leaned her back slowly onto the floor, never breaking contact with her delicious mouth as he slid one knee up between her thighs. She spread them eagerly, stretching her legs up around his hips, allowing him to settle his weight there more firmly. His now painful erection was pressed up against her and the friction of him felt so good there, even through their clothes, that she couldn't stop herself from rocking her hips up into him.

Ethan groaned through the kiss, shifting his hips into her again and running his hands over everywhere he could reach on her body at once. He stroked her hair, caressed her cheeks, and cupped her firm breasts through the material of her shirt before finally grabbing her hips and pulling her up into him again, grinding himself even harder there.

"Please!" Lily gasped around his strong lips, gripping and pulling at his shirt around his back, trying to lift it up but getting it bunched up around his moving arms. "God, please!"

Ethan pulled back long enough to get the offending shirt over his head, tossing it over in the corner before attacking her mouth again. She let out a blissful sigh once her fingers came in contact with his warm skin, sinking them into his back when she was treated to another grind of his pelvis.

He tugged at her shirt, pulling it up just enough to see her lacy bra. With another loud groan he buried his face in her cleavage, fondling and squeezing her breasts before yanking the lace down. A small rip could be heard as her dark, erect nipples were exposed to his ravenous mouth. He feasted on her swollen peaks, licking and sucking them while sliding one hand down between their bodies and cupping her sex.

"Are you wet for me?" he panted against her lips, bringing his hand back up long enough to slide it behind the waistband of her panties. She could only respond with a moan as she nodded and his fingers sank into her slippery wetness, giving him all the answer he needed. "Fuck," he gasped, quickly pulling his fingers free and shoving them in his mouth.

When the taste of her juices hit his tongue he snarled, a new wave of need washing over him. He had to be inside her body. If he wasn't buried deep inside her in the next minute he knew he would go insane. He sat back on his knees, knowing that she would follow. As soon as she had gotten up on her knees to face him, he kissed her one more time roughly before grabbing her and turning her around.

She arched back against him, bringing one hand up behind his head to tug on his hair, while at the same time rubbing her backside against the throbbing bulge in the front of his jeans. He grabbed her by the back of her hair and pulled her head back, nipping and licking at her lips.

"I need you," he groaned.

"Then I'm yours," she gasped.

Ethan bit back a growl as he began to pull on her pants, sliding them roughly over the swell of her hips while he nipped and licked at her neck. As soon as her pants were down around her knees and her delectable ass was uncovered, he ripped them the rest of the way off and pushed her forward to guide her onto her hands and knees. Perhaps later he could take his time and look her deep in the eyes while he lost himself inside her, but at that moment he didn't even have the patience to take the rest of her clothes off.

Fumbling with the fly of his pants, he wrestled his jeans down, and no sooner had he kicked them off and thrown them across the room than his leaking cock was in his hand and he was guiding it to her scorching heat. Arching her back, Lily offered him a perfect angle for entrance, and he thrust himself inside with one swift movement.

They both cried out at the sudden onslaught of sensation.

Ethan began pushing himself inside her, desperate to feel her climax on him again. He leaned forward enough to reach one of his hands around to the front of her, sliding his fingers through her wetness and swirling them around her clitoris in time with each thrust. She was shattering into a thousand pieces within seconds.

Lily wailed, her inner muscles gripping him tightly inside her. Ethan almost asked her to say his name, wanting more than anything to hear it falling from her kiss-swollen lips, until he remembered at the last second that she didn't even know it because he hadn't wanted her to. At the moment he couldn't quite remember why that had seemed like such a good idea.

He slowed his movements a bit, allowing her to regain some energy so that she didn't fall forward on her face. He was close, but he wanted her full participation. He ran his hands up her back, helping her take her shirt the rest of the way off until they were finally naked together. Once it had been tossed aside to rest next to his, she turned back and looked at him over her shoulder, a bright blush staining her cheeks.

"What could you possibly be embarrassed about right now, my beautiful girl?"

Lily moaned again, loving the sound of him calling her his. That was exactly what she needed to hear at that moment, especially considering what she was about to request. She swallowed down any nervousness she might have been feeling, knowing that this man was the only one she would ever want to share this with. Even if it was only while she was in this room, she was his. Body and soul.

"Come on, out with it." He smirked at her playfully, pushing his hips into her for good measure. Feeling him sliding inside her only served to distract her again, but after she remembered what the heck she had been trying to say, she smiled at him and felt her cheeks flame again.

"I was just...well...I've been thinking about what you did the other day, what you said. I think I'd—" She took a deep breath before continuing. "I think I'd like to try it."

She watched as the realization of what she was asking dawned on him. His mouth dropped open for a second before he could catch it and his gaze kept shifting from her eyes to her bottom. "Now?" he barely croaked. "Are you sure?"

"Yes," she whispered. "Yes, now, yes, I'm sure." She looked him directly in the eye before adding, "Yes—with you. Only you."

How he didn't come right there on the spot was beyond him.

Somehow the enormity of what she was asking of him outweighed the sexiness. He was suddenly very overwhelmed with the need to make this comfortable for her. He didn't know if he could promise total pleasure the first time, even though he would try, but he damn well wasn't going to give her pain.

"Dammit! If I'd only known you would be ready for this, I would have bought some lube. I don't have anything here that would work." He looked at her and gulped nervously. "I don't want to hurt you."

Scolding himself for his stupid mistake of ever being unprepared, he made a mental note to buy some lube the second he left again. While he was debating if he should be the world's biggest idiot and ask her to wait there while he ran to get some, his beautiful girl managed to completely surprise him once again.

Reaching down into the pocket of her pants that were bunched up beside her, she pulled out a small squeeze tube of lubricant and handed it to him. "I took this from the sample closet at work," she said quietly, a fresh wave of color tinting her cheeks.

Ethan briefly wondered where the hell she worked that she had access to samples of lube, but he stopped himself before asking her and crossing his own boundaries. "You've clearly given this some thought, haven't you?" he asked instead, still amazed by her boldness.

"Yes," she answered confidently. "I'm ready."

"All right," he whispered. Before he could talk himself out of it, he opened the tube and squeezed a generous amount of the slippery substance onto his fingers and brought them up to her rear entrance. He hadn't pulled himself out of her yet, wanting the feeling to stay pleasurable for her for as long as possible while he prepared her. "Now, this is going to feel just like the last time to begin with, okay? You liked that, right?"

"God yes," she moaned.

Ethan slowly inserted one finger inside her, gently moving deeper as her muscles relaxed to allow him entrance. She groaned loudly, pushing herself back against him slightly once she had grown accustomed to the feeling. Very carefully, he added a second finger, stretching her gradually as he massaged the lubrication inside her, coating her so thickly that his fingers began to slide in and out rather easily. By that point she was moaning and rocking back and forth and it took every ounce of his energy to keep from exploding at the sensation.

"Okay, okay…slow down, baby." He slowly pulled himself out of her gripping wetness, missing the contact instantly, but even more excited by what he was about to do. Holding himself firmly, he replaced his fingers with the tip of his erection. He had barely brushed against the puckered opening, but the sight of being so close to her there made his stomach flip over in anticipation.

"Now listen to me," he said quietly. "I'm going to go very, very slowly at first, all right?" When she nodded, he continued, "If at any point this gets too uncomfortable for you, I want you to tell me immediately, do you understand?"

"Yes."

"Do you trust me to try and make this as pleasurable for you as possible? You won't enjoy this at all if you can't relax your muscles, and you can't relax if you don't trust me."

"Yes," she whispered. "I trust you. I wish I knew why, but I trust you more than anyone I've ever met."

Rocked by her words, Ethan raised a shaking hand to her back, stroking her softly up to her shoulder where he squeezed her quickly and let go, as if in a silent thank-you. He brought it back down to brace her hip in place as he started to work himself inside her.

Slowly—so slowly that she barely registered any movement at first—his broad tip gradually entered her. He would move forward half an inch, only to withdraw even more, letting the lube do its job to allow him to slide along her muscles more easily. He heard her gasp and huff a few times, and each time he would ask if she was all right, but she would only grit her teeth and adjust her position, working through the initial discomfort.

He could feel her relaxing and stretching to accommodate his girth, and when he had finally seated himself inside her completely, he had to still his movements for a moment and take a deep breath. He wanted to let her get used to the feel of him before he started moving again, but the effort was making sweat stand out on his forehead. It was the softest, tightest sensation he had ever felt in his life, and he didn't think he was going to last longer than about two pumps.

Lily was breathing deeply, adjusting to the feeling of having him so deep inside her. It was uncomfortable, but she wouldn't say it hurt. He was being so slow and gentle with her that it was nothing more than a warm, stretching fullness. Yes…full. She could feel him everywhere inside her at once, like the blood that pounded through her veins. He was consuming her.

"I want you to bend down farther," he gritted through his teeth, breaking the silence. "Move slowly, we'll go together. You can prop up on your elbows and knees, but I need to lean forward on my arms." When she looked back at him, she was startled to see that every vein was standing out on his face and neck, and he was squeezing his eyes shut and biting his bottom lip. It was breathtaking to behold. Feeling her gaze on him, he opened his eyes, scorching her with their heat. "It's just so fucking intense. I need more leverage, and I'm afraid I'm going to lose my balance and hurt you."

Lily nodded quickly, touched by his honesty. She slowly moved forward until she was stretched out beneath him, braced on her forearms with her knees bent under her hips, thrilled at the sensation of his warm body covering hers. He propped himself up on his elbows on each side of her arms, kissing her shoulder a few times before she felt his shallow hot breath puffing at her ear.

"All right, I'm going to move now," he whispered. She felt him shifting his hips, pulling himself out of her slightly. He slid fairly easily, but her body still gripped at him so tightly that he whimpered as he moved. "Fuck," he groaned, biting her shoulder as he pushed back inside. He moved his hands closer until they were covering her own, lacing through the backs of her fingers, holding them tightly.

It didn't hurt nearly as bad as she had feared, and hearing him come undone was arousing her all over again. She lay there for a while, feeling the steady drag and slide of him as he flexed his hips back and forth slowly, and it didn't take long before his sultry voice was back at her ear.

"You're doing so good, baby," he panted, his voice shaking. "You are so fucking beautiful…you feel so amazing…God!" His entire body shivered above her. She felt his left hand release her fingers, sliding back up her arm and down her side, until he slipped it around her hip and settled it between her legs. The next time he thrust forward, she felt his fingers rubbing and circling her swollen clit.

"Oh!" she gasped. The dual stimulation was interesting.

Ethan was barely holding on. "Please," he begged, sounding desperate. "Please come for me, baby…I need to make this good for you… do you think you can?"

He kept up his swirling patterns on her throbbing bundle of nerves, and before long Lily was grinding herself against him, trapping his hand between her thighs for added friction. After only a few seconds they had built up an amazing rhythm together; Lily would rock forward into his hand and he would rock forward into her, over and over again.

"Oh…oh God…" Her body was shaking. He was everywhere… everywhere around her…everywhere inside her…and she was falling… falling into oblivion. "Oh *fuck*!" she screamed, her body convulsing as she rode out her release.

"Yes, baby, that's it…oh fuck yes, that's it…I can feel you squeezing me even tighter…oh…oh God…FUCK!" He threw his head back and cried out, finally losing control. His body tensed up painfully before exploding in the most intense, blinding pleasure he had ever felt. Between his ears ringing and his vision blurring, he wondered if anyone had ever died from an orgasm.

Gently shifting to the side and slowly pulling out of her, Ethan wrapped himself around her tightly, almost protectively. "Are you all right?" he whispered against her neck.

"Mm," she nodded, exhausted. "Better than all right." He had been so gentle with her; she had never felt so precious to anyone.

He wanted to take her into the shower and spend his time cleaning her and helping her wind down, but he was suddenly so sleepy that he hoped she didn't mind resting for just a moment or two first.

Burying his face in her hair and inhaling deeply, he barely had the energy to whisper one last thing to her before closing his eyes and drifting to sleep.

"Thank you for trusting me."

16

The next few days were full of more pleasure than Lily could have ever imagined in her wildest dreams.

By some great miracle, the Gods of Infidelity had been smiling down on her when she returned home Sunday evening. She had been all ready to go home and put on a brave face, making dinner while she suffered through the piercing agony of being away from her beautiful stranger yet again, only to find out that not only was her fiancé going out of town for the entire week, but so was her father. He was being sent to Springfield by the high school to help chaperone a student government field trip because the American History teacher had fallen ill and wouldn't be able to go. He was less than thrilled by the news.

She almost hadn't been able to contain herself when George told her over their bowls of venison stew. After she fought through the initial urge to jump up and down and do cartwheels around the living room, she still had trouble paying attention to him for the rest of the night. Her mind could only think selfish, joyous thoughts from that point on. No more dinners. No more excuses. No more rushing to the apartment and leaving within an hour or two just to go where she didn't even want to be.

Lily could get used to that.

From the next day on, the week had turned into one giant orgasmic blur, separated only by brief intermissions so that she could go to work and go home to sleep. She was sorely tempted to stay over for the night, but she was paranoid George would call the house while she was gone or that she might find her bored cats ripping the house apart in protest of being ignored. Spoiled rotten brats that they were.

It didn't help that her beautiful stranger's hints for her to stay were becoming less than subtle. Every time she would get ready to leave, he would find a new way to distract her into staying longer. Whenever they would nod off afterward out of exhaustion, which was pretty much every time, he would hold her tightly to him as soon as he felt her stirring. One time the bastard had even begun stroking her hair and humming softly in her ear, trying to lull her back to sleep. And that's not to mention the bed, which felt like lying on a cloud. It was getting increasingly difficult to say no when it was the last thing in the world she really wanted to say.

Lily sighed to herself, unable to concentrate on the buzz of office activities going on around her. Although she was supposed to be updating a patient's chart, she let her mind wander back yet again to the previous afternoon.

"I don't know the first thing about painting," Lily admitted, watching him apply broad strokes of color across the pristine canvas. "But I certainly do love to watch you do it." It didn't hurt that he was shirtless again.

"Care for a demonstration?" he smirked.

"Yes!" she squeaked. After the last demonstration he'd given her, she knew that the answer was always yes.

What she had assumed would be a silly lesson about doodling stick figures in a notebook quickly took a turn for the erotic. Before she knew what was happening, her stranger had rolled out a drop cloth across the floor and stripped her bare, laying her down right in the middle of it. With palette in hand, he slowly began painting lazy, sensual strokes of color along her fair skin.

He went through every brush in his case, explaining the difference

in each width and texture. When he ran out of brushes he smirked
again, telling her that it was time to explore the sorely underrated
art of finger painting. Dipping his long, slender fingers into a freshly
mixed dollop of a lovely shade of aquamarine, he proceeded to smear
the oils around her nipples and down her stomach. Before long, single
finger strokes were replaced with whole handprints across her flesh,
and the entire effect was mirrored onto his own torso once he covered
her body with his.

The amount of scrubbing and touching that was needed to clean each
other off later only served to ignite another heated sex fest in the shower.
It had been so steamy, and slippery, and—

"Yoo-hoo, Earth to Lily!"

"Huh?" She was startled back from dreamland, jerking upright when
she realized that Becky was sitting right next to her and waving her
hand in front of her face.

"Where were you just now? You looked like you were about to start
drooling any second."

"Oh…I, uh, I guess I just zoned out there for a minute." Hazy
images of her stranger standing under the spray with water streaming
down his back were still clinging to her conscious mind. They refused
to be shoved away for later, and who could blame them, really?

"I'll say. I was trying to get your attention forever."

"I'm sorry, Becky. What did you need?"

"Oh, I didn't need anything, really," she said, laughing lightly. "I
just came to tell you that I had to help that weird old lady again. You
know, the one with the Yoda forehead?"

"Ugh, yeah. That is the creepiest forehead I've ever seen on anyone,
especially a woman. It's even creepier than Mare Winningham's."

"Oh my God, isn't that the frumpy chick in St. Elmo's Fire? Man,
I never thought about it before. Her forehead *is* creepy!" They both

erupted in a fit of laughter that was interrupted by the loud beep on Lily's phone.

"What now?" Lily sighed before picking up the receiver. She didn't want to deal with Kim and her bad attitude today—she wanted to escape back into fantasies of her stranger.

Becky gestured that she was going back to work as Lily pushed the flashing page button. "Yeah?"

"Lily, you have a patient call on line four," Kim snapped. "They asked for you specifically."

"Okay, thanks." She clicked over to the other line. "Thanks for holding, this is Lily. How can I help you?"

"Lily?!" a panicked voice croaked. "It's Maggie Foster. Can you help me? I'm freaking out a little bit."

"Hi, Maggie. I'll certainly try to help. What seems to be the problem?"

"I'm spotting," she whispered, as if merely saying it out loud was painful. "And please don't give me the spiel about how this happens to most women. Nothing about my pregnancies has been what happens to most women."

"No, no, I wasn't about to say that. When did it start?"

"Overnight I think. It's not heavy, but it's there."

"All right, have you been doing anything strenuous? Have you had sex in the last twenty-four hours?"

"No! I've been too scared to!" she cried.

"Okay, okay, are you having any cramping?"

"No, not yet. Is there any way that you could squeeze me in for an ultrasound today? I'm not due for my next one for two more weeks, but this is exactly how all of the others started. I won't be able to calm down until I know the heart is still beating."

"I understand, but don't you live in Chicago? Wouldn't you rather go to a local hospital to be seen quicker? I can try to call in the order."

"I'm already in Aledo. My mother-in-law had me over for the weekend since Eric is out of town again."

"Let me see what I can do, all right? I'm going to put you on hold for a minute." Lily ran down the hall toward the ultrasound room, grateful to see the technician just dismissing a patient.

"Hey Lily, what's up?" she asked her after handing off a series of blurry pictures to a beaming woman.

"Heidi, I need a really big favor. I know you're overbooked today, but I've got a majorly important red sticker chart that needs an emergency scan. Can I have her come in?"

"I don't know," she huffed. "I'm never going to get out of here as it is."

"I know, and I'm sorry for making it worse. Believe me, though, Natalie will be insanely pissed if we don't jump for this one."

"All right, fine," she sighed, glancing down at her watch. "But she needs to get here as soon as possible."

"I don't think that is going to be a problem. Thank you so much." Lily spun on her heels and dashed back to her desk, already grabbing for the phone as she sat down. "Are you still there?"

"Of course!" Maggie replied with a shaky breath.

"Okay, I was able to work you in, but I need you to get here as soon as possible."

"I'll be there in ten minutes." The call went dead. She had already hung up.

Less than twenty minutes later, Maggie Foster was having a clear, warm gel applied to her abdomen by Heidi. She was joined by her mother-in-law, Barbara, who had refused to let Maggie drive herself to the office, and, strangely enough, Lily.

It was not customary for the nurses to be in the room with patients during this procedure, but when Lily had attempted to excuse herself after taking her into the room, Maggie had grabbed her hand.

"Please don't go," she whispered. "Barbara is going to cry in a minute. Eric is usually here to be strong for me, but he won't be able to get here for a few more hours."

"Uh, all right," Lily replied, unable to hide the completely baffled tone in her voice. "Just let me tell someone that I'm going to be in here." She walked back to her phone and paged the front desk.

"Reception," a sharp voice barked on the other end.

"Kim, it's Lily. You're going to have to shuffle some charts around up there. Natalie is going to be down a nurse for a while."

"What?" she snapped. "You've got to be kidding me! We're swamped!"

"Well, deal with it," Lily shot back. "If Natalie has a problem with it, just remind her that I am helping a red chart." She went to hang up but stopped the motion in mid-air, bringing the receiver back to her ear. "And if you have a problem with it, you can just kiss my ass." *Click.*

Now Lily was in the ultrasound room, standing next to the table where Maggie was laying, holding her hand. She noticed that the elder Mrs. Foster had already migrated to the back of the room and was hunched over in a chair, repeating a quiet prayer to herself under her breath.

"Okay, I'm going to start now," Heidi announced, dimming the lights slightly and sitting down in front of the machine. She fiddled with a few controls on the keyboard and held out the ultrasound wand, placing it in the middle of the gel on Maggie's skin. They all held their breath as they watched her moving it around, turning it in different directions and stopping frequently to enter data into the computer. At one point she switched on the volume only to turn it back off again quickly, but she hadn't been able to hide the sound in time. There had been nothing but static.

And silence.

Stopping the machine, Heidi set down the wand beside it and handed Maggie a towel to wipe off the messy gel. Once her hands were free again, she set them both gently on Maggie's arm and looked at her with eyes full of sympathy.

"I'm so very sorry, Mrs. Foster," she whispered.

Barbara immediately broke down into sobs, but Maggie sat there quietly. Lily was worried that she might be in shock until she felt her squeeze her hand tightly. "That's all right," she whispered. "I'm quite used to being a failure at this."

"Don't say that," Lily scolded. "You have a genetic condition, Maggie. That is *not* your fault. You did everything perfectly, it's just so hard to predict what will happen. There are women with your condition who only ever suffer one loss, and then there are those who lose seven or eight."

Their discussion was interrupted by another loud sob from Barbara. Maggie rolled her eyes and turned to look at her over her shoulder. "Mom, sweetie, why don't you go sit in the waiting room? I'll be out as soon as I find out what happens now, okay?"

"All right," she choked out. Barbara slowly walked to the door, stopping first to hug Maggie and kiss her on the cheek. "I'm so sorry, sweetheart." She wiped her eyes with a tissue and went out the door.

Maggie looked back at Lily. "I love her dearly, but I'm trying really hard to keep a tight rein on my own emotions. I can't handle her weeping like that right now. I know she feels badly for me, but the harder she cries, the more I feel like I let her down again."

Visibly uncomfortable with the awkward conversation, Heidi excused herself to give them some privacy. "I'll let Natalie know," she said quietly to Lily on her way out into the hall.

Once they were finally alone, Lily jumped in. "I'm sure that Mrs. Foster doesn't think you let her down."

"I've robbed her of four grandchildren now, Lily. And each one gets farther along, giving us all false hope. It's just…cruel to put her through."

"It's a cruel situation for everyone, not just her."

Just then a gentle knock sounded at the door and Natalie stuck her head in. "Maggie? May I come in?"

"Of course, Dr. Wilde. Thank you so much for sparing Lily right now. She's a great hand-holder."

"She's the best we have," Natalie agreed, and the praise sounded so genuine that Lily couldn't help the pink stain on her cheeks. "Let me just start by saying that I'm so sorry this happened again."

"Well, we knew it was a risk from the beginning." Maggie said, shrugging. The detached look on her face didn't reach her eyes, though. She was blinking back tears rapidly. "What do we do now? I've never found out like this, without anything really coming out first."

"Well, that's what I need to talk to you about," Dr. Wilde said, the tone in her voice leaving no doubt that it wasn't going to be pleasant information. "In some cases we can remove the fetus, but I'm afraid that won't be an option for us now."

"Why? I was hoping to just get this whole debacle over with as soon as possible."

"The fetus is too large now, Maggie. You've made it almost seventeen weeks—much farther than you have in the past. We can't remove the fetus here when it's that large. It's against our policy to perform a D&C on anyone past the first trimester. There are some locations that might, in a life or death situation, but I cannot. I don't want to get into specifics, but it's a grisly procedure that we don't perform here."

"I understand. I didn't realize it was that large already. I wouldn't want that done, either. But what does that leave us with, then?"

"We're going to have to admit you to the hospital. Once you are set up in the maternity ward, we will need to induce you. I'm sorry, but the only option is for you to deliver the stillborn fetus."

"Oh, God!" Maggie gasped as a rogue tear made its way down her cheek.

"I know it sounds terrifying, but it is quite similar to what your body would do on its own, except now we can monitor and control everything. We have no idea how long you would have taken to expel the fetus yourself, and this actually has less impact on your body than a D&C."

"How long will it take?"

"I'm afraid that's hard to say. Some women are done within hours, while others take a day or two. However, I can promise you any pain-killers you might need to get through the contractions."

"Jesus Christ!" Maggie wailed, putting her face in her hands. "Fine," she huffed after collecting herself. "But I want to be so doped up that I don't even know what day it is. I don't particularly want to remember this."

"I'm sure we can work something out to make you comfortable. Why don't you go home and pack a bag. Grab a bite to eat if you think you can. I'll get the orders sent over to the hospital and when you're ready, just head over there and get checked in." Natalie looked at Lily. "Would you come with me for a minute?"

"All right." She turned to Maggie. "I'll be right back, okay? Why don't you finish getting cleaned up and dressed?" Lily followed Dr. Wilde into the hall, closing the door quietly behind her.

"I think it would be wise if you stayed with her today, at least until her husband is in town. Her mother-in-law is a wreck out there. I honestly don't know if either of them are fit to drive right now."

"That's fine, but what about—"

"Don't worry about the clinic, we'll manage. And I'll pay you for the rest of the day." Lily had to stop her eyes from bugging out. Natalie never liked to part with help or money.

After grabbing an extra box of tissues and escorting the two desolate women outside, Lily took the keys from Barbara and began to chauffeur them home in a sleek red Mercedes. Lily insisted that it would be a hell of a lot safer to leave her own shitty old car in the lot and take the expensive vehicle they had driven.

"How are you doing, Maggie?" Lily asked over the loud sobs from Barbara in the backseat. "I mean, I know you aren't good, but do you need anything?"

"Honestly?" she replied, looking sideways at her from the passenger seat. "I'm just pissed. Of course I'm sad and depressed and doing everything I can to keep from acting like her," she nodded toward the backseat, "but overall I'm just pissed. And I want a large chocolate fucking shake. I've been eating so healthy lately and I want something horrible for me right now."

Lily turned into the closest drive through and ordered her the biggest shake they had, refusing to let her pay for it when she handed her money. "Put that away," she shoved at her hand. "This is probably the only nice thing I can do for you right now. Let me get you your fucking shake."

They drove for a few minutes in silence. Well, as much silence as could be had between one sobbing woman and another one making loud slurping noises. After Lily asked which way to turn to get to their house, she spoke again to Maggie.

"So, why are you pissed?"

"Because," she huffed after swallowing a large sip. "This is something I'm supposed to be able to do. It's one of the only natural, animal functions that we have left as humans. And even that is getting warped by all the women who refuse to breastfeed. I am being denied a basic function, and I want to wring someone's neck for it. I see so many women, so many young idiot girls, who spit out babies like it's nothing. They barely bother to get the father's name, but having a kid is just no big deal. And so many beautiful, precious children are neglected or raised by resentful grandparents. Nothing pisses me off more than seeing some dipshit preteen mother with five dirty kids by five different guys running around her unattended at the store, while I'm not allowed to have one. *One!* One baby who would be loved and nurtured by two parents who adore it."

"I know what you mean," Lily nodded. "You wouldn't believe how much of that I see at the office. There are some girls who deserve frequent flier miles for the maternity ward. Every time they come back in, all I can think is, Jesus, again?"

"Exactly!" Maggie took another long pull on her straw.

"Well, have you two ever thought of adoption?" Lily glanced in her direction before turning off the highway.

"We've talked about it. We had almost decided to start the process when we found out about the MTHFR mutation. We'd thought for the longest time that I just couldn't get pregnant, so we looked into adoption. Then I had my first miscarriage. After that, we kept trying since I had actually conceived, and after a few more losses they did the blood work that found my disorder. Once they finally put a name on it and told us what we needed to do to try and fight it, it sort of took over our plans."

"That's understandable, but it still isn't a guarantee. You could have more losses before the shots ever work. *If* they work, that is."

"I know," she sighed. "But I had to try. I couldn't live with myself if I felt I hadn't given this my all. I get very optimistic at the beginning, and then very bitter after each loss. Sometimes it even hurts to be around children for a while, and pregnant women make me want to cry."

Lily patted her shoulder, not knowing what else to say.

"Don't get me wrong," Maggie continued. "After this is over I'm going to have to do a lot of soul searching to see if I can go through it again. Poor Eric gets destroyed each time, watching what it does to me. Every time I think about giving up, though, I remember that my grandmother lost three babies and had an infant who died a few hours after birth, only to go on to have my father. If she had just given up, I'd never be here. That could be my child someday."

"You could always adopt now and try again later. I'm sure you wouldn't mind having two eventually, would you?"

"No, I'd love two children," she gushed, her smile beaming.

"Well, I have seen a lot of women who have struggled for years with infertility issues, only to have a baby with no complications the second they adopt. It's like having the child they always wanted helps them to relax and get rid of all the stress they've bottled up for years. I knew a girl in college who was adopted, and her brother was barely nine months younger than she was because their parents had a little celebration after they brought her home. You never know—weird things happen every day."

"Thank you, Lily," she whispered after a few minutes of silence. "For just being here. I know that I'm coming off as some sort of baby-obsessed moron right now."

"No you aren't. You've had some really horrible news today, and you have an even bleaker afternoon ahead of you. You're allowed to be emotional."

"It's just that I don't want you to think that I can't be happy with what I have. If we never have any children at all, we'll get by. I don't believe that only children make a family. My husband is my world, and his family has taken me in like another daughter from the first day I met them. My parents died when I was in college, and I have never felt alone."

Maggie turned to face Barbara in the backseat, reaching around the headrest to squeeze her hand. She smiled at her as she watched her wipe her eyes and blow her nose. "Take Weepy here," Maggie chuckled. "She's only so upset because this is happening to her daughter again. She isn't half as upset about losing a grandchild as I am about not being able to give her one."

Barbara smiled weakly at her and squeezed her hand in return. "I love you, sweetheart."

"I love you, too."

Lily pulled the car into the driveway of the largest house she had ever seen in the area. Parking in front of the main door, she was surprised when Barbara invited her inside.

"Don't sit out here like the help, Lily. Come in and have a bite while Maggie packs." She didn't leave much room for disagreement in her tone, so Lily turned off the car and followed the women inside. Once she'd closed the door and looked at the large, opulent surroundings, she couldn't keep her mouth from dropping open.

"I know," Maggie laughed. "I had the exact same look on my face the first time Eric brought me home with him." She draped her coat over the back of the nearest chair and turned back to Lily. "Why don't you come upstairs with me? You can help me figure out what to take."

"Don't you two want anything to eat?" Barbara called from the kitchen.

"We're going upstairs to pack first," she called back. "Maybe just a few finger snacks or something."

"All right, I'll make up a plate."

Maggie turned back to Lily before leading her up the stairs. "Don't worry, she's in her element now. Her brain functions much better once she can be physically doing something for someone."

She led Lily to a large room full of many different trophies and awards. "This used to be Eric's old room," she explained when she caught Lily eying the different pieces of sports memorabilia. "Barbara has offered to make him a trophy case downstairs, but he always groans about changing his room. Personally, I think it's because he likes to feel dirty, like he snuck his girlfriend in the house after curfew."

"So he's not just stuck in the past, reliving old glory days on the field?" Lily laughed.

"No way! He's more of the 'Big Man on Campus' type in the bedroom only. And when he gets around these damn trophies." Maggie winked at her and they both started laughing.

After a few minutes they had grabbed a few essentials and tossed them in an overnight bag. Talking easily back and forth, they joined Barbara in the kitchen for a snack of cheese and crackers. About twenty minutes later they were leaving for the hospital, and Lily was so involved in conversation that she never even noticed the large family portrait as they walked out the door.

Driving to Mercer County Hospital, Lily tried to keep the lighter conversation going for as long as possible, hoping to avoid another crying jag. "That was a beautiful painting on the stairway, Mrs. Foster. I don't usually pay much attention to art, but something about that one made me take another look."

"Oh thank you, dear. And please, call me Barbara. My son actually painted that." The pride was unmistakable in her voice.

"I didn't know Eric could paint, too!" Lily gasped, astonished at such talent coming from an amateur.

"No, not Eric. His brother, Ethan."

"Oh, I'm sorry, I didn't realize you had another son."

"We don't exactly see him much," Maggie explained. "A few weeks ago was the first time any of us had seen him in years." Before Lily could ask any more questions, Maggie's phone rang loudly to the tune of *Mr. Big Stuff*.

"Excuse me, it's Eric." She hit the SEND button eagerly, and her one-sided conversation was interrupted by brief pauses as her husband spoke in her ear. "Hi baby, where are you?... So that's only about an hour away, isn't it? Oh thank God!... Yeah, we're heading over to the hospital now, you might as well just head straight there... I know... I know... I'm not bad yet... I won't... I miss you, too. Love you, baby."

She ended the call just as Lily reached the hospital. After parking in the maternity lot, the three women walked inside and checked in at the front desk. Lily and Barbara waited in the room as the staff prepared Maggie, changing her into a gown and inserting an IV lock into her hand.

After a while, the nurse returned and told them that she was going to start the inducement drug, as well as a very weak morphine drip. She assured Maggie that if at any time her pain increased, she would up her morphine. Before long they could see that the drug was taking effect, causing Maggie to slur her words slightly as she spoke to them. Her eyelids had also gotten very droopy.

When Maggie started flipping through TV channels out of boredom, it sparked a discussion about the most annoying reality shows that they had ever seen. Barbara voted for *Jersey Shore*, Lily voted for *Cheaters*—which she couldn't help but find ironic—and Maggie once again named *Teen Mom*. Before they could finish their arguments for why each of theirs was the worst, a large man appeared at the door.

"Maggie?"

"Eric!"

The burliest man Lily had ever seen bounded into the room and sat down next to Maggie on the bed, scooping her up and squeezing her tightly in one swift movement. She pulled back to look at him, and as soon as their eyes made contact her tough facade finally crumbled.

Maggie Foster burst into tears.

"I'm so sorry, baby," he chanted over and over as he rocked her against his chest. "I should have been here. You go through too much alone." He stroked her hair and kissed the top of her head, treating her like the most precious gift anyone had ever received.

Something tugged at Lily deep inside when she watched them together, and she had to look away. As if sharing the same thought, she and Barbara both quietly left the room, leaving the couple to their privacy.

"They'll be like that for a while, I'm afraid," Barbara said softly. "He won't leave her side until she falls asleep, and maybe not even then." She looked wistfully at the door to the room. "Their love has always been such a powerful, tangible thing. From the moment they met they've been inseparable. She usually travels with him if he is going to be gone for very long, but they were both worried about the baby."

"It's nice to see a couple that is still so strong after so many years," Lily replied, still feeling something strange tugging at her when she thought of them. Her eyes were beginning to sting.

"My daughter is the same way with her husband. Must have been something they picked up at home," she blushed. After another moment she added sadly, "I only wish that my other son had been half as fortunate."

"I'm sorry. Did he divorce?"

"No, he never married her, thank goodness. I don't think it was meant to be. He never looked at her the way that my other children look at their spouses." She met Lily's gaze to add weight to her next words. "The spark never made it to his eyes. Does that make sense?"

"Actually, yes it does. It makes perfect sense." The curious stinging behind her eyes intensified, causing her to blink rapidly.

"Oh dear, you must be exhausted!" Barbara cooed. "Where was my head? It's been a long, emotional day for all of us. Let me take you back to your car so you can go home and rest."

The two of them traveled the distance in a comfortable silence, listening to the quiet music playing on the radio. They both seemed to realize that the afternoon's events were a bit too heavy to speak about at the moment, and the time for idle chitchat had passed.

Barbara pulled into the now empty lot of the clinic and parked next to Lily's monstrous 1976 Cutlass Supreme. "Goodness, is this beast yours?"

"That's right," Lily smiled.

"Well it certainly has character," Barbara smiled in return.

"That's what I always thought. Thanks for the lift," she said, turning to exit the car.

"Lily," she touched her shoulder gently. "Thank you so much for your help today. Maggie seems very attached to you, and I'm beginning to see why." With that, she leaned forward and hugged her close. When Lily finally stepped out of the car, she called after her one last time. "I hope that you'll visit us again sometime—under happier circumstances, that is."

Closing the door, Lily nodded and waved before climbing into her own car. Barbara waited until she had started the engine and drove off with a honk in the direction of the hospital. Lily watched as the car disappeared from view, and once she was truly alone she dropped her head onto the steering wheel and sobbed.

She sobbed for Maggie and the pain she was enduring. She sobbed for Barbara and her sorrow for her family. She sobbed for Eric and his grief.

But most of all, she sobbed for the love she had witnessed in that room.

The annoying tugging had turned into a burning ache deep inside her chest. She knew without a doubt that what she had with Scott would never feel like that, no matter how much effort and time she put into it. She had thought she could be content with him, that their friendship could be enough to nurture a deeper connection, but she was most definitely wrong about that. He would never make her feel as if he were the other half of her soul.

Without thinking, Lily threw the car in drive and skidded off down the street. She had no idea where she was going, only that she needed to go there right now. The tears were still flowing freely down her face, the images of Eric holding Maggie replaying over and over in her mind.

When the car finally screeched to a halt, Lily was startled to find that she was in the back parking lot behind the dance studio where the residents kept their cars. Weeping and sniffling, she climbed out of the car and tore off across the alley, the open door beckoning her.

As her feet hit the steps she ran even harder, pounding loudly along the way. She felt pulled, as if by a giant magnet, and by the time she reached the top she was completely out of breath and nearly choking on her sobs. Before she knew it the key was turning in the lock and she was shoving the door open so hard that it slammed against the wall. Any other time she would have been embarrassed at making such a spectacle of herself, but at that moment only one thing mattered to her.

He was there.

Ethan dropped his palette in shock when she barged in the door and had no idea what to think as she stood there regarding him with tears streaming down her face.

"My God, what happened?" he gasped. He barely had the chance to note that she was wearing burgundy scrubs instead of her usual workout clothes before she was across the room and in his arms.

An unfamiliar urge to defend and protect rose up in him, and for a moment his vision went red at the thought of someone harming her. "Are you all right?"

She couldn't speak, though. She could only bury her face in his neck and cry. Giant, wracking sobs that shook her entire body.

A sudden panic hit him. "You have to tell me what happened," he said to the top of her head as he held her. "Hey...hey! Look at me!" He grabbed her by the chin and forced her swollen eyes to meet his. "Did he hurt you? Tell me!"

Lily shook her head quickly.

"Then what's wrong?" The blinding rage began to subside, replaced quickly with the need to hold her as closely as possible.

"Just...it's just...I need...I need you..." her words were getting caught between her gasps and hiccups.

"You need me to what?"

"No...I just...*need* you!" His goddess looked up at him with enormous hazel eyes that were puffy and red, the wet lashes surrounding them sticking to her skin in dark points. She had never looked more beautiful to him. "Make it all go away! Please!"

Ethan leaned down and lifted her in his arms, carrying her into the bedroom. He laid her down gently and followed after her, kissing her soft lips and tasting her tears. She wrapped her arms around his neck and held him tightly, returning his kisses with a violent fervor. She would only let him go long enough for him to remove her clothing, and after each article was removed she would grasp onto him again, as if she were reassuring herself that he was still there.

Once he had worked his own jeans off he covered her completely, and when he slid himself into her welcoming heat they both cried out. He moved inside her slowly, worshiping her body with his own, and as each new tear fell he would kiss it away.

Many hours later, Ethan woke to a very dark room and a very warm body draped across his chest. It felt absolutely amazing, but he knew she would be angry if he let her sleep there through the night.

Rubbing her shoulder and kissing her lightly, he watched as she began to stir. "Hey, beautiful, it's getting late. Don't you need to leave?" She stretched her limbs for a moment and looked up into his eyes. With a big yawn she repositioned herself, snuggling even tighter against him.

"No," she sighed.

It was the sweetest word he had ever heard.

17

Lily woke before dawn, immediately feeling the deep ache in her muscles. As she moved and stretched, each sore spot brought back another vivid memory of the night before. Thinking back through the foggy, sleepy memories, she couldn't believe how her beautiful stranger had been there to help comfort her through the night.

She hadn't been able to sleep for longer than an hour or two at a time. It wasn't that she hadn't been comfortable next to him on the bed—quite the opposite, actually—but for some reason she kept waking up in a panic and reaching for him in the dark. His body was so in tune with hers that it was almost scary. Every time her hand would land on his warm, toned flesh, he would pull her to him and love her all over again until she was knocked out from sheer exhaustion.

The last time, he had been facing away from her on his side and she had simply rolled over and hugged him, pressing herself against his back to feel his smooth skin on her breasts, having every intention of drifting back to sleep. However, as soon as his body had recognized her presence, he had rolled back over and grabbed her, lifting her up and placing her in his lap, directly over his erection. When she had looked down at him she was amazed to see that he was barely awake, yet it didn't stop him from moving inside her and dragging her with him to a drowsy but passionate finish.

Now, completely sated and sprawled across his torso, she lay there for a few minutes and enjoyed the steady rhythm of his heartbeat and the rise and fall of his chest as he slept. Glancing down, she stifled a gasp, unable to believe that he was actually hard again. She knew that guys often got "morning wood," but didn't having mind-blowing sex four times overnight sort of negate that?

Looking at the long, smooth shaft curving back toward his stomach, Lily whimpered to herself, wanting so badly to crawl on top of him again. However, she could already feel the soreness growing between her legs; she knew that she was going to have trouble walking as it was.

Still, she thought to herself. *It would be a shame to let that go to waste.*

Moving slowly so as not to wake him, Lily slipped away and re-positioned herself between his legs. She watched his features closely, looking for any sign that he was stirring before leaning forward and dragging the tip of her tongue all the way up the underside of his erection. She started at the base and finished at the tip, flicking the bottom of her tongue a few times against his frenulum before looking up at his sleeping face.

He moaned softly, his brow furrowing in confusion, but his eyes were still closed. She repeated her actions, going even slower, and this time she swirled her tongue around the broad tip as she finished. He grunted a little louder, and she watched as his cock twitched in response, yet it still wasn't enough contact to wake him. One more time she licked him, but when she reached the top, she slipped her plump lips around him and sucked him deep inside her mouth.

"Mmm," he groaned, slowly coming to. Ethan opened his eyes just in time to see his goddess looking up at him, a wicked gleam in her eye as she bobbed her head up and down his length.

"Fuck!" He tried to keep his eyes from crossing, instantly feeling an overdose of sensation. Her mouth was so warm, her tongue so slick, and he could feel every stroke as it swirled around him. "God, baby," he gasped, locking eyes with her again.

Their gaze never broke as she moved on him, sucking him to the back of her throat and sliding back up again. When she saw him finally bite his bottom lip and close his eyes from the pleasure, it looked so erotic that Lily couldn't keep from moaning loudly around him, which sent a wave of vibrations down his length.

Ethan's eyes flew open. "Christ!" He sat up until he could brace himself on his elbows, allowing him a much better view of her lovely wake up call. The room was still fairly dark, but Ethan watched her so intently that his eyes quickly adjusted to the light. "You look so fucking sexy doing that." She met his eyes again and winked before setting up a steady pace, and the action was so arousing that he felt himself grow impossibly harder in her mouth.

Lily took her time and enjoyed herself, running her hands up the insides of his thighs lightly, causing him to jerk and twitch. When she reached the juncture of his legs, she cupped and stroked his balls until they tightened in response, which earned her another loud groan for her efforts. Feeling absolutely drunk with power, she pulled her mouth away slowly. Ignoring his whimper, she leaned down and swirled her tongue around them, gradually sucking first one and then the other in her mouth.

"Oh my God," Ethan panted, rolling his head back on his shoulders before looking at her again.

Lily devoured every inch of his sensitive flesh, licking her way back up to his broad tip and sliding her lips around him once more, eagerly bobbing up and down. She couldn't believe that she was completely aroused again, her swollen folds slick with excitement from the sounds he was making.

After a few more strokes with her mouth, Lily felt his hands tugging at her jaw, signaling her to stop.

"What's wrong?" she whispered, worried that she had somehow hurt him in her haste.

"Absolutely nothing," he groaned.

"Then why did you stop me?"

"I was wondering. Do you remember what we did together a few days ago?" Lily stared at him blankly, her mind wandering over all of the amazing things they had done together recently. "What you asked me to do?"

"Oh!" Lily blushed, instantly flashing back to their steamy interlude with the stolen bottle of lube. "Um, what about it?"

"Well, I've heard that it's supposed to be just as good for a man... during oral." He looked at her pointedly before smiling. "Sometimes even better."

"Have you ever?" Her cheeks were blazing now, but the thought of sharing something new with him was too intriguing to ignore.

"No. I've never—" he took a deep breath before continuing. "I've never trusted anyone enough to try it."

"Well..." Lily thought for a moment. He was telling her that he trusted her, above anyone else that he'd ever been with. There was no way that she was going to pass that up. "I can try. I don't want to hurt you, though. Is there any way I can make it easier for you?"

"Use this." Reaching over in the dark, Ethan grabbed the notorious stolen bottle that had been sitting by his bedside like a trophy ever since they'd used it. He kept it there just in case; he wasn't about to be caught unprepared if the mood ever struck her again.

Lily covered her fingers with the slippery gel before she took him in her mouth again, building him back up to a frenzy. As she worked him faster and faster and his moans grew more uncontrolled, she slid her hand down between his legs. Moving very slowly, she slid two of her fingers down to his rear entrance and made small circular motions, spreading the gel around the delicate skin. She heard his breathing hitch and felt him tense up involuntarily, but as she continued the slow movements he began to relax around her.

When she could tell that he was once again at ease, Lily started to apply more pressure with her middle finger, gently moving forward enough so that she was able to slip inside a tiny bit. He stilled his movements and held his breath; it was so quiet that she could have heard a pin drop. Hoping to distract him from any worries he might be having, she applied more pressure with her lips and tongue until he was moaning again.

Taking that as her cue, she pushed her finger deeper inside, feeling him opening to her slowly. This time, she didn't stop until it was all the way in.

"Fuck!" Ethan gasped. It felt full and tight and the pressure was… good. So good. He was completely lost in sensation by that point, feeling her delicious mouth swallowing him whole while she massaged him gently from the inside. It was one of the most intense feelings he'd ever felt in his life, and when she started sliding her finger in and out, he knew that he was gone.

"Oh…oh fuck, baby. Baby, look at me!" His words were interrupted by rapid panting and the sharp thrust of his hips.

The moment her beautiful eyes made contact with his Ethan cried out loudly, exploding in a violent torrent of fluid that sent hot spurts down her throat. Unable to keep his eyes on her like he wanted, he squeezed them shut and threw his head back, drowning in the powerful waves of his release. Lily sucked him even harder as he rode it out, refusing to stop until his shaking had abated and he began to twitch from oversensitivity.

When he finally looked finished Lily gently removed her finger and the firm grip of her mouth. Watching him closely for the verdict on how she had done, she was thrilled when he lifted his head again and she saw the fiery look in his eye.

"Get the fuck up here. Now," he growled.

Before she could scramble up his body, she felt his hands gripping her sides and lifting her, pulling her all the way up until she was perched over his face. He looked up at her long enough to grunt something that sounded like "so fucking good" before pulling her down on him, directly over his mouth. He used everything he had to stroke her swollen folds: his tongue, his lips, his nose, even his chin. Pulling her down against him, he devoured her, lapping up all of her juices until she was bucking wildly, grinding herself into his face.

When her own release hit her, it was enough to make her shake so hard that she fell over, crumpling into a heap next to him. He pulled her to his side, holding her tightly and kissing her with all of the passion that he could no longer deny. She kissed him back hungrily, only stopping when she was too exhausted to continue.

They collapsed together again, Lily resuming her favorite spot on his chest. As they both tried to catch their breath, she peppered his warm skin with light kisses while he stroked her bare back.

Lily looked up at him, gasping. "God…that was…"

"Un-fucking-believable," Ethan groaned.

"Exactly."

After a few minutes of recuperation, Lily rested her chin on her hands and smiled shyly up at him. She never wanted to leave the warmth of his arms, and she was doing her best not to dwell on how scary that thought was to her.

"What's that blush for?" he teased. "I can't imagine after the night we just had that you have anything left to be embarrassed about."

"I'm not embarrassed. It's just that…this is nice, being here like this. I don't have much experience with cuddling."

Sadly, it was true. Lily had never been one for the overnight adventure, much more comfortable with her own bed when she woke up. Most of the losers she'd dated in college were more than happy to end the night with a *bang*, and none of them ever complained about not being invited to stay over in her bed. Whether that was because they were already out the door before she could ask is hard to say, but she liked to think that it was her choice. Even Scott, on the rare occasions they ever found enough privacy to have sex, had never slept over—or held her this closely when it was done.

"I don't either, really," he smiled back. "But I'm starting to see what all the hype is about. This is definitely something I could get used to." He wiggled his eyebrows lecherously, making her giggle.

The morning light was starting to creep into the room, landing on the tips of his hair and making it glow the most amazing shade of flaming gold. Lily looked into his sparkling eyes, trying to ignore the violent pounding that it caused in her chest. There were times that his beauty alone could take her breath away, and combined with the warmth of his skin wrapped around her, she was ready to drift away into oblivion.

After a long stretch of silence had settled over the room, he spoke again. "Do you want to talk about it?"

"Talk about what?"

"Whatever had you so upset last night?" There was a genuine look of concern on his face, and it actually made her heart ache.

"I thought you didn't want to know specifics," she questioned.

"Well…" he ran his hands through his glowing hair for a moment as he thought. "I am simply pushing for anonymity. The only time people are truly honest about themselves is when it's anonymous."

"But how can I be honest about anything without giving things away?"

"I just don't want to know who you are supposed to be to the outside world. I want to know who you truly are here. That's all that matters to me. I never said that you couldn't tell me a few incidentals along the way. For example, I noticed you were wearing scrubs last night. That leaves me to assume that you work in some sort of medical office. I don't know if you are a doctor, a nurse, or a file clerk, but I don't really think that's giving too much away now, is it? I mean, you know what I do and still don't know my name."

"I never knew if that was your career or your hobby," Lily defended. "I just knew that you were unbelievably talented. And I'm a nurse, by the way."

"Thank you," he smiled. She wasn't quite sure if he was thanking her for her compliment or the added information. "Now," he grew serious again, "something upset you so badly last night that you brought it here, to us. I think that should concern me. Just be honest and tell me what you can."

"Okay." She took a deep breath, thinking of how she wanted to proceed. "Well, let me just say that yesterday some very sweet people went through something horrible. I wouldn't wish it on my worst enemy. I was there when they got the news and I had to witness their hearts breaking into thousands of tiny pieces." She glanced back up at him to make sure he was following her. He nodded in encouragement and began to stroke her hair gently; as she looked at him she could see his eyes soften in understanding. "The only thing they have to get them through this right now is their unbelievable love for each other."

"That does sound upsetting," he said quietly, still stroking her hair. It felt like warm silk threads under his fingers. "What made you come to me?"

"I didn't really think about it at the time, it just…happened. Like so many other things with us. I just sort of drove and ended up here. I needed you to hold me."

"You can always come to me," he smiled, kissing her forehead. "I will hold you all night long if that's what you need."

Ethan pulled her even closer, more touched by her words than he cared to admit. He didn't recognize the warm feeling that was flowing rapidly through his veins, but he knew that he didn't want it to stop. He had a feeling that she was still holding something back that she wanted to say, but he wasn't about to push her more than he already had. She would tell him eventually if it mattered enough.

"You did a whole lot more than just hold me last night, mister," Lily laughed into his neck before planting a few light kisses there.

"Only because that was what you needed. You asked me to make it go away, so I did. Don't get me wrong, I'm still reeling from how amazing last night was, but if you had told me just to hold you, I would have."

Trying to lighten the mood, Lily laughed. "I'm not sure we could be so chaste together. I probably would have jumped you five minutes after we lay down."

"Hey," he pulled her chin up, forcing her to meet his eyes. "I'm dead serious. You can always come to me."

"But for how long?" she whispered.

"What do you mean?" Ethan was puzzled by the instant look of sadness that took over her features.

"How long is 'always?' Are you planning on staying here permanently? For as much time as you spend here, you don't really seem to live here. I've always had the impression that this was a 'fun while it lasts' thing for you…that you might pack up and leave at any moment. Am I wrong?"

She really wanted him to say she was wrong. She wanted him to tell her that he loved her and wanted her forever. She wanted him to tell her that if he left tomorrow he would take her with him.

"Well…" Ethan had absolutely no idea what to say. He had never felt so put on the spot in his life. Why did she care when he left if she was getting married to that Neanderthal? Wasn't this just one last fling for her? He took a deep breath before answering. "You can come to me for as long as I am here, but as for how long that will be, I don't know yet."

"That's what I figured," Lily sighed.

"Hey, that's no reason not to still come to me now. I don't have any immediate plans to leave, and there's still so much for us to share together. It could be months yet." Panic filled him at the thought of never seeing her again. He couldn't leave her just yet, that much he knew, but he was no fool. He knew that he was already too attached to her as it was; once she got married he would have to let her go.

As much as he enjoyed her company, he didn't want to destroy her life.

Ethan knew she was just a young girl having a sexual awakening. She loved the thrill of it at the moment, but she would never want to leave everything she knew behind. If she did, he knew she would hate him the second she realized that she had given up love for nothing more than a good fuck.

Tucking her head back down into the crook of his neck, he kissed the top of her hair quickly. "We can just have as much fun together as time will allow, and when all is said and done we will have these unbelievable memories to cherish. How does that sound?" He was trying his best to sound positive, but the thought of leaving her ripped him apart inside, and for some strange reason his eyes were stinging.

"Okay, yeah," Lily whispered. "That sounds good." She was thankful that he had hugged her closer when he did, that way he couldn't see as she blinked away the tears that were welling up in her eyes.

They lay together like that for a few minutes in total silence. Suddenly Ethan's phone chirped in the other room, breaking the melancholy feeling that had settled over them both.

"I should grab that," he sighed, hating the coldness he felt the moment he let her out of his arms. "If someone's calling this early it might be important."

"Of course," Lily smiled at him. As soon as he left the room she sat up and wiped her eyes violently, cursing herself for her stupidity.

Forget it. Just forget it all. Have your fun and move along, idiot. You can't keep him.

In the front room, Ethan was surprised to see his mother's cell number on his display.

"Hello?"

"Ethan? Dear, are you awake?" Barbara's voice sounded thick and raw, as if she had been crying all night.

"Mom, is something wrong? Is someone hurt?" He wasn't used to getting calls from his mother very often over the last few years, and hearing her sound so obviously upset had him instantly on alert.

"I'm sorry to bother you so early, sweetheart. I just thought you should know that Maggie lost her baby late last night. She's finally resting now, but your brother is more than a bit broken up over it."

"Oh, I'm sorry to hear that." He had known Maggie since he was a teenager, and even though they'd never had the chance to get really close, she had always been sweet to him.

"Usually when this happens, Brandon is here for him to sort of lean on for emotional support, but he took your sister out of town for a long Valentine's weekend."

"Where is Eric?"

"We're all still here at the hospital. They are going to keep her here until tomorrow for observation."

"I'll be there in twenty minutes."

"Thank you. And Ethan?"

"Yeah?"

"You're a good brother."

"Uh…thanks." *Click.*

He didn't want to dwell on what she'd just said for too long; he knew it wasn't true. If it were true, he would have been there for him before now. If it were true, this wouldn't be the first he'd ever heard about them having multiple losses. Hell, he barely even remembered that she had been pregnant.

Lily couldn't help listening from the bedroom as she tried to find all of her clothes, but only hearing half of the conversation was more frustrating than not hearing any of it at all. She was surprised to hear that he actually had a mother: a real, flesh and bone mother. Until then she could have just as easily have believed that he had sprung full-grown from the head of Zeus.

When he returned he had a somber look on his face. "I'm sorry, but I have to go. There's a bit of a family situation."

"That's all right," she returned, pulling her shirt on over her head. "I really need to grab a shower and a change of clothes before work. I wasn't paying attention to the time." When she saw how stricken he looked she went to him and hugged him tightly. "I hope that it's nothing too serious."

"Well, the worst is done, but thank you. I'm just going to see if I can be of any help." He leaned down and kissed her softly one last time. As he pulled away he couldn't help raking his eyes down her body, appreciating the uniform she was wearing once again. "It's too bad we were interrupted," he said with a leer. "I would have enjoyed playing doctor."

"Really?" she said, astonished. "The scrubs do something for you?"

"Hell yes," he chuckled. "Now all I can think about is having you be my naughty nurse and giving me a sponge bath."

"All right, wow. I'm going to get the hell out of here before I take you up on that and we're both late." She pulled out of his arms and walked to the door. Before closing it behind her she turned and called to him over her shoulder. "Hey, stranger?"

"Yes, beautiful?"

"Next time, you bring the sponge and the bubble bath and I'll bring the scrubs."

His eyes began to smolder again. "Oh, it's a fucking date."

With that, his beautiful goddess smiled and closed the door.

18

Ethan arrived at the hospital fifteen minutes later to find his mother standing outside the room speaking quietly on her cellphone. Her eyes lit up when she saw him and she held up a finger, letting him know that she was almost done. He could see the dark circles under her eyes and hear the quiver in her voice as she spoke, giving him a fairly good idea of just how long the night had been for her.

"Darling, I've got to go, your brother just arrived." She listened for another moment. "Yes, sweetheart, I will. Give my love to Brandon. Let him know that we're all going to be all right. There's no need for him to drag you back here and cut your trip short."

She said good-bye and ended the call, turning her full attention to Ethan as he closed the distance between them and pulled her into a tight hug. Neither one of them said anything for almost a minute as he held her, slowly rocking back and forth.

Barbara broke the silence first, mumbling into his shirt. "Thank you so much for coming. I know it's terribly early."

"Shh," he scolded, patting her back lightly. "Don't be silly. I would have come in the middle of the night if you had called me." While Ethan would have hated to cut his amazing night with his goddess short, he knew that he was telling his mother the truth.

"Well, there was nothing you could have done at that point," she said, pulling back to wipe away the beginning of tears from her eyes. "I think Eric will be the one who needs you now, and he was too busy sitting with Maggie all night. He wouldn't have even known you were here."

"What can I do?"

"Just be there for him, dear. She's finally asleep—see if you can get him out of this damn hospital room for a while, even if it's just the cafeteria. He won't let himself relax while he's with her like this. He's always on alert." She sighed loudly, running her fingers through her hair in a gesture that was all too familiar to him. "Talk to him. Listen to him. Don't think that you need to cheer him up or make him laugh, that will just piss him off. If he wants to be distracted, he'll let you know."

Ethan hadn't really been there for anyone in so long that he felt completely out of sorts, but he knew that he owed it to his family to give it a try. "All right. Is he inside?"

"Of course. He hasn't left her side since he got here. He's been napping lightly for the last few hours since they gave Maggie something to help her sleep, but that's the most I could get him to do. Let's go see if he's awake yet."

They walked quietly into the large private room. Once Ethan's eyes adjusted to the darker lighting, he could see his brother sleeping on a couch in the corner and his sister-in-law resting in the large bed, hooked up to a few different machines. Her face looked sweaty and her always-perfect hair was matted to her head, but something about her appearance touched Ethan deeply in that instant. For the first time since he'd met her, Maggie's guard was down. Unable to hide behind her makeup and clothes, he could see how vulnerable and fragile she could be. Strangely, she had never looked stronger to him, or lovelier.

As if she somehow sensed his presence in the room, her eyes fluttered open. When her hazy gaze met his, the tiniest smile touched her lips.

"Hey, kid," she whispered.

"Hey, yourself," he smiled back. It was the same greeting they had exchanged since he'd been sixteen years old.

Maggie slowly raised a hand with IV tubes sticking out of it and held it out to him, motioning with her fingers for him to come closer. When he was at her side, Ethan gently took those same fingers in his hand and squeezed them before leaning over and kissing the backs of them, barely avoiding the looped tube that was taped in place.

"Such pleasantries," she teased.

"But of course. I'm ever the gallant gentleman." His smile faded as he looked at her. "I'm so sorry, Maggie. This whole situation is just bullshit."

"Tell me about it," she rasped back.

"Are you going to be okay?"

"Of course I will." She waved him off before glancing away. "Eventually." She met his eyes again. "I'm sort of used to it, you know? It's a shit thing to have to get used to, but it is what it is." Her voice dropped even lower as she angled her head toward the couch. "I'm more worried about him, though."

Ethan looked over at his brother, curled up in a ridiculous ball on what looked to be the world's most uncomfortable couch. "Taking it pretty hard?"

"You'd never know by talking to him, but I can see it in his eyes. Plus he's always so damn worried about me that he never lets himself grieve properly."

"Well that's why I'm here, actually. I was going to try to drag his lazy ass out of here for a bit while you rested."

"Oh, that would be wonderful!" Her sleepy eyes lit up more than he thought possible in her medicated state. "Get him the hell out of here. And don't let him stay in the building, either. He needs a little fresh air."

"All right, Maggie. Get some rest." Ethan smiled back at her and patted her hand before finally letting go. He crossed the room quietly until he was standing in front of Eric's balled-up form. After regarding his sleeping face for a minute, he lifted his foot and gently kicked at his shoe, which was sticking out over the arm of the couch. "Hey." He continued tapping. "Hey, Sleeping Beauty, get the fuck up."

"Fuck you," Eric mumbled, batting at the air before trying to roll over. When he realized that he couldn't move away from whatever the hell was annoying him because the couch was too damn small, he finally opened his eyes and looked around. Groaning, his gaze settled on Ethan.

"What the—? Is Maggie okay?" He sat straight up, his tone instantly panicked.

"Hey, calm down. She's fine. See, she's—" When he turned to allow Eric a view of her, he was surprised to find that she was already fast asleep. "Sleeping."

"Thank God," Eric sighed, leaning over and rubbing his face with his large hands. "She was up all damn night." When he looked up to meet Ethan's eyes again, it was with a look of suspicion. "What are you doing here, anyway?"

"I've come to kidnap you."

"That's what I was afraid of," he sighed again. "I'm not going anywhere."

"Oh come on, stop being a douche. You can't do anything for her while she's sleeping, and Mom is tired of not being able to sit on the couch. Let's go get something to eat. I haven't had breakfast yet."

"But who will sit with Maggie? What if she wakes up and I'm not here?" The worry in his voice was unmistakable.

"Mom's still here. Let's go and let them have some girl time. If anything major happens she can call us, all right?"

The battle of emotions that played across Eric's face was almost heartbreaking to watch. "Yeah…I suppose I can run downstairs for a bite to eat."

"Not happening, man. I'm not eating the nasty shit they try to pass for food here. I was thinking we could maybe go to the diner. I haven't had their pancakes in years. What do you say? My treat."

He looked at Maggie one more time before Barbara's voice rang out in the room. "Eric, go with your brother. I want to sit and read my book in peace."

Remembering his mother's presence for the first time, Eric nodded sheepishly and stood up, stopping to stretch and twist, which sent a loud round of pops and cracks echoing through the room. "All right," he groaned, "you guys win." Grabbing his jacket and throwing it on, Eric crossed the room and hugged Barbara, kissing her cheek as he pulled away. "Thanks for sitting with her. Do you want us to bring you anything?"

"No, your father is going to bring me something in a little while. We're going to eat together. Thank you for asking, though." She reached up and patted his cheek, doing her best to hide her sadness when she felt the coarse stubble that had grown in overnight and saw how strained his features were.

"All right, we'll be back soon. Call me if anything happens, okay?"

"I will, darling, but you really need to relax. They are only keeping her for observation now, Eric. The worst is over."

"I know. It's just hard to leave her." He looked over at Maggie one last time before turning and leaving the room. Ethan kissed his mother good-bye as well, and when he glanced at Maggie he could have sworn that he saw her close her eyes again quickly, as if she had been peeking under her lashes when Eric left the room. The little faker.

"What's so funny?" Eric asked as they walked outside, wondering why Ethan was chuckling to himself.

"Oh, nothing," he lied. "My mind's just wandering. Here, my car's over this way." He led him across the lot to the Audi, and once they were both buckled in he drove off to the local diner on the other side of town.

Grabbing a booth in the corner, they smiled politely at the young waitress who brought them their menus, who also couldn't seem to stop ogling the both of them as if she couldn't decide which one was hotter. Once they'd gotten her to stop drooling long enough to take their order, they settled in over coffee to have a nice talk.

"Sweet kid," Eric said, watching her walk away. "But way too young. She's gonna be trouble for her old man, acting like that."

"Oh, don't act like waitresses of all ages don't fall all over you, Mr. Football," Ethan teased.

"Hey, I haven't played in years," he blushed. "But sometimes, Maggie does get a little jealous. I keep telling her that fair is fair, because anywhere we go every man's eyes are glued on her."

"The trials of a gorgeous couple. My heart goes out to you."

"Oh, you're one to talk, Mr. Tortured Artist! I used to think you spent hours in the mirror trying to perfect that brooding pout of yours. Something must have worked, though, because Rachel certainly wasn't hard on the eyes." He looked up suddenly, realizing what he had just said. "Hey, man, I'm sorry. I wasn't thinking."

"Really, don't worry about it," Ethan waved him off.

"No, that was a shit thing to bring up right now. How are you managing these days? It's only been a couple weeks since you broke up."

"I'm…coping," Ethan replied quietly. "Besides, we're not here to talk about me. We're here to get you out of that damn hospital for a while and pig out on the best pancakes in town."

"We're doing that already," Eric smiled, nodding toward the young waitress as she delivered two heaping stacks of buttermilk pancakes to their table. Sighing wistfully, she looked back and forth between each of them and the warm maple syrup on the table before walking away. "Man, I don't even want to know what she's thinking."

"Yeah, me neither," Ethan laughed, pouring the syrup in question over his breakfast.

"Anyway, as I was saying, you've done your job. I'm out and eating something. We're having a nice talk and you are distracting me."

"Are you sure being distracted is what you really want right now?" Ethan asked quietly. "You can talk to me about anything, you know."

"If memory serves, I said the very same thing to you a few weeks ago. I think if anyone should be more ready to talk, it should be you." He looked pointedly at Ethan, calling him out for never confiding in him. "I'll come around soon—I always do—but you're the one who needs to realize that the world isn't going to end if you admit that you aren't always perfect."

"What's that supposed to mean?" Ethan snapped defensively.

"It means that I've never known anyone so worried about making a good show of things, setting the scene just right. It's okay to admit that you're upset about something, or pissed off even. Nobody should seem so level-headed after breaking up with their girlfriend of ten years."

"I don't like people to know my business." He especially didn't like it if it meant that they might hate him when they did.

"Know your business? Ethan, I don't even know *you*. Not anymore." Eric sighed and took another sip of his coffee. "I'm trying to get to know my brother again. I think if anyone has a right to ask you about some of your business, it's me."

Ethan finished chewing his bite and put down his fork. "All right, what do you want to know? And before you start, just know that I'm not sure how much I'm ready to talk about yet, so don't be offended if I pass on something."

"I understand. I won't dig too deep today, don't worry." Eric cracked his knuckles and sat up straighter, his enthusiasm coming off of him in waves. "You say that you are coping right now, but how? I couldn't even imagine being able to function if Maggie left me. I mean, I know you and Rachel must not have been in the best place there at the end, but still—how on earth are you handling it?"

"Believe me, Eric, 'not in the best place' is a fucking understatement. If I seem cold about it, I don't mean to, but I can't help it." He took a big drink from his coffee before continuing, forcing himself to divulge at least a few things to his brother. "In all honesty, I'm torn up about the way she left. The way it went down was really bad. But the whole relationship…it felt like a lie. And it would be a lie now to say that I miss her in my life."

He waited for Eric to process what he had just told him. "But I thought you two were, like…totally in love?"

"No. Not at all."

"What? I thought you guys were so far up each other's asses that nobody else mattered to you."

"Then you believed the lie," Ethan frowned. "What we had was sort of…an understanding. And it worked out for both of us at first, but things got very bad between us at the end."

"Dude, don't get pissed at me for asking this, but are you gay?"

"What? No!" Ethan's head snapped up and looked around, embarrassed at his loud outburst.

"You can tell me if you are. I swear I don't give a shit."

"No, Eric! What the hell made you think that?"

"Well, an 'understanding'? It sounded like you were describing some weird-ass beard arrangement."

"No, no," Ethan laughed, forking another bite of food into his mouth. "There just wasn't any love between us. It was purely physical to begin with, for me at least, and that sort of morphed into a warped friendship. I had problems that I'm not proud of at all, and then she had even worse problems after that. We were just toxic together and not doing each other any good."

"Why didn't you guys split up when you first realized it was that bad?"

"It wasn't part of the plan," Ethan whispered. "She told me how much talent I had, how successful I could be with her resources, and I believed her. I tried to stick it out for a while after I got out of rehab, but she started to get annoyed that I wasn't putting out the same amount of work that I had been when I was high. She started making thinly veiled threats about finding someone younger and more talented. I finally got fed up with the whole thing."

"Whoa, wait a minute," Eric said quickly. "What the fuck do you mean, *rehab?*"

Ethan blinked for a moment, a wave of panic washing over him. He hadn't meant to let that slip, but it had felt so good to talk to his brother that he hadn't been guarding his words.

"Uh…" He had no idea how to recover from his blunder. What would Eric think of him now?

"Ethan, don't bail on me now, man. Talk to me." The look Eric gave him let him know that he wasn't going to be able to weasel out of this. Ethan decided that even if it made Eric hate him, at least he would be able to say that he successfully distracted his brother from what was happening at the hospital.

"Well," Ethan sighed. "I guess you could say that I had a small cocaine habit."

"I didn't realize there was such a thing as a *small* coke habit."

Ethan flinched. This was going about as well as he had expected.

"That came out wrong." He fidgeted with his napkin as he tried to think of how to explain it so that Eric would understand. "I didn't mean that the habit was small. That shit did a fucking number on me. I just meant that it's not like I was strung out all this time, only for about a year."

"How the hell did you get wrapped up in that shit?"

"Rachel. She kept talking it up and suggesting that it would help me paint faster."

"Are you fucking *serious*?" Eric snapped, barely containing a yell. "That fucking bitch."

"Not that I feel like defending anything she's done right now, but I've come to accept my own role in it, too. I never should have started. I'd give anything to be able to go back and tell her to fuck off."

"Yeah, I'd like to go with you," Eric grumbled. "But you're all clean now, right?"

Ethan sighed and looked down at his hands. "Trust me, I have no desire to go through that bullshit again." He knew it didn't matter what he said, and that now he'd always be an addict in his brother's eyes.

"Thanks for telling me about it, man. That sounds really hard, and I think you're really strong to come out on the other side. I won't bring it up again, but just know that you can talk to me about it anytime."

Ethan's head snapped up and he stared at his brother. That was it? Eric didn't seem mad anymore, and he didn't seem ashamed to have an ex-druggie brother. He almost seemed…proud of him? Was that even possible? It was such a revelation that Ethan was stunned speechless until Eric spoke again.

"So after rehab you left?"

"I planned to, but she must have seen it coming because she beat me to it. We were in New York for a gallery opening. I was hoping that since we were back in the country it would be easier and more civil. We could go our separate ways and neither of us would be stuck in Europe alone, you know?" Ethan looked up from his coffee into his brother's caring blue eyes. "I underestimated how much she didn't want to be left. Not because she loved me, but because she had to have the upper hand.

Eric shook his head, trying to make sense of everything he was learning. "So rather than let you leave amicably, she dumped you first?"

"Well, I don't think 'dumping me first' is adequate enough to describe what she did. When I came home that night she had completely cleaned me out. Everything was gone from our room, even my luggage. She left me a note that said I had no more to give her. She went on to describe her new protégé and thanked me for providing her the startup money she would need to launch his career."

"She didn't!"

"You betcha. I checked and she had taken everything I transferred to my American account to get us by for months."

"That's really fucked up."

"I know."

"But—Rachel? I never would have pegged her as capable of something like that."

"I don't think any of you ever really knew her."

After a few moments of silence, Eric pushed further. "Do Mom and Dad know how bad it was?"

"Absolutely not. I'm not sure I want them to know." *But maybe it wouldn't be so bad.*

"Ethan." He wouldn't say anything else until Ethan met his gaze. "They'll understand. I know they'll be sad that you had to suffer through that, and Mom will cry and wonder why you never came home to us, but in the end they'll be supportive."

"I don't want to embarrass them," he whispered.

"What?" Eric's eyes bugged out. "Are we talking about the same people?"

"Think about it. The son who they think is a wonderful success in life is nothing but a cokehead who shut them out of his life for nearly ten years while he ran off with someone he didn't even like very much, who later stole all of his shit. How does that make me look?"

Eric thought for a second. "Okay, on paper, it's not great, I'll grant you that. But I'm not stupid enough to believe that's the whole story. I won't make you tell me anymore now if you aren't ready, but it's pretty obvious to me that she was seriously messed up from the beginning. I always felt like there was something funny about you guys, but Maggie just said you were probably snobs."

They both laughed at that, and their deep, husky voices pulled the waitress to them like a magnet, coffee pot in hand for refills. Once she'd left again, Ethan leaned forward and smiled, feeling lighter in his brother's company than he had felt in years. "Maggie wasn't exactly wrong, you know. I was a pompous ass for a long time. I thought I was above it all."

"Above what, though? Being in love?"

"Well…yeah. I've never really thought about it, but I guess that's right."

"Nobody is above it, man. It either happens or it doesn't. You just haven't met the right one yet. Don't think that because I was a goner at eighteen that everyone is supposed to be."

"I don't think I'd know it if it hit me over the head, to tell you the truth. I have no reference to go by. All I know is sex, and even that was fairly rusty until recently." Beautiful hazel eyes and soft pink lips flashed through his mind, and he ignored the warm feeling that it caused.

"Well, just don't fuck it up and mistake one for the other. If you find something worth keeping, you owe it to yourself to see it through."

Eric stopped his fork halfway to his mouth when he realized what Ethan had let slip. "Wait a minute. Did you say until *recently?*"

"Uh, pardon?" Ethan swallowed so hard that his brother could see it across the table.

"Dude, are you already fucking someone? *Here?*"

"Keep your voice down, asshole!" Ethan shot glances across the room, making sure nobody was paying attention to their conversation.

"Oh my God, you totally are! Who is it? Come on, tell me! Is it someone from high school? Some old crush wishing she'd never let you go?" He started batting his lashes and making kissy faces.

"Eric, shut the fuck up. I'm not going to talk to you about it."

"No way, that's so unfair. Do you remember how much you whined and begged until I told you about my first time? Payback is a bitch, isn't it? Besides, you're rebounding in a very small pond, brother dear. You might as well tell me, because I'm sure I can find out by other means if I have to."

Ethan put his head in his hands and groaned, cursing himself for not thinking when he spoke. "I can't tell you what I don't know," he mumbled, his hands muffling his voice.

"What the hell does that mean?"

Ethan's eyes darted around the room again before meeting Eric's expectant look. "It means that I don't know her name."

"Was it a one-nighter? Didn't bother to ask it?"

"No," Ethan felt his cheeks heating. "Uh, there have been numerous… encounters."

Eric stared at him for a minute in total silence. "Okay, forgive me if I'm coming off as thick here, but how the hell is that even possible? Do you just never speak?"

"No, we speak a lot, actually. She's really very lovely."

"Then why don't you know her name?"

"Because I demanded that she not tell it to me." At Eric's puzzled look, he explained in more detail. "I was upset about Rachel, I felt like everything was closing in around me, and then she just appeared, like some sort of angel or goddess. It was perfect, and I didn't want to sully it with names and facts about each other. I wanted to keep her as my own private treasure that only existed for me while I was here." He looked to see if Eric was following him. "When I'm with her, it's like nothing else matters."

"So why don't you swap names and start dating? It sounds like a little bit more than a fuck to me."

"Because I'm not available like that. I'm too damaged for anybody else right now, and with my art I might need to pack up and leave for New York any day."

"Don't give me that shit. You can paint anywhere."

"Not always. I have to be inspired. Besides, I don't think she's exactly single. This is just a fling to her, too. We're having our fun while it lasts and then that will be that." Perhaps if he said it enough he might start to believe it.

Eric arched an eyebrow as he studied his brother, smelling the bullshit from a mile away. "Mmhmm, well, if that's what you want to tell yourself, that's fine by me. I just hope you know what you're doing."

"I do!" he snapped, uncomfortable under Eric's scrutiny. "Now can we please drop this?"

"All right, you big baby, let's get back to the hospital. I want to see if Maggie is up yet." Eric stood up and reached for the check, but Ethan grabbed it out from under his hand before he could pick it up.

"I said it was my treat, remember?"

"Well yeah, but you entertained me with so much dirt about yourself that I figured I should pay." He smiled wickedly and reached for the check again.

"Ha-ha, very funny. And no way, I'm treating."

They walked up to the counter to pay, standing in line behind a middle-aged man who was picking up a takeout order. Eric looked at his profile long enough to make out the moustache and smiled broadly, reaching around Ethan and tapping the man on the shoulder.

"Hey, Mr. Blake, I thought that was you!"

The man turned around and smiled back. "Eric," he said gruffly, nodding at him. "How have you been? Are those Bears going to be worth a damn this fall?"

"I hope so! I only get at them after they're injured, though, so let's hope I don't see too many breaks next season."

"How's your father doing? I haven't seen him since he stopped in and visited me at the hospital after my injury. It's been, what? A couple years now."

"Oh, he's real good. Still a workaholic, but we love him. I totally forgot you were hurt a while back. Looks like you're up and around pretty good now, though. I didn't even see you limping."

"Well, I owe it all to my Lily. She moved down here to help me recover, and I don't know what I would have done without her."

"Is that your daughter?" When the man nodded, Eric's face lit up in recognition, knowing he had heard the name Lily a lot lately. "Hey, wait a minute! Does she work over at Dr. Wilde's office?"

"That's right." Mr. Blake paid for his order while looking back over his shoulder at Eric. When he was done he moved out of the way so Ethan could pay their bill. "Know her from there? I didn't think there would be much call for a guy your age to get a Pap smear."

"Cute, Mr. Blake," Eric rolled his eyes. "No, actually my wife just adores her. She said that she always goes above and beyond for the patients there. Maggie was just saying the other day that she wanted to have her over some time. I'll have to let her know she's your daughter."

"I hope that won't turn her against her," Mr. Blake chuckled. "I know your wife wasn't my biggest fan after the last time I saw her."

"Uh, heh, you remember that, huh?" Eric turned beet red. "Well, that was a long time ago, and we were just dumb kids."

"Oh, I know. But I must say that I was happy to hear you made an honest woman of her after that."

Looking to change the subject quickly, Eric saw that Ethan had finished paying and was turning around. "Hey, I'm sorry. Do you remember my brother Ethan?" He patted him on the back so hard that Ethan was shoved slightly forward.

"I don't think I do. I knew you had a younger brother, but I don't think I've ever had the pleasure." He reached out his hand and shook Ethan's, addressing him directly. "It's probably a good thing that I don't remember you, since most of the kids I'm familiar with were troublemakers."

"Nice to meet you, sir. I'm suddenly very happy that I was a book-worm in school." They all shared a laugh until Ethan realized they were holding up the line. "I suppose we should be going."

"Yeah," Mr. Blake agreed. "I need to get over to the school and eat my breakfast before it gets cold. I just got back in town from chaperoning the damn student government trip, and I've probably got a stack of papers on my desk a mile high. It was nice seeing you again, Eric. Nice to meet you, Ethan. Stay out of trouble, boys." He winked at them before leaving and jumping in his car.

"Nice guy," Ethan said as they walked to their own car. When they were both inside he looked at Eric and smiled. "So what did he bust you for?"

"Shut up and get going," he snapped back, turning even redder than before. When Ethan only continued to sit there and look at him, he finally caved. "He didn't bust me, exactly. He let me go with a warning."

"For?"

"Remember that first homecoming weekend when I brought Maggie home from college? Well, I took her to the football game to show her my old stomping ground. When we got in my car to leave that night, things…got a little heated. My car was the only one left in the parking lot when Mr. Blake drove up—I guess he forgot some papers in his office or something. Anyway, he saw my car there and expected to find a drunken teenager passed out behind the wheel, but instead he found Maggie blowing me."

Ethan threw his head back and laughed, wiping a tear from his eye as he started the engine. "And that's why I never tried anything like that in a car."

"Hey man, don't knock it. What you don't get caught doing can make the risk worth it!"

Ethan drove him back to the hospital, noticing that he hadn't felt so light in weeks.

Upon seeing the large building come into view, he also made a mental note to stop by the store on the way home. He definitely needed to pick up sponges and bubble bath.

19

There was no other way to say it.

Ethan wanted to fuck in a car.

Ever since Eric admitted to getting busted back in college with Maggie's head in his lap while parked in the high school lot, Ethan hadn't been able to shake the feeling that he'd missed out on a lot of fun activities when he was younger. He had gone from being a shy, bookish introvert to a pretentious snob who was above that kind of thing. By the time he had hooked up with Rachel—well, if designer sheets weren't involved, she wasn't interested.

But now? Now he had *her*.

Something told Ethan that his goddess wouldn't be adverse to a little bit of backseat bingo—if he could first get her in his car, that is. They'd never set one foot outside his studio together before, but he was hoping that since it was Valentine's Day he might be able to persuade her to try something different.

Although his goddess had spent a surprising amount of time with him that week, he hadn't been holding onto any expectations of seeing her on Valentine's. As much as he hated to think about it, Ethan knew that she had someone else in her life who had a much bigger claim on her than he did. He assumed that she would be spending the evening with the *other guy*, which is why he was blown away when she'd told him that morning that she would be back again later that night.

So he began to plan. He went to the store and picked up a few essentials to pack in a bag, not forgetting a fleece throw to finish it off—it *was* February, after all. Ethan was counting on hot, sweaty groping that would keep them both overheated, but there was nothing wrong with being prepared.

He was so excited by the idea of dragging his girl off somewhere different for a change that he could barely stop himself from attacking her when she let herself into the apartment later that afternoon. Lily was wearing her workout clothes again, some black sweats and a red shirt that said *THE LADIES GO CRAZY FOR MY SUGALUMPS* on the front, and she looked adorable. When he saw her reach for her jacket he finally remembered that he had a voice.

"Leave it on," he whispered, crossing the room to meet her at the door.

"Oookay?" she said with a puzzled look on her face.

Ethan grabbed her jacket by the collar, pulling it back up into place on her shoulders before looking her deep in the eye. "Trust me."

"You suddenly have a jacket fetish?" she teased.

"Very cute, but no. You'll need it to stay warm."

"Warm? What do you—?" Understanding dawned in her eyes. "Where are we going?"

He grabbed his own coat and threw it on before taking her hand and leading her to the door.

"You'll see."

Ethan led her down the stairway, pulling her behind him until they made it to the door at the bottom. When he reached out to touch the handle, she stopped in her tracks. He looked back at her to see what was the matter, surprised to find a worried look on her face.

"You okay?" he asked.

Lily's eyes shot back and forth between him and the door a few times before settling on his face. He watched as she took a deep breath and sighed, finally ending with a small smile.

"I think so," she replied. "Just nervous."

"Don't be. Can you trust me?"

Her cheeks turned beet red as she pictured the tube of lube that was still upstairs. "You know I can."

He smiled at her and kissed her quickly. "Then trust me now. I won't let anyone see you." Pulling her with him into the alley, Ethan looked around quickly for any witnesses before leading her to his car in the parking lot. Once they were inside and backing out of the spot he was in, he heard her quietly giggle to herself.

"What's so funny?" He looked at her across the interior, wondering what the hell could be so humorous when she had just been scared to even step outside with him.

She suddenly adopted a serious look, before replying in a completely deadpan tone, "I just never took you for an Audi guy." And then she burst into laughter.

"You are such an asshole," he chuckled, glancing at her again as he drove. "An adorable asshole, of course, but an asshole all the same. Besides, it's a rental."

They drove for a while in silence as the sky darkened around them. Ethan noticed that she had managed to scoot so far down in her seat that she could barely peek out of the window any longer. When nothing but a thick cover of trees came into view, she shot back up.

"Where are you taking me?"

He turned off the main highway onto an almost nonexistent dirt road before turning to look at her. "Far enough from town so that nobody can hear you scream." He arched his eyebrow in the most dastardly fashion he could manage and smirked at her.

"So this is when I find out that you're really a psychotic killer who travels the country seducing young women before making a belt out of their nipples?"

"Beautiful, I admit that I'm very fond of your nipples, but—wait, what?"

"Sorry," she blushed. "It was serial killer week on the Biography Channel." Lily watched for another moment as he turned off the road onto the grass and drove between the trees until they reached a clearing. "Seriously, where the hell are we?"

"Well," Ethan explained as he pulled to a stop. "This is a place where I used to come when I was younger. I would hang out here all day and sketch. Sometimes I would even bring some paints with me when I felt more colorful."

"What was so special about this place? It looks sort of drab to me."

"True. But you should see it in the summer. This clearing has some of the prettiest wildflowers I've ever seen."

"Wow, I never would have guessed this was hidden back here. Wait— you grew up here? You're actually *from* Aledo?"

"Why is that so shocking?" The amazed look on her face was almost comical.

"I don't know…look at you! You just don't seem to fit in here."

"I have no idea if I should be flattered or insulted right now," he laughed. "Although now that I think about it, I never really did feel like I belonged here." Just then a large crack of thunder could be heard in the distance, making them both jump.

"Oh no! I hope it doesn't rain!" She peered up at the sky, searching for storm clouds.

"Why? A little rain never hurt anybody."

"But didn't you want to show me this clearing? Won't a sudden downpour put a bit of a damper on whatever you have planned?"

"Believe me, rain won't factor into my plans at all." He gave her another evil smirk and leaned toward her, kissing her softly on the lips.

"Okay, now I'm definitely intrigued. What exactly are your plans?"

Ethan smiled widely and kissed her again, this time more slowly. When he pulled away he whispered, "Let's just say that they don't involve leaving the car at all."

"Oh, is that so?" she teased. "Well, since I don't exactly see a drive-in around here anywhere, that really only leaves one other thing, doesn't it?"

"I'm amazed that you could be so closed-minded," he laughed, turning around and reaching into the backseat, grabbing a box from his over-stuffed bag. "You didn't even mention the picnic."

"What picnic? You said we weren't leaving the car."

"It'll be a car picnic. It's not much, just some sandwiches, but I thought that I should at least feed you something if I was going to drag you out into the middle of nowhere to have my wicked way with you."

He handed her one of the sandwiches, expecting her to laugh at how poorly made they were, but was concerned to see an odd look on her face. Ethan watched as she stared at the sandwich, turning it over in her hands like she'd never seen one before. When she looked back up at him, he could have sworn that her eyes were moist.

"Is something wrong?" he asked. "Do you not like turkey? I have a ham and cheese one here, too, if you'd rather have that one." She still didn't say anything for a minute and it was beginning to worry him.

"You made this for me?" she finally whispered.

"Yeah, I know. Sorry. I probably should have bought something pre-made, huh?"

"No, no. This is perfect." A shy smile played on her lips as she blinked a few times. "It's just that I can't really remember the last time anybody made me something. Thank you."

Ethan couldn't understand why the hell anyone would be so touched by such a crappy sandwich, but he decided not to press the issue. They ate in silence for a moment, trying to ignore the awkwardness that was growing between them.

He finished his food as quickly as possible and dipped back into the bag, pulling out a lighter and a tiny jar candle that was scented like roses. Feeling her eyes watching him, he lit the candle and set it on the dash before grabbing one last thing from the bag.

"Happy Valentine's Day," he said quietly, embarrassed to feel his cheeks heating up as he handed her the small heart-shaped box of chocolates. Ethan couldn't help feeling like a stupid nervous teenager, experiencing things that he had somehow skipped over his entire life.

"Oh my God! That's so sweet!" She took the box from his hands and hugged it to her chest. When he saw that she was getting misty-eyed again he couldn't hold his tongue any longer.

"Please don't fucking tell me that nobody ever got you candy, either." Although he'd never actually given candy to anyone else in his life before that moment, it seemed like a goddamn crime to think of her never getting any.

"Oh, I've gotten candy before, it's just been so long! I think I was in high school, maybe. I don't really remember for certain."

"It is a bit of a high school thing to do, isn't it?" he said with a frown. "I just wanted to…I don't know…" He groaned and raked his hands through his hair, feeling like a first-class idiot. Ethan stared out the window after that, watching a bright streak of lightning in hopes of avoiding her gaze until his embarrassment had abated.

"Stop that," she whispered, placing a hand on his shoulder until he turned to face her. "It was an unbelievably sweet gesture that shows me you were thinking of me. It does feel like something from high school, but I think that's why I'm so touched. It's almost like we're sweethearts hoping our parents don't catch us." She smiled brightly and winked at him, and for some odd reason his heart lurched.

She opened the box eagerly, tossing the paper liner into the backseat without looking. When the small selection of chocolates was revealed, she leaned over and took a deep breath, inhaling the scent with a quiet moan. Ethan watched as she selected one of the dark chocolate creams and lifted it to her lips, biting down slowly.

As she chewed, her lids closed and she threw her head back. "God!" she gasped. "That's just sinful!" He watched as her tongue flicked out to catch any remnants of the flavor on her lips and could feel himself beginning to harden already.

"Like it?" he asked quietly, surprised to find his voice a little hoarse.

"Oh yes," She moaned again, causing him to shift in his seat. "Here," she said, smiling again before holding out the other half of the piece she'd just bitten. "You have to taste this."

Ethan was starting to wonder if he was becoming a total pervert or if she knew exactly what she was doing to him. From the mischievous look in her eye, he was beginning to suspect the latter of the two. Well, two could play at that game.

He leaned toward her and opened his mouth slowly, allowing her to place the sweet on the tip of his tongue. Before she could pull her fingers away completely, he caught the tip of one between his lips, wrapping his tongue around it and sucking lightly, refusing to let it go until he saw her lids begin to droop.

He chewed slowly, enjoying the velvety smoothness as it enveloped his taste buds. She was right; it was rich, decadent, potent—and sinful. But it paled in comparison to her.

Ethan reached forward and took the box from her hands, selecting another piece and raising it to her lips. She repeated his actions, sucking on his fingertip until his eyes were crossing, then hungrily eating the entire treat. "God," she groaned, "that's so fucking good."

He set the box down on the dash next to the small candle and leaned in until their mouths were almost touching. "You taste better," he whispered against her lips before flicking his tongue across the petal-soft skin.

She gasped and opened her mouth, kissing him hungrily. He could taste the tiniest hint of sugary fruit and chocolate as their tongues fought with each other. He gave in finally and let her lead, thrilling to the sensation of her hands yanking and pulling on his hair to bring him closer and angle his head better.

After only a few moments they were both panting loudly, straining for more contact. Ethan pulled away to catch his breath, resting his forehead against hers.

"I've never made out in a car before," he admitted. "I had no idea what I was missing."

"Holy shit, are you kidding me?" She looked absolutely dumbfounded.

"No, why?"

She regarded him for about five seconds before nodding sharply. "Come on." She turned around and opened her door, stepping out into the dark clearing.

"Where?"

"The backseat, silly! We're definitely going to need more room." He watched as she opened the back door and jumped in. When he didn't move for a minute, immobilized by pure excitement, she looked up at him in disbelief. "Well? What are you waiting for, big boy? You've got me right where you want me, and you're sitting up there with your mouth hanging open."

"Well, when you put it that way…"

Ethan joined her in the back, tossing his duffel bag in the front to give them more room. He had barely even closed the door before she was jumping on him, pulling him down on top of her and kissing him wildly. As soon as he made contact with her his body went up in flames. He couldn't touch her everywhere fast enough.

"Fuck," he groaned between kisses. "You are so beautiful…you smell so damn good." Ethan was so aroused it was painful, grinding himself against her as they groped and fondled each other through their clothes. He slid his hands down her body and began tugging on her sweats, hating the need to make even the slightest distance between them as the pants slipped over the swell of her hips. Once they were low enough she kicked them off, leaving herself clad in only a tiny scrap of red lace. "What the fuck is that?" he growled, staring at the barely-there fabric.

"My Valentine's Day present for you," she giggled.

"Is that a thong?"

"Mmhmm," she smiled, wiggling suggestively underneath him.

"You mean to tell me that this was hiding under those ratty sweats the whole time?" How he was speaking around the saliva that was pooling in his mouth, he'd never know.

"Yep," she gloated. "It matches the bra."

Ethan looked her in the eye for exactly one second as he processed what she'd said, before grunting and yanking roughly on the hem of her shirt. She laughed, a sexy, velvety sound that went straight to his erection. When she had finally struggled out of the offending item of clothing she was left in the most seductive demi-cup lace bra that he could ever remember seeing.

"Sweet Jesus," he groaned before burying his face in her cleavage and covering it with open-mouthed kisses. Her giggles quickly turned into moans as he started thrusting against her again, feeling the warmth between her legs much more acutely with her pants out of the way.

Somewhere in the background, Ethan heard the patter of rain-drops beginning to fall and slap against the windows, but when he glanced up they were completely fogged over. There was nothing to be seen but the soft glow of the candle—and the mouth-watering siren beneath him.

"Come back to me," she gasped, tugging him back down by his hair until his lips were covering hers again. She had somehow gotten him out of his shirt without stopping their kisses, and her hands were making excellent work of his button fly when a loud, obnoxious ringing tore through the car.

"What is that?" Ethan panted.

"What is what?" she asked, almost in a daze.

"That ringing. Don't you hear it?"

Lily looked around, reality sinking in slowly. When the shrill noise finally registered in her mind she bolted straight up. "Oh shit!" She dug through her jacket frantically until she located her phone. Shooting her stranger a worried glance, she crawled out from under him and sat up. "God, I'm so sorry. I have to take this."

"You've got to be kidding me! *Now?*"

"*Please! I'm sorry,*" she mouthed before lifting the phone to her ear and answering, trying her best not to sound out of breath. "Hello? Oh, I just got out of the gym."

As she listened to the loud, masculine voice on the other end of the phone, Ethan felt sick to his stomach. He could only make sense of her side of the conversation, but it was enough to make a red haze take over his vision.

"I'm sorry you keep missing me. I think there's something wrong with the charger for my phone, it keeps dying…yeah, maybe…okay… that's great…I'm glad it's going so great for you."

The more she said, the angrier Ethan got. There was no logic behind his rage, simply emotion. He was losing himself to it completely. He couldn't believe that her stupid Neanderthal would dare to interrupt his perfect night, and that she would let him.

"Oh, I'll probably just watch some chick flicks all night… No, don't be silly, I'll be fine… I know…yeah, I know… Okay…yeah, miss you, too... Thanks, you, too." Lily hung up the phone quickly and placed it back in her jacket pocket, refusing to look at him as she took a few deep breaths and wiped her eyes.

Ethan tried to hold his tongue; he tried really hard to bite it back. He could tell she was obviously very upset about what had just happened and felt horrible. But he wasn't sure exactly who she felt horrible for, and that pissed him off even more.

And then it just slipped out.

"Care to tell me why the fuck you just *had* to answer that right now?" Even he could hear the venom dripping in his voice.

"Please don't," she whispered, still not looking at him.

"Please don't?" he spat. "Don't what, exactly? Don't give a shit that I told you he didn't fucking exist when we were together? That I never wanted anything involving him to interrupt our time together?"

"What was I supposed to do?" Lily cried. "I tried to get that out of the way earlier, but he didn't answer."

"I don't give a fuck!" Ethan screamed. "He gets you every time you leave me. Every single time, you go back to him. It takes everything I've got in me to keep from thinking about what you do with him."

"Oh, like you give a shit! You said yourself that this was just for fun. You said you didn't care if I was a nun or married with five kids. *You* said that, *not* me. Why the fuck are you acting so possessive all of a sudden when you want nothing to do with me when I'm not riding your dick?"

Ethan couldn't believe that was what she actually thought. Part of him wanted to tell her that she couldn't be more wrong, but his stupid emotions got in the way. He was livid. He was seething. He was so angry that he couldn't see straight—and he knew that he had absolutely no right to be.

But it didn't stop him.

"If you remember, I also said that nothing from the outside was supposed to interfere here. I don't know about you, but I think this was a pretty big interference."

"Well shit fucking happens sometimes, doesn't it?" Lily snapped, getting visibly angrier by the second. "You had a call the other day and I didn't care. How can you even talk to me like that?"

"And you know damn well that I was talking to my mother about a family emergency, not someone else who I go home to every night and *fuck*!"

"Could be, how would I know? You certainly know more about me than I do about you. I don't know where you go at night, and I just have to accept that."

"And that's somehow worse than knowing for certain that you belong to someone else?" He wasn't expecting the sharp slap across his face.

"Fuck you!" Grabbing the door handle and shoving it open, Lily screamed, "I don't belong to *anyone*!" before running out into the rainstorm.

Ethan didn't know exactly what happened after that. He just knew that the combination of her saying those words and running away from him awoke some long dormant idiotic caveman. That was his only defense. It was as if his most base predator instincts decided to show up and pay a visit.

He ran after her.

"Where the fuck are you going?" he screamed at her, watching as she ran farther into the clearing. "It's storming and you're in your underwear!"

"It beats being in that car with *you*!" she yelled back. When she saw that he was following her she ran faster, but he overtook her easily in the center of the clearing.

"Now you listen to me, Goddammit!" Ethan yelled, grabbing her slippery shoulders and turning her around to face him. It was obvious she had been crying, but her tears were camouflaged by the steady stream of rain down her face. His own hair was falling in his eyes, and he shoved it back so that he could look at her. "I don't give a shit what you think. You *do* belong to someone!"

"No I don't! And if you hate talking about him so much, then why don't you just stop fucking talking about him?!" Lily shoved him and tried to run away again, but he held her tightly. When she realized that she wasn't going to get away, she began struggling in his arms, slapping at his soaking wet chest.

"I'm not talking about him, are you fucking crazy?" He shook her then, wishing he could somehow rattle some sense into her. "I'm talking about *me!*"

"Oh, that's rich," she laughed, her cheeks glowing with anger in the disappearing light. "I'm your plaything until you get bored and move on. Please forgive me for not being more enthusiastic."

"No!" Ethan screamed, blinking through the rain to see her more clearly. "You are mine until I have to leave, there's a big difference. My God, you think I could get *bored* with you?"

"Of course! You've made it more than clear." She sobbed loudly and shoved at him again, slipping from his grasp. He ran after her, pulling her to him roughly until their chests were sliding together.

"You don't understand a goddamn thing!" He slammed his mouth down onto hers, possessing her lips with a ferocity that he didn't know he was capable of. Grabbing her by her soaked hair, he forced her to look him in the eye. "I may not have any fucking rights to you when you aren't with me, but dammit, when you are, you are *mine!* It drives me crazy to think of anyone else's hands on you, to think of someone being able to kiss you whenever they want, to hold you at night! *Fuck!*"

Ethan kissed her again fiercely, not understanding why his anger was turning into lust. All he knew in that moment was that she was his, and he wanted nothing more than to mark his territory. He pulled her down onto the wet grass, ignoring her feeble protests. Once he had her hands pinned above her head so that she couldn't slap him again, he forced her to look at him.

"Admit it," he growled at her.

"I can't admit what's not true," she spat back at him. Lily's eyes were on fire, shooting daggers at him as if she were imagining his painful death, but it didn't stop her from wrapping her legs around his waist and shifting against his uncomfortably hard erection.

"Stop being a bitch and admit it. I'm not going to let you up until you say that you're mine!" Ethan ground his hips into her for added effect, leaving absolutely no doubt in her mind that he needed her badly.

"God!" she cried, wrapping her arms around his back and digging her nails into his slick flesh. Sobbing into his neck before biting him roughly, she snapped, "Just shut up and fuck me!"

"No!" he gritted through his teeth. Everything she was doing was painful, but it was also exquisite. He felt alive, and like he was exactly where he was supposed to be. Ethan thrust against her more firmly, digging into the hollow between her thighs. "Not until you say that you're mine! Tell me!"

He leaned down and pulled at her bra with his teeth, tearing the lace, exposing a tightly puckered nipple to his hungry mouth. Sucking on her chilled flesh, he continued his movements until he felt her grinding her hips back into his.

"Say it!" he snarled, feeling more possessive with every thrust.

"Oh God!" she sobbed again, digging her nails in deeper. "Yours," she croaked.

"Louder!"

"Goddamn you, I'm *yours!*" Lily screamed. "Now fuck me!"

Ethan had reached his breaking point. Fumbling with the fly on his jeans, he tore them open just far enough to free his aching erection before shoving his hand between her legs and yanking her thong to the side. Grunting and panting, he lined himself up at her entrance and slammed inside her, making them both cry out so loud that it echoed through the woods.

Ethan took note of the biting chill and the downpour of freezing water cascading over his bare back and onto her chest, but short of a lightning bolt striking two feet away from them, nothing was going to make him stop. He ground himself into her with one angry, possessive thrust after another, marveling at the scorching heat that was squeezing and milking every last ounce of sanity out of his cock.

"Yessssss," she wailed as he pistoned his hips faster, her head thrown back into the sopping wet grass and her eyes squeezed tight.

"Look at me!" he commanded, refusing to let her do anything that would shut him out of her senses. When her fiery gaze shot to his, he somehow felt himself growing impossibly harder inside her.

"What?" Lily spat out, furious at him for barking more orders at her. "I already told you what you wanted to hear! Isn't that enough?"

"No!" he yelled back. "It will never be enough! I don't just want you to say it, I want you to mean it. I want you to look me in the eye…I want you to know damn well who's fucking you right now!" He leaned down and sucked the water from her rigid nipple before swirling his tongue around it, biting it lightly as he ground into her again. "This is not some dipshit little boy trying to play house inside you right now. This is *me*," Ethan grunted as he thrust even harder. "And you. Are. *Mine!*"

He could actually see her resolve crumbling in front of him. Ethan didn't know if it was what he was saying to her, or what he was doing to her, but something finally made her snap.

"Yes!" she sobbed, wrapping her arms around him even tighter, her body starting to shake under his. It looked like fresh tears were pooling in her eyes, but he couldn't be sure due to the rain. "I'm yours! I fucking belong to you and I can't make it stop! I don't *want* to make it stop!" She began weeping freely into his neck before kissing the skin where she had bitten earlier. "Nothing else…nobody else… none of it means a thing to me when I'm with you! And sometimes I fucking *hate* you for it!"

"Well sometimes I hate you, too!" he gritted through his teeth, his body winding tighter, like a coil about to snap. It was true: there were times when Ethan hated even the thought of her. He hated her every time she left to go back home to *him*. He hated her every time he couldn't get to sleep without thinking of her. He hated her every time he would wake up in the middle of the night, painfully hard and alone, clutching his pillow because it still smelled like her.

He hated her every time he remembered that she wasn't his to keep.

"Just make me forget…make it all disappear!" Lily sobbed into his ear before taking it between her teeth and biting down on the lobe. "Be mine tonight, too! Belong to *me* for once!"

Ethan forced her to look at him again, holding her head in place while he wiped the rainy tear mixture out of her eyes.

"I already do," he said hoarsely. "I always have." And with that he leaned in and covered her mouth with his own, swallowing her kisses along with her tears.

Both of their bodies began to spiral out of control after that, finally reaching the point of no return together. Ethan sped up his thrusts as Lily bucked her hips wildly, and he was startled to feel her hands slide up and grab him by the back of the head. She yanked on his hair until he was staring down at her again before gasping, "Now *you* say it!"

"I just did," he grunted, barely holding on as they writhed together on the ground.

"Say it!" she cried, her voice breaking with an involuntary whimper. He could feel her inner muscles clamping down on him as he bucked his hips and had no idea how he was able to form a coherent thought.

"I belong to you," Ethan moaned. "You own me...body and soul."

And with that Lily exploded in a fit of screams, shaking and bucking beneath him as he quickly followed, pumping his seed deep inside her.

After a few minutes of frantic panting and attempting to regain composure, Ethan realized just how freezing his girl was: her teeth were starting to chatter and she was beginning to shake violently from the cold. He refastened his now-soaked jeans and scooped her up in his arms, holding her close to him as he carried her back to the car.

Sitting down in the backseat again with Lily on his lap, he reached forward into the front and turned on the engine, blasting the heat on high. After that, he grabbed the fleece blanket he'd packed and wrapped it around her tightly, tucking her against his chest as he rubbed her back, trying to generate more heat. Ethan held her close like that for almost an hour, stroking her hair in silence and watching her as her eyes slowly shut. When he tried to wake her up gently to help her get dressed before heading back into town, she surprised him by whispering against his skin.

"I'm sorry I ruined your plans for tonight." Her voice sounded tiny and frail, and full of sadness.

"You didn't ruin anything, beautiful girl," he replied, kissing the top of her head. "I did, with my bullshit temper. I hope you can forgive me. It was uncalled for."

"Forgive you?" she scoffed. "If that's what having a fight with you is like, I might have to piss you off more often."

Ethan could tell that she was putting up a wall between them again, making a joke when he was being serious, but he wasn't going to push her any more that night. Instead, he just smiled and kissed her gently before taking her back into town, dreading the moment when he would have to watch her leave all over again.

20

It had been two days since he'd seen her.

Two days, almost three.

After their awkward silence in the car on the way home from their disastrous attempt at an outing, he told himself that it would all be better the next day. Then, the next day came…and no goddess. Ethan reminded himself that it was the weekend and she no doubt had some sort of commitment that didn't include him, but that didn't stop the nagging feeling that told him something was wrong.

By Sunday night, he was grateful that he still didn't know her name, or else he would have driven up and down the streets of Aledo with his iPod dock looking for her, ready to become the world's most pathetic Lloyd Dobler impersonator. He didn't know what it was about this woman that made him regress to high school boyfriend mentality. He only knew that he felt horrible about the way things had escalated the other night and that he missed her terribly.

Monday afternoon found him pacing in front of a paint-smeared canvas, his mind too preoccupied to focus on the task at hand. Ethan normally had a routine of zoning out to his music when he painted and letting his emotions take over, leading him to paint from his subconscious until he found something tangible to work with for a subject. But now, every single time he tried to lose himself in his art, he would find another reminder of that night on the canvas when he was done.

First, it was a melted piece of chocolate that had quickly been scraped away with a loud huff. Next, it had been a half-eaten sandwich soaked with tears—that one had made Ethan pull roughly on his hair before squirting the whole thing down with turpentine and wiping it away. When he finally realized that his last one was shaping up to be the foggy view from inside the rain-soaked windows of his car, he cursed loudly and kicked the easel across the room before forcing himself to take a break.

He turned off the loud beats that were flooding the apartment and threw himself face down on the mattress, allowing himself for the first time to focus on the question that was really bothering him.

What if she never came back?

The only thing that scared him more than that idea was the fact that he cared so much.

Across town, Lily wasn't faring much better.

She had spent all weekend moping around the house, telling herself that there was always one more chore that had to be done before she could even dream of going anywhere. The house had never been cleaner, George and the cats had never been fed better in their lives, and now Lily was completely out of distractions and excuses.

She'd even gone so far as to call up Scott out of the blue and talk his ear off for the better part of an hour before he finally told her that he was really happy to hear from her, but he had to get back to work. It turned out that Ryan's buddy in St. Louis also ran his own garage, and they were down a mechanic since their best one skipped town with his seventeen-year-old pregnant mistress the week before. Now that he and Ryan had two cars, Scott offered to stay behind and help them out for a few days until they could find a replacement.

Lily could tell from how happy he sounded on the phone that if it weren't for his drunk-ass nagging father, and the fact that he had a fiancée back home, he might have decided to stay quite a bit longer than a few days.

Her thoughts were only half-selfish when she found herself wishing that he would.

Once she had absolutely nothing left to feign interest in, she curled up in a ball on her bed for hours and tried desperately to forget how embarrassed she was over her actions Friday night. She kept telling herself over and over again that she never should have taken that phone call. The night would have gone so much smoother. She'd been so thrilled to be able to help her stranger live out a fantasy—they'd been so damn close—and then she had to fuck it all up by answering a stupid call that she didn't even want to take. It could have waited… it really could have.

Then she had gone and cried like a big baby when he got angry, and she still felt completely humiliated by the things she'd said and done after that. How could she ever look him in the eye again?

And why would he ever want her to?

That was the thought that dug at her the most. Every time she nearly caved and ran out the door to go to him, she was struck with the fear of what she might be greeted with when she got there. Would it be indifference? Resentment? Or, even worse, pity? Pity for the poor girl who thought she could actually make him hers, even for just one night?

She knew that she could never take back the things she had said, and she was convinced that he had only agreed with her to shut her up. Nevertheless, she missed him so much it hurt. The longer she stayed away, the worse the pain inside her became.

Monday at work was an even bigger disaster than the weekend. She was so sad and distracted that even her patients were asking her what was wrong, and Lily discovered that there was hardly a situation more awkward than someone offering you a hug when you were just about to test them for chlamydia.

By the end of her shift she knew that she couldn't stand it any longer. She had to see him again, regardless of how he received her.

As she walked up the long, dark stairway to the apartment, she couldn't shake off the feeling that something was different. When she clearly heard the key turn in the lock, she realized that it was the total silence that seemed off. Where was his blaring music? Was he not there? It was so quiet in the living room that she could actually hear the melodic strains of a waltz drifting up from the dance class downstairs.

Before she could call out for him he appeared in the bedroom doorway, like some sort of dark angel who knew when he was needed without ever being asked. He stood there for a moment, watching her from across the room, looking her up and down as if he were afraid she was going to disappear. When he seemed satisfied that she was real, he approached her slowly, and Lily was pleased to find no hint of pity or sarcasm on his face—only relief.

When he was no more than five inches away from her he stopped, his head ducked down as if in shame, as if he were afraid to meet her eyes. Lily watched as he carefully reached out and slipped his hands around her waist, and only then did he seem to breathe, a deep, loud sigh. He pulled her to him quickly and buried his face in her neck, not doing anything but holding her tightly and inhaling her scent. It wasn't until Lily hugged him back that she felt his stiff body start to tremble before finally relaxing around her.

They stood there together like that for almost a minute, simply holding each other and soaking it all in. Lily was busy marveling at how right it felt to be in his arms again, while Ethan couldn't stop trying to commit every single aspect of her scent to his memory. After nearly three days without her in the apartment all of his reminders of her had just about faded away.

They probably would have been content to stand there like that all night if it hadn't been for the loud *thump, thump, thump* that echoed up through the floor, followed by a muffled "Again!" as Mrs. Knight scolded the class and started the song over again from the beginning. However, the interruption didn't force them to move away from each other. Rather, it brought them back to reality just enough to hear the music.

As the violin drifted around them, Lily was surprised to feel her stranger grip her tighter and begin to sway to the beat. When she looked up at him with a puzzled expression, he merely smiled gently and stopped long enough to push her jacket off her shoulders, letting it fall to the floor before kicking it away. By the time she had followed its motion across the floor with her eyes, he had taken her right hand in his left and lifted it to their side, his other hand sliding around to grip her hip firmly.

"What are you—?" she gasped as he took two elegant steps toward her, forcing her to move backward with him.

"Shh."

"But I have no idea how to—"

"Shh!"

With that, he took her other hand and placed it on his shoulder before grabbing her by the hip again and taking another small step in her direction, guiding her backward with the pressure of his grip. She watched as he slid sideways after the second step, moving her body with him, and she realized that he was slowly gliding them in a box step, commanding her to follow with only his touch.

Lily shut up and allowed herself to be led, never taking her eyes off his. She was afraid if she tried to look down at her feet she might stumble, so she concentrated on the smoldering jade gaze in front of her. He pulled her with him as he stepped backward before turning her slowly and repeating the motion all over again. At one point, he shifted and dipped her back deeply. When he lifted her back up she giggled nervously, imagining how foolish they looked doing the waltz in grubby workout sweats and paint-splattered clothes, but when she met his eyes, his heated gaze nearly did her in.

There was nothing foolish about it.

Ethan took his time whirling and twirling her around the room, never losing control of the beauty in his arms. Whenever the music would change in tempo, he would spin her out the full extension of his arm before snapping her back to his chest and dipping her again. He eventually twirled her around so that her back was pressed against his chest. After a few more gliding steps back and forth, he spun her around and pulled her to him one final time, dipping her sharply while his hand slid down her back, caressing the swell of her ass before lifting her thigh up and wrapping it around his hip as the beautiful song finished.

He leaned over and kissed her gently, barely brushing her soft lips with his own before resting his forehead against hers and closing his eyes.

"I missed you," he whispered, his eyes still shut tight.

"I missed you, too," Lily replied, surprised at the loud exhale he made, as if he'd been anxiously awaiting her response. He opened his eyes and looked at her intently, slowly lowering her body down beneath him. The soft feeling of the mattress hitting her back finally made her pay attention to her surroundings. The sexy motherfucker had danced her into the bedroom and dangled her over the goddamn bed.

She opened her mouth to tease him about dancing with ulterior motives, but something about the look on his face made her stop. There was such a deep longing in his eyes that she instantly knew this wasn't the time or place for jokes.

"I was worried you weren't coming back." His voice was so soft and quiet that she barely heard him, even though he was only inches away from her face.

"I—" she swallowed thickly, "I was worried that you wouldn't *want* me back."

Ethan planted his knee between her thighs and braced his weight on his hands beside her head, doing nothing for almost a full thirty seconds but staring at her face. His eyes lingered on hers before falling to her lips, then back up to her eyes again as if he couldn't decide which was more captivating. Very slowly, he lifted one hand to the side of her face and caressed her cheek, dragging his long thumb across her bottom lip in the process.

"Silly little girl," he breathed. "I'll always want you. I just have to accept that I can't always have you."

With that, Ethan could wait no longer. It had been entirely too long since he had tasted her lips properly, and he was going to remedy that immediately. Closing the distance between them, he covered her mouth with his own, deepening the kiss as he settled his weight on her more firmly. His body screamed to life when he felt his goddess respond eagerly, wrapping her arms around his neck and shoving her hands into his hair as if she were holding on for dear life.

When the slick tip of his sweet tongue probed at her lips for entrance, Lily feared that she might faint, the intoxicating flavor of him making her dizzy. She accepted him slowly, both savoring the experience and doing her best to stay lucid. The languorous drag of his tongue against hers was its own form of exquisite torture, and they both moaned at the sensation when they began to swirl them together.

Ethan couldn't resist sliding his hands lower, down her sides and over her hips, touching everything along the way as he kissed her. When he switched direction and pushed them back up, he hooked his thumbs under the hem of her shirt and lifted it, raking his fingertips over her bare flesh as he moved. Lily lifted enough for him to remove the offending article of clothing, but whimpered when he had to pull his mouth away long enough to raise it over her head.

Just as hungry to feel his skin, she barely had enough clarity of mind to return the favor, tugging on his paint-splattered T-shirt until he took the hint, raising up on his knees and yanking it off before tossing it across the room. Lily quickly removed her bra, throwing it in the same direction as his shirt, and lay there looking up at him in all of his bare-chested glory. He watched her for a moment, panting, before smiling and lowering himself back on top of her, nearly jumping at the electric jolt he felt when their flesh made contact.

Ethan began kissing her again, each shift of his lips and tongue more ravenous than the last. He went no farther than kissing for a while, though, happy to simply have her in his arms again with her skin touching his.

Lily didn't know what to make of it at first. He would normally start speeding up their actions in a rush to move on to better things. Now, he slowed down even more, kissing her so deliberately and deeply that her eyes began to cross.

When he finally moved to touch her, it was so light at first that she barely felt it. He started at her face, dragging his fingers down her soft skin as he kissed her, following the column of her throat until he was cupping her breast. He loved her with his hands, almost tickling her sides as he stroked her flat belly.

When his hands met the top of her pants he slid his fingers underneath the elastic, reaching around her to pull them down around her backside, taking her panties with them. When her pants were bunched up around her ankles he noticed that he hadn't even removed her shoes yet, so those were thrown haphazardly over his shoulders without looking, quickly followed by her wadded-up sweats. Ethan couldn't be bothered to take his eyes away from her gloriously nude body to see where they landed.

This time he moved even more slowly, drinking in the sight of her, from her feet upward until he followed his gaze with his hands. He circled each of her ankles with his long fingers, dragging them up her calves before sliding his hands to the front of her thighs, moving even higher. His thumbs barely brushed against the tightly manicured hair at the apex of her thighs before continuing on, circling around her navel.

When he had reached her breasts again he stopped, looking up to meet her eyes before he grabbed them more firmly, making sure that she was watching. He rested his weight on his elbows and settled between her legs, causing Lily to wrap her long limbs around his jean-clad hips. They both watched as he swirled his thumbs around her aching peaks, causing the tissue to tighten and swell, before he released a loud groan and covered one of her breasts with his mouth. Suckling her greedily, Ethan made sure to lavish attention on her other breast with his hand, squeezing and pinching her dusky nipple with his fingers as he continued to work the other with his tongue.

She tasted so good that he knew he could get lost in her flavor, but after a while he made sure to switch over, not wanting the other nipple to feel neglected. He worked her breasts for so long that Lily was becoming unglued beneath him, never having felt anything quite so intense before. He had always enjoyed her chest whenever they'd been together, but nothing like this. It felt like he was worshiping her.

After a few more minutes the constant stimulation began to make Lily squirm. She was delirious with need, her body aching and feeling more hollow with each new stroke of his tongue. She was swollen and wet, her throbbing sex weeping to have him inside her. Before long she began rocking her hips against him, eager to find some sort of relief.

Ethan tried to keep himself away from her for as long as possible, wanting to focus his energy on her body first, but feeling her writhing underneath him made him thrust forward involuntarily, grunting loudly around her hardened flesh.

After she ground herself into him a few more times he pulled back, not trusting himself to stay that close without losing control. Sliding his hand in between their bodies, he slipped his fingers between her swollen folds and groaned at the feeling of them slipping through her wetness. Her hips bucked sharply at the contact, and the loud moan that tore from her body startled them both.

"Do you need that, baby?" he whispered as he slid two fingers lower and circled her entrance. "Right *there?*" He pushed them deep inside her to accentuate his question.

She couldn't answer. She couldn't think. She could only feel, and it felt fucking amazing.

Lily could barely manage a squeak and a slight nod, but it was more encouragement than he needed. Without removing his fingers, Ethan slid down between her legs and licked her silken petals with one long, broad stroke. Lily groaned incoherently and shoved her hands into his hair, moving herself against his hungry mouth when he began worshipping her there. He licked and sucked at her with more vigor than he had either of her nipples, drunk on the taste of her, and when he curled his fingers upwards inside her, she exploded around them, shattering into what felt like a million pieces.

Moving back up her body slowly, Ethan took the time to appreciate every aspect of his beautiful girl's climax: her flushed features, her dilated pupils, the rise and fall of her breasts as she tried to catch her breath. She was absolutely addictive.

He honestly didn't know how he had ever lasted so long without her.

He told himself that he was only referring to the last few days, but the longer he looked at her, the less sure he became.

"Where did you go?" she panted, reaching up to hold his face. He snapped out of it, meeting her curious gaze. She stroked his cheek gently before slipping her hand behind his head, pulling him down closer to her lips. "Come back to me."

"I can honestly say there's nowhere else I'd rather be right now."

He closed the distance between them and kissed her deeply, thrilling to her touch as she pulled him to her eagerly and moaned into his mouth. It never ceased to amaze him how responsive she was with him, and today was no exception. Her arms wrapped around him, squeezing him tightly before she slid her hands down the muscles in his sculpted back. When she reached his firm backside she cupped it, grimacing at the feel of the denim he was still wearing.

"I need you," she gasped, breaking the kiss just long enough to make him understand her desperation. "Please," she begged as she tugged on his jeans. "I feel so empty without you inside me."

Ethan didn't need to be asked twice.

Their hands tangled together in the rush to get his fly undone. The sounds of the buttons popping open were the only noise that could be heard in the room over their wet kisses. When he had finally freed himself from his jeans, Ethan kicked them the rest of the way off before settling back between her legs, bracing his body above her with one arm as he guided himself to her entrance.

Lily felt his broad tip sliding along her slick folds, nudging at her opening briefly before probing her gently, stopping once it was just barely inside. She glanced up into her stranger's eyes again, wondering what had made him stop, and the expression on his face nearly made her weep. He was staring at her closely, as if he were memorizing every detail of her features, and once again the only word that came to her mind was worship.

"Is there anything wrong?" she asked after a few more seconds of silence. "Why aren't you moving?"

Just as he was about to slide inside her, business as usual, Ethan was struck with the realization that his time with his goddess was undeniably limited. The last three days had been merely a sample. He had no idea how many more chances he would have to be where he was right at that very moment, and he didn't want to take it for granted any longer.

"I just…realized that I've never watched your face when I enter you," he whispered. "I've usually got my eyes closed or my head thrown back because of how amazing you feel. That just doesn't seem right. I need to know what you look like."

Lily had no idea what to say to that. She was feeling completely overwhelmed with a thousand different emotions at once, so she surrendered herself to her body and let them take over. Her hips shifted forward, welcoming him deeper, and she cried out in pleasure when he finally made the first thrust. It was shallow, pushing in only halfway, before he pulled back again.

"Look at me!" he grunted when she instinctively closed her eyes. He may not have been all the way in yet, but he still felt so damn good that it was nearly impossible for her to concentrate. When her eyes were finally locked with his again, he began to roll his hips, continuing with very shallow movements as they watched each other. He went a little bit deeper with every thrust, and after the fourth or fifth she could see the veins popping in his neck with the force of his restraint.

"Do you feel me?" he gritted through his teeth, eyes blazing. "Can you feel me moving inside you?"

"Oh God…*yes*," she gasped, trying harder with each movement to pull him in farther, using her thighs around him for leverage.

"Now let's see how deep I can go," he growled, leaning over to claim her lips in a possessive kiss before rearing back and thrusting, seating himself inside her to the hilt. Ethan watched as her eyes rolled back and she moaned, and the sight was almost more powerful than the feeling of her tight walls gripping him. He grabbed her hands and pinned them beside her head, holding her fingers tightly as if it might ground him to the only sanity he knew anymore.

"Yes," he groaned, rocking into her more forcefully with each thrust, never taking his eyes off her face. "Do you think I can touch your soul like this?" he panted before kissing her again.

She met every movement eagerly, bucking and moaning underneath him and trying her damnedest to keep her eyes open, but before long it was all just too much. He felt too good inside her, the words he said were too perfect, and his face was just too painfully beautiful to look at any more.

Lily clamped her eyes shut, unable to process the onslaught of stimulation. Her body wound itself tighter and tighter around him as he moved, each shift in angle hitting her in a more interesting spot. When he swirled his hips one final time and groaned that he was close, something inside of her snapped wide open. She felt him deeper than she ever had before, and knowing that they were both about to explode made her frantic. She wrestled her arms free and reached down to grab his ass firmly, locking him in place as she ground herself against him, pulling him deeper into her with every buck of her hips.

"Oh fuck!" Ethan cried out in shock at her sudden fierceness, the tight grip of her body milking him as he spilled deep inside of her. The feeling of him letting go triggered her own release, and as he watched her face in ecstasy, he couldn't stop the emotions from overflowing and the words from spilling out of his mouth.

"You're so fucking beautiful…so perfect," he panted. "You feel so amazing!" With that, his lips crashed down on hers, devouring her whimpers and moans.

Lily had never felt so cherished in her entire life. He had made her feel beautiful and precious. They had experienced plenty of sex together, but never like that. Today she had been loved—even if only for one day.

Bittersweet emotions made rivers of hot tears flow down her cheeks. She clung to him as they kissed, afraid to let him go, as if he would disappear at any moment, knowing deep down in her heart that he could. She kissed him all over—his lips, his cheeks, his neck—physically unable to break their embrace.

When she tasted salty tears on her lips, she assumed they were her own.

21

Three hours later, Lily walked into her bedroom at home. She hadn't felt like fixing dinner and since George was out late at a PTA function she'd simply grabbed a container of blackberry yogurt and followed her cats upstairs.

Once she was changed into some pajamas she threw herself back onto her bed, sprawled out with her legs spread wide, and stared up at the ceiling. She didn't move when Boober curled up into a furry ball between her legs and went to sleep. She didn't move when it got so dark in her room that she couldn't see anymore.

She just kept staring up at her ceiling.

It wasn't until Wembley padded up and yowled in her face that she snapped back to reality. Turning her head to look at his fuzzy face in the dark, she sighed deeply.

"Wembley, what's Mama gonna do?" He just stared at her for a minute before licking her nose.

"Some help you are," she huffed. "I love him. I love him and there isn't a damn thing I can do about it. If I tell him, he'll just run away even faster."

The cat had grown quite bored with her whining by then, turning away and jumping off the bed to go sit on the windowsill and clean himself. *Men.*

Wiping fresh tears from her eyes, Lily sighed again.

One thing's for sure. Scott and I are going to have to have a long talk when he gets back. No matter what happens, this just isn't right or fair to him.

She let the tears flow freely then, mourning the loss of their future together.

When she realized that the thought of not being with him anymore didn't even hurt, she sobbed even louder.

About twenty minutes later, after she was all cried out and almost asleep, Lily jumped as her cellphone started ringing on the nightstand by her head. She didn't recognize the number, but she could tell it was local and figured it might be important.

"Hello?"

"Is this Lily?" a lovely female voice asked through the phone.

"Yeah. Who's this?" The voice sounded familiar, but she couldn't imagine who would be calling her at such a late hour.

"Oh, good! I was hoping this was the right number. This is Maggie Foster."

Lily glanced over at her bookshelf in the moonlight, her gaze landing on the now-ragged copies of Maggie's books. This was just too surreal. "Um, hi, Mrs. Foster."

"Please, call me Maggie."

"Um...okay, Maggie. How can I help you?"

"Well, I hope you don't mind my calling. I know it's terribly late, and I had to pull a few strings at Dr. Wilde's office to get ahold of your number." After a moment of silence that Lily didn't have a clue how to fill, she continued. "Can we talk?"

Her voice dragged Lily out of her self-induced pity coma.

"Of course," Lily replied, sitting up on her bed quickly. "Is something wrong?" As she listened she leaned over and turned on the small lamp on her nightstand, illuminating the room in a soft glow.

"No, no, nothing bad this time," she laughed lightly. "Actually, I realized that I never had the chance to thank you properly for everything you did last week. I would have called you sooner, but this is literally my first minute of alone time. I love my family dearly, but they tend to hover and cling when someone is unwell. Eric is the worst of them all!" She spoke the last sentence in a dramatic stage whisper, bringing a smile to Lily's face.

"Don't be silly, Maggie. I was only doing what anyone would have done."

"Well, see, that's where you're wrong. I don't think I've ever met anyone who would have gone above and beyond the way you did for me. Someone else might have given me a ride, but that's where it would have ended. You gave me comfort, and I'd like to think friendship as well."

Lily swallowed a lump in her throat before replying. "Of course I'm your friend, Maggie—if that's what you'd like."

"I would. I'd like that very much. I don't know what it is about you, but I get the feeling that you are a good friend to have."

Lily wasn't quite sure how to respond to that, but it was her turn to talk, so she tackled the subject that was making her feel the most uncomfortable. "All right...I have to ask you something."

"Sure."

"Is it weird that I'm a big fan of your books?"

"You *are?*" Maggie chuckled lightly at first, and it grew into a full belly laugh. "Oh, I'm sorry to laugh, but I haven't so much as giggled in the last few days and it just feels so good." She took a deep breath before continuing. "Why on earth would that be weird?"

"I don't know. I guess it always feels a little surreal to me that you even know who I am. I was reading your stuff before I ever moved here."

"Hey, I'm just a bored housewife who got totally lucky and sold some sleazy daydreams that I put down on paper, and I'm flattered that you enjoy reading them. Why should that be weird? I would have more fun talking about them with you than my mother-in-law, that's for sure!" Her voice dropped down to another dramatic whisper. "I can just tell that she's wondering how many of my love scenes I've acted out with her son and that always grosses me out."

"How many?" Lily asked, before clamping a hand over her mouth in embarrassment. She hadn't meant to ask, it had just slipped out.

Another loud laugh echoed over the phone. "*All* of them, darling, all of them!" After Maggie had calmed down again, she cleared her throat. "Listen, there was another reason I called. Have you ever done karaoke?"

That was probably the last thing that Lily expected to hear. "Not since college, why?"

"Well, we sort of have this twisted little tradition. Whenever something bad or depressing like this happens to one of us, we hit up the closest bar that does karaoke and make fools of ourselves. Now it just so happens that one of the little dive bars here in town has karaoke on Friday night."

"Karaoke? That's your twisted tradition?"

"I know it doesn't sound like it, but the way we do it, it is. Emma and her husband usually tag along with me and Eric, and once we get a good buzz going we take our turns butchering the most ridiculously outdated stuff. It's pretty scary, actually, but they will do anything to get my mind off things and make me laugh. I was wondering if I might be able to talk you into joining us."

"Wow," Lily replied, more than a bit stunned by how much she really wanted to hang out with Maggie. "Thank you. But are you sure? That sounds an awful lot like private family time to me, especially considering the circumstances."

"The circumstances are exactly why I'd like to have you there, Lily. I've had my mope this week. I've cried my tears. Now I want to get drunk, be tone-deaf, and laugh. Something just tells me that having you around would make for a fun night. What do you say?"

"Well, I don't know." She had to remind herself that the world wouldn't spin off its axis if she actually went out and had fun one night.

"Please? It would mean the world to me."

Lily took a deep breath and a leap into the unknown—it was a feeling she was beginning to recognize and enjoy. "Okay," she exhaled loudly, shoving her messy hair back off her face. "Okay, yeah. Why not?"

"Really?" Maggie all but squealed. "Oh, that's great! I think you'll have a fun time. Now," her tone changed suddenly, all business, "Wear something kind of sexy-flirty. We make the biggest asses of ourselves and completely overdress for the occasion, and it's a blast. Karaoke starts around eight, so we'll be there to pick you up about seven thirty."

"Wait, you're picking me up? Why?"

"Never turn down a carpool to a group outing, Lily. It's much easier to relax and enjoy the ride."

"Okay," she sighed with resignation. "Did you want my address?"

"I don't think so. You're still living with Mr. Blake, aren't you?"

"Yeah, that's right. Wait, how do you know my dad? Or where he lives?"

"Jesus Christ, Lily, it's *Aledo*! Everyone knows where your dad lives. Besides, your dad and I go *way* back." The evil laugh that followed made Lily decide to ask her to explain that statement at another time, when she wasn't quite so scared to find out the details.

"All right, so you'll pick me up Friday," Lily steered the conversation away from whatever wicked memories were making Maggie laugh. "Should I look for your car?"

"No, we wouldn't all fit in that. Just keep an eye out for the most garish, outlandish SUV that you've ever seen in your life."

"All right, now I'm officially intrigued," she laughed.

After a few more minutes of small talk, they said their good-byes and ended the call. As Lily crawled into bed that night she found herself wondering how long it had been since she'd made a new friend.

She honestly couldn't remember.

"Why, nurse! I don't think I'm dirty there."

"Trust me, Mr. Smith. I've seen what you do with this when you think no one is watching. It's positively filthy!"

Lily gripped the sudsy sponge around her stranger's engorged flesh, slipping it up and down his length underneath the warm water. She watched as he rolled his head back and forth against the wet tile and groaned loudly, temporarily dropping their playful banter as the pleasure flooded through him.

When his eyes met hers again there was a new fire in them. "Why don't you join me in here, nurse?" he practically purred.

"Don't be silly, Mr. Smith. You're the dirty one here, not me. Besides, that little tub isn't big enough for both of us to sit in." Before Lily could say anything else, her unruly patient splashed a large handful of foamy water at her, effectively drenching the front of her scrubs.

"There," he replied smugly. "Now you're dirty, too." The look he gave her was steamier than the water. "I think there's just enough room for you in here if you sit on my lap."

Within seconds, navy blue scrubs joined paint-splattered jeans in a heap on the wet floor as Lily eagerly straddled her beautiful stranger and sent a large wave of water splashing over the edge.

Neither of them noticed.

It had been that way all week between them, playful and lighthearted and *happy*. It was as if something had shifted since their argument, but Ethan couldn't put his finger on what it was.

He only knew that he wanted her more than any woman he'd ever seen, and he was alarmed that he seemed to need her more and more each day.

And he didn't want it to end yet.

The week flew by, and Friday night arrived faster than Lily expected.

She was brushing through her hair one final time in the bathroom mirror when she was startled by an obnoxiously loud horn honking outside the house. Dropping her brush in the sink, Lily ran downstairs to see what the hell was making that ungodly sound.

When she opened the front door she found two gorgeous women on her porch. Maggie Foster, looking like a voluptuous Playboy model, was poised with her arm in mid-air, ready to knock. Standing next to her, looking like a sleek supermodel, was the waifish woman with the sandy-blond pixie cut that Maggie had brought with her to her doctor's appointment a few weeks ago. Behind them, parked at the curb and sounding exactly like an idling semi-truck, was an enormous yellow Hummer H2.

Lily couldn't help but think that "garish" and "outlandish" had been understatements.

"That's your idea of sexy-flirty?" Maggie scoffed, bringing Lily's attention back to her visitors.

Glancing down quickly at her faded jeans and bulky sweater, she couldn't help but shrug in response. "I don't know…I don't have much in the way of flirty. And why are you so early, anyway? It's not even seven yet."

"It's an ambush, Lily. You remember my sister-in-law Emma, don't you?"

"Yes, of course. It's nice to see you again."

"Same here!" Emma practically chirped with excitement. She was so visibly worked up that she was nearly jumping out of her skin. "Now step aside and show me to your closet."

"I beg your pardon?" Lily couldn't understand if it was a joke or if Emma was actually tweaking on something and looking for an excuse to raid her medicine cabinet.

"Maggie thought you might need a little help getting ready since you felt a little weird about hanging out, and I can see that she was right. We came early to get you sorted out." And with that Emma was gone, blowing past Lily through the door and already making her own way up the stairs toward her bedroom.

Lily was left standing dumbfounded, not quite sure what had just happened, while Maggie patted her shoulder reassuringly. "Don't worry, sweetie. It happens to the best of us. Emma is like a force of nature, and it's best to just stay out of her way. Now let's go up and see what the hell she's up to."

"But what about the guys?" Lily asked, gesturing to the two men in the horrendous SUV. One of them she quickly recognized as Eric, but she was fairly certain that she'd never seen the dark-haired man sitting behind the wheel.

"Believe me, this won't take long." Maggie glided right past her through the open door, a bit more gracefully than her speed-freak sidekick, grabbing Lily's hand along the way. When they reached her bedroom at the top of the stairs, it was to find Emma already rifling through her drawers.

"What the hell?" Lily snapped. "Ever hear of respecting some-one's privacy?"

"I'm sorry about her," Maggie said from behind her. "Just think of her as your own personal Tim Gunn."

"Christ, Lily," the subject in question growled as she slammed another drawer shut, heading to the closet. "Do you own anything other than Flight of the Conchords T-shirts and scrubs?"

"Well, no, not really. I guess I don't get out much."

"Don't you own any skirts?"

"I'm more of a blue jeans kind of girl."

Lily quickly got over her irritation with the privacy-invader, standing back in awe as she watched her move with lightning speed. She was ripping through the hangers aggressively, clearly a woman on a mission, when suddenly she let out a loud "Aha!" Turning to look at them triumphantly, she held up a hanger high above her head. "No skirts, huh? Just what do you call this?"

Lily's mouth dropped open when she saw what was in her hand. "Uh, I call that a Halloween costume." She flashed back to the night five years ago when her roommates had dared her to dress as a slutty cheerleader and groaned. The tiny black skirt dangled on the hanger, somehow mocking her.

"Well, it just looks like a mini skirt."

"No way." Lily started shaking her head vehemently. "Nooooo way."

"But knife pleats this cute never go out of style!" Emma marched toward her like a drill sergeant. "Put it on. Now." When it looked like Lily might possibly cave, she went in for the kill. "Just try it on for now. Let's see how it looks while I try to find a top that will work with it." A victorious light flashed in her eyes when her Lily took the bait, feeling like prey. Clearly, Emma had no intention of letting her take it off.

As Lily begrudgingly changed into the skirt, Emma returned to the closet. In the very back, price tags still attached, hung a dark teal silk top with a drooped boat neck and short sleeves that split at the shoulders and dangled loosely at the sides.

"Hallelujah!" Emma cried, grabbing the hanger and turning back to face her audience once again. "Why the hell have you never worn this? It's adorable."

"That thing?" Lily groaned. "My mother sent that to me two Christmases ago. She said it was for me to go clubbing in." She couldn't stop from rolling her eyes. "I didn't have the heart to tell her that it was nowhere near my style and that there isn't a club around for about a forty-mile radius. I don't exactly hit The District in Rock Island every night."

"Well it's your style tonight." Emma nodded sharply. "Put it on. It looks like it's probably the only form-fitting thing you own. Why do you have so much baggy stuff? Are you afraid of your boobies?"

Maggie chuckled while Lily simply shrugged. "I don't know," she replied. "I've just never been big on displaying them. I like a guy to look me in my eyes first, I guess."

"Boobs are the best accessory a woman owns," Emma explained as she tore off the tags and handed the top to her. "Men are visual creatures. You need something to capture their eyes before they even bother thinking about looking into yours. It doesn't matter what size they are and they don't need to be hanging out, it just needs to be clear that you have them."

Once the outfit was in place and her guests *oohed* and *ahhed* over how she looked, Lily was told to sit down at her desk while Emma threw her hair up in a high ponytail. She was informed that it would look best for her to show off her neck and collarbone and there was no time for a haircut. After adding some larger earrings and a bit more eye makeup, they were ready to go.

The entire ordeal took less than twenty minutes.

When they climbed into the ridiculously large vehicle outside, Lily was formally introduced to their escorts for the night. Eric shook her hand, giving her an appreciative once-over before flashing the largest set of dimples she had ever seen in her life.

"So this is the Lily I've been hearing so much about," he said. "I'm sorry I didn't get a chance to thank you at the hospital last week for helping Maggie."

"No problem, really. It was my pleasure."

"Well, thanks anyway. I was happy someone was with her." His smile dimmed slightly as he remembered the day's events, but he composed himself quickly and gestured to the man behind the wheel. "This right here is my sister Emma's much better half. Say hello to the lovely lady, Brandon."

Brandon looked up into the rearview mirror, meeting Lily's gaze in the reflection. She could tell from the crinkling around his eyes that he was smiling.

"Nice to meet you, Lily."

"You too," she nodded. As the bright yellow behemoth rumbled to life and pulled away from the curb, Lily couldn't resist laughing. "I must say, Brandon, this is some truck."

"Why thank you, but it's not mine. It's actually Emma's."

"Really?" Lily laughed louder, looking at the woman in question.

"Mmhmm," she nodded happily. "It's my baby! I used to have a little sports car, but there was just no room in it. After a year of driving in Chicago traffic, I opted to go for size rather than speed. Now if someone won't get out of my way, I just drive over them!"

The group talked easily on the way to the bar and Lily was surprised at how comfortable she already felt with them. They joked and teased each other the way that only people who had known each other for years seemed to be able to do, but they never once made her feel left out. By the time Brandon had managed to find a parking space big enough for their massive school bus, Lily was feeling right at home.

Two hours later, they were all well on their way to being two beers past tipsy.

Maggie hadn't been kidding when she said they made complete asses out of themselves. All night long they had been taking turns with the other locals, singing cheesy, rude, borderline offensive songs that had kept Lily laughing so hard that her sides hurt. When Eric and Brandon got up to share the spotlight again and broke into an obviously practiced routine during "Hoochie Mama" by 2 Live Crew, she had to fight hard not to spit her beer on the table.

Eric would yell a line and Brandon would jump out from behind him and shout the chorus. By the middle of the song, Maggie and Emma had begun booty dancing behind them and Lily had needed to make a beeline for the restroom after laughing so hard she nearly peed herself.

When that was done, their husbands took their seats and the girls stayed up there to perform a rousing rendition of "Shoop" by Salt-n-Pepa. Maggie really got into it, circling Eric's chair as she propositioned him through song, finally sitting on his lap and handing him the mic when it was time for the male solo. Lily realized that they must have done this one a lot, since he didn't even need to get up and look at the lyrics.

It didn't stop there; the boys jumped back up and did some Beastie Boys followed immediately by Tenacious D. Lily had no idea if anyone else in the bar even wanted to sing anymore after that; they all sort of sat there hypnotized as the Fosters got more creative.

Another round of beers later, everyone started hounding Lily to get up on stage. She kept waving them off and blushing, but Eric sealed her fate when he yelled, "C'mon, Blake! What are you, a big scaredy cat?"

Throwing back the last of her drink, she glared at him coolly as she walked up and gave her request to the DJ. She hadn't ever done the song she was thinking of in front of anyone before, but it was one of her favorites by Liz Phair, and she knew that the ridiculous lyrics would make Eric eat his words and prove that she wasn't too scared to embarrass herself. She looked around the room nervously one last time as the music kicked in, and after taking a deep breath she opened her mouth and gave it her best shot.

When Lily finally finished the song about a woman begging for her man's semen due to its cosmetic properties, every man in the bar stood up and applauded, some of them even whistling and blowing kisses at her. All four of her companions stared at her with their mouths hanging wide open for a good thirty seconds before screaming and clapping loudly.

"Damn, Blake!" Eric laughed, pounding her on the back when she sat down. "You are fuckin' *made*! Far as I'm concerned, you're an honorary Foster from now on!" Lily simply smiled and fought back another blush, but she was surprised by how much his words affected her. She hadn't felt that accepted in…well, ever.

It wasn't until later, when Eric and Brandon were teaching everyone "The Humpty Dance," that Maggie voiced the question.

"Lily, are you single?"

Emma overheard and perked up like a prairie dog, speed-slurring an interruption. "Oh my God, Maggie, I know exactly what you're thinking!"

"Why do you ask?" Lily hedged, suddenly feeling a chill. She glanced down at her now-bare ring finger, thinking of the engagement ring hidden away in her desk drawer until she could give it back to Jake properly.

"Well, it's just that we've never really talked about your life much, and I've never thought to ask before. Besides," she glanced between her and an eagerly nodding Emma. "I think you should meet my brother-in-law. It might be a bit soon because he recently got out of a bad relationship, but something tells me that he would really enjoy meeting you."

"Oh, no," Lily replied quickly, shaking her head. "No, no, no, no. Thank you so much for thinking of me, but I'm really not the best person to consider for that right now."

"Why?" Emma piped up, her gossip detector going off.

Lily looked back and forth between them both before promptly bursting into tears. She had always gotten overly emotional when she drank, and the combination of the guilt that she was feeling mixed with the sweetness of Maggie's suggestion was more than she could take.

"Oh my God, what's wrong?" Maggie leaned in, stroking her back reassuringly. When Lily let out another loud sob, she began to get concerned. "Sweetie, whatever's bothering you, you've got to let it out."

"I...I'm..." Lily paused to wipe her eyes before looking up at her new friend. "I'm supposed to be engaged."

"What do you mean, 'supposed to be'?" Emma probed, causing Maggie to wave her question away in dismissal. She could tell that Lily would need to be coaxed gently rather than forced to answer any questions.

"Don't listen to her, Lily. She's just nosy. You take your time and just tell me what you think you can when you're ready."

"I'm supposed to be, but I don't want to be," Lily whispered. "He's such a sweet boy, he really is. He's always been very kind to me. I love him, but not like I should." She paused to look at the two women, one with the face of a spectator, the other with a look of understanding. "I thought I did," she cried. "I thought I had everything I needed to be happy in life—or at least as close as I'd ever get."

Maggie gently patted her hand. "And then you met someone, didn't you?"

"How did you know?" Lily asked. Emma simply shifted her eyes back and forth between them as if she were watching a gripping tennis match, loudly slurping her mixed drink through a straw.

"I don't know how I didn't put it together earlier tonight, honestly. You seem different lately. More alive, if that makes any sense."

"I do?"

"Yeah. You look like a woman in love."

"Well, fuck!" she groaned. "It's all pointless now, anyway. I'm head over heels for a guy who's leaving town any day and I'm too damn scared to tell him."

"Why?" both women asked in unison.

"Because I'm terrified it will just make him run away that much faster. He doesn't seem to be the kind who sticks around."

"How can you know that for sure?" Maggie asked.

"I broke the rules," Lily sighed, hanging her head low. "It was just supposed to be a fun distraction while it lasted and then we'd each go our separate ways. I was never supposed to get attached. Now every time I see him it hurts even more than the last when I have to leave."

"And he doesn't feel the same way at all?"

"That's what kills me! There are moments when I could swear that he feels it just as strongly as I do. He sometimes acts so jealous and possessive, but any time I've tried to hint at possibly wanting more, he changes the subject."

Maggie thought about what she said for a minute. "Is it possible that he's trying to convince himself that he doesn't feel that way?"

"What do you mean? Why the hell would anyone do that?"

"So he can try to keep from becoming attached, too. Does he know that you're engaged?"

"Yes," Lily whispered, thinking back to the moment when he had discovered the ring on her finger.

"Well, think about it. He sees you willingly staying with another man. In his mind, you've already chosen someone else, no matter what you do with him. And I don't care what you say, some men just don't respond to hints. They need it spelled out for them with capital letters and small words."

"Mmm, boys are dumb!" Emma mumbled around her straw before sucking up the rest of her drink.

"You got that right," Lily huffed. "Well, anyway, I've decided that I have to end the engagement. It's not right to keep it going when my heart isn't in it, with or without anyone else in the picture. I'm only sorry that it took my dishonesty to make me realize how unhappy I was."

"I think that sounds like a smart idea. Better to deal with a little pain now than a lot of pain later. Now, enough of this talk." Maggie summoned the waitress. "Let's have another round! Oh, and just remember, if it doesn't work out, I know a guy." She winked at her, making Lily laugh for the first time since they'd started the conversation.

She felt so much lighter just by telling someone what she had been so torn up about. She also felt better about the situation after the way Maggie described her stranger's possible perception of things. In fact, she felt so much better about it after one more drink that she decided she wanted to see him as soon as possible.

Excusing herself from the table, Lily told them that she wanted to step outside and get some fresh air. She didn't want to lie, but she had the feeling that Maggie would insist on escorting her to his door if she knew what Lily was contemplating.

Her thoughts were so fuzzy from the drinks and so concentrated on her stranger that she wasn't paying attention as she walked out the door and straight into the warm wall of someone's chest. Strong hands gripped her arms to steady her, and when she looked up to apologize she gasped loudly.

Smoldering jade eyes looked back at her, just as surprised as her own.

22

Ethan looked down into the warm eyes in front of him and felt his heart skip a beat. He wasn't sure if it was from the shock of seeing her there or the uncontrollable delight.

"What the hell are you doing here?" he gasped, still gripping her shoulders firmly. His goddess blinked a few times to focus on his face, as if she almost didn't believe what she was seeing, before smiling widely and wrapping her arms around his waist.

"Hey, Stranger!" she said with the tiniest of slurs.

When the smell of alcohol drifted up to him he looked at her more closely, finally noticing how glassy her eyes were and how heavy her lids appeared. "Are you drunk?"

"Lil' bit," she giggled. "I was just about to go find you!"

"You were, huh?" he teased briefly before he remembered where he was. Looking up quickly, he darted his eyes over her shoulder toward the door. A tipsy goddess could be entertaining, but standing there waiting to see what she did next wasn't worth the explanation that would be needed if his family or her fiancé suddenly walked outside. Dragging her farther away from the door, he turned back to her. "Are you alone?"

"Well, my friends are inside, but I was leaving to go see you." She couldn't take her eyes off his beautiful features, concentrating longer than necessary on his lips while she spoke.

"But...*he* isn't here?"

"Huh?" Lily asked, finding it very difficult to process the actual words that accompanied his velvet voice. It was so rich and sexy that she wanted him to let her crawl inside his throat and live there. It wasn't until she managed to drag her eyes back up to meet his that things seemed to click into place. "Oh! No, no. He's still out of town."

Ethan let out a relieved breath, and it wasn't until that moment that he realized he'd been holding it in. Allowing for a brief second to collect himself, he finally glanced down long enough to notice her clothing—and felt his heart stop all over again.

"What the fuck are you wearing?" he growled.

"Do you like it?" She smiled, turning around in a wobbly circle in front of him. "I had a makeover!"

"I'll say," he muttered under his breath. When his heart finally started beating again it was only to force all the blood in his body to his groin. She had never looked so sexy before. Well, she had never looked so *intentionally* sexy before. He had never found a time when he didn't want her—every look she had drew him in like a moth to a flame—but this particular look was custom-built for seduction.

And it was working.

Her eyes were accentuated with a smoky liner that made them pop even more than usual, and her hair was swept up off her shoulders enough to show off her mouthwatering cleavage. The color of her blouse against her creamy skin as it hugged her delicious curves could have been described as a religious experience, but the absolute showstopper was her skirt: it made her legs look ten miles long and filled his mind with filthy images of bending her over the nearest object and flipping it up.

"Oh!" she blurted out, interrupting his train of thought. "I wanted to talk to you."

"What about?" he asked, doing a bad job of hiding his repeated glances at her legs.

"Well, it's private. But I think you'll like it. Maybe. I hope you will."

Ethan forced himself to look away from her outfit long enough to say, "I'm sorry, what? I have no idea what you just said."

She startled him then by reaching out slowly and squeezing his bicep through his jacket sleeve.

"Can you give me a ride?" she all but purred. "I was going to go to the apartment to talk to you, but I don't care where we go, really. I just wanted to be alone with you."

Ethan only picked up on "alone," "apartment," and "ride," but it was enough to set him in motion. He glanced down at his watch quickly before shooting another look toward the door, making his decision with a sharp nod of his head. "All right, come on," he said, rushing her away with an arm behind her back.

It took everything he had to keep from sliding his hand underneath her skirt as they walked.

He led her down the side of the building and around the corner, into the dark outskirts of the parking lot where he had finally found a spot for the Audi. He quickly ushered her into the passenger side and shut the door, casting a few more furtive glances around the lot before joining her on the other side of the car.

"So," he said after a moment of silence in the dark of the front seat. "Do you want me to take you back to the apartment, or did you just want to talk in the car? I could drive you home if you like."

"No you can't," Lily giggled.

"Why?" He wondered to himself again if she lived in that shack he'd seen on the outskirts of town and realized that if she did it probably wouldn't be wise to risk her being seen with him in the car.

"Because then you would break one of your own rules, silly!" She giggled again, reaching out to brush her fingers down his cheek. "That would tell you something about me."

She stared at his mouth again, tracing it lightly with her finger-tips. "But who knows? Maybe you won't mind so much after we talk." Her voice had dropped to a mere whisper, and Lily had managed to hypnotize herself by not pulling her eyes away from his lips.

Ethan was having a very difficult time of his own trying to concentrate when her fingers were stroking him like that. She wasn't making any sense, and he didn't know if it was because she was drunk or because she was touching him.

"Um," he blinked a few times and tried to clear his head. "How about we head back to the apartment for now? We probably shouldn't just sit here."

"Fine by me," she clearly purred that time. Lily knew that if he didn't make a decision soon, she wouldn't even remember what it was she wanted to talk to him about. Her mind was becoming cloudier by the minute as she looked at him, wanting to taste his mouth again.

As Ethan went to turn the key in the ignition, he cursed to himself when he remembered why he was even there. "Shit! Just a minute," he apologized as he fished his phone out from his coat pocket, firing off a quick text message.

Sorry, man. Something came up last minute.

A reply buzzed in his hand before he could even put his phone away.

What was that, your dick?

Ethan rolled his eyes before typing back a response to his brother. It was scary how perceptive he was, even by text.

Ha ha, real funny. Fucker. There's just something I have
to take care of and it can't wait.

OK. Whatever u say. But if u punk out on dinner tomorrow
b4 we leave, mom is gonna have your ass. Speaking of
ass, spank your mystery girl 4 me.

Fuck off. And don't worry, I'll be there.

Ethan shoved his phone back in his pocket with a huff, wondering
how the hell so little got by Eric. "Sorry about that," he said, turning
to face his tipsy goddess again.

"Hey!" She looked back up at him with a huge grin on her face, not
even noticing that he'd been texting. "We're in your car!"

"That's right," he couldn't resist a small chuckle. She was unbelievably
adorable and carefree like this. "We were just leaving, remember?" As
he placed his hand on the key ring again, he was surprised to feel her
small hand cover his own.

"Wait." Her voice carried through the dark of the car, caressing his
ears seductively before making its way down to his straining erection,
causing him to bite back a groan.

"Is something wrong?" he gritted through his teeth, wanting her so
badly he could taste it. Her scent was filling up the car quickly and
even the slight hint of alcohol couldn't dilute its potency.

"Yes." Somehow her voice had gotten huskier, which he didn't
think was even possible.

"What is it?" he squeaked out. He was trying to stare straight ahead,
afraid that the sight of her in her skirt might be his undoing, but a
sudden shifting in her seat made him glance sideways just in time to
catch a small scrap of material sliding down her bare legs.

"This is wrong." She pulled his hand away from the ignition and placed it between her thighs, pushing his fingers forward until they were touching her wet flesh. "You aren't in here right now."

Ethan's heart stopped yet again and his eyes rolled back into his head. His voice was shaking when he finally found it again. "Are you sure about this? We're in public…and you're drunk."

Lily pulled his hand away and shoved his fingers into his mouth, making him groan and whimper as he sucked them clean.

"Does that mean you don't want to fuck me in your car anymore?" She leaned over and licked the outer shell of his ear for good measure.

Reluctantly pulling his fingers out of his mouth, he turned to her and grunted. "I'm just trying to do the right thing here. I don't want you to regret this after you sober up."

She chose that moment to pounce, climbing over him quickly and planting herself in his lap. It was a tight fit, crammed between him and his steering wheel, but there was nowhere else she would have rather been in that moment.

"Fuck regret!" she panted before grabbing him by the back of the head and slamming her mouth down on his. She could still taste herself on his tongue and it was enough to make her dizzy with need.

Any resolve that Ethan had left snapped in that moment. Snarling loudly into her mouth, he shoved his hands under her skirt, gripping her bare ass and grinding her into his throbbing erection. He thrust up against her as they devoured each other, and after mere seconds he could feel the front of his jeans getting damp from her moisture.

Everything seemed to happen in a blur after that.

Deciding that they didn't have enough room, he reached down and slid the seat all the way back. He tore his hands away from her backside to wrestle with his button fly, only to have her beat him to it. With loud panting that was peppered with kisses and lots of fumbling, they both worked to yank his jeans down over his hips enough to allow his erection to spring free.

There was just enough light in the car for Ethan to see her rise up on her knees and maneuver him between her legs, gripping him by the base of his weeping cock and positioning the tip at her entrance. He was panting so heavily that in the back of his mind he wondered if he might hyperventilate, and as he watched their bodies connect he was afraid that he might start crying in agony at how slow she was going.

Once just the very tip had been inserted, she stopped moving completely, waiting for him to stop whimpering and look up at her. When their eyes finally met again, Lily placed her hands on his shoulders and leaned forward, kissing him softly before pulling back and watching his expression as she sank down on him in one swift thrust.

It was her favorite part, watching his face. Sure, it felt good as hell, but there was nothing like seeing that look of shock and amazement cross over his features. No matter how many times he'd been inside her, he never failed to look simply awestruck at how good she felt—and it was one hell of an ego boost.

This time was the best one yet.

His eyes widened and his brow furrowed, and he somehow managed to look scared at how good it felt, as if it just wasn't humanly possible for anything on earth to feel so right. The panicked look he gave her was almost a silent demand for her to explain herself, to admit to some sort of black magic or voodoo that had him under her spell.

Holding his gaze, Lily began to move on him, using his shoulders for leverage as she bounced up and down. Rocking her hips into him with every upward stroke, it wasn't long before she had built up an amazing rhythm that made them both throw their heads back and groan.

Her beautiful stranger had begun a steady litany of, "Oh God… Oh God… So good… So good…yes…yes…yes yes yes so fucking good!" and by the time he grabbed her ass to pull her onto him harder so that he could thrust up inside her even faster, he had regressed to nothing more than grunts and snarls.

Ethan was completely beside himself. He had just enough presence of mind to know that he was just as drunk as she was—only he was drunk on her. He couldn't have been stopped at that point if the car had caught on fire. He might have tried to finish faster, but he knew he couldn't have stopped.

He couldn't understand how she managed to feel better to him every single time they were together. Once he'd been with Rachel a few times, it had become old news. It had been enjoyable, but there'd been nothing new between them, and before long, it had all felt the same. He'd assumed that was simply normal, and that that was probably why so many people stepped outside their relationships for a little variation.

But this girl—this girl made him want more and more and more.

Her body gripped him so tightly that he nearly started to weep from the pleasure, and each new shift of her hips made him want to cry out his thanks to the universe that this treasure had been delivered to him, that she was literally dropped into his lap.

Hungry for more of her scent, he buried his face into her cleavage, kissing and sucking her soft skin and whimpering louder when access to her breasts was denied by the fabric of her shirt. Somehow understanding his primal noises, she moved her hands long enough to pull her top up to her shoulders and yank the lace of her bra cups down, allowing them to spill out over the edges for his ravenous mouth to feast on.

Ethan licked, sucked, and bit each taut peak repeatedly, unable to focus on only one. His growls and moans were creating the most delicious vibrating feeling around her nipples, which caused Lily to buck her hips sharply into him, setting off a whole new round of snarls. It was a delicious cycle that neither of them wanted to end.

Before long Ethan felt the familiar tightening of his muscles, signaling an approaching release that promised to make his spine snap in two. Wanting to feel her finish first, he slid his hands up and gripped her hips, lifting her up and down on him as he slammed up into her as hard as possible.

"Ungh! Fuck!" She yelled at the sudden change, her body beginning to tighten itself around him.

"Yes baby…that's it!" he moaned, watching her cheeks becoming more flushed by the second. "Touch yourself for me. We're both so close…I want to feel you come all over me."

She complied quickly, sliding her hand down between their bodies until she was rubbing at her tightened bundle of nerves furiously in small circles. The added stimulation caused her to fall over the edge, her body squeezing and milking him as she found her release.

She only had enough sanity left at that point to look him in the eye and beg him, "Please! Come with me!"

She needn't have worried—he was way ahead of her.

"Oh God!" he cried out. "You're so fucking wet…so fucking tight…I can't…I can't get enough of you… Fuck!" And with one final thrust of his hips he emptied himself inside her, filling her to overflowing.

Lily collapsed against him then, every ounce of energy disappearing with her powerful orgasm, and her exhaustion began mixing with her alcohol intake. Ethan held her tightly, tucking her head under his chin as he stroked her back. He had no words that could come close to anything that he was feeling, so he simply squeezed her tighter and kissed her forehead, wishing that he could bottle that moment up to keep forever.

When he noticed that she was beginning to drift off to sleep, he figured that he should get her into bed. No matter how much he loved the moment, he was willing to bet that she wouldn't be thrilled to wake up in a ball on his lap at four in the morning with his limp dick all sticky inside her.

"Baby. Baby, wake up," he whispered into her ear. She rubbed her eyes a few times before yawning loudly, and managed to open them only long enough to smile at him. "Baby, if you want me to take you anywhere other than home with me, you need to tell me right now."

"Mmm," she murmured with her eyes closed. "You, always you."

Lifting her carefully, Ethan set her on the passenger seat next to him and did his best to adjust her clothing so that she was covered. Spying her panties still wadded up on the floor by her feet, he reached down and picked them up, using the small scrap of fabric to wipe gently between her legs before also cleaning himself up as well as he could manage and readjusting his own clothing. He shoved the panties into his jacket pocket, only to take it off a few seconds later and drape it over her sleeping form when he saw her shiver.

As he backed the Audi out of the gravel parking lot he thought to himself that no matter what else happened in his life, this would always be his favorite parking lot in the entire world.

Once he was back at the apartment, Ethan scooped her up in his arms and carried her upstairs, stopping only to fight with the key in the lock one-handedly because he refused to put her down. When he sat her gently on the bed he somehow managed to whisper the right words to convince her to help him take her clothes off so that she could be more comfortable.

Watching her barely raise her arms above her head so that he could slip her top off had the strangest effect on him—it was such a trusting action, and for some reason he felt himself swallowing a lump in his throat at the thought of her letting him care for her. He'd never thought of himself as much of a nurturer or caregiver before, but he knew that if she got sick in the middle of the night he would be there in a heartbeat to hold her hair back for her.

When she was finally stripped bare, he laid her back on the sheets and covered her up with the fluffy blanket, only leaving the room long enough to grab the wastebasket and a glass of water from the bathroom. He set the can on the floor near her head in case she woke up sick and then woke her back up long enough to drink the water.

"C'mon, baby. You'll feel a hell of a lot better in the morning if you get this in you now." He cradled the back of her head until she had swallowed a few sips. Once he was fairly certain that it wasn't going to come right back up, he laid her back down and removed his own clothes quickly, tossing them across the room in his rush to get back to her.

He hadn't intended on cuddling with her. He had wanted to leave her as much room as she needed to get up in case she felt ill, but as soon as he climbed in beside her she rolled over and snuggled right up against his side with her head on his chest.

"Mm…thiz iz nize," she mumbled against his skin, kissing him lightly on the chest.

"Yes, it is," he smiled into the darkness, rubbing his hand up and down her back slowly, stopping every once in a while to stroke her hair back from her face.

"Hey, you never told me what you wanted to talk about," he whispered, chuckling lightly as he wondered if it had all been only a tipsy attempt at seduction. If so, it was certainly successful.

"Mmm…" she rubbed her eyes without opening them and yawned again, resting her hand back down on his chest and patting it lightly. "Wanted to talk…tell you…love you." She yawned once more before giving in to the dead weight of sleep. "Night, night." And with that, she was out.

Ethan lay there for a long time after that, doing nothing but staring up at the ceiling with wide eyes.

23

The next morning was slightly awkward, but from what Ethan could tell she didn't seem to remember saying anything out of the ordinary before she fell asleep. She'd been startled to find herself waking up next to him, and had blushed terribly when the night's events came back to her, but it had only looked like typical "morning after" embarrassment to him.

He offered to pick her up some breakfast and coffee, but she insisted that she was fine and only wanted to go home so that she could shower properly and lay back down in her own bed. He didn't want to let her go when she told him that she thought it would be best if she walked home, but he finally agreed, sending her off in an old pair of sweats and a pullover. He also tried really hard to keep from thinking about just how perfect she looked in his baggy, oversized clothes.

Before leaving, she thanked him for being so sweet to her and gave him a hug, kissing him gently before pulling away. As she was opening the door she stopped one more time and turned to look back at him, another blush coloring her cheeks. When he asked her what was wrong, she simply shook her head and said it was nothing, closing the door behind her.

For the next hour, Ethan took the longest, most introspective shower of his life. He kept seeing her bright blush before she left, wondering what she'd been thinking. Had she finally remembered what she had told him last night? Had she meant it?

He told himself that she couldn't have meant it. She'd probably just said it out of habit. She was drunk and cuddling with a warm body—who knew who she was thinking of when she said it?

The thought of her saying that to him while thinking of that muscle-bound asshole made him so angry that he threw the bar of soap he was holding, and it shot over the top of the shower curtain, making a loud crack as it slammed into the mirror over the sink.

"Shit!" he yelled, not sure if he was angrier about his thoughts or the broken mirror.

He stood under the spray of hot water, thinking back to earlier in the evening. He had been so damn surprised to see her there, but what a way to end the night. She had been just as desperate for him as he'd been for her, and even the mere thought of her climbing on top of him had him stroking himself furiously within seconds.

He kept seeing her eyes, how determined she'd been to fuck him senseless in a parking lot full of cars, in the front seat of a shitty rental, no less, fulfilling one of his fantasies. And she'd felt so good. So fucking good.

He gripped his shaft harder, bracing himself against the shower wall with his other hand, squeezing himself as tightly as her body had the night before. When he bit his lip and closed his eyes, he was back in that car, listening to her moaning and panting as she rode his cock. The harder he stroked, the better he could hear her groans and cries for more.

Yes...please...harder...so good...ungh...yes...right there...love you...love you...love you—

"Fuck!" he cried, erupting violently over his fingers with thick spurts of fluid.

His orgasm was so powerful that he instantly felt weak in the knees, and he leaned forward until his forehead was braced between his hands against the wall, warm water trailing down the taut muscles of his back. He was so shaken that he didn't move for a while, hearing those same words repeated over and over again in his mind.

…love you…love you…love you…

Squeezing his eyes shut tightly as if it would make the words any less true, he finally allowed his own reply to slip through his gritted teeth in a harsh whisper.

"I think I love you, too."

Hours later, after Ethan had finally dragged himself out of the shower and forced himself to move on with his day and stop dwelling on things that he had no control over at the moment, he pulled into his family's driveway for dinner.

Walking into the house, he was comforted to hear the typical chitter chatter of his mother and sisters in the kitchen. Rather than stop in there first and to be fussed over by his mother, he instead hunted out Eric, following the loud yelling in the family room—a clear sign that he was battling Brandon in another round of video games. He walked in and sat down on the couch, trying not to be resentful of the playful back-and-forth between the two men who were clearly as close as real brothers.

Ethan knew that if he was going to stay around much longer, he was going to have to get to know Brandon better. He seemed nice enough, and it wasn't Brandon's fault that Ethan was jealous of his relationship with his brother.

"Hey, Pud!" Eric called to him when he noticed him on the couch. Brandon waved somewhat nervously from the opposite side of the room where he was positioned for the next round of bowling.

"Fucker," Ethan said in greeting, then nodded back to Brandon with a smile. There wasn't much else said between them until the game was over and Brandon went to join the ladies in the kitchen, giving the brothers a moment of privacy.

As soon as the room was clear, Eric turned to him in frustration. "So what the hell was up last night, you douche nozzle?"

"What do you mean?" Ethan attempted to play dumb.

"Don't bullshit me, man. I can't believe you didn't show. Would it have really killed you to break yourself out of your pity cocoon for one night? I know you've never really hung out with us like that, but I think you would have had a really great time."

"Eric," he sighed, running his hands through his hair. "I swear I was going to go. I was running late, I know, I got sidetracked on a painting, but I actually physically went there. It's just that—well, I wasn't lying when I said something suddenly came up." He gave him a stern look before adding, "And that's all I'm going to say about it."

"Holy shit! Mystery girl really did show up, didn't she?"

"Eric!" Ethan hushed him, looking around the room to make sure they were still alone. "I said that was all I was going to say."

"Dude, I'm not gonna push for particulars, but isn't this the ass that you've been getting on a fairly regular basis lately?"

"What's your point?"

"My point, pudwhacker, is that you might have been able to keep it in your pants for one night to spend time with your family! Or God forbid, invite her in with you."

"You know I can't do that. Besides…I don't know how to say this right so that it makes sense, but it wasn't about not wanting to hang with you guys. It's just *her*—she has this power over me. When she's around, I can't focus on anything else. I've never felt anything like it before."

Eric closed the distance between them swiftly and slapped him upside the head.

"Ow! What the fuck was that for?"

Eric crouched down in front of him so that they were at eye level with each other. "That, my darling idiot brother, was reality slapping you into consciousness. Wake the fuck up! Those strange tingly feelings you're getting in your no-no zone for this chick? It's called love, you fucking idiot. That's how people feel when it first sets in. Some people are lucky enough to always feel it, like me and Maggie. Now do yourself a favor and tell this phantom no-name woman that you want to spend forever with her doing the mommy-and-daddy dance."

Ethan dropped his head in his hands and swallowed a thick lump. When he looked back up, Eric could see that his eyes were damp. "It's not that easy! I'm willing to admit that I have feelings for her, but she's fucking engaged, Eric!"

Eric stood up, dragging Ethan up with him as he went. He patted his shoulder a few times before speaking again. "You know what? Engagements can be broken. Fuck, marriages can be broken pretty easily these days. It's not the end of the world. If she's what you want, you owe it to yourself to try."

"But she doesn't want me. She's had plenty of time to end her engagement and she hasn't. There are times that I think she feels something, too, but then it's gone as quickly as it appeared. And what if she did end it? What kind of life could I give her? I have no permanent home, and she would be throwing away everything she knows to gamble on me. Me, who's done nothing but make the wrong choices his entire life."

"But what if she's the right choice for you?"

"And what if I'm the wrong choice for her?"

"Shit, man. You sure know how to bring down any conversation,"

Eric sighed. "You know what I think? I think you should just focus on getting her out of this engagement for now. Work your Foster magic, man. Get her single, and give yourselves a chance to grow into something more. Nobody said you have to run off and elope tomorrow. Get to know her first. Start by asking her name!"

"You make it sound so easy! I know deep down, that's exactly what my heart wants to do. But whenever I think about it too much, my head gets in the way. I start feeling caged in and panicky, like I'm just going to fuck it all up again and end up with another Rachel. Or I'm going to make this poor girl resent me so badly for taking her away from the only life that she knows. I can't stand this pressure, feeling like I have to jump off a cliff right now or forever be miserable."

"Dude, relax." Eric patted him on the shoulder calmingly. "You are getting yourself way too worked up right now. Take a deep breath, do some fucking Lamaze breathing if you have to. You've got time to think about it all. Now let's go see if dinner's ready, okay? Mom's making her homemade lasagna. That can cheer anybody up."

"All right," Ethan sighed, knowing that he was right. He only wished he could look at things as simply as Eric did. He decided that he would worry about it another time. He owed it to his family to relax and enjoy their time together. Nobody there was pressuring him to do anything he wasn't ready to do.

As they walked into the dining room the doorbell rang. Maggie jumped up, yelling, "I've got it!" as she ran into the foyer.

Ethan made his way over to his parents before they sat down, hugging them both before letting his mother fret over the length of his hair and insist that he wasn't eating enough. As he walked toward his seat at the table he heard Maggie again, but this time she wasn't alone.

"So what happened to you last night, anyway? You went out for some fresh air and never came back."

"I know, I'm sorry."

Ethan stopped in his tracks. He knew that voice. As it got closer, he began to feel a freezing chill working its way down his spine.

"I, uh, ran into an old friend outside. We got to talking and left to get some coffee. I'm sorry I didn't come back in and let you know."

"Hey, I'm not your mother," Maggie laughed. "I don't care who you go home with. We were just worried something had happened to you!" She rounded the corner and walked into the room, and right behind her was none other than his goddess.

"Hey, Mom, look who finally accepted my dinner invitation."

Barbara turned around and gasped, running over to violently hug the person who couldn't possibly be standing in his mother's dining room.

"Oh, darling! I was so worried we'd never see you again! I'm so happy you came!" She turned to Maggie and smacked her shoulder playfully. "Shame on you for not letting me know! I would have made something nicer."

"Oh, be quiet! Your lasagna is heaven and you know it. Besides, there's not much of a surprise if I tell you about it."

Ethan stood frozen and forgotten as the entire family fussed around their dinner guest. Was this some sort of joke?

He watched as she was presented to his father, apparently the only fucking person in the room who didn't somehow know her already, who within seconds was smiling fondly and talking to her as if she were family.

Finally Eric remembered that Ethan was even there, and he smiled broadly and brought her over, his arm thrown easily around her shoulders. Somehow she hadn't noticed him standing off in the corner yet, but as his brother brought her closer, Ethan saw her features change from the thousand-watt smile as she beamed up at

Eric to the look of a deer in headlights, which he assumed matched his own expression.

"I think this morose one over here is the only one you haven't met yet," Eric announced, laughing loudly. "This is Ethan, my younger, much worse-looking brother." He held out his other hand and clapped Ethan on the shoulder so hard that he rocked on his feet, but Ethan didn't feel a thing.

"And Ethan, this is Lily. She can do a mean-ass karaoke! Something you would have seen for yourself if you'd bothered to show up last night," he teased. "This pretty little thing is practically our new sister!"

Practically our new sister.

Fuck.

24

Lily couldn't believe what was happening.

Somehow the world was still turning and life was continuing on around her, but inside it felt as if everything she knew had just tilted on its axis.

Her stranger was there, and he had a name. Ethan.

Ethan.

Could it really be so simple? Would she have ever guessed it?

Ethan.

It suited him.

But that didn't answer the most pressing question at the moment: What the fuck was he doing there?

She could hear Eric talking, but as soon as she'd seen her stranger's face in the room she'd tuned out everything else. He'd said something about "karaoke" and "brother," but that couldn't possibly be right. *Brother?*

Suddenly, everything began to click into place in Lily's mind. All of the things she had somehow not paid attention to before came tumbling back at once: Barbara's other son, the artist; the strangely familiar painting on the wall; Ethan's mysterious family emergency last week. When she finally added them all together she wanted to smack herself for not making the connection sooner.

Eric was continuing with the introductions, somehow oblivious to the fact that the two people he thought had never met before were both locked in a death stare.

"This pretty little thing is practically our new sister!" he enthused, squeezing Lily warmly around the shoulders.

She could have sworn that her stranger—*Ethan*, that is—flinched at Eric's words, but he recovered quickly. She watched as he blinked a few times before slowly extending his hand toward hers, reaching out his long, graceful fingers that her body already knew so well, apparently preparing to fake their "first meeting" for the eyes of his family.

Lily began breathing rapidly, feeling a mini-panic attack approaching. She didn't know if she could handle touching him in front of his family. She was certain that the moment their skin made contact, everyone would just know.

She took a deep breath, never moving her eyes from his fingertips, slowly willing herself to calm down. It was only a handshake. She could do that for him. Counting to ten in her head before moving, she gently placed her hand in his, using every ounce of her energy to keep from jumping at the instant electric jolt that ran between them as he finally closed his fingers around hers.

"So, *Lily*, is it?"

The only thing that was able to break her gaze from their joined hands was his velvety voice saying her name for the first time, the sensation of it sliding over her body like liquid sex. Her eyes were pulled up to his again as if they were magnetic, and this time she was surprised to find that the jade pools had become molten and fiery.

He looked beautiful. He looked sexy. He looked confused. He looked *angry*.

"Uh...yes, pleased to meet you." She shook his hand quickly and tried to pull away, but he held her fingers tightly, squeezing them for a moment too long before finally letting them go.

"Likewise," he replied coldly. Lily had no idea why he was so angry at her—she was just as surprised and confused as he was.

Eric glanced at his brother. *His brother*—the thought still made Lily feel faint, as if he had suddenly sprouted a second head. The glance proved that this level of coolness wasn't customary when he was introduced to someone new.

There was an odd moment of silence between all three of them before Eric jumped to fill it.

"You remember me talking about Lily, don't you, man? Remember, when we were talking to Mr. Blake at the diner? I said how much Maggie loved her and appreciated her *help*." He emphasized the last word, conveying a blatant warning to his sibling that he'd better ease off their dinner guest.

Ethan blinked a few times, reaching for a memory that seemed like years ago now, before snapping his attention back to the newcomer.

"You're Mr. Blake's daughter?"

Lily blushed furiously before nodding quickly. "Yes, that's right." It was barely a whisper.

Ethan's mind was flooded with images of all of the depraved things he'd done to this woman's body, over and over again, ending with the very naughty, very public encounter they'd shared only the night before in his car. He then pictured her father tapping on the glass and busting them just like he had Eric and Maggie so many years ago. That would have gone over *great*.

Before any of them could utter one more awkward word, Maggie appeared at Lily's side. "All right, no monopolizing the guest, guys. That's my job!" Smiling brightly, she took Lily's hand and pulled her away from the bizarre encounter. "Come on, sweetie. Don't get sucked into any sort of conversation between these two on an empty stomach. Eric won't shut up about football and injuries, and Artsy Fartsy over there will bore you to death talking about Dali and Monet and Impressionism versus Surrealism."

Eric laughed and lovingly flipped her the bird as they walked away, causing Maggie to stick her tongue out playfully before showing Lily to her seat at the table—a seat that turned out to be directly across from Ethan. She had no idea how she was supposed to concentrate on what anyone said to her while he was facing her all night.

As if on cue, Richard chose that moment to speak. "So, tell me about yourself, Lily," he smiled warmly. "My wife tells me that you're a nurse?"

"Yes, that's right, sir." She did everything she could to keep her eyes trained on the attractive older man at the head of the table, but realized that the longer she looked, the more physical similarities she saw between him and his youngest son. They had the same cheekbones, the same long, elegant nose, and what looked to be the same jawline.

"Please, call me Richard." He smiled again, interrupting her train of thought. "And you work under Natalie Wilde, is that right?"

"Yes sir—I mean, Richard."

"She's good," he nodded. "Probably the best OB/GYN we've had in this area for years. She's also one of the most…ambitious doctors I can remember meeting in a long time."

"That sounds like her," Lily laughed quietly, and they shared a knowing look that made her feel instantly comfortable talking to him.

Ethan didn't like it one bit.

In fact, Ethan hadn't liked one damn thing that had taken place since she'd walked into the dining room. It was all too much for him to process, and having so many witnesses around made him feel like he was under a microscope and about to snap at any moment. Who the hell did this girl think she was, infiltrating his family and making every single person he cared about fall in love with her? And why was his mother mooning over her like she was the second coming? And what was with that look his father gave her just now, like they were best friends sharing an inside joke?

He wasn't ready for this.

This was *his* girl, his own private angel. He didn't like the thought of sharing her with anyone when his feelings for her were so new, and he definitely didn't like that they all knew her name before he did. It wasn't supposed to play out like this. It was supposed to be some hot, no-strings-attached sex while he was in town. Now it appeared there were strings attaching every which way he looked.

What bothered him the most was how meant-to-be it all felt, as if he had absolutely no say in the matter. He had just spent a decade of his life being bossed around and having all of his decisions made for him, and now here was another decision that he didn't get to make—it just *was.* He had been trying so hard to take back control of his life, and now it seemed as if everyone was conspiring against him to decide what he would do next, as if fate was actually forcing this girl on him whether he was ready or not.

He felt himself getting angrier and angrier, mentally preparing himself to start digging in his heels. Fuck fate. What had fate ever done for him? If he was ever going to give in to his driving need to be with this woman, it was going to be on his own fucking terms, not because she had somehow snaked her way into the heart of his family.

He sat there at the table, barely touching his food, watching her talk with everyone easily—even Brandon, who Ethan had yet to befriend. There he was, feeling as if he were literally going to explode from the tension, and she was just laughing away and fitting in nicely. Fitting in perfectly. Sitting in the chair that Rachel had never been able to fill properly.

That realization hit him on a primal level. He felt punched in the gut, immediately wanting to avert his eyes from how *right* she looked in that chair, but not having the strength to do it. And that made him angrier still.

Since he couldn't stop watching her, he tried to find any sign that she was even remotely as uncomfortable as he was with the odd situation. The only change in her behavior came whenever their eyes met, when she would glance away quickly and blush. It wasn't much, but it was something. Well, if looking at him made her uncomfortable, then dammit, he was going to find a way to make her just as uncomfortable as he was.

"So, Lily," he spoke, interrupting her exchange with Emma about a possible shopping excursion. "How long have you been living in town?" Everyone stopped eating and looked at him, surprised that he had finally found his voice. He got what he wanted, though, because the moment he said her name she turned a deep shade of scarlet.

"Um, about three years or so now," she said, her voice cracking in the process. She could barely look at him, casting nervous smiles around the table at everyone else as she spoke.

That would never do.

"And where did you live before then?" he pushed, loving the sight of her finally starting to squirm.

"Uh…Minneapolis, actually. I grew up there with my mom."

"And what brought you here, to tiny little Aledo?"

"Well, my dad was injured. He had a heart attack while driving and crashed his car. It shattered his hip. He was laid up for a while and needed help around the house, and I hadn't seen him in a long time. I decided to make a change and move down here."

"Oh, dear!" Barbara chimed in. "And you nursed him back to health by yourself? How long did that take?" Ethan tried not to snarl as his mother derailed his attempt to hold her attention.

Lily turned to her, a quiet sigh of relief escaping her lips before she replied. "About six months until he was ready to go back to work. He healed faster than I thought, but I think he liked having a little time off for once."

"Oh, I'll bet," Barbara chuckled knowingly. "Men! They love to be taken care of, don't they?"

And waited on hand and foot, from the sound of it! Ethan thought to himself. He'd never heard anything disparaging about Mr. Blake before, but it certainly sounded like he enjoyed taking advantage of his daughter's caring personality.

"So you were just his nursemaid for six straight months?" Ethan butted in again, forcing her eyes back to his. "That sounds lonely, especially in a small town where you don't know anybody." His tone was harsher than he intended, but his emotions were getting away from him.

"It was a bit…claustrophobic, yes, but I would do it again if I had to. He doesn't have anybody else." She didn't flinch when she answered him that time, and Ethan could tell that she was quickly shifting from uncomfortable to annoyed.

Richard reached out and covered her hand with his own, patting it lightly. "Of course you would, dear. He's very lucky to have you." Ethan watched his father give her the warmest smile he'd ever seen and had to fight from swearing out loud.

"Anyway, Lily, as I was saying," Emma jumped back in, clearly trying to diffuse the strange mood that had settled over the table. She shot her brother a *what-crawled-up-your-ass* look before finishing, "the Quad Cities have some decent stores, but you should really come visit us in Chicago some time. They have the best shops!"

"Oh, yes!" Maggie clapped. "That would be so much fun! You could come over for a weekend sometime soon. One night at Emma's and one night at my place."

"Or we could just slumber party!" Emma squealed.

"Totally! And then go shopping in the daytime!" Maggie was practically hopping in her seat at that point.

"That might be fu—" she started to reply before Ethan couldn't hold it in any longer and cut her off.

"I'm sorry—Lily, right? Could you please pass me the salt?"

"Son, that was rude. Besides, the salt is right in front of you." Richard gave him a disapproving glare.

"Oh, so it is," he said, reaching out and grabbing it, shaking it into his hand slowly before sprinkling it on his food and licking his fingers clean where some had stuck to his skin. Without taking his eyes from hers, he pulled his thumb slowly from between his lips and practically purred, "My apologies...*Lily*."

She looked away quickly, not wanting to let him affect her in front of so many people.

The dinner was fairly uneventful after that, full of nothing more than the typical banal conversation Ethan was used to hearing at these get-togethers: shopping, sports, cars, history, and, of course, medicine. He kept his mouth shut for the rest of the meal, choosing instead to watch her in silence. After his little trick with the salt she refused to even look in his direction again, but he was certain that she could feel his eyes on her skin, and it was just as effective at making her squirm.

When everyone had finally deemed dinner over, Barbara announced that the men were in charge of clearing the table and cleaning the dishes. It was a routine trade-off in the Foster household: whoever spent time preparing dinner got to rest while the others cleaned up afterward. Ethan was forced to watch as the women in his family dragged his mystery girl away to show her embarrassing old photo albums while he was left to scrape out serving dishes.

Maggie cracked another bottle of wine and joined all of the ladies in the family room, who were currently huddled around an old book that Barbara had shoved in Lily's lap. "Oh, Jesus, Mom, you're going to bore the shit out of her and she's never going to want to come back."

Barbara held up her glass and waved her hand, shooing her away once the glass was full. "Oh, stop! I never get a chance to enjoy such lovely dinner guests. Lily, dear, am I boring you? Feel free to let me know, I won't be offended."

"No, of course not. I love looking at old photos."

"Oh, now you're just being nice."

"No, really. I'm an only child, and my mom was not the best photographer. She would lose rolls of film and forget to pick up others she had developed. If it wasn't an annual yearbook photo, there just weren't many in the house. I think it's fun to look at candid moments and hear the stories that go with them."

"Wow, I don't know what's worse," Emma said, flipping over another page, "never having any photos to look at, or being forced to suffer through years worth on every major holiday."

"I bet if you lost them all tomorrow you would miss them terribly," Lily replied, looking wistful for a moment. "Just look at all of these amazing family memories."

She looked over the page full of aged snapshots from the 70s, stopping on one that caught her eye. It was so washed out that it was sepia toned, and it had a thick white border. It showed a much younger Barbara, sitting on a loud-patterned sofa, holding two tiny babies in her arms while a toddler with huge dimples and brown curls played on the seat next to her with one of those old, brightly colored xylophones. It was obvious that the toddler was Eric—nobody else in the world had dimples that huge—but the two infants surprised her.

"Twins?" she gasped.

"Oh, yeah. Ethan and I are twins," Emma stated matter-of-factly, as if anyone in the world would be able to tell.

"Wow, I don't see any resemblance. You look much more like Eric."

"Well, I have his coloring, but Ethan and I both have green eyes. We got those from Mom, and he got her hair color. Everything else he seems to have gotten from Dad."

"Oh, my little mix-n-match of genetics!" Barbara cooed before hugging Emma tightly.

"Okaaay, Mom, I think that's enough wine for you," she teased.

Lily continued to flip through the pages, seeing the children progress in age. Plaid dresses and corduroy pants switched over to denim jackets and tight-rolled jeans. Emma had gone through a very large bangs phase, while Eric had apparently gone through a Metallica period.

The only one who didn't seem to change very much was Ethan. His clothing changed with the fashion of the times, but he always looked like a poster boy for that year's "American Teen." There was picture after picture full of Izod, Polo, Abercrombie, Old Navy, and Lacoste. His hair always looked a little bit unruly, no matter the length, and for some reason he always appeared bored. He epitomized the brooding smart guy who just knew he was meant for better things.

She knew without a doubt that if she had gone to high school with him, he would have been the golden boy that she always fantasized about but never had the nerve to speak to.

"Hey, Lily," Maggie said, draining the last of her wine. "What do you say I give you a proper tour of the house?"

"Okay, sure." She handed the album off to Emma, who was still being cuddled by her tipsy mother, and followed Maggie out of the room.

"Let's start at the top and work our way down, shall we?"

Maggie led her up to the third floor first, pointing out a guest room that was lavishly decorated, followed by another room that had the door closed. "That's Ethan's old room. He still uses it from time to time, but Barbara redesigned it a while back. It's really lovely now, no cheesy old trophies and pennants like the ones my husband refuses to pack away. I'd show you, but he gets really moody when people mess with his things."

"I understand," Lily whispered, feeling her eyes drawn to the closed door, as if it held some long-hidden secrets about her beautiful stranger. "He seems like he gets moody easily," she added, still unable to shake off the effect of his antics over dinner.

"Yeah," she sighed. "That's just Ethan. I have no idea why he was being such a prick to you earlier, but I've known him since he was a teenager, and he was always a moody little shit. He's very sweet deep down, but it takes a while for him to warm to anyone. Shit, he still barely knows Brandon, and he's been married to Emma for almost eight years now."

"Wow, don't they get along?" Brandon seemed like a perfectly likable guy from what she could tell.

"No, that's not it. You have to actually know someone to not get along with them. They've barely spoken more than a few times."

"Why?"

"Well, Ethan's been gone for so many years, I don't think he's ever made time for it. And he's been so preoccupied with his nasty breakup lately that I doubt anything else has seemed very important to him yet."

Lily stopped in her tracks. "His…breakup?" She vaguely remembered Barbara telling her something at the hospital about her other son recently ending a bad relationship, but she had barely been paying attention at that moment, eager to flee the scene of so much heartache.

"Yeah," Maggie frowned. "About a month ago now, maybe a touch longer. I guess it was really ugly," she whispered, as if they weren't completely alone in the hallway. "I don't know all the particulars and he isn't sharing yet, at least not with me. I get the feeling that he told Eric some stuff, and I've been itching to pry it out of him. Anyway, I guess that explains why he was such a grouchy fucker tonight. I'm sorry you got caught in the crossfire."

"I guess I understand," Lily said, not really understanding at all.

"You know, it's funny, I was actually thinking of trying to set you two up sometime, before you told me about your little *situation*. How's that going, by the way?"

"Oh, it's still going—I think." Lily wanted to laugh at the circumstances that had led her to that moment in time, having a conversation about her secret lover with said secret lover's sister-in-law. "I haven't really had the chance to make any major changes yet, though. But I hope to soon."

"Well, I hope it all works out for you. You deserve some happiness." And then Maggie did something completely unexpected. She hugged her.

Lily was surprised to find herself blinking back tears.

"Okay, that's enough sappy girl time," Maggie teased. "Let's go downstairs." They went back down another level, Maggie pointing out rooms as they walked by. "That's Emma's old room, they stay there whenever they visit, and of course you remember the football hall of fame that is our room. Richard and Barbara sleep down there at the end of the hall."

They continued down the hall until they reached a back stairway, which led them down into the kitchen. Maggie chattered away happily as they walked into the room, not paying any attention to the men who were still scraping and washing the dishes. Lily tried to concentrate on what she was saying, but she couldn't help noticing when Ethan straightened up and spun around, tracking her movements like a hawk. She felt his eyes boring into her back as they crossed the room, stopping at yet another door.

"Now this," Maggie paused for dramatic effect as she opened the door. "This has been my favorite room since I first came home with Eric to visit." She started down yet another set of stairs into what had to be the basement. At the bottom was simply a small area with a fancy washer and dryer set and a folding table set up next to a drying rack.

"The laundry room?" Lily said, unable to hide the disbelief in her voice.

"No, silly, through here." She opened a door to the left that Lily just assumed was for storage, and when they both walked through it she could barely keep her mouth from hanging open in shock.

It was an enormous rec room that spanned the entire length of the house, complete with a pool table, an air hockey table, a pinball machine, and three full-sized arcade game machines. There was an area set up for watching movies, along with about three different gaming systems.

"Oh my God!" Lily said, feeling lightheaded as she took it all in. "I thought they played video games upstairs. Why would they bother when this is down here?"

"Well, that's just for killing time. This room...this is for getting serious. When we hang out down here, we can go missing for days. That's why the kids lucked out and inherited the room from Richard. Barbara got tired of him never leaving his man cave."

"This is Dr. Foster's?"

"It was, but he would spend long hours at the hospital and then every waking hour down here when he was home. Barbara can only handle so much air hockey before she starts yelling. Once the kids hit high school she convinced him to hand it over, thus skyrocketing them into superstardom for the best parties practically overnight."

"Wow. I just…I could never imagine having this kind of stuff at my disposal growing up."

"Yeah, it's a lot to take in at first. When I first met Eric I was worried that his family was going to be a bunch of stuffy, rich pricks, but they sooo aren't!"

"I know, they are so sweet," Lily agreed, turning to look at her hostess. "You all are."

Maggie blushed slightly before socking her on the arm. "Hey, don't get all mushy on me, Blake. I am fully prepared to beat your ass at any game here."

"Oh, bring it!" Lily laughed, and it was the best she'd felt all day. "I haven't played air hockey since college, but I'm sure I remember enough to send you home crying."

The gleam that ignited in Maggie's eyes at Lily's words was almost scary. "Oh, it is fucking on!" She started to walk across the room toward the machine in question, only to be interrupted by Eric's voice at the top of the stairs.

"Baby!" he called down, making them both jump.

"What?" she yelled back, rolling her eyes in annoyance.

"What's the best container for all of this lasagna?"

"Jesus, Eric, ask your mother!"

"I can't. Emma said she fell asleep on the couch."

"Then ask Emma!" she huffed.

"Are you kidding me? I want to *store* leftovers, not give them a makeover."

"Ugh, fine!" she snapped before turning back to Lily. "I'm sorry. I better get up there before he finds a way to blow up the kitchen. I'll be right back."

"Of course, take your time," Lily said, still laughing at their exchange.

"Okay, feel free to check out anything you like while I'm gone.

They're all rigged to play for free, so you don't need any quarters." She disappeared through the door and stomped loudly up the stairs.

Lily made her way over to the pinball machine, laughing when she noticed that it had a cheesy, dated vampire theme. There was a large black coffin inside that looked as if it popped open to let the ball drop down into it for extra points, as well as little bats that lit up when they were hit. She'd always loved playing pinball on the few occasions when her mother would let her go to the arcade while they were shopping at the mall, so she eagerly stepped up and started a game.

The moment she heard the dinging bells and saw the flashing lights, Lily was transported back to her childhood, a time when things were so much simpler. She didn't have to care about things like broken hearts and responsibility; she only had to be a kid and have fun. Granted, that hadn't lasted very long since her mother had turned into a bigger kid than she'd ever been, with her multiple marriages and selfish behavior, but it still made for fun memories.

A few minutes into her game, she heard light footsteps descending the stairs behind her. Without looking back, she called out to Maggie, "Man, I hope you brought your A-game today. I am on fire!"

"And I hope you can explain yourself," a deep, velvety voice said from right behind her, causing her to jump nearly a foot off the ground before spinning around, clutching her chest to keep her pounding heart from bursting through it.

"Goddammit!" she gasped. "Was that absolutely necessary?" She avoided making eye contact with him by looking over his shoulder, afraid of being swayed by his unearthly beauty.

"I don't know, was it absolutely necessary to show up at my fucking house with my fucking family?" The venom that fueled his words finally made her cave and look at him, not understanding why so much anger was directed at her.

"Excuse me? What the hell is that supposed to mean? You act like I planned this whole embarrassing evening!"

"I don't know, *did* you?"

Suddenly so furious that she couldn't even think straight, Lily raised her hand to slap him, only to have him catch it in midair.

"I don't think so, princess," he growled, pinning her back against the pinball machine with his body. "You already got away with that once. Do it again and I'll slap you back."

"You wouldn't dare!"

"Do *not* fucking push me tonight. I really don't know what I'm capable of." His gaze dropped to her lips quickly before shooting back up to her eyes. "Now. Explain yourself."

"Why are you so angry with me?" Lily whispered, trying hard to focus on anything but how good and solid his body felt against hers.

"How would you feel if your dad rolled up one night for dinner at the diner with me sitting in his car next to him? Wouldn't that make you feel just the tiniest bit blindsided?"

"Of course it would, but you can't possibly think that I planned this!"

"I don't know what the fuck to think anymore!" he snarled, now only inches from her face.

"Oh, stop being ridiculous! I had no way of knowing that was your family. I met Maggie at work, and she's the one who wanted me to hang out with them. Last night was the first time we ever went out, and if you'll remember, I left early to find you!"

"That may be so, but I don't like this one fucking bit." Ethan looked down at her again, letting his eyes roam more freely. "I don't want you hanging out with them anymore."

"Well, that's not your decision to make, now is it? They're my friends, and I like them!"

"I can't handle it!" he growled again, forcing himself even closer.

"Just what is it that you can't handle? That your dirty little secret is around to rub your nose in the fact that you aren't exactly devastated about your breakup like they all think?"

"That is none of your fucking business!" he hissed through his teeth, grabbing her by the arms roughly. "And that's not what I can't handle!"

"Ethan, stop! You're hurting me!"

He froze, easing his grip but not letting go. "Say that again." It was a harsh whisper, like a dying man in the desert begging for water.

"You're hurting me?" she asked, not understanding what he wanted.

"No."

"Ethan?"

With a loud groan he pulled her to him, crashing his mouth down on hers. His hands were everywhere at once, roaming over her body before settling in her hair, holding her head in place while he ravaged her lips with his own. He reached down and grabbed her ass, gripping it tightly before lifting her up and setting her on the pinball machine, wrapping her legs around his waist.

Lily could feel him, hard and pulsing against her wet heat. She wanted to stay angry, she wanted to yell, but none of that could top how much she wanted him inside her at that moment.

He kissed his way down her neck, licking and biting as he ground himself against her. "I can't handle how much I need you," he panted against her skin. "It's too much," he groaned. "It's all too much! I can't take wanting you like this in front of them, too!"

"Shh," Lily whispered soothingly, running her fingers through his hair. "Don't think about that right now. We'll sort it out somehow. Just fucking kiss me!"

He complied happily, sucking her bottom lip between his teeth before flicking the tip of his tongue against her mouth, probing for entrance. She opened hungrily, swirling her tongue with his, tasting his need. Ethan shoved his hand in her hair again, holding her to him tightly while letting his other hand cup her bottom so he could pull her into his thrusts as he swallowed her moans.

They heard Maggie's voice before the sound of her feet on the stairs.

"Eric, just figure it out! I helped you with over half of it. You and Brandon are big boys, I'm sure you can finish the rest. Now hurry up and get down here so you can watch me kick Lily's ass."

They both froze, staring at each other in a moment of panic. Looking down at the tangled mess they were in, they jumped apart quickly, but not before Ethan whispered in her ear, "To be continued."

Ethan ran over to the other side of the room and started up the PlayStation while Lily resumed her pinball game. They both did their best to steady their breathing, and Ethan was grateful that he could sit down to hide his blatant arousal.

"Okay, Lily, sorry about that," Maggie apologized as she walked in the room, stopping in her tracks when she noticed there was someone else with them.

"Oh, Ethan. I didn't know you were down here. I thought you snuck out and went home."

"No, I thought I'd play a few rounds before I took off."

She looked back and forth between them for what felt like an eternity. Lily was positive that she was doing a mental checklist of everything about them that was disheveled, but she simply shrugged and walked over to the air hockey table, turning it on.

"So, Lily, are you ready to feel the pain?"

"Uh…absolutely." She tried her hardest to sound excited, hoping that it didn't come off as awkward as it felt.

For the next two hours, Lily was subjected to numerous competitions. Once Eric, Brandon, and Emma finally joined them it became all-out war. They played pool, darts, Donkey Kong, Rampage—just about anything they could turn into a battle. There were one-on-one bouts as well as team matches, and they even whined enough that Ethan agreed to play a few with them.

Aside from the initial awkwardness of almost being caught grinding with her new friends' brother on a pinball machine, it was the happiest two hours of Lily's life.

When she noticed that Ethan was beginning to signal her when the others weren't looking, she shrugged her shoulders, not knowing what he wanted. He nodded toward the clock on the wall and raised his eyebrows at her, willing her to understand.

"Oh! Is that the time? I really need to get going, guys. I'm sorry." It was a horrible performance, but probably the best of Lily's life.

"Aw, really?" Eric whined. "I wanted a rematch!"

"Next time, I promise."

"I should probably get going, too," Ethan piped up as Lily headed to the door. They all said their good-byes, everyone hugging Lily tightly before releasing her.

"We'll walk you out," Maggie said, dragging Eric along with her behind them.

"Oh, you don't need to do that. I can find my way."

"Nonsense. You're my guest, and I insist."

They made their way up through the kitchen and out the front door, saying their good-byes to Richard as they passed, asking him to thank Barbara once she woke up. When they reached the front steps, Lily thanked them again profusely for inviting her, hugging them both one more time. Ethan kept walking, barely acknowledging any of them with only the slightest of nods as he got in his car.

"I'm going to call you about that weekend in Chicago," Maggie called after Lily as she walked to her Oldsmobile. "Don't think I'll forget."

"Good, I can't wait. I think it sounds like fun." She gave them a final wave before hopping in her car, following Ethan out of the driveway.

Maggie stood with her hand behind Eric's back and her head on his shoulder, both of them watching as the vehicles traveled farther away from the house.

"So," she sighed, "do you think they're even going to *bother* taking different directions, or just race each other straight to his place to screw?"

"Oh, definitely race," Eric chuckled, stroking her arm lovingly before kissing the top of her head.

25

"What the hell was all of that about?" Lily barked at Ethan as she slammed her heavy car door after pulling up next to him in the lot behind the apartment building.

"Inside," was all he said, not even looking back at her as he crossed the alley to the dimly lit door. When he reached it he held it open wide, turning to face her with an exaggerated, sarcastic bow. "After you, my dear."

"Very cute," she mumbled under her breath as she passed him, unable to decide whether to slap him or kiss him. The moment he closed the door behind them she spun around and faced him. "Okay, spill it. Why the hell were you so shitty to me at dinner? In front of everyone!"

He took a deep breath before gritting through his teeth, "I said *inside.*"

"We are inside."

"No, we're at the foot of a very dark stairway. I want to get upstairs behind locked doors if you insist on continuing this discussion."

"No. You just want to lock out the real world again. It's not going to be that easy now."

"Goddammit!" he growled, grabbing her by the arms and shoving her up against the wall, pressing himself against her until their noses were almost touching, his toned chest and firm legs warring with his words for her attention. "Don't you think I fucking know that?" he said, his sweet breath flowing over her lips. "My entire life has just been turned upside down! Cut me just the tiniest bit of slack. I'm so fucking torn apart right now, I don't know whether to scream at you for screwing up everything perfect that we had going, or rip your clothes off and fuck you where you stand!"

"*I* screwed it up?" she snapped, trying to ignore the feeling of his muscular thigh sliding between hers, pinning her more thoroughly to the wall. "How the hell was I supposed to know that was your family? I have exactly *zero* friends in this town! Maybe I should blame you for fucking up the first invitation I've ever had to a dinner that I didn't fucking cook."

"Do you think I don't know how crazy I sound? None of this makes any sense to me, my reactions most of all!"

"Well, you need to at least try to think before you speak. I didn't screw anything up about us that wouldn't have gotten screwed up eventually, and believe me, it was not perfect to begin with. It was bound to fall apart—we always knew that. We just didn't know how."

"But I'm not ready for that!" he hissed before taking a deep breath and calming himself. When he spoke again it was almost a tortured whisper. "I still need this." He ran the tip of his nose against her cheek, back and forth, until he was next to her ear. He couldn't look her in the eye when he choked out his next words. "I still need *you.*"

Lily's heart soared at his admission. "You still have me. You just know my name now."

He groaned and buried his face against her neck, kissing the tender skin of her throat lightly before flicking it with his tongue.

"Lily," he whispered, and he could feel her soft moan vibrate beneath his lips. He felt her hands sliding up between their bodies until she was gripping the back of his head. What he heard next was only a muted gasp in the dark, but it was enough to set his soul on fire.

"*Ethan.*"

Angels couldn't have sounded so sweet.

His mouth quickly covered hers, inhaling the rest of her moans and gasps. He was painfully hard and couldn't resist shifting his hips so she could feel what she had done to him. When he felt her starting to rub herself back against him, he groaned even louder and slipped his tongue between her lips, flicking at the tip of hers before swirling his own around it.

Before long, his hands had gone from gripping her shoulders to groping her breasts through her shirt. He felt her nipples harden into tight peaks in his palms, and when that wasn't enough contact, he started rubbing them more firmly with the pads of his thumbs.

The only sounds that could be heard in the dark stairwell for some time after that were a series of grunts and gasps as the two lovers grinded against each other. Lily had completely forgotten everything she had been angry about, only wanting to feel more of him.

The sound of her loud moan echoing in the narrow entryway reminded her all too quickly that they were in a stairwell. A dark, dirty stairwell.

"Wait," she somehow murmured between kisses. "Ethan—wait!"

"God, yes!" he growled into her mouth, thrusting her harder into the wall. "Say it again!" He couldn't hear anything but the sound of his name leaving her lips.

"No—wait!" Finally her voice broke through his lust-induced stupor, but only after she gave a good tug on his hair for emphasis.

"What's wrong?" His face was completely baffled, as if dry humping against the wall of a creepy stairwell was nothing out of the ordinary.

"We need to get upstairs. *Now.*"

"Oh. Is that all?" He smirked wickedly before grabbing her ass tightly and holding her to him as he turned around and started up the stairs. "Ask and you shall receive, my lovely."

Lily squealed and wrapped her legs around him tightly. "Oh, God! Don't drop me!"

"Baby, if you keep wiggling against my dick like that, I'm going to toss you down right here on the stairs." She immediately stopped moving, anxious to get up into the apartment. "That's what I thought," he teased. He was also very eager to get her inside, hoping to make her squeal like that again—but for very different reasons.

Not wanting to set her down until he was poised to thrust inside her body, Ethan pinned her up against the wall by the door as he fished his key out of his pocket, which pressed his body even more firmly into her and made her cry out with the ache he was creating. She couldn't stop herself from grinding back into him and leaning forward, biting his neck to stifle her scream.

"Fuck!" he snarled, shoving the door open finally and kicking it closed behind them, spinning around quickly to slam her against it. "Did you just fucking *bite* me?" He didn't think he'd ever been so turned on in his life.

In answer, she simply grunted and bit him again on the other side, well past the point of words. Dragging her tongue up the side of his neck, she sucked his earlobe between her lips before clamping her teeth down and biting that, too.

The guttural moan that ripped from his throat startled both of them.

Grabbing her roughly, he kissed her so hard it was almost painful, his need for her eclipsing any other thought in his mind. He turned and walked with her, stumbling into the bedroom and kneeling on the bed, silently cursing himself for never buying any more furniture. He would have liked to just fuck her on a couch or a chair in the heat of the moment, rather than always needing to go into the bedroom or risking her discomfort on the hardwood floors.

Dropping her on the mattress, he immediately went to work on the zipper of her jeans, needing to be inside her body more than anything else in the entire world at that moment. He knew it would not be sweet. He knew it would not be slow. He was consumed with a driving urge to claim, to conquer. Nothing else would be right in the world until he felt himself pumping his hot seed deep inside her as she shattered around him.

By the frantic way that she tore at his clothing, she apparently agreed.

When she was finally nude, he leaned back on his knees long enough to rip his shirt over his head and unbutton his jeans, stopping only briefly to gaze at her porcelain skin in the darkness. Just the sight of her underneath him again made his body quake with need. He pushed his jeans down over his hips, barely enough to free his throbbing erection before he fell on her with a loud growl.

"Fuck, I need you," he moaned into her breasts as he licked and sucked them, lining himself up at her entrance quickly before driving into her deeply. Her scorching wet heat engulfed him, stretching to accommodate his girth as he moved in her. They both cried out at the contact, her inner walls gripping him tightly.

He paused long enough to catch her gaze in the dark. "Say it."

She wrapped her arms around his waist, grasping his firm ass and pulling him farther inside her. "Ethan," she gasped as she thrust up to meet him.

"Yes!" he growled loudly, completely overcome with the primal feeling of claiming her. Something about hearing her finally say his name while he was buried deep inside her body set him off like nothing ever had before. "More!" he growled, shoving himself inside her to the hilt, over and over again, kissing and sucking her tender skin everywhere he could reach, unable to touch her in enough places at once to satisfy him.

She kept a firm grip on his toned cheeks, digging in her nails so hard at one point that it hurt, pulling him inside her eagerly, deeper and deeper. "Ethan," she would cry out with every thrust, feeling him hit places inside of her that she didn't even know she had. "Ethan... Ethan... Ethan... Ethan!"

His growls and snarls grew louder and louder, and by that point he was near feral with his need to consume her. It wasn't enough. It would never be enough.

"Who—" he panted, barely able to speak with the amount of need he felt, his powerful thrusts leaving him breathless. "Who is fucking you right now?"

"You are!" she cried. "Ethan." Another hard thrust and grunt.

"Who do you belong to when you're here?" he gasped between more grunts and snarls.

"You...you...only you!" she panted, bucking her hips with even more force, pulling on him roughly. "*Ethan!*" His loud growl vibrated her skin before he bit her nipple, sucking it into his mouth afterward to soothe it.

When he felt her inner muscles starting to clamp down on him, he knew that they were both close. "Who is going to make you come so hard that you see stars?" He slid his hand between their bodies and began stroking her, rubbing her swollen clitoris in tight circles as if to prove his point.

"*Ethan!*" she screamed, her body poised on the brink of explosion.

"And who is so fucking crazy about you that he can't think straight?"

"Oh, God...Ethan!" She wasn't even answering him that time. Just the thought of him feeling that way about her sent her flying over the edge, screaming her release. Her entire body began bucking wildly, milking him dry as he followed her into the abyss.

"*Lily!*" he roared, exploding so powerfully inside her that he thought for a moment he might pass out. Thick ropes of fluid filled her as he pumped his hips frantically, desperate to leave every drop behind.

After what felt like hours, but was most likely only a few seconds, Ethan rolled off of her and collapsed at her side. Not wanting to let her go, he pulled her close to him, settling her on his chest with her head resting on his shoulder.

"Wow," she sighed deeply, snuggling into him more completely, loving how warm his skin was underneath her.

"I think 'wow' is an understatement," he chuckled, stroking her back lightly. "I would have said something along the lines of *holy fuck sonofabitch.* To put it mildly."

"Well said."

They stayed there together in the dark for a while, simply existing, enjoying the feeling of being so close to each other. Ethan had almost drifted off to sleep when he heard a quiet whisper next to him.

"Ethan?"

"Mm?" It was still so odd to hear her say his name so easily, and he was ashamed to feel himself twitching in response again.

"You know we still have to talk, right? Don't think you distracted me that much."

"Ugh, dammit," he sighed. "And here I thought I was getting away with it." He ran his fingers through his hair, leaving it sticking up in many different directions. "What, exactly, do we still need to talk about?"

"Well, how about the entire evening, for starters?" she said, propping her forearms on his chest to look him in the eye.

"What about it?" he asked, stalling.

"Like I asked you earlier, why were you so shitty to me? Couldn't you tell that I was just as freaked out as you were? At least *you* were in familiar territory—I was surrounded by a bunch of people I barely knew in a place I'd never been."

"I know. I have no idea what came over me. It was all just so damn intense. I felt like I was going to fall apart at any moment. I totally wigged out." He stroked his hand through her hair, running his thumb across her bottom lip when he finished. "I'm sorry. I think I just wanted someone to feel as freaked out as I did, so I lashed out."

"So what set you off so bad? Just the fact that I was there? I was too busy freaking out that you were related to Maggie."

"Well…everything!" he sighed. "Yes, I was totally thrown that you were there and that was how I had to 'meet' you, but then, seeing you with them like that? I mean, you know my entire family! They all love you! They want to have you over for sleepovers, for fuck's sake—and I didn't even know your name. It was more than a tiny bit overwhelming."

"Why does it bother you so much that they like me?"

"I told you, I'm not ready to share you with them." He swallowed hard, trying to find the best way to say what he was feeling without putting his foot in his mouth again. After another loud sigh he continued. "I don't know if I'll ever be ready, honestly. You're fucking engaged, and my life just fell apart! I don't particularly like them acting as if they're about to pick out our china patterns already."

"I hardly think that's what they were doing. You're just being paranoid."

"Bullshit, I know my family. That was a setup. They might as well have posted a sign above the door that said '*Wife Interviews Inside.*'"

"Oh, whatever," she rolled her eyes, trying to ignore how much the word "wife" affected her, and then she remembered her earlier conversation. "Well, Maggie did say that she'd thought about trying to set us up before she knew I wasn't available."

"She knew you were engaged?" he said, his eyes going wide.

"Yeah, so I wonder why she would think—hmm. Maybe it was because I told her I was going to end it. She must have hoped I'd be so moved by her beautiful brother-in-law that everything else would go out the window. Ha! Little did she know that I was already sleeping with him!"

She laughed lightly, finding the irony of the situation way too funny. It wasn't until she looked back up at him that she realized something she'd said had upset him. There was a grave look on his face, and his jaw was clenched.

"What's wrong?"

He didn't speak for a moment, and the silence in the room was deafening. When he finally opened his mouth, it was to speak through gritted teeth.

"You told her *what?*"

"I just said that out loud, didn't I?"

"Yeah, you did."

"I…I meant to tell you last night. That's why I was looking for you. But then we got in your car and I just sort of lost control."

"Don't try to distract me with car sex talk," he snapped. "You're ending it?"

"Yes," she said in an exhale that ended with a sharp nod, as if she were only just then making up her mind. "I just haven't had the chance to yet because he's still out of town."

"When is he coming back?" Ethan felt a pain in his gut even mentioning him.

"I'm not sure. Soon, I think."

"I hope you're not doing that for *me*. I never told you to." His delivery was as abrupt as a slap in the face.

"No, actually," she replied, trying to ignore the sting that his words left. "It's just become obvious to me that I'm not happy with him anymore—if I ever was."

"Are you sure you want to do that?" he pried.

"Excuse me? Is this the same man who is so jealous that he can't even stand to see the ring?" She tried very hard not to sound pissy, but his odd reaction to her news was a little bit less than what she'd been hoping for. No, she wasn't only ending it with Scott for him, but she wondered if a little bit of enthusiasm would kill him.

"Wait, Lily, hear me out." He put his hand on top of hers on his chest, stroking it lightly with his warm fingers. "I'm not telling you not to...I just don't want you to regret something later that you didn't think through all the way first. This has all happened so fast, and today certainly just sped things up way more than *I'm* comfortable with. I don't know about you."

"Your family doesn't need to affect this. Today was an odd day that nobody could have predicted. I'm not asking you to do anything drastic just because they like me."

He thought for a moment before speaking carefully, trying to make her understand. "I'm trying to not let anyone force my choices but me for the first time in my life, and I think you should do the same. I know what we have here is...intense, and addictive, but is it worth throwing your life away?"

Yes. She didn't say it out loud, but she felt it to her very core.

"I mean, are you absolutely positive that you don't love him anymore? That you can hurt him like that? That you aren't just going through some sort of sexual...awakening or experimentation? Can you honestly say that you can't work it out with him and make it better?" It hurt him so much to even think those questions, but he had no idea if they had even crossed her mind. If she did something based solely on fleeting emotions without thinking it through, she could end up hating herself for it one day—and him.

"You think all of that hasn't been going through my mind for a while now?" she asked, blinking back tears. "I realized recently that

I've never loved him the way that I should. *Never.* I do love him, a lot, but more like a friend or a brother. He's got his problems, but he's a very sweet man underneath it all. I think it's more hurtful to him to keep that charade going, don't you? He deserves the chance to find someone who can love him with her whole heart."

"All right." Ethan stopped pushing, cringing inside at any mention of her history with him, but he couldn't stop himself from wondering how much of her revelation was fueled by their illicit activities. "I only wanted to make sure that you knew what you were getting yourself into."

"Believe me, I've thought about it," she snapped. "And I've got to say, I really thought you would be a little bit happier about this. You can't stand to hear about him and you never want me to leave whenever I'm here…I'm sorry, but those are some extremely mixed signals from what I'm hearing right now."

"I *don't* like hearing about him. I fucking *hate* it! But that's me, not you. I know what it's like to make a horrible decision without giving it enough thought. I don't want the same for you, especially if *I'm* that horrible decision."

"Are you talking about your breakup?" she asked, wiping her eyes quickly and giving him a serious look. "I heard it was bad. Can you talk about it?"

"I can," he growled, "but I don't particularly like to."

"Is it too painful? I understand that it was recent." She hated the thought of him hurting. She wanted to wipe away any ounce of pain that he'd ever felt in his life.

"Well, honestly, the entire relationship was painful, and I don't know if I really want to go into it all right now. Let me just say that we weren't exactly a match made in heaven and we brought out the worst in each other. I barely recognized the person I became, and I can't say that I miss her at all." Ethan looked at her for any sign of judgment, but only saw patience and understanding. It made him want to continue, just to make her see that he wasn't completely heartless. "We'd been on the outs for a long time. I was in the process of finally trying to end it when she took everything I had with me—money, clothing, art supplies—and gave it to somebody else." His expression clouded over as he was struck with the memory of finding her note again.

"Oh my God!" Lily gasped, scooting closer so that she could cup his cheeks in her hands. "Ethan, I am so sorry. Nobody should have to go through something like that." She leaned forward and kissed him gently, his lips, his nose, even his eyelids.

It was the most cherished Ethan had ever felt in his life, and he had no idea what to think about that.

He lay there in silence, running his hands along her back in soft patterns for a few minutes before pulling her the rest of the way on top of him. "I don't want to talk about this anymore," he whispered, enjoying the way her body easily molded to him as she straddled his waist.

"You don't have to," she said between more light kisses on his chin. "Let me make you feel better, baby." She kissed him again and again, moving all over his face as she began shifting her hips against him, trying to feel how ready he was. She was pleased to find that he had already begun to grow hard between them, so she decided to expedite matters a bit. Leaning forward, she flicked her tongue up the side of his neck, biting and sucking his earlobe before whispering, "*Ethan.*"

He groaned loudly, grabbing her hips and pulling her down on him more firmly. She continued shifting and wiggling against him, working until his erection was pinned between them, sliding her wet folds back and forth over the bottom side of his shaft.

"Fuck, that feels good," he panted, lifting his hips up toward her.

When she felt him trying to pull back enough to change his angle so he could penetrate her, she lifted off of him slightly. "Ah ah ah," she scolded, holding herself just above him. "I'm running this show now."

"Oh, God," he practically whimpered. "Don't fucking tease me. I can't take it. I need to be inside you!" He pulled down on her hips for emphasis, trying to get her where he needed her to be.

"I told you, *Ethan*, I'm going to make you feel better." She smiled wickedly at the loud moan he let out when she said his name again. "However, I think I'm going to make you a little crazy first." He grunted and jerked his hips upwards again, trying in vain to enter her. "Now be good, or I'm going to make you squirm even longer."

He lay perfectly still beneath her on the mattress, trying his hardest to obey, but the longer she kept it from him, the more insanely he wanted it. It didn't help that she began to fondle and caress her breasts above him, moving and gyrating her hips over him in the most sinful display he'd ever seen. He knew it would only take one well-placed thrust to shove himself inside her to the hilt, and the thought of that was killing him slowly, but he loved that she was being playful with him. He didn't want to ruin her fun just yet.

However, if she kept it up much longer, he wouldn't be responsible for what he did.

"Now, don't you dare move," she commanded, circling herself over him until the broad tip of his cock was lined up perfectly with her dripping entrance. With the tiniest shift of her hips he slipped inside, but only the tip. The need to thrust was excruciating, setting his entire body on fire. He could feel her scorching heat surrounding him, all centered at one point on his body.

"Please," he gritted through his teeth, his veins standing out on his neck with his restraint.

"Not yet," she replied easily, as if they were talking about something as mundane as the weather. "But I like the begging. Let's have more of that." And with that she wiggled her hips a bit more, slipping down another inch on his length before pulling back up.

"Goddammit! *Please!*" he ground out again, sweat beads beginning to form on his brow.

"Please, what?" she said, reaching down to pinch his nipples roughly, causing him to hiss.

"*Lily*. Please, Lily!"

"That's more like it," she smiled, allowing herself to drop another inch. "You aren't the only one who likes to hear your name." She rocked her hips on him then, sliding a bit more up and down. His loud groan was music to her ears.

"Can you feel that?" she asked innocently, bracing her hands on his chest as she raised and lowered herself, never going farther than halfway down his shaft. "Can you feel me gripping you?" For added effect, she clenched her inner muscles around him, causing his eyes to roll back in his head. "Can you feel my pussy dripping all over you?"

"Fuck!" he cried out. "Lily, please! I need to feel you. I need to be inside you. Now!"

"Don't get demanding," she snapped. He would have thought she was completely unaffected if it weren't for her heavy panting. She was loving this. "I told you, I'm running the show. Now tell me: whose pussy are you desperate for right now?" The up and down sliding never ceased, never going deeper, never stopping. He was going to come without ever being all the way inside her if she didn't change it up fast, and the thought of that made him want to cry.

"Oh God…Lily!" Ethan looked up at her, pleading with his eyes, and was met with the most primal, animalistic look he had ever seen in his life. It took all of his energy not to explode right at that moment.

"And who's about to fuck you into next week?" she growled.

"Lily!" he gasped. "*My* Lily." And with that she pulled all the way back, hovering for merely a second over him before slamming herself down on him to the hilt.

They both threw their heads back and howled, she from the unbelievably deep intrusion and he from the almost transcendent release from agony.

She rode him hard after that, each thrust slamming her down on him, gripping him tightly, and pulling him inside her to oblivion. She grabbed his hands and shoved them on her breasts, holding them in place for leverage as he gripped and squeezed, loving the feel of her consuming him. Every single thrust brought him closer to the edge, and he couldn't stop from gasping her name every time she sank down again.

"Yes," she moaned, beginning to tremble around him. "Ethan… God, yes!"

Just watching her face nearing her release was enough to set him off. "Oh fuck…baby…baby, I'm gonna come. I can't hold it back any more. Please…please come with me!"

But by then it was too late, and he shattered into a million pieces, exploding violently inside her. "Oh God, *Lily!*"

And that was all it took for her. Feeling him spilling inside her while crying out her name sent Lily reeling into a release of her own, causing her body to clamp down hard while she shuddered above him.

It was the most beautiful thing he'd ever seen in his life, and he hoped he would remember it forever.

They had another fairly sleepless night after that, Ethan never letting her drift off completely. He would let her rest long enough to get her energy back, but then he would be right back again, rock hard and needy. He was like a man possessed, even worse than the first time she'd stayed the night, licking and kissing every bare inch of her skin before driving himself into her over and over again. Sometimes he was slow and gentle, other times he was hard and rough, but every time felt full of emotion.

Lily wanted to tell him to calm down, that they had all the time in the world to explore each other now, but there was something inside her that liked him craving her, like a starving man devouring his first meal in weeks.

It wasn't until the soft light of dawn filtered into the room that he finally let her collapse on his chest, half asleep before she closed her eyes.

"Ethan," she sighed, wrapping her arms around his sweaty torso. "I just want to be with you." And with that, she was out. If she'd managed one last look up at his face, she would have seen the hot tears streaming down his cheeks.

"I love you, Lily," he croaked out, leaning forward to place a gentle kiss on the top of her head before wiping his eyes and allowing himself to sleep.

26

After she'd managed to get a few hours of uninterrupted sleep, Lily woke feeling sore and wonderful. She grabbed a quick shower, not wanting to go home reeking of sex like the entire room did, and leaned over Ethan one more time to kiss her sleeping man good-bye.

"Mmm," he moaned, rolling toward her. "Leaving so soon?" he spoke without opening his eyes.

"Don't wake up," she whispered. "You're so beautiful when you sleep." She kissed his cheek before standing up. "I have to go home for a while. I'm sure the laundry is a mile high. But I'll try to come back later if I can get away."

"M'kay," he mumbled, starting to roll over, but the sound of her shoes on the floor as she walked away made him open his eyes. "Lily, wait!" he said, sitting straight up. She paused halfway across the front room and turned around to see the glorious sight of a completely naked Ethan striding toward her.

"What on earth are you doing?" she laughed. Not that she minded. No, not one little bit.

"I just…wanted a hug." His cheeks reddened slightly at his admission. "In case you can't come back later, I didn't want your last memory of me today to be a lazy slug who can't say good-bye properly."

"Well, there was nothing wrong with Sleeping Beauty," she chuckled, wrapping her arms around him tightly. "But this is definitely the better option." She slid her hand down and patted his bare bottom, giving it a quick pinch before squeezing him in another hug.

"Good-bye, Lily," he whispered into her hair.

She loved this new affectionate side of him, but it startled her when he kept holding her as she tried to pull away. "Ethan, I'll be back before you know it."

"I know, I know," he sighed, finally pulling away. "I just don't want to let you go." He held her face with both hands as he slowly covered her mouth with his, giving her the sweetest kiss she'd ever had.

"Wow," she said on a sharp exhale. He had taken her breath away. "You really know how to make a girl not want to leave." She kissed him on the cheek before pulling away. "Now get your sexy ass back in bed or I'll never get out of here."

Closing the door on such a perfect vision was one of the hardest things she'd ever done, but it left her with the motivation to get back there as fast as possible.

When she pulled into her driveway, she was surprised to find her father's car in the drive. She had thought he was going to be gone hunting most of the day. Taking a deep breath, she prepared herself to do the walk of shame in front of her father and went inside.

"Where the hell ya been, Lil?" George was perched at his usual chair in front of the TV, *Sports Center* blaring in the background.

"Uh, I was out late at the Foster's for dinner. I had a little too much wine, so they let me crash in one of the spare bedrooms." She congratulated herself for thinking quickly. "I didn't realize how late it was. I meant to be home earlier. I thought you were going hunting. What happened?"

"I didn't feel up to hunting today. My hip's been acting up some." He rubbed at his leg absentmindedly as he spoke.

"Are you all right?" Lily asked quickly. "Do you need me to help you do some more stretches?"

"No, I'll be fine," he answered, waving her off. "The weather just gets to me sometimes. I was looking forward to one of your Sunday breakfasts, though," he grumbled.

"I'm sorry, Dad. Do you want me to make you something now?"

"No, no. I grabbed something. I can feed myself, believe it or not." He huffed again before looking at her. "I'm sorry I'm being such a grouchy ass. I didn't get a lot of sleep last night from the pain, and I guess I was just hoping to spend some time with you this morning. I feel like I haven't seen you all week."

"I'm sorry. I guess I've been gone a lot lately." It didn't matter that it was probably the first time she'd been away from her father in three years. Lily instantly felt guilty for her implied neglect. "Are you sure you're feeling okay, Dad? You're not letting the school overwork you, are you?" As frustrating as George could be at times, she still loved him and wanted to make sure he was staying healthy.

"Yeah, I'm good," he sighed, turning off the TV and getting up. "Just tired. Think I might take a pain pill and try to nap for a while." He started to head for the stairs before stopping and turning back to her. "By the way, there's something in the kitchen for you." Lily's eyes followed his outstretched arm to where it pointed at the kitchen table. On it sat a vase with a few pink and white carnations. "Scott was here looking for you a while ago. I didn't know where to tell him you were. I think he left you a note."

"Oh," Lily said quietly, feeling the color drain from her face as she looked at the vase.

"So the Fosters, huh?" George continued rambling behind her as he walked up the stairs, but her gaze was locked on the flowers. "They're a nice family. Good friends to have. I'm glad you're finally meeting people, Lily. Well, anyway, off to bed. See you later, hon."

"Later, Dad," she said automatically, barely hearing him, never taking her eyes off the flowers.

She waited until she heard George's door shut, then slowly approached the vase as if it were highly explosive and she was on the bomb squad. Reaching her hand out carefully, she grabbed the folded-up note that had been scribbled on the back of a gas station receipt in Scott's clumsy scrawl.

> *Hey, babe. Sorry I missed you. Was trying to surprise you, but George said you must have left early. I couldn't stay, my dad is riding my ass for being gone so long. I'll try to catch you later. Hope you like the flowers.*

Lily let out a breath she hadn't known she was holding. She was greatly relieved that he hadn't found out where she'd been—nobody deserved to find out like that—but now that he was home again, she felt a deep sense of dread at the upcoming conversation she was going to have with him.

Walking into the other room and grabbing her phone, she pulled up his number and hit send. After a few rings his familiar voice answered.

"Hey, babe! Back home? Did you like the flowers?"

"Uh, yeah. They were pretty, thanks," she replied, feeling guilty that she couldn't even remember what they looked like.

"Yeah, I figured I kinda owed you a Valentine's present," he chuckled sheepishly.

"They were lovely, Scott. Listen, can you get away for a while? We really need to talk."

He groaned loudly, "Ugh, are you pissed at me, too? Dad hasn't laid off me since I walked in the door. Keeps saying I abandoned him. I have a list of chores a mile long that he wants me to do for him today."

"No, I'm not pissed, but I really need to talk to you."

He sighed before speaking. "I can try to get out there later, but it might not be until tomorrow."

"That's fine," she huffed, telling herself that one more day wasn't going to kill her. "Just come tomorrow."

"Are you okay? Is everything all right? I can try harder if it's urgent."

"Yeah…just come tomorrow, okay?" She ended the call, feeling a mixture of relief and aggravation that she'd been given more time.

Doing her best to put it out of her mind so that the heavy feeling in the pit of her stomach would go away, Lily busied herself with things around the house. She did three loads of laundry, cleaned the bathroom, and packed George an extra large lunch to try and make up for missing breakfast. When that was done, her lack of sleep started to become noticeable, so she decided to sprawl out on her bed for a while and give Wembley and Boober some sorely needed cuddle time with Mama.

It was after five o'clock when she heard a light tapping on her door. She looked around the room groggily, realizing that she must have fallen into a deeper sleep than the light nap she'd planned.

"Lil, are you up?" George called through the door.

"Yeah," she groaned as she sat up. "Sorry, I slept later than I meant to. I'll be down to make dinner in a minute."

"Don't worry about that. I just wanted to let you know that I was going to meet some friends over at the diner for a while. Did you want to come and grab a bite?"

"No thanks, I think I'll just eat something here later."

"Okay, then. I'll be back in a few hours."

She listened as he made his way downstairs and got into his car. Almost instantly, she was struck with the thought that she was finally alone again and free for the night.

Jumping up and running to her dresser, she changed her clothes quickly. Looking over the few items in her drawers, she thought to herself that perhaps a shopping trip to Chicago was just what she needed. Once she was ready to go, she threw some food out for the cats and ran to her car.

She knew it was crazy to rush off to see him again so quickly, especially when she knew she should have fought harder to get Scott to come over so she could end things officially, but she was well and truly addicted and would have done anything at that point to be with her stranger—no, *Ethan*—again.

She drove quickly across town, weaving through traffic as if her life depended on it. As soon as she was there she turned into the alley much faster than she should have and pulled into the parking lot. As she got out and ran across the alley, she noticed the Audi wasn't there, but since he knew she might be coming back tonight she figured that he wouldn't be gone long.

Smiling at the thought of using her key again, she pulled it out of her pocket as she ran up the stairs, thinking of different naughty ways that she might wait for him. When she reached the top she eagerly unlocked the door, more than excited to spend more time in his warm embrace.

But when she opened the door wide with a smile on her face, it was only to find an empty apartment.

Completely empty.

It was all gone. Everything.

The easel. His canvases. Even the few drinking glasses he'd had in the kitchen and the one towel he'd had hanging on the rack.

She walked around like a zombie, not believing what she was seeing. There was no note. No sign of his existence.

She finally made her way into the bedroom, afraid to look.

The bed was gone, too.

Lily backed slowly out of the room as if she were in a trance. She shuffled backward blindly, shaking her head in disbelief. It wasn't until her back hit the opposite wall in the hallway that her knees gave out. Sliding down the wall until she was crumpled on the floor at the top of the stairs, she choked on the sobs as they stuck in her throat, her vision becoming one messy blur as her eyes filled with rivers of tears.

The
Blank Canvas
Book Two

For Luke
Who stood by me through rewrite after rewrite
and was convinced that all it needed was more cock

Thanks for the suggestion, babe.

1

Lily had no idea what time it was.

She had been lying there on the hallway floor for the better part of the evening, barely noticing when the light began to dim through the windows. Her eyes were swollen and red, completely drained of any moisture, and her top lip was puffy and sore from being contorted into various shapes as she wailed out her heartbreak.

He was gone.

Her beautiful Ethan had left, taking everything with him, including her heart.

When she was finally able to process anything other than that, she thought back to their good-bye that morning and wanted to smack herself for not seeing the signs. He had been so insatiable, so clingy. It had been his body's way of preparing to let her go.

That thought only set off another round of dry sobs, causing her to clutch her chest at the pain of knowing he would never be in her arms again. Her entire body felt sore and raw, and in the back of her mind she wondered how long she could curl up there before someone came looking for her.

Suddenly, an obnoxious noise broke through her lament, and after a few moments of looking around hopefully, she realized that it was coming from her pocket—and she recognized the ringtone. Fishing it out quickly and sitting up in the darkness, she lifted it to her ear and answered.

"Hello?" she croaked.

"Whoa, babe, did I wake you up?" Scott chuckled on the other end.

"No," she replied gruffly, "why?"

"You sound like hell, that's why. Is something wrong?"

"No, I just…think I might be coming down with a cold or something," she lied quickly, coughing a few times to clear her throat. "What did you need?"

"Oh, well, I was finally able to get some free time tonight. Dad fell asleep earlier than I thought he would, so he's not barking in my face anymore." Lily knew he really meant Sam Walker had passed out drunk exceptionally early that night. "Did you still want me to come over?"

Lily glanced through the open doorway into the dark living room and was hit with a fresh wave of panic. Panic that her horrible crying jag was going to be the last memory she ever had of this wonderful, crappy old apartment. She didn't want that, but she had no idea what to do about it. At that point, her body was so frazzled and exhausted that she could barely think straight.

"Well…" She didn't even want to think about seeing Scott at that point, but she'd promised herself that she would end things with her fiancé as soon as possible rather than keep him dangling any longer. She figured that she already had her heart ripped out, so how much worse could the day get? Might as well tackle things while she was feeling numb. "Yeah, that's fine. Only I'm not at home. Why don't you head over to the house and I'll meet you there?"

"Okay, sure. See you in a bit."

Less than fifteen minutes later, Lily pulled into her driveway only to find that Scott had beaten her there and was sitting on the front steps with his head hung low, looking like a scolded child awaiting his punishment.

As she walked toward him, she couldn't stop from thinking about all of his good qualities that she was about to throw away. Scott was sensible. He was dependable. He would never leave her without looking back. He wanted to marry her. Scott was quite possibly the best offer she would ever get.

I could try to be better, Lily thought to herself in a brief flash of doubt. She could refocus her attention and be more enthusiastic. She could be the woman he deserved.

But she also knew that no matter how hard she tried for him, *she* would be miserable—and living a lie.

"Hey, babe," he said quietly when she had reached the bottom of the steps. "So how mad are you?"

"I'm not mad at all," she replied.

"Really?" he said with a smile, jumping off the steps to sweep her up in a huge bear hug. "Mmm, you smell good. God, I missed you."

Lily couldn't help thinking that she smelled good because she had foolishly showered off every remaining trace of Ethan's scent. Now she would never smell him deep in her skin again. She'd never be able to curl into his pillow and fall asleep while she breathed him into her.

"Um, thanks." She forced a tight smile as he put her down, shoving her rogue thoughts back into the dark corners of her mind before they made her cry again.

"Okay," he sighed at her tone. "Let me have it. You *are* pissed at me, aren't you? Be honest."

"No. Honestly, I'm not." The truth was she had barely remembered he even existed while he was gone.

"Well, pissed or not, I'm sorry that I was gone so long." He reached up and stroked the back of his fingers down her cheek. It was a gesture she used to find endearing, but now it only made her want to jump away. His fingers weren't the right fingers.

"I believe you," she said stiffly. "Let's go inside." She unlocked the door and held it open for him as he followed her into the house.

"I don't have any excuse, really," he admitted, a slight blush tinting his cheeks. "It just felt so damn good to be of use at that shop. Does that make any sense?" He looked at her quickly for confirmation before continuing. "Those were some great guys, Lil. I mean, I really like Ryan and the gang, but there just isn't enough work here to keep us all busy, you know? I really felt in my element there." He thought for a minute before adding, "They seemed really sorry to see me go. It was...nice, I guess. First time I felt like a real mechanic."

"That's great, Scott." She smiled again, and it was her first genuine smile of the night. She couldn't remember the last time she'd seen him this excited about anything, including her.

"So, where were you when I called?" he finally asked, glancing around after the room grew quiet.

"Well..." Lily took a deep breath. "I just found out that the apartment over the dance studio is available again."

"Available for what?" he sneered. "Demolition?"

"It's not that bad," she said, fidgeting nervously. "The right furniture could really make it a cute place."

"I don't know if I could ever picture anything cute there, sorry."

"Well, I think it's full of...*potential*." She wanted to say memories— vivid memories that lived in every corner of the room. Quick flashes shot through her mind: Ethan, shirtless and painting... Ethan, rolling around on the floor with her after smearing her body with colors... Ethan, preparing her lovingly for something she would never trust another man enough to do.

"Eh," he shrugged, sitting down in her dad's recliner with a practiced movement.

"Well, I'm going to take it," she said decisively.

"You *can't* be serious."

"Why?" she demanded.

"Well, it's right over that damn dance studio, for one, and you know you would hear a bunch of old farts doing the two-step all night."

Lily knew for a fact that he was wrong: you could hear lovers doing the waltz. She shut her eyes against the onslaught of memories as Scott continued. "Second, it's a dump! It probably looks like some squatter's paradise, or a crack house!"

"Oh, whatever! It's nowhere near that bad." She rolled her eyes, unable to hide her frustration.

"Lily, I really don't understand why you want the place."

"I thought it would make a nice apartment for me," she whispered. "I'm tired of living with my dad. I need my own space." What she didn't say was that she needed to keep just one last piece of Ethan alive.

"*What?* That doesn't even make any sense!" he bellowed, standing up again so he could look her in the eye. "Why the hell would you get an apartment—especially that piece of shit—so soon before the wedding? Why would you bother moving out now when we're only going to move to my house after we get married?"

Lily stopped pacing around anxiously and stared at him, her expression as shocked as if he'd slapped her in the face. She'd been about to tell him that she was getting an apartment because there wouldn't *be* a wedding, but his words interrupted that train of thought.

"Excuse me—what did you say? We're going to do *what?*"

"Move to my house?" He said as if it were a question, unable to see why she was so upset.

"And when, exactly, did *we* decide that?"

"That's what I've always planned for us. You knew that."

"Uh, no, I most definitely did not!" she snapped. "Where the hell did you picture us living all this time, the garage?" It wasn't even about her getting the apartment anymore; she was absolutely livid that he'd been planning their entire life for them for over a year and never once said a word about it.

"No, in my house. My room is big enough for us."

"Scott, your room isn't big enough for *you*!" Suddenly she realized what he was really saying, and she sucked in a breath. "Wait a minute—you thought we would live with your *father*?!"

"Who the hell is gonna take care of him if we don't?" he screamed, his own emotions bubbling to the surface. Sam was always a sore spot with Scott, a burden he chose to carry through life even though it made him miserable.

"How about rehab, for starters?" she yelled back, knowing that she was treading in dangerous waters, but not caring anymore. She knew that she was striking out in pain and anger, and it had probably been the worst possible time to start this conversation, but the dam had broken and she wasn't going to keep quiet anymore.

"Don't go there," he said with a warning tone in his voice.

"Oh, I think it's *way* past time that I went there, Scott."

She felt the truth in her words the moment they left her lips. She knew now, without any remaining doubt, that she really did need to end it, even without the beautiful new man who had interrupted her life. This wasn't going to work, no matter how much she might try to force it. She couldn't go through life smiling and nodding blankly while she was hollow on the inside.

"You know what my dad's like," he stated simply, as if that was all the explanation she needed. She did know what Sam was like, and she also knew that Scott was only going to grow more bitter by the day if he kept letting himself be a slave to his father—just as she had let herself become one to George. At least her father was somewhat gracious about it; the only thing Sam knew how to do was bark orders and get drunk.

"Yeah, I do. And I know you need to get the hell out of there before you become just like him."

"I can't just abandon him like that, Lily! I'm all he has left!"

"Well that's only because your mother was smart enough to take off! Why should you be stuck with your life on hold?"

"I'm not stuck—I'm helping him. He needs me. And don't bring my mother into this," he growled.

"Scott!" She threw her hands up in exasperation. "Your father was an abusive, overbearing jerk to her until she finally gave up and left. And you know what? I don't blame her! Your dad is a prick! He always was, even before the stroke!"

Scott reached out and grabbed her by the arms roughly, shaking her as he screamed in her face. "Don't you dare fucking bring up the stroke! My dad lost everything after that! His dignity, his wife! I'm the only one he's got!"

Refusing to be silent in the face of his rage, Lily kept going. "So because he ruined his body with meth and emotionally abused your mother so much she abandoned her own son to save herself, you're bound to him forever?"

"Shut up!"

"No, I won't," she said more calmly than she felt. "Just because she made the mistake of leaving you here with him doesn't mean that you are stuck here forever. I understand wanting to help him through a hard time, but he has done nothing in all these years but get worse! Why do you think my father can't stand to be around him anymore? They used to be best friends, for God's sake, and now whenever I mention Sam's name my dad gets sad. He tried so hard to talk him into getting help. It broke his heart to watch him become what he is today. When your mother left, that was the last straw. I think he's always blamed himself for not doing more for you. Hell, I'm pretty sure that's why he wants us to get married so badly."

"What is that supposed to mean?"

"It means that he loves you like a son, and he's hoping that I'll scoop you up and take care of you the way that I took care of him. I'm pretty sure he's hoping that I'd get you *out* of that situation, not get myself sucked into it."

"But it would be better with you there, I just know it. My dad likes you! He's on his best behavior when you're there. And you're a nurse. You could help me take care of him."

"Are you even *listening* to yourself? Do you hear what you're saying?" Lily couldn't believe that after she'd spent so much time dreaming of a life in which she wasn't waiting on someone hand and foot, her own fiancé had been planning on signing her up for indentured servitude.

He let go of her and stepped back, dropping his gaze to the floor. When he spoke again, it was a quiet whisper. "You're acting like I'm some kind of monster just because I want to help my dad."

Lily felt her heart go out to him, finally seeing just how confused and misguided he had become. Closing the gap between them, she hugged him and put his head on her shoulder. Stroking his hair, she sighed before finally speaking.

"Scott, you're not a monster. You love him, I know that. But what you're doing now isn't helping him. He needs *real* help, not the kind you can give him. And if he refuses that, there's no reason you should throw your life away making runs to the liquor store for him and helping him to bed every night. And it's totally unfair to expect me to throw my life away."

"Then what? What do I do? I thought I had everything worked

out, but now I don't have a clue." She could hear him swallowing a lump in his throat. "I really thought you were the answer." He seemed to finally understand.

"I know," she whispered. "But this just isn't right. I think you know that now as much as I do."

He looked at her, slowly reaching up to cup her chin. "I really do love you, you know."

"And I love you. I always have. But I don't think either one of us feels the kind of love we're supposed to feel. We're like best buddies. You deserve to go somewhere and find a girl who will love you with her whole heart."

"But everything is so much easier with you," he chuckled. "We hardly ever fight and you put up with my shit."

Lily smiled softly, but her eyes were sad. "That's because there's no passion between us, sweetie. I know that now." Her mind flashed through so many heated encounters with Ethan that she lost count. "When that kind of passion is there, it makes the fighting and nagging worth it, because the good times are so much better."

"I've never had that before," he said quietly. "I just thought that we clicked so well that it had to work."

"We would have been comfortable, but deep down we both would have been bored to death."

"Yeah, you're probably right." He looked at her for a moment before leaning down and kissing her softly. They both knew it was nothing more than a friendly gesture, the comfort of a good friend. "So what happens now?"

Lily reached into her pocket and pulled out the ring she had hardly ever worn. "You should have this back," she whispered, holding her open hand out to him. "You saved up a long time for it. I'm sure you could use the money for a fresh start."

"Wow," he sighed, taking the ring from her small hand. "I can't believe this is really happening." He turned it over in his huge fingers, watching the slight sparkle from the small stone. "Do you really think I can start over?"

Lily stood up on her tiptoes, kissing him soundly on the cheek. "Absolutely. I think you can do anything you set your mind to. You just have to try."

"Thanks, Lil."

"Thank you for understanding."

A little over an hour later, Lily sat alone in her father's kitchen. She still felt completely raw, as if her entire body had been turned inside out, but she was pleased to notice a new lightness in her chest. She hadn't realized just how much the guilt of stringing Scott along had been weighing her down, and she was happy that they were able to end things so amicably.

A part of her wondered if she should have come clean about her affair, but she couldn't find any reason to hurt him more than necessary. If it had come down to it—if he hadn't been so understanding and had demanded another reason—she would have told him. But as it was, she was just happy it was finally over. She knew that telling him anything more now would only serve to lessen her guilt, and in her mind that guilt was her own punishment to bear.

She looked around the dark kitchen, food the furthest thing from her mind, and wondered what she was going do now. She had finally started down a new path, but she wouldn't be able to spend it with the person she cared most about. Sighing deeply, she pushed back her tears and forced herself to think about the topic at hand.

George.

She knew he would be home any minute, so she spent what quiet time she had left preparing herself for the inevitable confrontation.

He walked into the kitchen about ten minutes later, surprised to find her waiting for him in a silent house with a mug of hot cocoa in her hand. It was still fairly full, since her diminished appetite had only allowed her a few sips, but she figured it might be helpful to have something to do with her hands during the upcoming conversation.

"Lil?" he asked, sensing something was up. "What's going on?"

"Pull up a chair," she said as calmly as possible, trying to keep her voice from wavering.

"All right," he said hesitantly. Once he was seated across from her, he sighed loudly. "Want to tell me what this is all about?"

"Listen. I have some news, and I don't think it should wait."

"Are you pregnant?" he asked, a slight enthusiastic edge to his voice.

"No!" she gasped. "God, no! Why on earth would you think that?"

"Well, you said you had news. Forgive me for jumping to conclusions. So? Whatcha got for me?"

Lily took a deep breath. "I'm moving out."

There was a beat of silence. "Oh," he replied quietly. "So soon?"

"Soon? Dad, it's been three years."

"I know. I guess I just figured you two would wait until closer to the wedding. So, where are you guys going to live?"

"Actually, that's the other part of my news. I'm moving out alone. The engagement is off."

"Are you all right?" he asked quickly. "What happened? Did you fight? Did he hurt you? Do I need to kick his ass?"

"Slow down, Dad. Take a breath."

"Tell me what happened, Lil."

"We ended it."

"Care to be more specific?" George asked sarcastically.

"We both agreed that we aren't the right people for each other. There wasn't any one thing that happened, Dad. We aren't mad at each other, there was no big fight. We just aren't together anymore."

"Not right for each other?" he yelled. "What are you talking about? You two are a perfect couple!"

"Not even close, Dad."

"I just don't get it," George sighed, running his hands through his hair. "He's a great kid, Lily. He's always treated you well."

"If you love him so much, why don't *you* marry him, then?" she snapped, regretting it instantly when he winced. "Listen, I'm sorry. I didn't mean that. But you're supposed to care about what I want and need, and it's not Scott. It hasn't been for a long time, and I finally found the courage to admit it to him. I didn't think we had any business getting married when we just weren't in love."

"But he loved you. That was easy to see."

"Yes, he loved me. And I loved him. But it wasn't the right kind of love, Dad. I hope you understand because I need that to be enough for you."

"I'm sorry, this is just a lot to take in. You swear you're okay?"

"Yes, I'm fine. And so is Scott, don't worry. I know you care about him. You can still hang out with him whenever you want. I won't mind. But I'm not going to be here to bust my ass making you both dinner anymore."

"You mean you're still moving out? Why?"

"Dad, really? I'm almost thirty, single, and living with my father. It's time for me to be on my own."

"But...but who's gonna help me out around here? You know my leg still bothers me."

"Your leg is fine. You've just gotten used to having me wait on you hand and foot, and now you don't like the thought of going back to what it was like before. Well, if I remember correctly, you used to whine and moan when I first moved in, telling me over and over again how you somehow managed to get by on your own for over twenty years without my help. Now's your chance to prove it."

Lily could see him blinking rapidly, and on closer inspection, she noticed that his eyes looked watery.

"That's not it," he whispered, swallowing a lump in his throat. "I'll be fine. I admit I've gotten a little lazy, but I think I can remember how to use the microwave. It's just that I'm really going to miss you around here. I love you, Lil."

She could probably count on one hand how many times she had heard her father say that.

"I love you, too. And it's not like I'm going back to Minnesota and you'll never see me again. I'm just moving into an apartment across town. I'll even have you over for Sunday breakfast someday."

"I guess that's not so bad," he said. Lily watched as his thick mustache twitched at the corners, eventually turning up into a smile. "At least you'll finally get those damn cats out of here."

"Hey! Don't knock the Fraggle twins. I know you secretly love them."

After a few uncomfortable moments of silence he glanced at his watch. "I should probably be getting to bed. I have to be at the school early tomorrow." He stood up from the table, wiping at his eyes quickly when he thought she wasn't looking. As he turned to leave, he stopped and looked at her one more time. "Are you sure you're going to be okay, kiddo?"

"Yeah, Dad. I think everything is going to be just fine."

She almost believed it.

After George went to bed, she slowly made her way upstairs and got ready to turn in herself. It wasn't until she was settled underneath the covers that she finally lost control of her thoughts, allowing all of the memories to come flooding back again.

Ethan, holding her tightly in the dark, stroking her bare shoulders and kissing her softly.

Ethan, waking her up in the middle of the night with his wandering fingers.

Ethan, smiling and laughing as she tickled him playfully.

When she couldn't take any more, Lily rolled over onto her side and cried herself to sleep.

2

———

"Jesus Christ, Lily, would you just pick one already?" Emma slurred as she drummed her manicured nails impatiently on the coffee table.

"Seriously!" Maggie groaned from the other end of the table.

"Hey, lay off! I rolled exactly the right number to try for another pie piece, but I don't know which color I should choose. Pink is my favorite category, but I gotta get that fucking green one out of the way. I hate Science & Nature. I always blank on the answer, even when I know it."

"Lily, everyone loves pink," Emma chided. "Entertainment is the easiest category."

"Speak for yourself, bitch. I like sports."

"Oh shut it, Maggie. We can't all be married to the NFL." Maggie stuck out her tongue childishly at Emma before tipping back her margarita and slurping loudly. Emma flipped her the bird and looked back across the table without losing her focus.

"All right, Lily, *today!*"

"Fine, pink. Do it before I change my mind." Lily finished the rest of her drink as Emma fished out another card from the box.

"Okay," Emma cleared her throat before continuing. "In the Steve Martin remake of *Father of the Bride*, what was the final head count at his daughter's wedding?"

"Five hundred and seventy-two," Lily answered without even blinking.

"Holy shit!" Maggie blurted, almost spitting out her drink.

"How the hell did you know that?" Emma asked, her mouth still hanging open.

"Girls, let me tell you, if it's a movie that I was remotely interested in when I was younger, I can probably quote the entire thing to you. I just have this strange knack for remembering useless bullshit, and movies were one of my favorite ways to kill time. Now shut up and give me my pink pie piece," Lily teased, holding her hand out across the table toward Emma, who had announced at the beginning of the game that she always hands out the pie pieces.

"All right, Rain Man, don't get your panties in a wad," she laughed, handing her the tiny plastic triangle. "Maggie, you're next."

"Wait," Maggie replied, getting up from her kneeling position on the carpet. "I call break. We're out of margaritas and I really need to pee." She grabbed the empty pitcher and headed to her enormous kitchen, which currently looked like a disaster area, covered with bags and boxes of junk food.

The Foster girls knew how to do a girls' night right.

"Hey, how are you doing, Lily?" Emma whispered as soon as Maggie was out of earshot.

"Oh," she sighed, "I'm okay, I suppose. Every day goes by a little easier."

"Good." Emma smiled, reached over, and patted her hand. "I'm happy to hear that."

It had been over three weeks since Lily had started living on her own, and she had been in contact with one or both of the girls nearly every day from the beginning. It all started when she had tried to go in to work the Monday after Ethan left. Maggie had come in for some final blood work before going back to Chicago, and Lily took one look at her and promptly burst into tears.

It hadn't taken much prodding on Maggie's part to get her to admit why she was so upset, and as soon as she'd learned that Lily's "mystery man" had left her without one word of explanation, she was just about shooting flames out of her ears.

"That stupid, arrogant, selfish prick!" she snarled, grabbing her cellphone and scrolling through her speed dial violently.

"Who are you calling?" Lily asked, wiping her nose with the tissue Maggie had handed her. She appreciated Maggie sympathizing with her, but she hadn't expected such venom on her behalf.

"My idiot, shit-for-brains brother-in-law, that's who!"

"Oh my God, you know it's Ethan?!" Lily gasped, positive that she was in her own custom-made nightmare.

"Oh, please!" she snapped, pressing the SEND button and holding the phone to her ear. "You two were eye-fucking each other all night after dinner. It didn't take a genius to figure it out, Lily."

"What?! Wait, you can't call him!" She reached for the phone frantically.

"Why the hell not?"

"Because it was his decision. He obviously didn't want any more contact with me, or he would have left me his fucking number."

"Oh, bullshit! He's just being his typical broody, overdramatic self. I'm getting to the bottom of this right now." His voicemail picked up, and just as Maggie was about to repeat that entire sentence verbatim for Ethan to enjoy, Lily began to beg so pathetically that she stopped and looked at her.

"No! Please, no! Please, not right now, Maggie. Please! Not like this."

Maggie debated for a moment before finally ending the call. "Okay, fine. But this isn't over, and I make no promises about not talking to him."

"Duly noted. Just please let me deal with this my own way. I'm already better than I was yesterday, and I won't be able to put him out of my mind if you're talking to him right in front of me. Besides, I don't want him to think I went running to his family and tattled on him."

"All right, but you need some girl time. You need to be able to vent or cry or whatever girly shit you feel like doing, and we can't do that here. We're hanging out tonight, whether you like it or not."

And that was the beginning of Operation Cheer Up Lily.

Maggie and Emma spent the next weekend helping her decorate her new apartment, giving her a few pointers about curtains and knickknacks but otherwise allowing Lily to truly make it her own space for the first time in her life (aside from a veto that forbade the Flight of the Conchords posters from going up in the living room). They helped her find a good deal on a little loveseat and dining set, and the shitty little place had actually become damn near cozy.

After that, they made sure that one or both of them called her every day, keeping her occupied and laughing on the phone. It didn't stop the memories from coming back as soon as Lily hung up and tried to go to sleep, but she found that they were becoming less and less painful to remember. Nothing would change the fact that she missed him terribly, but it comforted her to know that one day she might be able to think of their time together with nothing but fondness.

The girls had whined and begged Lily for weeks, finally ganging up on her in a three-way Skype chat until she agreed to come to Chicago for the weekend. They spent all of Saturday dragging her around from store to store, forcing her to try on one new outfit after the next, as if she were their own personal My Size Barbie. When she'd finally had enough and vowed to happily vomit on the next thing they handed her, they grudgingly relented and dragged her back to Maggie's penthouse for margarita game night.

Now, only two rounds of *Trivial Pursuit* and three pitchers later, Emma did what Maggie made her promise not to do for the entire weekend: she brought up "the situation" and "He-Who-Must-Not-Be-Named."

"Oh shit!" she swore to herself, looking at Lily apologetically. "Is it okay that I asked how you're doing? I know I'm not supposed to mention anything about the situation, but I just had to make sure that you were feeling better about...you know, *him*."

Lily simply chuckled and shrugged. "Emma, he's your brother, not Voldemort! Don't think that you can't ever talk about him."

"Well, I just didn't want you to think I was being insensitive."

At that moment Maggie came back in the room with a full pitcher, shaking her head. "Dammit, Emma! You did it already, didn't you?"

"But she just said I could!" Emma whined before grabbing her glass and draining what was left, eager for a refill.

"Of course she did, you dolt! She's being nice! I told you not to make her uncomfortable," Maggie scolded as she sat back down on the carpet, crossing her legs Indian style and scooting up to the coffee table.

"Guys!" Lily interrupted, holding up her hands in front of them before they could get into it even further. When they were quiet, she continued. "I really don't mind. He's part of your family, and I'm a big girl. If you want to talk about your brother, there's no reason you should stop on my account."

"Yeah, but it's not like we ever used to talk about him that often before," Maggie explained. "We hadn't seen him for so long that I'd nearly forgotten all about him until that bitch left."

"Maggie!" Emma gasped.

"Oh, don't 'Maggie' me. You know damn well it's the truth. There is no reason we need to talk about Ethan any more now than we ever did before the last time he ran off and cut everyone out of his life. Don't get me wrong. I love the boy, and I will always be there for him if he ever pulls his head out of his ass again, but I don't think we need to keep bringing him up right now. He hurt our friend by being a selfish prick, and until he's ready to stop being one, I don't see what there is to talk about."

"But why does that make Rachel a bitch?"

"Oh, she's a cunt, Emma! You wouldn't believe *half* the shit that Eric told me about her after I pried it out of him. I promised him I wouldn't divulge the details—and it's a promise I intend to keep—but believe me when I say that leaving Ethan was probably the nicest thing she ever did for him."

After almost a full minute of silence, Emma finally whispered, "I *knew* it. I never did like her." She looked up at Lily and felt the urge to explain herself. "She was just so damn stuck up, always looked down her nose at everyone. But she was who my brother said he wanted."

"You guys really don't need to explain this stuff to me," Lily said, grabbing the pitcher and filling up their empty glasses. "I'm not asking or trying to pry. If you want to talk about him, talk about him. If you don't, then don't."

"But doesn't it hurt you even more?" Maggie asked, reaching out and grabbing her hand before she could pick up her glass.

"What do you want me to say? I'm not going to lie and say that I don't still miss him every day. Missing him hurts. Not having him in my arms at night hurts. Hearing about him—well, that also hurts, but it also lets me know that I didn't dream the whole damn thing. He really existed. For a short, beautiful time, an amazing man was in my life. I would never trade in those memories, even if it meant never feeling any pain."

"Are you more hurt, or angry?" Emma asked.

"What do you mean?"

"Well, be honest. You just uprooted your entire life, and it sounds like it was mostly triggered by him—by the hope of being with him.

And that very day, he disappears without a word to any of us. That's gotta piss you off just the littlest bit."

Lily thought for a moment before giving the most truthful answer she could manage. "Yeah, I suppose I'm angry. But if anything, I'm angry about how he went about it. I'd like to think I'd have more respect for him if he had the guts to tell me to my face that this wasn't what he wanted anymore. Without actually hearing it from him, I feel like it's not over, like maybe there's more going on under the surface. I hate feeling like I'm reading more into it than I should, and that makes me angry. I don't want to be one of those clingy girls who just can't take a hint. I mean, he left. Most people would get the message loud and clear, not lie around pining for him."

"Sweetie, I don't think you need to worry about that," Emma smiled. "It's not like you locked yourself away in your room for six months and stared out the window. You *are* getting on with your life. You moved out on your own, you aren't waiting hand and foot on everyone around you—hell, just you being here is a big deal. Getting you out of the house used to be like pulling teeth!"

"She's right, Lily," Maggie joined in. "You are becoming a new person. I always liked you before, but I really love who you have become. You're sassy and you don't take our shit, and that's just the kind of friend we need. It's inspirational to see you blossom like this." She smiled wickedly before adding, "In fact, the whole situation is inspirational. If your relationship had ended better, I totally would have stolen it for my next book. When I first figured out what was going on, my fingers were just itching to start typing!"

Lily rolled her eyes and sighed loudly. "Well maybe you can write me the happy ending that I didn't get."

"Would you take him back if he showed up tomorrow?" Emma asked.

"Jeez, Emma, we're trying to get her to move on from this topic, not beat her over the head with it."

"I want to know how she feels," Emma explained. "Besides, how can someone really learn and grow from an experience if they never really know how they felt about it?"

"Wow, that's almost profound," Maggie teased. "When did you get all deep and shit?" She hiccupped loudly, reminding them all of just how much they'd had to drink. Emma flipped her the bird again, and they all started laughing.

"I don't know," Lily finally said after some of the giggling had died down. "My pride tells me that I should tell him to shove it up his ass and slam the door in his face, but if it ever actually came to that, I really don't think I could do it."

"Aw, really?" Maggie pouted, her glorified image of *Lily the Superbitch* dashed in a heartbeat.

"I'm sorry, I can't help it. *He* ended it, not me. Just because he can apparently shut off his emotions in a split second doesn't mean that I can."

"You still love him, don't you?" Emma whispered.

"Of *course* I do," Lily groaned, dropping her head down on the table with a loud thud. "Ow." She rubbed at her forehead quickly before continuing. "I think what hurts the most is that I had just really come to terms with how much I loved him when he left, so now I'm all alone and missing him, wishing I had only told him sooner. I don't know if it would have mattered enough to make him stay, but at least I'd have the peace of mind knowing that I gave it my all. He was the first person to make me feel like I really had anything worth giving. I never found anything I wanted enough to fight for before him." She looked up when she realized how quiet it had become and found both women both staring at her, hanging on every word. "What?"

"That's kinda beautiful," Emma sighed.

"Yeah," Maggie nodded.

"Well, whatever it is, I can't just turn it off because he's gone. All I can do is get on with really living my life for once and hope that the pain will go away eventually. I know it will happen if I give it long enough and force myself to not obsess over it. But if he came back tomorrow?" She paused. "I think things would definitely have to be different than before, but deep down, I really just want him back. I want the chance to see if we are as good together as it felt like we'd be."

"Even after he did that to you?" Emma said in amazement.

"I think I get it," Maggie said sadly. "I think I'd be the same way if Eric ever left. I can't imagine him ever doing that, but if he was just suddenly gone, I wouldn't know what to do with myself. He's like the other half of me. Nothing would feel right until he was back."

"He's gone all the time, Maggie."

"It's not the same, Emma. That's work. We talk all the time and I know he's coming home to me when he's done. And I'm here with all of his things around me, always reminding me of him." She suddenly gasped and looked at Lily. "Oh man! I just got it!"

"What?" the other two said in unison, both startled at her sudden outburst.

"I just realized why you took that apartment."

"What do you mean?" Lily asked nervously.

"Well, I always thought it was a little creepy that you rented the same place where you used to hook up with him. No offense or anything—it's a totally cute place now—but it just didn't make sense to me why you would want to torture yourself like that."

"Do you care to share with the rest of the class?" Emma prompted, making a rolling gesture with her hand to signal her to continue.

"It's all she has left of him, Emma. I thought it was maybe some odd way that she was conquering her demons or something, but that's not it at all." She turned to look at Lily again. "It's just your only way to be near your other half, isn't it?"

"Pretty much," Lily sighed, hugging her knees to her chest. She didn't want to draw their attention to the oversized Aledo High School sweatpants and pullover she was wearing—the same thing she'd worn to bed every night since she'd found them in her laundry after Ethan had loaned them to her the morning after her drunken night of karaoke. She knew it probably wasn't healthy to become so attached to his clothes just to feel him around her at night, but she wasn't ready to give them up, and she silently hoped the girls wouldn't suddenly remember that she'd never even gone to Aledo High School. She also couldn't fake that she'd bought them recently if they noticed. Aledo High School didn't even exist anymore. It had merged with another school a few years back and become Mercer County High School, a fact that still irked a lot of former students.

Just then, Maggie's phone started playing "Mr. Big Stuff" from under a pile of scattered cheese popcorn. Her face lit up and she scrambled for it, wading through the junk food.

"Speak of the devil!" she smiled, answering it excitedly. "Hey, baby!"

"How are all my girls doing tonight?" Eric laughed, hearing the slight slur in his wife's words.

"We're doing margaritas, that's how we're doing!" she giggled, holding out the phone and waving at the others to say something.

"Hey, Eric!" They both yelled into the phone before Emma began making kissy noises in the background and Lily started making whip crack sounds. They loved teasing him about being whipped whenever he would call. Eric never forgot to call and check in, no matter how late it was or how short the call was. Neither one of them could sleep right if they hadn't spoken at least once that day.

"You bitches," he laughed, wishing he was in town and could witness their drunken antics.

"How's Denver, baby?" Maggie asked when she put the phone back up to her ear.

"Eh, you know, Broncos, Shmoncos. I miss Chicago."

"Well, Chicago misses you too. You'd be so proud, I totally kicked ass on all the sports questions in *Trivial Pursuit*."

"That's my girl! What have you guys been up to besides drunken trivia?"

"Oh, you know. Talking about the selfish prick."

"Ah...I knew Emma would bring him up. Is Lily doing okay?"

"Yeah," she answered, smiling at Lily as she spoke. "Turns out that our little girl is all grown up. She can talk about big girl things without me looking out for her every step of the way."

"I told you she could handle it, hon. She's got balls bigger than mine."

"Well, I don't know about *that*," Maggie purred.

"All right, that's my cue to hang up. I can't have you start talking sexy now or I'm gonna have to jerk it again before I go to sleep, and I'm fucking exhausted. Rain check?"

"Of course!" she smiled, clearly thinking of the fun they would have the next night when she was alone again. "I love you." The girls watched as she ended the call, but before she set the phone down on the table again she made a face as if remembering something and fired off a quick text message. "There," she said to herself as she set it back down.

"Forget to tell him something nasty?" Emma teased.

"Yeah, something like that."

3

On the East Coast, a loud beeping noise could be heard in a dark hotel room.

Ethan rolled over and swatted at the alarm, but as he reached for it he realized that the noise had already stopped. Peeling his eyes open slowly, he groaned when he saw that it was barely one in the morning.

"Fucking Maggie," he grumbled as he reached for his phone instead, realizing that it must be time for his nightly text. He wasn't pissed at the content of the texts—he'd gotten used to it—but he was frustrated that he had actually managed to fall asleep that night. It happened so rarely anymore.

His foggy brain was still swimming with flashes of warm brown and soft pink, so he sat up all the way and turned on the small table lamp, hoping to chase them away. As he looked around the dimly lit room, he could make out the various shapes of different canvases stacked along the wall, none of them finished. Looking at them disturbed him even more, so he forced his attention back to his phone and opened up that night's message.

Have I mentioned lately that you're a selfish prick?

"As a matter of fact, you have," he whispered to himself as he scrolled back through his very full inbox. When he had first left, he'd been bombarded with calls and text messages from his family, some of them wanting to know what had happened, others seeming to know way too much. Emma, Eric, Maggie, his mom and dad, and even Emma's husband, Brandon, whom Ethan hardly knew, had all chimed in:

OMG! Where R U? What happened?

You are such a prick. I know what you're running from, you chickenshit. Big Mistake.

Honey, are you OK? Your brother said you left town. Please call and let me know.

Dude, WTF? I thought you wanted this. I really wanna kick your ass right now.

Sweetheart, where are you? Just let me know you're all right.

Ethan! Stop ignoring me! I'm worried!

Prick.

Hey, I know we don't know each other well, but your sister is going batshit crazy worrying about you. Plz call her.

Son, you are breaking your poor mother's heart. Again.

You've made every woman I care about cry, including Lily. It's official. Next time I see you, I'm kicking your ass.

Asshole.

Your brother explained that you may be having some personal problems right now. I won't bother you, but if you need a good therapist, let me know.

The texts starting dwindling after he refused to answer them (or return any calls), but he found it almost touching that Maggie and Eric were still in it for the long haul.

Hope you're still alive, prick. You threw away the best thing you ever had, but I still don't wish you dead. Neither does she, surprisingly.

Get your shit together, bro. I miss you. We all do. Still punching you in the face, tho.

Ethan sighed loudly and hit DELETE, finally clearing out the messages that had been stacking up. He knew that one day soon he would need to get in touch with someone, but he'd been too busy hiding his head in the sand to worry about it yet. He kept one message, unable to get rid of it, and read it over a few more times.

Neither does she, surprisingly.

He couldn't stop reading that sentence, so he forced himself to exit his inbox and start in on the voicemails. As he listened to each member of his family yell at him in turn, he found his mind wandering yet again to some of the text messages.

It was apparent that some of his family members, if not all of them by now, had found out about their secret relationship. He wondered briefly if she had told them, but what would have been her aim? She clearly hadn't sought them out to get his phone number, because she was the one person who *hadn't* sent him texts and left him messages. He'd expected something from her by now—even a simple "fuck off"— and he didn't know what to make of the complete lack of contact.

He kept telling himself that he'd been dreading it, that he hadn't wanted to hear her screaming and crying at him. That he'd wanted her to move on quickly, to get back to her normal life so she could be happy. But no matter how many times he told himself those things, they never got any easier to believe.

He had been absolutely terrified when she told him what her intentions were. He couldn't imagine that she really knew what she wanted that easily. When he'd heard the words "I just want to be with you" come out of her mouth, he felt the most amazing rush of happiness, as if he could finally get everything that he had ever wanted.

But just as quickly, the panic set in.

How could he possibly deserve her? She was good in every way that he was horribly wrong. She had no idea what she was saying. How could anyone really want a man who could take such a sweet, innocent soul and corrupt her against everything she had ever known? Less than a month with him and she was ready to break up her impending marriage and most likely desert the only family she had in the area. All of this for a man with nothing but a history of selfishness, always putting himself before everyone else.

The thing that his dear sister-in-law didn't realize was that this was the most unselfish thing he'd ever done in his entire life.

Leaving Lily had been the hardest thing Ethan had ever forced himself to do. It was as if someone had placed the most glorious diamond in the palm of his hand and said it was his for the taking—

as long as he didn't care about ruining the lives of everyone it had ever come in contact with. And he had wanted it. Badly.

He had imagined scooping her up that very night, throwing her in his car and just driving until they ran out of gas, away from anyone they knew. If he asked, he knew that she would go. He saw himself dragging her to the first courthouse he could find for a quick elopement, then racing to the closest motel so that he could fuck her stupid for the next three days straight, maybe five, only stopping to eat—and when they ran out of food he would live on her sweat and her moans and her cries of pleasure.

And then it hit him: an image of his family, ashamed of him for stealing such a precious girl away from her family. That was quickly followed by a vision of Lily, lonely and scared, far away from home and bored out of her mind in a foreign country while he disappeared for days on end to paint. She had no one to talk to, and her father refused to speak to her ever again for what she had done. Ethan knew without a doubt that she would grow to hate him. She would blame him for wrecking everything, knowing that he had taken advantage of her naiveté so he could keep her as his own precious jewel.

He also knew without a doubt that seeing that look of hate in her eyes would kill him.

So he did the only thing he knew how to do.

He ran.

He ran away like the chickenshit Maggie called him, hoping that Lily would go back to the life that she had always known, the life she had been perfectly happy with before he bulldozed into it. He hoped that after a few weeks, she would forget all about him.

He just hadn't taken into account how hard it would be to forget *her*. He saw her everywhere, in every passing smile, every bubbly laugh—even the sunset had shades of gold that reminded him of the highlights in her hair. He also wasn't sleeping again, but this time, it wasn't because of Rachel's cruel departure. It was because of the lack of Lily's warmth in the dark, the smell of her sweet skin, the sound of her breathing softly as she slept.

He just fucking *missed* her.

He couldn't listen to his music anymore; every song made him think of her. If the lyrics were sad, all he could think of was how badly he wanted her to be there with him. If it was a happy tune, he would immediately think of the fun, playful times they had shared together. And he didn't even want to think about the sexy songs. Those opened up a floodgate of memories that kept him paralyzed with need for hours on end.

Of course, not being able to listen to his music had made painting nearly impossible. He couldn't focus—his thoughts were always leading back to her, and when he would step back and look at his canvas he would see her eyes or her lips or some other feature that his subconscious was fixating on at that given moment.

So now he had a large collection of half-finished paintings stacked up, all of them some version of Lily, all of them screaming at him to finish them properly and admit that he wanted nothing more than to be with the real thing. Just thinking of them made him glance across the room at the canvases before he could stop himself, which caused him to shut his eyes tightly and repeat his newest mantra over and over in his mind.

You did the right thing. You did the right thing. You put her before yourself for the first time. You weren't what she needed. You did the right thing.

It helped for the most part. Whenever he was hit with moments of doubt it usually calmed his nerves, but lately there had been times when he found himself doubting whether he actually *had* done the right thing.

He hadn't even asked her what she wanted; he'd simply decided what was best for her. When these thoughts struck him, he would try to convince himself that she was only infatuated with him, that there was no way she could have actually loved him, and then he would berate himself for assuming that he knew about love any better than she did. He'd never even been in love before, so what gave him the right to assume that his feelings were more honest and real than hers?

"Fuck!" he yelled out, throwing one of the wadded-up pillows next to him across the room. He couldn't stand the nagging feelings of doubt that were creeping in and taking over his brain. What if he had made a split-second decision based on fear, and rather than saving her from herself, he had sentenced her to a life with someone she truly didn't want? What if they were *both* miserable right now?

No, he thought to himself. *She will move on. She will marry that big oaf and have his babies and never think of you again.*

"God dammit!" he roared, chucking another pillow, this time knocking over a figurine on the mantle across the room and sending it to the floor where it shattered into a million tiny pieces. Just the thought of that fucking guy's hands anywhere near her body made him feel sick to his stomach.

He reminded himself that this was what he wanted for her, regardless of how horrible it was to think of her being with that Neanderthal. But what if she *didn't* end up with her fiancé? She was going to eventually let someone else touch her. A girl that passionate wouldn't be alone for long. She was going to be someone's wildest fucking dream come true when they realized what a firecracker she was. And she had only him to thank for tapping into the passion that was hidden deep down inside of her. He had left her there, all alone, ripe and ready for the plucking.

"Mine!" he growled loudly, chucking another pillow across the room.

The nights were the worst for Ethan.

All he wanted was to drift back to sleep and shut out all of his traitorous thoughts, even if it meant dreaming of her. But once he was tossing and turning and these thoughts set in, he knew that he would be up for the rest of the night. He glanced at his luggage across the room, eyeing the side pocket that contained his treasure, and mentally scolded himself, knowing it would never get any better for him if he kept depending on such a pathetic crutch.

Focusing instead on his voicemails again, he continued plowing through them, using all of his energy to keep his mind from wandering. His phone played them in reverse order, from most recent to oldest, and he listened to his family's anger morph backward to their initial worry. When he finally reached the last one, which must have come in right after he left, he expected more of the same and nearly dropped the phone when he heard the last thing he'd ever expected to hear again.

Lily's voice.

She wasn't calling him—her voice was muffled, like the phone was being held away from her—but he would know her voice anywhere.

"No! Please, no! Please, not right now, Maggie. Please! Not like this."

Click.

Somehow he had missed the message when it had first come in. Some of the others he'd heard already, before he'd started just flat-out ignoring them. All this time without her, and he'd had her voice right there in his phone the entire time.

He had no idea what the call was about. The only thing he could assume was that Maggie tried to call him to bitch him out when she'd first found out what had happened, and Lily must have been there.

She sounded so broken, so sad.

Stop! You did the right thing. You did the right thing.

He listened to the message again and again, barely letting it finish before starting it over. When he closed his eyes he could see her as clearly as if she were lying next to him, her long tresses spread out over the sheets as she smiled up at him. Before long the sound of her voice on the recording began to bleed into his imagination, and then his beautiful goddess was looking up at him with tears in her eyes, begging him for an explanation, begging him not to leave.

She was haunting him.

As much as it killed him to think of her like that, he couldn't bring himself to stop. He kept telling himself that he needed to forget her, but he missed her so fucking much that he knew he would take whatever small piece of her he could get to keep her alive in his memories—even if those memories were painful.

It felt as if part of him had been ripped away, as if he had somehow become an amputee. Glancing at his luggage once again, he sighed loudly, finally admitting defeat. Whenever that feeling showed up, he knew it was useless to fight it anymore.

Slowly getting out of bed and walking toward the bag in question, he quietly unzipped the side pocket, as if at any moment someone would hear and call him out for being the pathetic, perverted loser that he truly was. Pulling the item out quickly, he returned to bed, clutching his prize to his chest as he reached for his phone.

Pressing PLAY yet again, Ethan lay back on the only remaining pillow, listening to her scared, sad voice on repeat until he finally fell asleep, a dark blue scrap of lace knotted in his fist.

4

As the natural light began to fade from the windows, Ethan looked up from his canvas and saw that it was already after 7:00 p.m. He couldn't remember the last time he'd even glanced at the clock, and the loud growl in his stomach indicated he certainly hadn't eaten.

Without moving his eyes away from his latest project, he backed away slowly until his legs bumped into the small desk behind him that held the phone. Dialing the extension from memory, he quickly ordered up a pot of coffee and a turkey sandwich, not wanting anything that would take his attention away from his painting for longer than a few bites. He knew he should probably have gotten something more substantial, but considering he had gone almost three days on an empty stomach, he figured that anything was better than nothing.

Within a heartbeat he was back in front of his easel, swirling and streaking different colors across the stretched fabric. Zoning out in front of his paintings had become his typical day for...how many days? He couldn't remember. All he knew was that he had finally given himself over to his body's driving need to paint, and he had gone back and finished every single piece he'd started, as well as many new ones.

The last time he could remember being so focused and immersed in his work, he'd been on a four-day bender and Rachel had only interrupted him to refill his nose candy. But this time felt completely different. He wasn't rushing to meet a deadline or trying to impress anyone. This time, he had somehow found his own world...his own version of paradise filled with nothing but memories of Lily...and he never wanted to leave.

In what felt like less than five minutes but was likely closer to twenty, there was a loud knock on the door. Swearing to himself under his breath for not thinking to unbolt the damn thing in advance so that room service could just come in without his needing to stop, Ethan set his palette and brush down and made his way across the room. Feeling through his empty pockets as he walked, he grumbled even louder as he reached his destination.

"I hope I can sign your tip on the room, man," he called to the door as he reached for it. "I'm all out of cash."

"Oh, I'm sure we can work something out," a deep, menacing voice answered as Ethan pulled back the door to reveal a very large, very angry looking man.

Ethan stared for a moment, blinking, not believing who he was seeing.

"Eric?" he whispered.

The large man allowed an evil grin to spread across his features before replying. "Hey, bro."

And then he proceeded to pull back one of the biggest fists that Ethan had ever seen and pound it straight into the side of his face.

Before he could even register the sickening thud, Ethan saw sparks flash in his vision as he was catapulted across the room, landing flat on his back as the world went dark around him.

The sound of clinking china was the first thing Ethan registered.

As he opened his eyes slowly to get his bearings, he noticed two other things right away. One: only his right eye was cooperating with him and no matter how hard he tried to open his left, it just wouldn't budge. And two: he was flat on his back on the carpet while Eric was sitting at the small table above him, apparently drinking his room service coffee.

He tried to shift so that he could sit up, but the action only sent a wave of pure agony straight to his face. His loud groan sounded more like a wounded animal than a man, but it simply made Eric smile wider as he poured himself another cup.

"Awww," he teased. "Does the widdle baby got a booboo?" Ethan peered up at him through the one eye that wasn't already swelling shut, causing a ridiculous winking expression that set Eric off into a fresh fit of laughter. "Dude, you look like Popeye!"

"Fuck you," Ethan grunted out through clenched teeth as he finally struggled into a sitting position, propping himself up with his hands on the floor behind his back.

"Oh, fuck *me*?" Eric raised an eyebrow sharply as he looked at the disheveled man in front of him. "Let's not start with that, my friend. My 'fuck you' list is longer. I'll win." He stared him down for a moment before chuckling again. "Besides, I took it easy on you. That was only about half power."

"Bullshit," Ethan whined. "I feel like my face is on fire. Everything's swelling up." He slowly pulled himself up by the edge of a chair and sat down on the other side of the table, gingerly prodding at his sore cheek with the tips of his fingers.

"Not my fault you're a lightweight, bro." Eric slurped loudly from the tiny china cup and merely winked when Ethan flipped him off.

"How did you find me?" Ethan asked after settling back into his chair with a groan.

Eric sighed deeply before finally setting the cup down. "You think the NFL has never had to track down some asshole player on a bender? We have our ways." He meticulously unfolded a linen napkin as he spoke, scooping up a large handful of ice from a bucket before wrapping it up and handing it to him. "Here. Put this on your eye. It's still gonna be an ugly son of a bitch, but it should help with some of the pain and swelling."

"Thanks," Ethan grunted, gingerly applying the makeshift icepack to his cheekbone.

"Anyway," he continued, "I knew that New York was the last city you were living in before Rachel took off. When one of the Giants needed help after a torn ACL this week, I thought there might actually be a chance of finding your dumb ass."

"Oh."

"Yeah, 'oh.' Did you think that none of us would find you or did you just think that nobody would ever bother looking?"

"Nobody ever did before," he said quietly.

"Well that's because you acted like a pompous shithead who had no time for his family," Eric gritted out between clenched teeth, years of resentment spilling out. "We didn't want to bother you when you made it more than clear that your lives were much too fabulous for us," he mocked.

"But that's not—"

"Yeah, yeah, yeah," Eric interrupted, waving him off. "That's not how it ended up. I know that *now*, but that's sure as shit how it started out," he sighed. "Believe me, I wish that bitch were still around so I could put my boot up her ass for putting you through that, but none of us would have let you go on that way if we'd had one fucking inkling of how depressed you really were. Shit, Mom would have backpacked through Europe with attack dogs if she'd known what was going on."

Ethan stared down at the table, unable to meet his brother's eyes. Eric was totally right. If he hadn't allowed Rachel to feed his already overgrown ego, things never would have gotten as bad as they'd become. If he'd only forced himself to speak up when he first had his doubts, things might have turned out completely different.

"Here, eat something," Eric said, an odd catch in his throat as he looked at Ethan closely for the first time since he'd barged in. He shoved the untouched turkey sandwich toward him across the tabletop. "You look like hammered shit."

Ethan knew he must. There were dark rings underneath his eyes from numerous sleepless nights, and his skipped meals had caused his cheekbones to protrude. His skin had taken on a sallow hue from his lack of sunlight and fresh air, and he couldn't remember when he last showered.

They sat together for over a minute in total silence as Ethan ate, wincing at the pain in his face every time he had to chew. When he swallowed his food, Eric could have sworn his Adam's apple would slice right through his throat as it bobbed up and down, his neck had gotten so thin.

Clearing his throat nervously, he forced himself to speak. "All right, fuck it. I'm just gonna ask. Are you strung out?"

"I beg your pardon?"

"Cut the bullshit, Ethan!" he roared, slamming his fist down on the table and causing the fragile teacup to rattle on its saucer. "Are you fucked up right now, or not?"

"Why would you think I was fucked up?"

"Because I have eyes!" he yelled. "You look horrible! You've lost weight! You obviously haven't been sleeping. I saw all those canvases in the other room. You've been working yourself to the bone! As soon as you disappeared I got worried that you were going to fall off the wagon. I've been fucking terrified for almost three goddamn months that you were going to turn up dead!" He grabbed the small rattling cup and threw it against the wall; it shattered into tiny pieces. "Now, are you actually going to sit there looking like that and tell me that you're not snorting that fucking poison again?"

"It's been three *months*?" Ethan whispered.

"You *see*?" Eric bellowed. "You don't even know what fucking day it is, do you? How about the month?"

Ethan looked down at the table in silence, trying to remember whether the cleaning staff had changed the sheets yesterday or not. He had told them that he didn't want to be disturbed more than a few times a week, so they had set up a schedule to clean on Mondays, Wednesdays, and Fridays only. After wading through caffeine-induced moments of clarity, he concluded that no one had been in his room for two full days.

"Is it Sunday?" he guessed.

"Jesus Christ, man. You really aren't sure, are you?"

Ethan took a deep breath and looked up to meet his brother's angry glare. "I'm not high, Eric." When Eric made to stand up and began pulling his fist back, Ethan waved his hands in front of him. "Wait! Wait! Hear me out!"

"Start talking, asshole. You've got about thirty seconds before *both* of your eyes are swollen shut."

"I swear I'm not high. I haven't touched that shit in well over a year. I can't lie and say that I'm not a little strung out, I guess, but it's not drugs."

"Then what the fuck is it?"

"It's *her*," he choked out.

"Who, Lily?"

Ethan visibly flinched at hearing her name again, as if he'd been slapped in the face. Unable to speak, he simply nodded, a deep look of anguish etched on his features.

"What the—?" Eric started, cutting himself off and breathing deeply before finishing his thought. He was determined to calm down and get some answers out of his halfwit brother if it killed him. "Why the fuck did you break her heart and take off if you were only going to hole up here and pine away for her?"

Ethan let out a loud sob, reaching forward and grabbing onto Eric's wrist with all of his strength. "Please," he begged in a harsh gasp, "Please tell me that I did the right thing."

"The *right thing*? How could anything that you've done lately be called the 'right thing?'" Eric clearly wasn't trying to be hurtful with his question—it was simply honest bafflement speaking.

"Tell me that she forgot about me and married that guy. Tell me that she's happy and moving on with her life. Tell me that I didn't give her up for *nothing*!" His last word was strangled by another sob. Eric watched as his brother completely broke down in front of him, burying his head in his hands and finally allowing the dam that held back the last of his emotions to shatter.

"Dude, I don't understand anything you're saying. I thought you were into her. You were just talking about wanting her to end her engagement and then the second she says she will, you bail. I'm sorry, but that makes no fucking sense whatsoever."

"I got *scared*!" he yelled into his hands before looking up at him. "I was convinced that there was no way she could be feeling what I was feeling. I was terrified that she would give everything up to be with me and then realize that I'm not fucking worth it!" Ethan wiped blindly at his eyes with the back of his hands, yelping when he rubbed his bruising flesh too roughly. Taking another deep breath to calm himself, he waited a moment before continuing. "I didn't want her to ruin her life to be with me. I've been a selfish fuck my whole life, Eric. This was the first time I've ever tried to put someone else first. I knew she would eventually be miserable with me, so I took myself out of the equation."

"So you've been here this whole time, wanting and missing her and wishing you'd never left, but trying to sacrifice your happiness for hers? Am I hearing this right?"

"Yeah," he sniffled.

"Then why did you ignore all of us? You could have told us that a long time ago and spared us the worry that you were going to turn up dead any day!"

"I'm sorry! It's just that, after the dinner party, I saw how much you all loved her. Here was this sweet, young, lovable girl who only ever wanted to help people, and I was corrupting the shit out of her. I had her ready to throw away everything she knew for me and I fucking loved it!" he admitted. "I was so consumed by her. She was all I wanted. And when she told me that she was going to end her engagement, I had this flash of all of your faces being really pissed at me and being ashamed of me for letting you down again. And you know what scared me the most?"

"What?"

"I didn't even fucking care! I heard her say those words and even though I knew how disappointed everyone would be in me, all I wanted was to pick her up and throw her over my shoulder and disappear into the sunset and forget about everyone else."

"So, what stopped you?"

"Don't you see? I was doing it all over again. I was being the selfish prick who never thought about anybody else but himself. I stayed in town after Dad's party to try and find a way back into the family. I missed everyone so much, but it was all so different after being gone for so many years. I felt so much shame about what I had let my life become, and there I was getting ready to do it all over again! I just couldn't face you guys after that. I just couldn't."

"Ethan, when are you going to get over this crazy delusion that Mom and Dad are going to disown you or something? I've done a lot of stupid shit in my life and they have always been there for me. So you dated a total bitch and got hooked on booger sugar—so what? You're still their son, and they will always love you. The same goes for me and Emma." He thought for a moment and chuckled to himself. "Shit, I'd really like to keep beating the crap out of you for this, but it doesn't make me love you any less."

Ethan couldn't hold back a smile at that, no matter how much his face ached. It was short-lived, however; the moment his thoughts returned to Lily, he began to choke up again. "I don't know how to fucking exist without her, man. I know it sounds stupid. I hardly knew her. We spent less than a month together!"

"But you don't feel right when you're alone in your bed at night, do you?" he asked knowingly.

"No! I can't even sleep! She's everywhere. She's haunting me."

"You think about her all day, and if you manage to fall asleep, she's in your dreams, too."

"Yes! Why can't I shake it? Why can't I let her go? I keep telling myself that with enough distance and time, I will finally be able to focus again, but it's only getting worse! Fuck, detox didn't hurt this bad."

"That's *love*, bro," Eric answered simply. "I tried to tell you that. You finally got bitten by the Foster bug. I don't know what it is about us, but we don't love lightly—or gently. Look at me and Maggie. There are times I think I could strangle her with my bare hands, she gets under my skin so bad, but I couldn't fucking function without her in my life. She's like my oxygen. She's really my other half, and whenever I have to leave her for work, I feel like I've been ripped in two."

"That's how I feel, and it scares the shit out of me! There's no way she could have felt anything like that for me, even if she was having a good time. That's why I've been hoping she got married, and at least something good came from my leaving."

"Ethan, pull your head out of your ass!" Eric yelled, his frustration reaching a breaking point.

"Huh?"

"That is not what you want, and you know it! You just want to be able to not feel guilty for leaving her that way. And like it or not, you can't just decide what other people should and shouldn't feel. Who the fuck do you think you are to belittle her feelings and assume that she isn't capable of that kind of love?"

"Wait, no. It's not that I don't think she's capable. It's just that…"

"What?" Eric growled, clearly growing tired of his excuses.

"Well, why the hell would she feel it for *me*?" he asked, his voice dripping with insecurity. "I'm not worth it. I didn't bring anything to the table but my dick, and that is not enough to base a relationship on."

"Do you honestly think you're the first couple who hooked up before they worked out the finer details? Shit, Maggie sucked me off at some frat party before I even learned her name. We were just drawn to each other. It was insane. And I don't think Emma and Brandon spoke more than ten words to each other the whole first year they were dating—they were too busy fucking like rabbits."

"But this is diff—"

"Ethan, she still called off the wedding," Eric cut in, allowing his words to hang in the air as his confused brother attempted to decipher them.

"But—but she—" Ethan stammered.

"And she moved out of her father's house." Eric looked like he was starting to enjoy making Ethan squirm.

"She moved? Where? Did she leave town?" Ethan was breathing rapidly, only seconds away from a total meltdown.

"Oh, you don't like not knowing where someone you care about is living?" he replied with an evil grin. "Does the possibility of her disappearing off the face of the earth and never hearing from her again bother you?"

"God dammit! Where the fuck is she?!" Ethan snarled, reaching forward and grabbing Eric by the shirt with clenched fists.

"Not so nice, is it?" Eric calmly replied, unflinching in the face of so much rage. He watched as realization slowly dawned on Ethan, his face morphing from one of fury to one of anguish. He could actually see the moment when it all sank in, and Ethan finally knew what he had done to his family and the woman he loved.

Releasing Eric's shirt gently and sitting back in his chair, he ran his hands over his face and up into his hair, fisting dirty handfuls with a loud groan. "I've really lost her, haven't I?" he choked out.

"I don't know, man," Eric answered honestly. "She was really hurting for a long fucking time. For as much as she's changed, there's still a sadness in her eyes. I don't know if she would take you back now or not, but if there's a chance that your sorry ass is the only thing that will make her happy then it's my job to drag you back there."

Ethan's eyes lit up. "So she's still in Aledo?"

"Yes, asshole, she's still in Aledo," he sighed.

Ethan's face fell as another possibility dawned on him. "But what if she won't see me? What if she refuses to take me back?"

"Then that's her choice to make, but at least you gave her the choice. It's a hell of a lot better than making all of her decisions for her and running off with your tail between your legs. Besides, even if she makes you jump through hoops, I really can't see her blowing you off completely. She's fucking shacked up in that piece of shit apartment just to be close to you."

"She's living there?" he gasped, a whole new feeling of hope sweeping through him.

"Yeah. I think it's fucked up, personally, but she just tells me to butt out, so I do."

"Then what the fuck are we waiting for?" Ethan snapped, jumping up and running into the bedroom. He stopped short in the entrance when he noticed that all of his bags had already been packed and were sitting in the middle of the freshly made bed.

"Our flight's in three hours," Eric said behind him, clapping his large hand down on his shoulder. "I didn't know what you wanted done with the canvases, so I'm sure you'll need to make some calls."

As Ethan nodded eagerly and made to reach for his phone, Eric squeezed harder on his shoulder and yanked him back to his side. "Not so fast, stinky. Do us all a favor and get your skinny ass in the shower. I'm not taking you anywhere looking like that."

An hour later, Ethan was cleaner than he'd been in days. His scruffy three-day beard had been shaved off, but it only served to highlight his newly bruised skin. He'd arranged for his paintings to be shipped and was bouncing around excitedly as they grabbed his bags and left the hotel.

"Dude, I'm glad to see you so lively and all," Eric said as they entered the cab for the airport, "but I hope you know that you aren't going straight to her."

Ethan's face fell as if someone had flipped a switch. "What do you mean? I need to see her!"

"Yeah, I know. But you need to get yourself together first. You're in no shape to go wooing, douchebag. Besides, the entire family is waiting for me to drag you back dead or alive, so I'm pretty sure the inquisition is going to happen as soon as you walk in the door."

"Oh God," Ethan groaned.

"Yeah, I know," he said again, chuckling this time. "But you need to let them love you, bro. Give them the chance to show you that they aren't judging you. They may beat your ass worse than I did at first, but it's only because they've been so worried."

They were both silent for a while as they drove through the busy streets, staring out at the bright lights as they streaked by in the darkness.

"Eric?" Ethan's quiet voice broke the silence.

"Yeah?"

"Thank you."

Eric nodded quickly and didn't say anything, but that didn't stop a small smile from reaching his face as he turned to look out the window again.

For the first time in years, he had his brother back.

5

Ethan pulled his crappy Nissan rental car—the only one he could get on short notice—into the familiar parking lot and couldn't stop a fresh wave of nerves from overtaking him when he saw the monstrous Oldsmobile parked in his old spot.

She was there.

She was there, and he had absolutely no idea how she was going to receive him—or if she *would* receive him. He hadn't exactly called her to give her a heads-up that he was in town; in fact, he still didn't even have her phone number.

Truthfully, he didn't want to give her the chance to run away before he could see her again, and there was also a small part of him that hoped she might give him her number herself—if he was brave enough to ask for it. It hadn't escaped him that while he had done just about everything under the sun with her sexually, he was still terrified of something as simple as asking for her phone number. That was the kind of thing you were supposed to do when you first met someone you were interested in. *Not* fuck them roughly on a kitchen counter.

They certainly had a knack for doing things backward.

Ethan made his way across the lot, slowly approaching the familiar staircase that led up to the apartment. As he quietly walked up the steps, he couldn't help but recall the last time he'd been in that very spot, carrying an eager Lily upstairs to screw her six ways from Sunday. It had been the same day he'd learned her name.

Once again: backward.

He had to force himself to think of something else, already feeling his body responding to the memory. He couldn't help it lately—just the slightest thought of her caused him to react that way. When combined with specific memories of what they had done together, it was damn near painful. The whole time he had been gone, he had felt dead to the world, numb to every sensation but his grief. However, over the last week since he'd been home again, he found that he was more high strung than he'd been in years, as if his entire body were on high alert for Lily—as if it could sense she was close.

When he finally got control of his thoughts and his flesh, Ethan stepped forward the last few feet and raised his hand to knock. His knuckles were less than an inch from the door when a muffled voice inside made him pause. He pressed his ear to the wood, hoping to make out whom the voice belonged to. If she was entertaining company or had a…guest…he didn't want to disrupt her night.

"No, Mom…I'm fine. Why do you keep asking me that?"

It was definitely her voice and just the sound of it caused a deep ache in his chest. He listened for a reply, but there was none, only Lily again. "It's been months now, for God's sake! You didn't even know Scott, why do you care that it's over?" More silence. "Oh, *please*! I know you're just concerned, but I'm a big girl. I'm the one who ended it, remember? I wouldn't have done that if I wasn't ready to be alone."

She was obviously talking on the phone, but it didn't stop Ethan from listening further. The topic itself was interesting enough, but what he couldn't get over was how lovely her voice sounded. He had somehow forgotten that. He knew it was beautiful, but he had forgotten the way it made him feel whenever he heard it.

"No, I don't feel guilty. I actually just spoke with him the other day, and he's doing great… Yeah, really. He took that garage job I told you about in St. Louis after Sam kicked him out...I know, he was always a dick. Anyway, he loves it there and he's even dating already...I don't know, some girl named Abby or something, that's not important right now. What's important is that he called me up out of the blue to *thank* me. He said that he never would have had the courage to move on if I hadn't called bullshit on our entire relationship."

Ethan wanted to smack himself after hearing that. If he had only given her a little more time, if he had only trusted her to know what she wanted in life, then they would be together already rather than him standing outside their—*her*—door like a stalker.

He heard her groan in frustration before speaking again. "No, I do not feel lonely all by myself. I actually do way more now than I ever did living at Dad's and dating Scott. I go out with friends from work now. Hell, I actually *have* friends from work now. I have a life again. I'm sorry if you think I need a man to make the world go 'round, but I am perfectly content to let it happen in its own time. We can't all be defined by the men we marry. How *is* number four, by the way?"

He could hear her pacing around the front room as she listened to her mother, back and forth across the floor, and he could almost taste her desperation to end the call. Not allowing himself to stall another minute, he rapped lightly on the door.

"Hold on a sec, someone's at the door... I don't know who... No, I *don't* have a peephole... Yes, Dad has already told me that I should install one. My God, would you please be quiet for a second?"

Ethan held his breath as her footsteps approached, but nothing could have prepared him for what the sight of her would do to him.

Lily opened the door with her cellphone held against her collarbone, a look of mild curiosity on her face. She was still in her scrubs from work—a fact that he was trying very hard not to focus on—and her long hair was swept up into a loose bun. She looked flushed and healthy, and even more beautiful than he remembered. He instantly felt as if someone had punched him in the gut, knocking the wind out of him and causing him to feel lightheaded.

Once Lily realized who she was looking at, she froze like a deer in headlights, dropping her phone to the floor with a loud thud. Her mother's voice could be heard throughout the room—a distant, tinny sound, as if some mouse had suddenly wandered into the apartment and started yelling. When Lily made no move for the phone, continuing to stare at him as if a ghost had appeared, Ethan slowly bent over and picked it up. Without ever taking his eyes from hers, he carefully lifted it up to her face as if she were a caged animal that might strike out at him at any moment.

Her mother's voice still squeaked out between them. "Lily?! Are you all right? Do I need to call your father? *Hello?*"

He watched as she blinked a few times rapidly, as if noticing the voice for the first time. She glanced at the cellphone and swallowed quickly, reaching up to pull it from his fingers without allowing their skin to touch. When she had a firm grasp on it again she held it to her ear.

"Mom, I'm sorry, I have to let you go." Her eyes were back on his as she listened for another moment. "No, everything's fine. I just dropped the phone…but I do need to hang up now. Talk to you soon." Without waiting to hear another word, she ended the call and tossed the phone on the half-round table against the wall.

Lily stared at him for another thirty seconds in complete silence.

"What…what are you doing here?" she finally whispered.

Ethan fought off the urge to pull her close, wanting nothing more than to hold her in his arms again, but knowing that he needed to go about things very carefully to avoid scaring her away.

"May I please come in?"

She rocked on her feet briefly, startled by the effect his words had on her body. The velvety richness of his voice washed over her in a tidal wave of heat, and for a second she felt as though she had just been given her first drops of water after wandering the desert for days.

He looked different to her somehow, but still achingly beautiful. He was a bit thinner, and there was a less haunted look to his eyes. Instead, they looked more…determined. And bruised.

"What happened to your eye?" she gasped, stopping her hand in midair as she reached out to touch the yellow and purple skin, then dropping it back down to her side quickly.

"Eric."

"Oh." Her face fell. "Is that why you're here?"

"No," he answered instantly. "Well…yes and no," he said, trying to be as truthful as possible.

"What is that supposed to mean?"

"If you'll let me in, I'll try to explain it the best that I can."

"Oh, an *explanation*?" she replied sarcastically. "Why on earth would you think I deserved one now? You never did before." She was surprised by her own bitterness, having thought up until that point that she would be happy just to have him back in her life in any way possible.

"I know…and I'm sorry. I want to fix that. Can we please go inside and talk?" It was taking all of his strength to keep from touching her. Even the slightest brush of his fingers against her bare arm might set him off, and that was not the impression he wanted to make at that moment.

"I'm shocked you didn't just barge in here like you still owned the place. I mean, it's only been three fucking months, why would that be odd?"

If she only knew how close he'd been to doing that very thing.

"Lily…please," he choked out.

"All right," she sighed, unable to handle the look of anguish on his face. That combined with the bruising was just too much. Standing aside, she ushered him inside with an exaggerated wave of her arm.

"Thank you," he said quietly as he passed her, stopping in the middle of the room as she shut the door. After an awkward silence in which they simply stared at each other, Ethan took a deep breath and bit the bullet.

"So…" he exhaled loudly.

"So…" she returned, visibly as nervous as he was. Her emotions were running the gamut from angry to worried to excited. She honestly had no idea why he was standing in front of her in the little room that had once been their own private sanctuary. She only knew that something deep inside of her finally felt right again, despite her anger.

Ethan glanced around, really taking notice of his surroundings for the first time. "Wow…I can't believe this is the same place." He turned slowly, making mental comparisons to what it had looked like before. "It's so…comfortable. So lived in."

"Thank you," she said sincerely. "I really like it. Emma and Maggie helped me put it together."

"Yes, I heard that. It seems that they are all fond of you. Especially Eric," he added with a grimace, gently touching his discolored cheekbone. It had made amazing progress healing over the last week. The swelling had gone down and he could open his eye easily again, but the dark splotches were slower to disappear.

Fighting back the urge to show concern for his face again, Lily was overcome with a sudden rush of rage. "Oh really? You'd heard that, huh? Well, it seems that one of us is at a disadvantage, because while you were apparently getting regular updates on me, I haven't heard one fucking *word* about you!"

Ethan made to grab her shoulders to calm her down, but stopped himself halfway and simply held his hands up in surrender between them. "Hey...it's not like that."

"I think you need to start talking *now*, because I'm getting angrier by the second," she fumed.

"Here, let's sit down," he said, gesturing to the love seat. He ignored the new, comfortable-looking—though much less lavish—bed that he saw from the corner of his eye when they passed the bedroom door, refusing to think of his fond memories of that room and his desire to create new ones.

When they had settled on the cushions, both instinctively sitting as far away from the other as they could, they turned to face each other with their backs against the armrests. Lily tucked one of her legs up under her other knee and crossed her arms, giving off the impression of hostility, but really hoping to just hold herself back long enough to keep from jumping on him.

She was angry. She was confused and upset and unsure of her own shifting emotions, but that didn't make him any less attractive to her. She wanted to kiss his bruises and hold him for hours. Then she wanted to throttle him.

Ethan cleared his throat nervously. "Well, first off, let me start by saying that I wasn't getting regular updates on you. Nobody even knew where I was until last week when Eric showed up out of nowhere and punched my lights out."

Good, Lily felt like saying, but held her tongue. She couldn't allow herself to say it when she knew that she didn't mean it. She didn't think that violence was the way to solve things and she hated to think of him swollen and in pain. But she also knew Eric well enough by now to know that he must have been very scared, worried, and hurt to have done that to his own brother. It didn't exactly excuse it in her eyes, but she could certainly understand it.

"And where *were* you?"

Ethan watched her mouth form the words as she spoke and felt a pang of desire in his stomach. When he realized that she had actually asked him a question, he shook his head quickly and fought to regain his composure.

"Uh…holed up in a hotel room in New York." He brushed his hands roughly over his face and hissed when he bumped the sore flesh. "Ouch. Anyway, I sort of cut myself off from everyone. I wasn't even taking their calls."

"How could you *do* that to them?" she gasped. "They care so much about you!"

"I know that—now," he sighed. "There's a lot of backstory between me and my family that you don't know, and I've just begun to see how much time I've truly lost with them. But luckily, it seems like their love outweighs their frustration with me."

That was another thing that Lily could certainly understand.

"Am I ever going to hear any of this backstory?" she asked, her curiosity piqued.

He smiled gently. "Actually, I'd love to tell you anything you'd like to know about me. And there's even more that I want to learn about you." He looked into her eyes and took a deep breath. "Will you allow me the chance to get to know you, Lily? To *really* get to know you?"

"What…um…what did you have in mind?" she whispered.

"Well," he swallowed roughly, "I was thinking that we might…go out? For starters, that is."

"You want to take me on a date?" she asked, her head swimming with a mixture of apprehension and elation. "Like…a *real* date?"

"Well…more than one, if you'll let me." He started to fidget a bit and she could have sworn she saw a hint of a blush tinting his cheeks.

"I'm sorry, I'm terrible at this, I know. It's just that I've never really done this before."

"What, dated?"

"Yeah. I don't think I've ever even asked anyone out before." He definitely blushed that time. "I went from being a shy kid to a snobbish adult stuck in a miserable relationship for years, and it was like all of those things just…happened to me. Does that make sense? Like I was sort of being led about, never making my own choices in life."

"I guess I get it," she said after thinking about it for a while. "But it also sounds like you allowed it to happen to you."

"What do you mean?"

"Well, you didn't *have* to be *stuck* with her. Once you found out what she was really like, you didn't have to stay with her as long as you did. It sounds like you just…sat back and took what was handed to you, without ever bothering to search for anything better." She looked him in the eye again, suddenly worried that she had misspoken. "I'm sure that's oversimplifying your situation, I hope that doesn't offend you. I know that I don't have all of the details yet."

"No…I'm not offended," he said slowly, a bit rattled that she had hit the nail on the head so easily. "That's actually pretty accurate. I guess I just never thought that anything better was really out there. I figured it would all just be more of the same." He met her gaze again before adding, "I've never had a reason to want to make a choice before."

Lily gulped so loudly that he could hear it. "But you do now?" she barely squeaked out.

His eyes began to smolder, becoming a bright, scorching jade before he answered her. "I do now."

She felt like she was drowning in those eyes, about to go under and not really caring anymore.

"Lily, may I please take you to dinner tomorrow night?"

The breath in her lungs whooshed out, making her feel instantly lightheaded. She was balanced on the edge of a cliff, wobbling back and forth. It was there in the distance, she could just see it out of reach. *Surrender*. All she had to do was let go.

Lily closed her eyes and jumped.

"Yes."

"Really?" he smiled, and it was brighter than the sun. "Thank you, Lily. Thank you so much. I know I haven't given you any reasons to give me a chance." He leaned forward without thinking and placed his hand on her knee.

They both froze.

Both pairs of eyes stared at his hand as if it might start talking.

Lily braced herself against the onslaught of emotions—fear, resentment, need, lust—coursing through her body as his fingers rested on her knee. Her emotions were all battling each other for dominance, and none of them were winning.

Their skin wasn't even touching—she was still wearing her scrub pants, but she would swear on a stack of bibles that she could feel the electric current passing between them once again. It was scary... but familiar. It instantly reminded her of the many heated encounters that had taken place in that very apartment.

And judging from the panicked look on Ethan's face, he too was remembering them all.

"I should go," he blurted out, standing up quickly. Lily forced herself not to whimper at the instant chill she felt at the loss of his touch.

"So soon?" she said, still a bit dazed from the unexpected contact. She stood up slowly and followed him to the door, trying desperately to clear her mind of all the cobwebs.

"Yes," he nodded curtly. "I think it's for the best."

"But I thought we were going to talk? You still haven't given me much of an explanation."

"I know," he sighed, his hand resting on the doorknob. He kept his back to her, never looking back at her as he spoke. "It's coming, I promise. I was just hoping that we could discuss it all over dinner tomorrow."

"Ethan...what's wrong?" She could see a shudder pass through his body when she said his name.

"Nothing," he gritted out between his teeth.

"I don't think I believe you," she huffed. "If this is how things are going to be already, then perhaps we should just forget it." It killed her to say that out loud, but having him near her wouldn't mean anything if she was always worried that he was ready to bolt for the door at the first sign of discomfort.

She wondered how she would ever be able to trust someone who had always chosen flight over fight. He was going to need to fight for this if he wanted her to take him seriously.

"No, please!" he gasped, finally turning to face her completely. He didn't move any closer, but he made eye contact. "Lily...please."

"Then tell me what's wrong."

He looked uncomfortable and embarrassed, and it was the oddest thing she'd ever seen. Ethan always owned any room he was in, and his self-confidence practically oozed out of his pores. She had never seen this vulnerable side of him before, and if someone had asked her about it three months ago, she would have sworn that it didn't exist. Even when she first met him and he seemed so broken, he still had a carefully constructed wall around him. She could tell that he desperately wanted something to hide behind as he stood there under her scrutiny.

"Lily..." he begged one last time, but when she crossed her arms and arched an eyebrow, he knew it was now or never. He exhaled loudly, visibly defeated. "I'm sorry to end the night so abruptly. I had really only hoped that you would hear me out long enough to agree to go to dinner. I knew that was a long shot in itself, so I wasn't really prepared to…stay longer."

"What do you mean?" she asked. "What does it matter if we talk tonight or tomorrow?"

"I wasn't…" he took a deep breath. "I wasn't ready for this." At the hurt look on her face he was quick to clarify, "Not *this*, as in you and me." He gestured back and forth between them with his hand. "I've dreamt of nothing more than that for longer than you'll ever know."

Lily suddenly wondered how gravity actually worked. She knew she was still standing in there in front of him, but her heart was soaring somewhere up in the clouds.

"I meant that I wasn't ready for how intense this would feel, being back here again. Being this close to you again. I want to give you time to get used to the idea of us…but if I don't get the fuck out of here right now I'm going to do something we'll both regret."

"Why would we regret it?" she whispered breathlessly, her mind flashing to vivid images of his sweaty flesh as it covered hers in the darkness.

He groaned at her words, closing his eyes briefly to strengthen his resolve. "Because," he answered honestly, "I think that you would be angry with yourself for not waiting until you got some more answers out of me."

"And you?" she pressed, choosing to ignore how right he was. "What would you regret?"

"That's easy. I would hate myself for not making you believe how much you mean to me first. I spent way too fucking long allowing you to think that you were nothing but a warm body to me. It's not true…and I need to make you believe it."

She knew then that her heart had returned to her body, because it was suddenly beating so loudly that she was surprised he couldn't hear it across the room. "Okay…so tomorrow night, then?" she said, knowing that if he didn't leave soon she couldn't be held responsible for what she did to him.

"Yes," he smiled knowingly. "Is it all right if I call you tomorrow to set up a time? I need to make a few arrangements."

"Call me?" she mumbled. The thought seemed so absurd to her. They had shared so much together and yet had never even spoken on the phone. "Yeah, sure. Call me tomorrow."

"I need your number," he said nonchalantly, as if he asked beautiful women for their numbers everyday, as if the mere thought of her giving him her number didn't make him want to cry from happiness.

"Oh!" she said, wanting to smack herself in the forehead. "That might help, huh? Let me see your phone." She held out her hand, slowly walking forward until she was standing right in front of him.

Ethan pulled his cell from his pocket and dropped it in her open hand, careful to avoid making contact again. As he watched her quickly enter the number he'd been obsessing over all day, he took a deep breath, tasting her as he inhaled. Fire shot through his veins, traveling along his body rapidly until it settled into his fingertips, making them itch to touch her.

"There," she smiled, holding the phone back out to him. "All programmed."

"Thank you." This time he allowed his fingers to slightly brush against hers as he took it back from her, watching for her reaction.

Lily gasped quietly and froze, staring up at him with heavily lidded eyes. "Um…I think you should probably go now…*Ethan*." Her voice dropped to a husky whisper when she said his name, causing his aching erection to twitch.

He nodded, knowing that it was her way of telling him that she wanted him just as badly, but that she was allowing him to set the pace. Taking her cue, he opened the door quickly and stepped into the hallway, as if being on the other side of the wall might actually weaken his desire enough that he wouldn't still want to attack her.

It didn't.

"Until tomorrow, then. Good night…Lily."

She slowly closed the door, never breaking eye contact with him as the opening became smaller and smaller. He made no move toward the stairs for as long as he could still see her, and right before the door clicked shut he shot her a wink and licked his lips.

The loud whimper he could hear through the wall as he walked away had him chuckling to himself all the way to his car. It certainly hadn't helped the epic state of arousal he was in, but just knowing that Lily obviously still wanted him and was willing to give him a chance was enough to make him feel lighter than he had in…well, years. She'd always had a way of making him feel alive when no one else could, but now she was giving him something really worth living for.

Ethan made the lonely drive back to the edge of town, where his parents were probably waiting up as though he were a teenager. They were eager to learn how his first attempt at wooing had gone. They had been so full of support for him over the last week, and it made him feel even more foolish that he'd waited so long to turn to them.

When he first arrived back home with Eric, scrawny and bruised, everyone had different reactions. Maggie had damn near ripped him a new asshole before tearing up and hugging him, whispering that she would have kicked him in the nuts and punched him if she had found him. Emma was as hyper as a hummingbird, asking him thirty questions a second and bouncing up and down until she had her answers. Brandon simply stood back and reeled her in when she got out of control, which Ethan would be eternally grateful for. Barbara just cried and hugged him, begging him to please come home if things ever got that bad again. Richard was unsurprisingly the most stoic of the group, simply putting his arm around Ethan's shoulders and patting him on the back, mumbling a quiet "welcome home, son" as he wiped at a suspicious drop of moisture in the corner of his eye.

None of them judged him for his lifestyle or his addiction; they were simply hurt he hadn't had the faith to trust in them. They were also thrilled with his hopes for him and Lily, none of them chastising him for the fact that he'd been secretly seeing her when she was still engaged. Perhaps if they hadn't already known her as well as they did, they might have frowned on it a bit, but while he'd been gone they had all formed close attachments to her. Apparently his entire family had a better idea of just how unhappy she'd been in her previous life than he did.

It seemed that actually talking about things helped you to understand quite a bit about people.

After his siblings returned to their homes in Chicago, his mother made it her personal mission to fatten him back up. She'd been cooking the most heart-stopping, stick-to-your-ribs meals all week, and he'd already gained five pounds. He was still a bit on the thinner side compared to how he'd looked before, but his cheekbones had some flesh around them now and his eyes no longer looked empty. Although he knew that last part had much more to do with the love and support of his family than any food he ate.

As Ethan pulled the car into the driveway, he wasn't surprised to see a light on inside. Just as he'd suspected, Richard and Barbara were both sitting in the kitchen, casually playing a game of cards. When he walked into the room his mother's face lit up.

"Oh, Ethan, dear! You're back early."

"I was just going to say that you're up late," he returned.

"Nonsense, it's not even ten o'clock yet."

"Yes, but aren't you both usually up in bed by now, watching television?"

"Don't be silly. We sit up playing cards all the time."

"All right, Mom. If you say so," he rolled his eyes. His father at least had the decency to look sheepish, knowing their ruse hadn't worked. Ethan looked back and forth at their expectant faces and decided to go easy on them. "Would you like to hear how my evening went?"

"Only if you care to share, sweetheart," Barbara answered, and he nearly laughed out loud. If she moved any closer to the edge of her seat, she'd fall off.

"She was a bit hesitant at first, but she's agreed to let me take her to dinner tomorrow night."

"Oh, that's wonderful!" his mother gasped, jumping up to hug him tightly. "I'm so proud of you for refusing to give up. Where are you going to take her?"

"I have no idea," he blushed. "I was so worried about getting her to say yes that I didn't plan that far ahead. What the hell is there to do in Aledo?"

"Hmm…" she paused in thought. "Well, not a lot, honestly. There are some casual things to do with someone you are already dating, but nothing for making great first impressions. You'll probably need to take her into the Quad Cities for dinner—there are some nice restaurants in Moline and Davenport."

"Thanks. I'll look into it," he smiled, leaning down to give her a hug.

Barbara kissed his cheek as she pulled away and sighed loudly.

"I'm just so happy for you. Things are going to be different now, I can feel it." And without another word, she turned and went up to bed.

Once she had left the room, Richard walked up to him and stared him down. "So…you spoke with Lily. Is that *all* that happened?"

Ethan turned beet red before answering, "Not that it's any of your business, but yes, that's all that happened."

"Good for you, son," he smiled, clapping him on the shoulder. "I'm glad you listened to me. I know that you two have unbelievable… *chemistry* together, but she'll never be able to take you seriously right now if you're always trying to get in her pants."

"Dad!"

"What? Just because it's your old man talking doesn't make it any less true."

They shared an awkward good-night after that, and Ethan went up to his bedroom. He sat up sketching a few different ideas for a new painting for a while before he decided to call it a night. As he climbed into bed, a thought struck him that made him jump back out and grab his phone.

Scrolling through his contact list, his breath caught when he found it—Lily's number. He finally had the woman of his dreams only the press of a button away. As much as he wanted to call her and hear her voice before bed, he figured she would probably be asleep already. He also knew that hearing her voice at that moment would get his hormones going all over again, so he decided to just send a quick text message. That way she could see it when she woke up in the morning.

> Just realized that I never gave you my number. Now you can reach me in case you ever need anything.

Feeling instantly better knowing she had the message, he sat his phone next to him on the nightstand and settled into bed, ready to sleep comfortably for the first night in months. What he hadn't expected was to hear his phone buzzing with a reply. He picked it up with a shaking hand and opened the message.

> Great, thanks! But I'm trying to be good, so I won't tell you what I really need right now. Looking forward to tomorrow. ;-)

Well, apparently he could achieve a raging erection without hearing her voice, too. She had done the job just as well by text. Sighing loudly in the darkness, Ethan rolled over and set the phone back down, sliding open the drawer underneath and pulling out a certain small bottle of lube. As he squirted some in his hand and rolled onto his back to take care of business, he wondered how the hell he was going to make it through an entire evening without attacking her.

6

The following day was Saturday, which gave Lily time to get herself ready. She spent all day pampering herself, going to her favorite salon in the Cities for a facial and a mani-pedi—and even though sex was supposedly off the table for a while, she threw in a wax for good measure. Hopefully it wouldn't be too long, and it was always good to be prepared.

She had hoped he might text her back after her little note the night before, but he hadn't taken the bait. It wasn't that she didn't appreciate what he was trying to do, but she was hoping they might have a little bit of fun in the meantime. And really, what could be more fun than some naughty sexting with Ethan?

Around 1:00 p.m. her phone rang and her heart skipped a beat when she heard the new ringtone she had set for him: "Business Time" by Flight of the Conchords. He called to let her know that he would be picking her up around 6:30 p.m. that night to take her to a restaurant in Bettendorf. When everything was finalized, she told him that she couldn't wait to see him again, and he made a funny choking sound and told her he needed to go.

When she got back home that afternoon she started the horrible task of trying to find something to wear. Although she had a closet full of new clothes after her trip to Chicago with the girls, it was still no easy task. There was almost too much to choose from now and her head started to spin. Sighing in defeat, she reached for her phone.

Emma picked up on the second ring. "So? Any big plans tonight?" she asked when she answered, as if they were already mid-conversation.

"How did you know?" Lily asked with a huff. "And don't think I'm not totally pissed at you for not telling me he was back in town."

"Hey, don't take it out on me. I would have called you that night if I could have, and Maggie would have, too. He swore us all to secrecy because he wanted some time to get his shit together."

"I'm just saying a little heads-up would have been nice. Maybe *I* had some shit to get together."

"Lily, you've had three months to do that. You're much more ready for this than he is, so you're actually at an advantage here. You can call all the shots this time."

"I don't care about calling all the shots. I just want to feel comfortable with him again. I feel like I'm a high schooler getting ready for the prom, for fuck's sake!"

"It will come in time, don't worry." She sounded so calm that Lily wanted to slap her. "So, what did you call for, anyway? Was it just to yell at me or did you need something?"

"I hate doing this because I know you're going to squeal…but I need help deciding what to wear." She held the phone away from her ear, the loud screeching on the other end echoing throughout the room. "Good lord, are you done yet?" she teased when she felt brave enough to lift up the phone again.

"Oh this is just perfect! I will bring you over to the dark side yet, young Skywalker." Emma loved to picture herself as the head of an evil empire of fashion fierceness.

They spoke about the date: where they might be going and how formal it might be. After deciding on an elegant wrap dress and the perfect pair of heels, Emma's voice grew concerned.

"Hey, all of the fun stuff aside, are you really okay with this?"

"Okay with what? Having you help me? Of course, or I wouldn't have called."

"No, no. Everything with Ethan. This date. Giving things a real try with him even though he hurt you so badly."

"I'm not sure," Lily said honestly. "Part of me feels like I'm walking on eggshells, and the other part feels like a giddy schoolgirl who's getting everything she ever wanted. I'll admit that I'm still feeling a little resentful and I'm not completely sure that I trust him yet, but I've only ever wanted him back…that's never changed. Now that I have that chance, I really don't want to spend the rest of my life making him eat shit."

I also don't want to spend the rest of my life waiting for him to freak out and leave again.

"So you're just going to forgive and forget it all? I mean, I love my brother dearly and I hope this all works out, but if it were me, I might make him sweat a bit."

"Yes, but what you guys keep forgetting is that he promised me nothing before, and I was the one who hoped for everything. I wasn't even officially single and I had planned my whole future with him. I should have ended it with Scott a lot sooner than I did, and made myself truly available. I'm the one who set myself up to be hurt so badly, so while I might appreciate an explanation from him as to why he took off like that, I still couldn't ever imagine putting *all* the blame on him."

"Wow, you're better than me. I would be trying to find ways to get even."

"But get even for what, Emma? Not saying good-bye? Yeah, that stung like a motherfucker, but even if he hadn't been such a chickenshit about it and had told me why he was leaving, it was still his right to leave. Just because one person is okay with how something is working doesn't mean the other person is. That would be like saying nobody ever has the right to end a relationship if the other person is content."

"Yeah, I guess, but—"

"But what?" Lily interrupted. "Think about it. He didn't cheat on me, he didn't lie to me, and he would never hit me. He just…left. It hurt and I missed him like crazy, but if he's willing to give it a real try and not run away at the first sign of trouble, then so am I."

"Well I guess you have your answer now, don't you?" She could tell Emma was smiling.

"You little shit. You did that just to drag my real feelings out, didn't you?"

"But you're sure now, aren't you?" Emma giggled.

"Okay, I'm letting you go now. You're too evil for me, Darth." Lily ended the call, frustrated but laughing.

When six thirty finally arrived, she was dressed in a curve-hugging, dark-blue, silk wrap dress and a killer pair of black high-heeled shoes. Her hair hung in loose curls down over her shoulders and she wore a light dusting of makeup to even out her skin tone. She was watching the clock nervously and pacing around the room, hoping she wasn't making the biggest mistake of her life.

When the knock sounded at her door a few minutes later, she almost jumped, somehow missing the sound of his footsteps on the stairs. She rushed to the door, stopping briefly to take a deep breath and calm down. It turned out to be pointless once she got a good look at her date.

Ethan was literally breathtaking.

He was standing before her wearing a mouth-watering charcoal gray suit that she could only assume had a designer label, and a sleek black tie. It was clearly tailored to fit his broad shoulders, and it somehow even made his bruised face look civilized, as if he were some bad boy rich kid who got punched out at a casino in Monte Carlo. Simply put: Ethan was fuckhot.

It took her a moment to find her words, and before she could speak he cut her off. "Wow," he breathed. "You look...amazing."

"That's funny," she laughed softly. "I was going to say the exact same thing about you."

"Here, I brought you these," he said as a telltale pink colored his cheeks. She looked down to see his hand holding out a gorgeous bouquet of pink stargazer lilies.

"Oh, Ethan, they're so lovely! Please, come in while I put them in some water."

"I hope that you don't think lilies are too predictable, since that's your name and everything. I just wanted to bring you something different than the standard roses."

"No, I love lilies! I love all kinds of lilies, but these are actually my favorite," she said with her own blush.

As she walked into the kitchen he followed behind her, leaving the front door wide open on purpose—secretly hoping that having it open might prevent him from grabbing her and throwing her down on the floor. She looked so unbelievably sexy in that wrap dress, just thinking about what one tiny little tug on the tie could do had him adjusting himself in his pants already. Also, he'd never seen her wearing anything other than sneakers or boots. The full-on fuck-me heels she was sporting now were worthy of their very own fetish.

He hovered in the entrance to the kitchen, leaning against the doorframe as he watched her grabbing a vase under the sink. The sight of her bending over made him groan under his breath, but it was masked by a loud yowl from down by his feet. He looked down to see a tubby orange tabby cat pawing at his legs.

"Well, hello there," he smiled, bending down and scratching the cat's head. "I don't think I've met *you* before." Another yowl came from behind him. Ethan turned his head to see an identical cat staring up at him before it stood up and perched its front paws on his thigh. "Or you!" he laughed.

"I see you've met my babies," Lily chuckled, crouching down next to him and flashing a decent amount of cleavage as she did so. "Ethan Foster, this is Wembley and Boober."

"I guess we're down at Fraggle Rock, huh?" he laughed loudly, scratching each one on the head simultaneously. "Those are great names. But how on earth do you tell them apart?"

"Well, Wembley's the fat one."

"I hate to break it to you, but they're both on the portly side."

"I know, I know. I guess I'm just used to them. They have different stripe patterns around their eyes if you look close enough. Anyway, I'm all done if you want to get going."

"Okay, great," he smiled, scratching each cat on the head one more time before standing up.

"C'mon guys, stop being beggars. Mama already fed you, and he doesn't have any treats," she said to the cats, shooing them away from the kitchen.

"Why didn't I see them here last night?" he asked on the way out the door.

"Oh, they were at my dad's house. Sometimes when I'm working and he's not, I drop them off there for the day, sort of like kitty day care. I don't need to, they're perfectly fine on their own for a while, but ever since I moved out, my dad sort of misses them. He's the one who suggested it," she laughed.

Ethan escorted her downstairs to his waiting car, and she gasped when she saw the sleek silver Lexus. "What happened to the Audi?"

"That was a rental. I have a different one now back at the house, but this one is my dad's. Is it too pretentious? I just wanted to take you out in style."

"No, not at all," she said as she got in and adjusted her seat belt. "I think it's very elegant. Thank you for going to so much effort for me tonight."

Ethan turned to face her, illuminated by only the dashboard light. "You're worth it, Lily."

She was thankful that the darkness of the car hid her blush.

They made polite conversation the entire way to Bettendorf, each of them sneaking longing looks at the other when they had the chance. When they pulled up in front of the restaurant she was surprised that it looked like such a simple place from the outside. She'd assumed that Ethan would hunt down the most lavish place available in an attempt to wow her, but The Red Crow Grille just looked like a basic restaurant at the end of a strip of businesses.

Until they went inside.

It was the fanciest place she'd ever been taken by far. The waiters wore long aprons and described the menu items at length. They had food she'd never heard of, paired with wines she'd never tasted. To say that she was out of her element was putting it mildly.

"I hope you don't think it's too much," Ethan whispered as they were led to their table. He had reserved one of the special oversized red booths by the pianist. "It was one of the nicest places in town, and I really just wanted to make this evening special."

"No, not at all…I think it's charming, actually. I've never…oh, never mind."

"Please," he said as they were seated. "What were you saying? You've never?"

"Well…I've never had anyone put so much thought into anything like this for me. Don't get me wrong, I don't need to be wined and dined to be impressed—but this?" She gestured around the room. "This is impressive."

Ethan smiled and reached over the table, taking her hand in his. He stroked his thumb across the backs of her knuckles in small circles as he looked deeply into her eyes. "I'm happy you're enjoying yourself."

He didn't add that there was no reason she should be so moved by a simple restaurant when there were places he'd taken Rachel that cost more than most people's car payments. She hadn't even batted an eye at the cost, either, taking it all in as her due. That was one of the things he was beginning to treasure about Lily: she actually appreciated things. Hell, just thinking of how she'd teared up when he made her a fucking sandwich was enough to make him want to shower her with diamonds and sapphires. And then shower with her.

They talked and laughed as they ate, feeling more comfortable with each other by the minute. Lily updated him on all of the new changes in her life, including the fact that she was saving up for a trip to New Zealand and hopefully Australia as well if she could swing it. She had no idea how long it would take her to save enough, but even if it was still a few years away, she didn't care. She was just happy to finally be doing something for herself.

After a while, Ethan took the conversation in a more serious direction, needing to finally be up front with her about why he left. He explained his fears and hesitations, and how he had truly thought he was doing right by her. He filled her in briefly on what she still needed to know about him and Rachel and their rocky past full of addictions. He apologized again for leaving the way he did, and then shared the story of how Eric had found him and literally knocked some sense into him.

"When I asked you last night if that was why you were coming to see me, you said 'yes and no.' What did you mean by that?" Lily asked, handling the subject matter much better than Ethan had anticipated.

"I guess I just meant that technically, yes, his punching me out was what finally got me motivated to get off my brooding ass and come back here to fight for you. But no, it wasn't what made me want to do it." He reached over and took her hand again, fighting to ignore the instant jolt he felt at the contact. "You've got to believe me, Lily. I thought of nothing else for months…I just honestly figured you had gotten married and it was too late. I let myself get sucked into some sort of downward pity spiral, convinced that I was too damaged and not good enough for anybody, even my own family. I should have given them more credit than that…and I should have had faith in you."

Lily wiped her eyes quickly and patted the back of his hand with her own. "I should have ended things with my ex so much sooner and told you how I was starting to feel about you—your little privacy rules be damned. I guess I was too scared that you would reject me."

He swallowed uncomfortably. "Man, I guess I didn't help that perception by running away like a thief in the night, did I? I have to be honest and say that I think I also panicked because things went from playful to serious way faster than I expected. It was all such a romantic notion, having this unattainable secret lover…it made me want you for myself even more. And then when I found out that not only were you actually leaving him, but you were also friends with my entire family and they loved you? I just started freaking out, trying to convince myself that nothing could be so perfect. I was so wrong… because to me, you *are* perfect."

She wiped another tear from the corner of her eye, blinking rapidly until she could see him clearly again. "Maybe you should wait 'til you get to know me better. I'm far from perfect, Ethan."

"But that's another thing that makes you perfect for *me*."

After they had lingered at their table for over two hours, sharing dessert as they talked, Ethan signaled for the check. As they walked to the car he asked her if he could take her out for a drink before they headed back.

"Of course, but they had a full bar at the restaurant," she said, confused.

"I know, but there's a place I've been meaning to check out just across the river in Rock Island, over in The District. They have live music."

"That sounds great," Lily smiled.

He drove them to The Rock Island Brewing Company, RIBCO for short, and although it was obvious they were way overdressed, Lily found the place charming. She had heard about it before from friends at work but had never been to a show there.

They grabbed a small table in the back and listened to an adorable girl on tour from San Francisco, Uni & Her Ukelele, who sang the most quirky, beautiful songs about unicorns and rainbows and love and heartache, all while playing a mean ukulele. They sat with their heads together for almost an hour, whispering questions and answers during the song breaks about their favorite music and artists. Lily leaned her head on his shoulder at one point and he wrapped his arm around her, pulling her even closer to him in silence, both of them touched by how right it felt.

When the set was over, Ethan bought two CDs from the singer (intentionally overpaying for them), and thanked her for a great show. When Lily asked why he bought two, he explained that this way they could each have one as a souvenir of their first date together.

She knew without even listening that it was already her new favorite.

7

The drive back to Aledo was fairly quiet, both of their minds preoccupied with arousal and self-restraint. When they arrived back at her building Ethan walked her upstairs, both of them stopping to face each other in the hallway when she opened the door.

"Lily…thank you so much for joining me tonight," he said quietly. "I had a great time and I hope you did, too."

"I had an excellent time! Thank you."

The silence was deafening as they stared openly at each other's lips. As if pulled together by magnets, their bodies drifted toward each other almost unconsciously. When they were only mere inches apart, Ethan raised his hand slowly and cupped her cheek, as if he were holding the most priceless, fragile treasure in existence.

"Lily," he gasped, and she could feel his hand shaking.

"What's wrong?" she whispered, almost against his lips. She could tell he was holding back even the simplest of kisses.

"I just can't believe that you're really in my arms again. Dreams aren't supposed to come true twice…I don't want to fuck this up."

"Ethan," she whimpered, "please kiss me!"

Unable to resist her plea, he finally closed the distance, covering her mouth with his own. He had intended for it to be soft and gentle, only a small taste of a still-forbidden fruit, but when she cried out and shoved her hands into his hair, he went a little mad. A loud groan tore from his throat as he drove the tip of his tongue between her succulent lips, instantly tangling it with hers. The silky texture he felt brought so many memories flooding back to him that he feared he might cry, both out of frustration and the joy of being able to experience them again.

His arms wrapped around her waist tightly as he shoved her against the doorframe, grunting into her mouth when he felt his erection brush against her stomach. Lily moaned and rubbed herself against him more firmly, causing starbursts to explode behind his eyes.

"Ethan," she panted as she came up for air. "Do you want to come inside?" She knew if she hadn't spoken, things probably would have continued on seamlessly, but she also wanted it to be his conscious choice after the way he'd acted the night before.

She could see the very moment that awareness of his surroundings entered his heated gaze, and suddenly it was his turn to whimper. Dropping his forehead to her shoulder, he took a few deep breaths before slowly pulling away.

"It's not a question of *want*," he choked out, squeezing his eyes shut tightly and pinching the bridge of his nose. "Of course I *want* to, but I promised myself that I wouldn't. Not yet."

"What is it that you're waiting for?" she asked softly, trying to hide the rejection she felt.

"I need to make you truly believe how important you are to me first. I don't think I've done that yet."

"Ethan, I'm not looking for penance."

"I know…but there's something that I'm arranging, something that I hope to do very soon. If we can manage to wait until then, I think you will finally see."

"That doesn't make any sense," she huffed. "It's not like there's some magical event that will erase everything that's happened between us. We have an awkward history that we have to get past together. How is some grand gesture going to change that?"

"This isn't just about waiting for a grand gesture, Lily."

"Then will you try to explain this to me so that I can understand it better? Because the way I see it, we're consenting adults and can have sex if we want to." When he opened his mouth to protest she held up a hand to signal that she wasn't finished yet. "Now, I'm willing to hear you out and you don't have to spill the big surprise, but I need you to *stop* leaving me out of decisions that affect both of us." She crossed her arms in front of her and looked up at him expectantly.

"*Shit!*" Ethan sighed loudly and ran his hands through his hair in frustration. "I'm fucking doing it again, aren't I? I'm totally deciding what's best for you."

"He finally gets it," Lily said with a smirk.

"I'm sorry," he groaned in embarrassment. "I have no idea how to do this. I *told* you I've never dated before."

"I understand that this is new for you." Her voice lost its irritated edge when she realized that he genuinely felt bad. "Listen, I'll understand a lot more when you decide to *communicate* with me."

"I'll try," Ethan whispered, leaning in to kiss her on the forehead sweetly. He was immediately hit with a wave of her intoxicating perfume. "Christ, you smell good!" He leaned down by her neck to inhale her deeply, which sent a shockwave of arousal through his body that caused him to shudder against her. It took him a few moments to collect himself and think clearly before he spoke again. "I promise to try my best if you promise to be patient with me."

"Deal." Lily smiled brightly, happy that he seemed willing to compromise, even happier that he was clearly still as affected by their proximity as she was. "Now tell me why you think we should wait."

He took a deep breath, choosing his words carefully. "I guess I'm worried that if we start getting physical right away that's all it'll ever be. I get near you and all I can think about is having you again. Feeling your body moving underneath mine—"

"*Not* helping!" Lily interrupted, her breathing suddenly shallow. If Ethan kept talking like that she wouldn't be responsible for what she did to him right there in the hallway.

"Sorry. See? I can't even give you an explanation without it turning sexual." He watched the rapid rise and fall of her breasts as she tried to gain her composure, forcing himself to look her in the eye when he spoke again. "This is what I'm talking about. I love that we have so much chemistry together, but I don't want that to be all we are. I want the whole experience with you."

"Whole experience?"

"The dating experience. I want to court you, as lame as that may sound. I want to woo you. I want to take you out to a movie. I want to cuddle with you in front of the TV and watch old reruns. I want to talk to you for hours and get to know you more than anybody else ever has."

"You mean my 'true soul that I hide away from the rest of the world?'" Lily asked with a shy smile, using the same phrase he'd used when they first started their affair. The beauty of those words had always stuck with her.

He looked at her then, deep into her eyes, and there was no mistaking the heat that was radiating from his gaze. "I meant that then, but it's even more true today. I want to learn everything I can about you, not just certain parts that conveniently fit into my life."

Lily couldn't help herself after that—she simply had to kiss him. Her arms went around his neck and pulled him to her roughly, causing their bodies to crash together at the same time as their lips. She led the kiss, probing the spicy depths of his mouth with her tongue and conjuring a loud moan from him for her efforts.

Ethan allowed himself to enjoy the surprising embrace for a few moments longer before slowly forcing his traitorous body to back away from her. He could feel every muscle scream in protest as he did so, but he knew that he couldn't let his resolve weaken so quickly.

"Lily," he whimpered when he saw the blazing desire in her eyes. "Please tell me you understand." He took an extra step back from her as he waited for her reply, not trusting himself to remain so close.

"Are you saying that we can't even make out?" She sounded out of breath and slightly panicked. "Because most couples make out, you know."

"Oh, we're going to make out," Ethan growled. "I plan on making out a *lot*, don't you worry. I just hoped that we could build up to it a little bit when we're together, or at least try. Does that sound okay?"

Lily thought for a moment, trying to ignore how kiss-swollen his lips were. She felt a strong tug deep in her belly that told her to drag him into the bedroom and show him how silly he was being—yet another part of her couldn't deny that she wanted to see how this would play out.

"I guess a little wooing might be nice," she finally answered, feeling the truth in her words as she said them.

Ethan sighed loudly in relief and hugged her tightly. "Thank you! Thank you for being so understanding."

"Well, thank *you* for making me understand. I appreciate you explaining it to me and I'll do my best to take it slow, but we both know that it's going to be *hard*." To emphasize the word she brushed against the front of him again, his prominent erection dragging across her stomach.

"I know," he groaned almost painfully, forcing himself not to thrust his hips. "All we can do is try."

"Okay then. But for the record, I am ready and willing whenever you are."

Ethan groaned again and nodded, kissing her chastely on the cheek before pulling away from temptation.

"I'd better go. Thank you again for tonight," he smiled weakly. "I'll call you soon."

"I'd like that."

Lily stood in the doorway until he was gone, missing him already. She felt hollow and swollen, and parts of her that she had previously left for dead ached.

Taking her time getting ready for bed, she skipped pajamas due to the heightened state of arousal her body was in. Slipping under the covers, she had just begun to slide her hand between her legs when her phone rang. She would have ignored it completely and called whoever it was back later, but it was Ethan's ringtone.

"Hello?"

"Lily?" his velvety sexiness oozed through the receiver. "I know it's late, and I just left you, but would it be ridiculous to admit that I really wanted your voice to be the last thing I heard tonight?"

She realized with rising excitement that the wooing had already begun.

"No," she smiled. "Not at all. I was just thinking of your voice. Well, not only that, but it's wonderful to hear again right now."

"Are you angry with me about earlier? I hope you believe how much I wanted to stay."

"Of course I'm not angry. It's actually a very sweet notion. It just doesn't help how...*tense* I am right now."

"You and me both," he groaned.

"Oh really?" she said, smirking in the dark as an idea came to her.

"Well, let me ask you a question," she said, dropping her voice to a husky level.

"Yeah?" She could hear his thick swallow over the line.

"Where does *talking* fall into your plan of things? I mean, we wouldn't touch each other. We would still be waiting. Just helping each other to relieve a little bit of this tension."

"Oh shit," he groaned, and she could swear she heard him drop the phone. After some quick fumbling in the background, he spoke again. "God, I don't know. Are you sure you want to?" His resolve was audibly weakening by the second.

She would gladly respect his wishes about actual touching, but she'd be damned if they were going to go another day without *some* kind of connection. Taking a deep breath, she went in for the kill.

"Come on, Ethan. We had our beautiful, romantic date...but now it's over. I know there's still a dirty boy inside there who's dying to come out and play."

"*Fuck!*" he grunted. As if someone had flipped a switch, her beautiful stranger was back. "Take off your clothes," he commanded.

"Way ahead of you," she sighed.

"You've been lying there naked this whole time?"

"Yes. I was just about to start touching myself when you called."

"God! I'm almost sorry I interrupted you," he groaned. "Almost."

"I'm not. This way I can hear you, too."

"Fuck...okay, baby...I need you to touch yourself for me. Tell me how wet you are."

Lily slid her fingers between her slippery folds, moaning at the feeling. "Oh...so wet. I'm so fucking wet for you."

"What does it feel like? Tell me everything."

She swirled her fingertips around a bit more, trying to find a good way to describe the bliss she felt. "Everything's so soft and swollen...I can barely feel my flesh because there's so much wetness." She could hear his breath coming in soft pants on the other end. "Did you already start? I don't want to miss that, either."

"Don't worry baby, you won't. I haven't started yet…I'm just getting so turned on I can't see straight. Keep going."

"It's throbbing so badly that I know I'll explode in two seconds if I rub my clit, but I don't want to be finished yet."

"Nobody's finishing anything yet," he said roughly. "Even if you come, I'm not finished with you yet. Now, slide two fingers inside yourself. Tell me what it feels like."

"God, Ethan…it's so hot…and tight…and slippery," she gasped.

"Now slide them in and out," he panted. "Does that feel good?"

She did as she was told, sliding them in deeper, already feeling familiar tingles shooting up her legs. "Oh…it feels so damn good. I'm so wet that I can hear everything I'm doing."

Ethan groaned loudly on the other end, his panting getting louder. "Baby…do something for me. Put the phone down there and let me hear you."

"Really?" she asked. She was always a little embarrassed by the wet noises.

"Fuck, yes! I miss that delicious little pussy so much I'm about to start crying. If I were there right now I would be lapping up every fucking drop. *Now let me hear it*," he growled.

"Okay…I'm putting you on speaker. I want to hear you, too." She threw the covers back and slid the phone down between her legs, not wanting to miss one single grunt that he made. Pumping her fingers a bit more roughly so that he could hear, she was rewarded with a loud snarl coming through the phone.

"Fuck! I just want to bury my face in there," his voice echoed in the darkness.

That did it. "God, Ethan! I can't hold it!"

"Then come for me, baby. Set the phone down next to you on the pillow and use your other hand to rub your clit for me. I can hear you fine…God…please come for me!"

Ethan was going absolutely crazy on the other end, hearing every swirling motion of her fingers as she pleasured herself for him. He wasn't lying when he'd told her that he hadn't even started, wanting to really savor every little sound first, but the moment she let go and started screaming his name, he honestly worried that he might explode without even laying a hand on himself.

When her breathing had calmed a bit, she turned her face toward the phone. "Oh my God…that was intense. But I didn't get to hear you," she pouted.

"Oh, we're not quite done yet," he answered, hoping he could last long enough to enjoy this properly. "That was just foreplay, Lily. Tell me, do you still have that purple toy? The one that you said would always be me?"

"Yes," she moaned. "It's right here in my nightstand."

"Good. Because I'm going to fuck you now…and it's not going to be slow *or* gentle."

"Promise?" she moaned again, reaching over and grabbing the toy in question. "God, Ethan…are you hard for me?"

"Are you fucking kidding me?" he laughed. "I'm throbbing so badly right now that it's painful."

"I miss your beautiful cock so much," she whimpered. He could hear her trying to catch her breath, and it took every ounce of his strength to keep from jumping in his car and driving straight over there.

"Fuck…it's yours, Lily. Only for you. And we'll be together again before you know it."

"I want you to touch yourself now, Ethan. I need to hear you, too."

"Absolutely, baby. Now, I want this to feel as real as possible, so why don't you tell me how much lube I should use. A little bit?"

"No," she groaned. "A lot. I'm fucking dripping for you."

He squirted a huge dollop in his palm, holding it for a moment to warm it up. "Okay, baby, I'm ready. Do you have me where I need to be?"

"Yes…I'm ready." Lily held the toy in position, waiting for his word.

Ethan shut his eyes, remembering the last time they'd been together, when she rode him so hard that he'd nearly passed out. She had been perched above him, looking down into his eyes lovingly before she'd fucked him into submission. Grunting at the memory, he clenched his fist tightly, holding it right over the broad tip of his erection.

"Now, baby," he gasped, sliding his tight fist down his shaft at the same moment she pushed the toy inside her to the hilt.

They both cried out, feeling each other as if they were together. In that moment, they truly were making love to each other…only on the opposite sides of town.

"Now," he panted after a moment, "I'm going to move. Feel me, Lily."

"Oh god!" she sobbed. "I missed you…I missed you so much! Can you feel me, too?"

"Yes," he hissed as his fist began pumping faster. "You're so fucking tight and wet. You feel like home to me…I'm fucking you harder now…shoving myself as deep as I can go. I want to hit that spot that always makes you scream."

"Ethan," she gasped, "I want you to fuck your hand for me. Don't just stroke your cock…I want to know you're really fucking me."

"Tell me what you want, baby," he gritted through his teeth. "Anything."

"Stop moving your hand for a minute…just thrust your hips. You can move it again in a bit, but I want to know that you're thrusting inside me at the same time."

"All right...pull that toy all the way out to the edge. *Now*," he said as he flexed his hips, shoving himself into the tightness of his palm. Lily moved in time with him, pumping the toy all the way inside her again.

"Yes!" she cried out.

"Is that what you want, baby?" he moaned.

"Yes...so good! You?"

"It feels amazing. I'm going to again...now...now...yesss...fuck... faster...oh God!"

Lily began bucking her hips furiously, timing every thrust with the sound of his voice. "Ethan, move your hand now. I'm so fucking close...I want you to feel me pushing back into you."

At the sounds of his loud moans, she felt herself tightening around the toy, and she was suddenly possessed with the need to hear him finish first.

"Ethan, baby...come for me...please!"

"But...you...first," he grunted, barely holding on.

"No...please, baby...I need to hear you so badly. I need to hear you to help me finish. Ethan...come for me...come inside me...let me feel you spilling inside me."

"Oh fuck!" he cried out. "Lily!" He exploded violently, spurting his release all over his hand and stomach.

Just as she'd expected, hearing him finish set her off like a chain reaction, and before he was even done moaning and thrusting, she had thrown her head back and was howling like a banshee.

When they had both stopped orbiting the planet several times over, they each rolled over in the darkness, gasping into the phone.

"That was..." he panted.

"*Incredible*," she finished, just as out of breath as he was. After a moment of silence Lily giggled.

"What's so funny?" he smiled.

"Oh, I was just wondering if you'd be able to get to sleep now. I know I will."

"God yes. I can barely keep my eyes open. You wore me out from across town, woman."

"Good," she smirked. "I suppose I should let you go, then. Thank you, Ethan. Thank you for sharing that with me."

"Oh, it was absolutely my pleasure. Thank you for asking… I don't know if I would have had the nerve just yet."

"Good night, Ethan." And then, because it finally felt right, and she felt freer than she had in months, she added, "I love you."

It was only the beat of a second before she heard a sigh and a quiet whisper.

"I love you, too, Lily."

8

———

They actually said it.

And she said it first.

Ethan's mind was still reeling the next morning, almost positive he'd hallucinated the entire evening's events. There was just no way such a perfect night could have happened between them so soon. He had been so worried that it would take him days, if not weeks, to get her to agree to spend time with him. The fact that she was willing to put aside her misgivings long enough to give him a real chance spoke volumes about her maturity—and her strength.

It was clear she had no interest in playing head games or doling out punishment; she simply wanted to get to a place where they could finally be together and put some real effort into it. For the first time since he'd met her, they were both on the same page.

And rather than feeling like a chore, it was absolute heaven. If their first date was any indication of the future, he wanted to spend the rest of his life putting effort into his time with Lily. How could something so enjoyable even be considered effort?

He was so proud to take her out in public, wanting to shout out to anyone who would listen that she was his. Everything about her was breathtaking, from her dress to her conversation, and what still amazed him was that it had all been so easy. He had fretted over whether they would be comfortable enough together to actually say more than five words to each other, but he'd worried for nothing. The moment they started speaking, it was as if he had finally found his way home after a very long journey.

Lily was his home.

He already knew without a shadow of a doubt that he was madly in love with her, but it was news to him that she felt anything close to the same after everything he'd put her through. Thanks to her bravery and newfound ability of cutting through the bullshit, they already had their first declarations out of the way.

It was almost comical how simple it was to say the words when the moment came.

Ethan had been thinking them over and over in his mind on a constant loop for the entire evening, even during their phone call. He'd wanted nothing more than to blurt them out, but he was nervous that it was still too soon and they wouldn't be received well. Thank goodness Lily had enough balls for the both of them, because once she put it out there, it was as easy as breathing to say it back.

The moment the words left his mouth, he felt his world shift, as if he'd been tilted off his axis for longer than he could remember, and telling her that he loved her had somehow set things right again. Now *she* was the center of his universe…but how could he make her believe it?

Sobering instantly at that thought, Ethan grabbed his phone and called one of his contacts. It was answered on the first ring.

"Foster, I wish you would stop checking up on me," a gruff voice spoke in his ear.

"I will when you give me a set date," he replied. "Any news?"

"I told you I would call you the second I heard anything, didn't I? You've given me zero notice here. These things take time to organize— you should know that by now. Everyone has been booked up for months."

"I can't believe that's the best you can do. What the fuck have I been paying you for all these years?"

"Well, with all due respect, you've never been on this side of it before. You were just the talent, and you were perfectly content to let Rachel handle all the gory details. She would have at least understood that what you are asking for now is damn near impossible."

"Well Rachel's not with me anymore, now is she, Greg? I guess that means you're stuck with me. At least, if you still want my business, that is."

A loud sigh could be heard on the other end. "Of course I still want your business. I'm not saying that it can't be done, only that it might take longer than you want."

"How long?"

"At least a good six to eight weeks."

"Are you fucking *kidding* me?" Ethan shouted.

"That's not unreasonable for the size of the venue you need. You have to understand that."

"And you have to understand that I don't have that kind of time. I need this done yesterday!"

"Would you please calm down? I'm doing the best I can, I promise you. I still have a few calls out, so nothing is final yet. I just want to prepare you for the worst."

"Please just work your magic. I'm counting on you, Greg."

"I know. Listen, Foster. All differences aside, I'm happy you're working, and that you still thought of me for this." His voice dropped to a whisper as he added, "I was very concerned that I wouldn't hear from you again after the fiasco with Rachel."

"Yes, well…I guess I should thank you for the concern." He sighed loudly. "Last I heard, she was smearing my name everywhere to make room for her new protégé."

"I wouldn't be too concerned about that," Greg replied. "The fucking kid is a joke. She can promote him all she wants, but he'll never sell the way that you do."

"I appreciate that. Hey, I'm sorry I'm being such a prick about this. I know Rachel usually handled this stuff for me, and she did a much better job at it. I just *really* need this, man."

There was a beat before Greg spoke again, all business. "I think I have a few more contacts I can call. Somebody in Chicago owes me a favor."

"Thanks, man," Ethan said before ending the call.

Deciding that he needed something to lighten his mood, he opened his list of contacts again, glancing at the clock quickly as he pressed his favorite new number. It was already after 10:00 a.m. and he couldn't help wondering what she'd been doing with her morning. Just thinking about hearing her voice again was putting a smile on his face and he hoped that she wouldn't mind him calling her again so soon.

"Hello?" she practically purred when she answered. Well, perhaps she was speaking normally, but it sounded like a purr to him.

"Morning, beautiful," he said, allowing his smile to stretch even wider across his face.

"Hi there," she giggled, and he could practically see her blush. Just knowing that she was remembering their call from the night before was making him lightheaded—all of his blood flowing to a location farther south on his body.

"What have you been up to this morning?"

"Well, my dad just left. I make breakfast for us sometimes on Sunday mornings before he goes out hunting."

"Still taking care of good old dad, huh?" he laughed.

"Not quite like before," she chuckled. "Now it's really just a way for us to stay in touch. Like I said, he misses me."

"And your cats," he smiled.

"And my cats, that's right."

"Well, I'm sure you're wondering why I'm calling again so soon."

"Not really, should I?" After a moment of silence in which he didn't quite know how to respond, Lily continued. "You don't need a reason to call me, Ethan. I'm happy simply talking to you and hearing your voice."

He took a deep breath before finally speaking. "That's really nice to know, Lily. That would make me happy too. But I actually did have something to ask you."

"All right, what is it?"

"I was wondering what you have planned for the rest of the day."

"Laundry," she said with a groan. "I was just about to head out to the laundromat."

"Oh really?" he said excitedly, sitting up straighter on his bed. "Why don't you do it over here?"

"I don't know. I'd hate to impose."

"Impose? I'm inviting you. I was hoping to spend some more time with you today anyway, so why not take advantage of our laundry room?"

"Really?" Lily said, biting her bottom lip in contemplation.

"Definitely. How about I come pick you up? You can throw your clothes in the wash and we can grab some lunch here while you wait. I know my mother would love to see you again."

"Barbara will be there?"

"Yeah…is that all right? Oh man, I sound totally lame now, don't I?" He laughed and began speaking in a higher voice to mimic a little boy. "Gee, Lily, wanna come play at my house? My mommy's gonna make us lunch!"

"Don't be silly," she laughed. "I enjoy spending time there, and I haven't seen her in a while."

"I keep forgetting how well you know them all."

"Does that still bother you?" she asked, remembering how angry he'd been when he first discovered their connection.

"No, not really. Although, I'll admit that it's a bit…disconcerting sometimes when I think about how much our lives seem to be intertwined."

"I know what you mean," she sighed. "It has a huge feeling of inevitability, doesn't it?"

"Exactly!" he laughed. "But it also saves me a lot of time worrying and hoping that you'll get along with my family."

"You know, now that you mention it, I think this has all been a bit too easy for you," Lily teased. "It's like the universe just decided that you needed a new girlfriend and literally dropped one in your lap."

"Yeah, I noticed that, too. Once I finally pulled my head out of my ass, that is. But at least now I can appreciate it." Lily was about to make another joke about him being the universe's bitch when he suddenly spoke again in a near whisper. "You know, I like hearing you say that word."

"What word?" she asked quietly, wondering quickly why she was also whispering.

"*Girlfriend.*"

"Oh, that," she replied, instantly feeling her face go up in flames.

"Yeah, that. Girlfriend. I like the sound of it. '*My* girlfriend' sounds even better."

Ethan had the sudden urge to drag her all over town on the off chance he might run into someone he knew, just so that he could introduce them to "my girlfriend, Lily." He briefly considered letting her follow through with her original plans to go to the laundromat just so that very thing might happen, but thought better of it when he remembered how much more comfortable it was at his parents' house. And how much more privacy they would have.

"I think you're right," she smiled, thrilled that he hadn't wigged out on her for dropping the g-word. "That does sound even better."

"So, how about it? Laundry day at my place?"

"Oh, I suppose I could be forced to spend some time with you in your gorgeous house with your adorably sweet mother."

"Great! I'll be there in fifteen minutes."

Ethan was already jumping up and running to the stairs before Lily realized that the call had ended, and by the time she had loaded everything into her laundry basket he was knocking on her door.

"Wow, eager much?" she teased as she opened it to let him in.

"For you? Always."

Lily tried to ignore how much the simplest compliment made her heart beat erratically. Ducking her head to hide her telltale blush, she motioned him inside while she grabbed her purse from the kitchen.

"I just can't believe what you've done with the place," he called out to her as he stood in the center of the room and slowly turned around, looking at every detail more closely in the light of day. When his gaze landed on the vase of flowers sitting in the middle of the tiny dining table he couldn't help but feel a swell of pride. She had kept his flowers.

"Thanks," she said as she re-entered the room, slinging her purse over her shoulder. When she was right in front of him, she stopped and looked up into his eyes. With a small smile playing at the corners of her mouth, she added, "I always knew it had amazing potential."

Ethan wasn't convinced they were still talking about the apartment.

In an effort to lighten the mood, and to keep from tackling her to the ground and covering her entire body with kisses, he quickly changed the subject. "I'm surprised there are no Conchords posters, though," he joked.

"They were vetoed," she sighed.

"I was only kidding!" he laughed. "You were seriously going to put some up?"

"Hey, this is the first place I've ever lived by myself. I was anxious to display all the things I love."

"Then why didn't you?"

"Emma and Maggie both thought they would make it look like a dumpy dorm room," she frowned. "I see their point, but still."

"Well, I suppose they do lose their charm once you grow out of your twenties," he chuckled. "At least for a living room. But you could always frame one and hang it in your bedroom or something."

"True, but I'm not so sure that having a poster of Jemaine Clement near my bed is the best idea. I mean I'd probably never leave."

"Fair enough. I'd hate to be jealous of a poster." He smirked playfully and winked at her. Lily thought she might actually faint.

"Um…let's get going," she said awkwardly, suddenly too aware that they were only three feet from the bedroom in question. She went to pick up her laundry basket but he beat her to it, refusing to let her carry it to the car.

"I'm not a weakling, you know," she grumbled behind him as they walked down the stairs.

"Oh, stop pouting and let me enjoy this," he called back to her.

"What exactly is there to enjoy about carrying my dirty clothes? I *despise* laundry day." They stopped at the side of his car while he opened up the back door and tossed the basket into the backseat.

"Well, think of it this way," he said, turning to look at her as he shut the car door. "I never got to carry anybody's books in high school. This is the next best thing."

"Wow," Lily sighed.

"What?"

"I can't decide if that's really sweet or really lame." It was actually one of the sweetest things she'd ever heard.

"Oh really?" he smiled. "Are you leaning in either direction?"

Lily cocked her head to the side and looked at him, holding her chin with her thumb and forefinger as if in deep thought. "Hmm…I'd probably vote sweet, but only because you're so cute." She stood up on her tiptoes and gave him a quick peck on the cheek, only to squeal when he reached behind her and swatted her bottom.

"Brat," he growled with laughter in his eyes.

"You know it."

Ethan leaned down and captured her lips in a chaste kiss, pulling away before either of them could respond more passionately. "Delicious brat."

"You know that, too." She did that purring thing again with her voice and it was beginning to make him feel dizzy. They stood there for a moment doing nothing more than stare into each other's eyes, both of them feeling the electricity grow between their bodies.

He was the first to break away that time, blinking rapidly as if waking up from a dream. Opening the passenger door for her, he smiled and bowed deeply with his arm extended as if she were royalty. "Your chariot awaits, milady."

"Why, thank you, kind sir." She grabbed his hand as she lowered herself into the seat, biting back a moan when he kissed the back of her hand. She watched him through the windows as he walked around to the driver's side and got in. "So…this is the new rental, huh?" They both looked around at the interior of the Nissan Maxima.

"Yep," he answered as he turned the key in the ignition.

"It's nice. I miss the Audi though."

He hit the brake hard, turning to look her in the eye. "Believe me, I do, too. There were some…*fond* memories in that car." The rest of the drive to the Fosters' was spent in near silence, both of their minds flickering over rainstorms and parking lots.

When they arrived, Barbara was just finishing the soup and sandwiches she'd happily started making when Ethan announced he would be bringing Lily over for the afternoon. He had been a little hesitant at first, worrying that she might smother them with attention and make Lily feel awkward, but as soon as he saw the loving hug between them, he knew he had done the right thing by including his mother in his life for a change. Spreading the love was a new concept to him, and he was finding it to be quite rewarding.

They sat at the small, informal table in the kitchen, talking easily as they ate. Ethan was amazed by how comfortable the two women seemed to be together, laughing and sharing more in thirty minutes than Rachel had with his mother in ten years. Watching them like that only served to drive home a fact he'd recently learned to accept: Lily belonged there, in every aspect of his life.

When they were finished with lunch, Barbara didn't linger. She thanked Lily again for visiting and made her promise to return soon, then excused herself, claiming that she had some errands to run in the Cities for the day and that she would be back later. He hadn't even asked her to leave, but when she hugged Lily one more time, she looked at him over her shoulder and winked.

Leave it to his mother to be the best wingman he'd ever had.

As soon as they were alone, Ethan grabbed her laundry basket again and headed toward the stairs to the basement. Lily followed closely behind him, reclaiming her dirty clothes once they were standing in front of the washing machine. She sorted them quickly into two loads and threw the darks in first, turning to face him after she was done.

"Okay, that should be almost an hour before this load is ready to go in the dryer. What do we do now?"

Ethan smirked knowingly. "That depends on which game you want to lose first." He turned around and disappeared into the darkness behind them, flipping on the light switch to reveal the enormous rec room. "You remember this room, don't you?"

"Well, I certainly remember the pinball machine," she choked out, already turning a deep shade of red.

His smirk bloomed into a full-on wicked smile. "Yeah…if I remember correctly, I was just about to hit the high score before Maggie interrupted us."

"Uh, no!" she huffed. "You weren't about to hit anything, thank you very much!"

"I think we remember things differently."

"What are you talking about? Your entire family was upstairs! There is no way I would've let it get that far."

"Maybe not intentionally," he teased, "but I don't think either one of us had our wits about us that day."

Lily thought for a moment and sighed. "All right, I'll grant you that. Now stop being so smug and get over here so I can kick your ass at pool."

"Awful sure of yourself, my dear."

"I'm pretty…not bad," she smiled.

"Well I've also been known to be pretty not bad," he replied as he grabbed two cues from the rack on the wall.

She walked up to him slowly, reaching out and wrapping her fingers around the cue that he held out to her. "And I've been known to play dirty," she whispered, stroking her hand up the long, smooth shaft a few times while licking her lips seductively.

Ignoring the twitching in his pants, Ethan took a deep breath and smirked again. "Two can play that game, baby."

"Then rack 'em up."

What followed next was the most sexually tense game of pool in the history of rec rooms.

Every time Lily took a shot, she made sure to lean way over, strategically displaying her ample cleavage right in front of a nearly drooling Ethan. She would then slide the cue back and forth between her fingers, looking up at him through her lashes as she did so. Whenever she had to take a shot from close to where he was standing, she would make a show of leaning over slowly and sticking her ass out, never failing to look back over her shoulder before striking the ball.

To say that Ethan was distracted would be an enormous understatement. However, he wasn't completely unarmed in their little game. Rather than trying to distract her during his own shots like she was doing, he would wait and make his move while she took hers. When she would lean over with her cleavage on display, he began meeting her gaze with his smoldering jade eyes, licking his lips and adjusting the now prominent bulge in his jeans.

While she was visibly affecting him with her tricks, his were clearly working as well. Her shots grew increasingly sloppier the more obvious his arousal became. When she bent over in front of him again, he closed the distance until he was leaning over her back, whispering tips into her ear.

She missed the ball altogether, and he gently placed his hands over hers and guided her, brushing his lips against the outer shell of her ear as he breathed, "Like this." And then he proceeded to gently rub himself against her backside as they followed through the shot, causing Lily to moan and throw her head back, squeezing her eyes shut against the sudden pleasure of feeling him so close again.

He stilled his movements, trying to decide through his haze of arousal if he should take advantage of the situation or back away quickly to stop things from going any further.

Lily chose for him.

She threw the cue down on the table and brought her hands up behind his head, effectively trapping him against her. She leaned back into him, rubbing her bottom against his painful erection as she pulled his mouth down to her neck. Between her luscious scent and the extreme pleasure of feeling her grinding back against him, Ethan was quickly drunk with desire.

He parted his lips and left wet kisses along her neck, punctuated by soft nips with his teeth. Her groaning in his ear only fueled his desire, causing him to buck his hips against her more fully. He reached his hands around the front of her, sliding them under her shirt and anchoring her with one large hand pressed against the soft flesh of her stomach. The other hand had a mind of its own, roaming higher until he was cupping one of her breasts, squeezing it roughly when he felt her nipple pebbling up under his palm.

She gasped loudly and spun around in his arms, pressing herself against the front of him as his hands slid down to grip her ass. Their mouths met frantically, each of their tongues fighting as they swallowed each other's groans of need. Ethan desperately wanted to touch her everywhere at once, so he lifted her up by her backside and sat her down on the edge of the table.

Positioning himself between her legs, he growled against her lips when she wound them around his waist eagerly. It felt like home to have her wrapped around him again, even through all of their clothes. He suddenly needed her to know just how right it felt to be back with her, both physically and emotionally, where he had so badly needed to be. He reached up to hold her face and pulled back so that he could stare into her heavy-lidded eyes.

"I love you, Lily," he whispered, surprised at how easy it was to say now that he was certain it was true.

"I love you, too, Ethan," she smiled, and he felt a jolt of elation rip through his chest. "Can we please keep kissing this time, though?" she panted, glancing between his eyes and his lips.

"Yes, my beautiful girl," he chuckled.

"Oh, thank God!" She pulled him back to her lips, igniting a whole new kissing frenzy. Shoving her hands into his hair, she yanked and pulled at it as she sucked on his lips and tongue. He moaned deeply, wondering if his eyes might completely roll back into his head at some point from a pleasure overdose.

When Lily needed more, she began to lean backward, pulling him down with her. Ethan followed happily, climbing onto the table on his knees as she continued to pull him down on top of her, sliding farther back to allow him room. When he finally settled the full weight of his body on hers she cried out, wrapping her arms and legs around him and holding him tight, as if she were afraid he could disappear at any moment.

He slid her shirt up high enough to expose her black lace bra, and with a hungry groan lowered his head and sucked on her swollen peaks through the material. His hands began gripping and squeezing them as he feasted, and before long he had to yank the material down and taste her sweet flesh. The moment the hot wetness of his mouth came in contact with her aching nipples she almost wept, and the intensity of it caused her to buck her hips wildly underneath him.

They both felt it at the same time then, the first full contact of his straining erection against her heated sex. They stopped moving and locked eyes, hers questioning and his conflicted. After only a few seconds he smiled again, rocking his hips more fully into her. They both cried out that time, and the frantic way she was clutching at his back only drove him on.

He resumed his position at her breasts, alternating between squeezing, sucking, and licking. Lily began to moan incoherent words and phrases, sinking her fingers into his hair again as they continued to move together, the feel of their clothing creating a new and interesting friction between them. Each thrust of his hardness against her made her see stars and fireworks when she closed her eyes, and they eventually set up a steady rhythm that kept him rubbing exactly where she needed him.

"You're so fucking beautiful," he groaned against her flesh before he kissed it again. "Everything about you feels so perfect!"

"Oh, God," she panted, her breath shaking as she felt herself winding tight like a spring, climbing higher and higher and loving every moment of it because he was with her again. "I missed you," she cried out, on the verge of something explosive. "I missed you so much!"

"Never again," he groaned out, moving up to look her in the eye, his thrusting becoming more erratic as his release neared. "You'll never be without me again." He kissed her deeply, pouring everything he was feeling into it, begging her with his body to feel what was in his heart.

"Oh...oh, God, I'm right there," she moaned when their lips broke apart, causing him to speed up his movements and press himself more firmly against her.

"Yes, baby," he gasped between thrusts. "Yes...let me hear you," he begged. There was so much warm, wet heat between their bodies that it felt amazing, and he was barely hanging on.

When the tightly coiled spring finally snapped inside her, Lily threw her head back and wailed, her entire body spasming beneath him. The feral beauty of her climax triggered his own, and Ethan buried his face in her neck and began rambling so fast that she barely understood him.

"I love you so much! I love you, I love you, I love you, oh fuck!" His hips jerked a few last times before he collapsed, laying his head on her rumpled shirt and still-exposed chest.

They lay there together like that for a few minutes in silence, Lily stroking his hair lovingly as he tenderly kissed the spot over her heart.

"Was this...okay?" she finally asked him, hating to break the comfortable quiet in the room.

"It was more than okay," he whispered against her skin, sounding as if he could fall asleep at any second. "It was amazing."

"We didn't go too far for you?" she asked, feeling guilty for provoking him now that the heat of the moment had passed.

"No, I don't think so. As much as I want to date you properly and get to know you all over again, we can't exactly ignore this insane attraction between us. Things are bound to happen. I just don't want that to be all it's about anymore, and I'm really trying to hold off a little longer before we make love."

"*Aw*...you called it making love," she smiled. "I don't think I've ever heard you call it anything other than fucking."

"Well," he explained, propping himself up on his elbow to look down at her. "I think there's raw, nasty, sweaty fucking, but I now know there is something on a deeper level that can be shared between two people when the time is right. I think we've even come close to it before without realizing what we had. Hopefully I'll have the opportunity to do both with you so often we lose count. But the next time I'm inside you, I want to be making love to you."

"Why can't we do that now?" she asked, pouting. "We both know how we feel about each other."

"Because in my mind, I haven't earned it yet."

"But, Ethan—"

"Just listen," he interrupted. "I know you've forgiven me, and for that I will be eternally grateful, but I haven't completely forgiven myself."

"I don't want to spend all our time together with you treating me like some delicate, fragile thing, putting me up on some pedestal." Lily huffed. "I happened to like how things were before, at least physically. I just wanted us to get to know each other more and let each other into our real lives."

"Oh, don't get me wrong," he smiled. "There is way too much heat between us to ever become boring. I adored what we did too…but I need to find a way to balance out the hunger with the sweetness. I want to be in a real relationship and actually try to make it work. I've never really dated before. I've never had to try. To me, you're worth it."

"Dammit," she sighed.

"What?"

"Well, that was so damn beautiful I want to cry, and now all I want to do is throw you down and have my wicked way with you!"

"You think I don't want the same thing?"

"We're adults, dammit!" she pouted again. "If we want to have sex, we should be able to have sex."

"Normally I would agree with you, and that's also why I know things are going to happen between us no matter what. I just really want to feel like I've deserved something for once in my life, and if I cave now I know I will always regret it."

"All right," she grumbled. "I guess I see your point. It's just so easy to forget when you're on top of me like this."

"I know, baby," he laughed, shifting to her side. "It's going to be a struggle, but it will make it that much more worth it in the end."

"How long are we talking, here?"

"That's the hard part. There's an actual event that I'm trying to set up, and I'm having trouble finalizing a date. Hopefully it won't be too long."

"Will you tell me what it is?"

"No, of course not! It's a surprise."

"Will I like it?"

"I really hope so," he sighed.

"Hey, look at me. If it's something that you spent this much time and energy and sexual frustration on, I'm sure I'll love it."

"Thanks," he smiled, leaning down and kissing her softly. "Now, we should probably get cleaned up. I'm going to run up and change into a different pair of jeans. Things are starting to get a little…sticky," he blushed.

"Just bring those back down with you and I'll throw them in my next load of laundry."

"Thanks, that would be great. I'll see if I can find a spare pair of Maggie's jeans in Eric's room." Ethan turned on the television for her before he left because she didn't feel like playing any more games. When he returned less than fifteen minutes later, he tossed his dirty clothes in front of the washer and joined her on the couch. "Well, I couldn't find any jeans. All she had were pajamas, so I grabbed you a pair of shorts. I figured that your clothes will be done drying before too long anyway, so you won't need to wear these for very long."

"That'll work, thanks."

"There's a small bathroom over there if you want to go change, then you can throw the next load in."

Lily changed quickly and switched out the laundry, happy that all of her other jeans were going into the dryer and she'd be able to change back soon, before Barbara saw her in Maggie's shorts. She returned to sit by Ethan on the couch, feeling her heart soar when he comfortably wrapped his arm around her and pulled her against his side. When she snuggled against him even closer and rested her cheek on his shoulder, he leaned over and kissed the top of her head.

"This is nice," he sighed.

"What, the *Dukes of Hazzard* marathon? I was going to ask if we could change it. I can only take so much unbuttoned beefcake."

"No," he laughed. "Being together like this." He handed her the remote. "Here, put on whatever you like. I can't believe you aren't feeling the good ol' boys."

"Oh, I used to love this show when I was little. I had the hugest crush on Bo Duke. Now it's kind of embarrassing when I think about it."

"I always loved Rosco and Flash."

"Oh, me, too! I always wanted a basset hound that looked like Flash, but my mom would never let me have one." She looked at him and then back at the TV. "Funny, I would have thought you'd have been into Daisy."

"Oh, I never said I wasn't," he laughed. "Just look at those shorts!"

"Okay, that's enough of that," Lily huffed, turning the channel quickly. "There, *Top Chef*. Not a single pair of shorty shorts in sight."

"True, but there's always Padma Lakshmi's post-pregnancy cleavage."

"Ugh!" She reached for the remote again and he laughed loudly, grabbing it out of her hand.

"My God, you're jealous! Of the TV!"

"No, I'm not," she protested.

"You totally are! That's hilarious," Ethan laughed even louder. "It's damn adorable, actually."

"No, I'm not a jealous person. I don't *get* jealous. All of my old boyfriends back in college thought I was the coolest girlfriend ever, because I can talk about how sexy women are and play 'spot the falsies' while watching porn."

"Spot the—? Wait, aren't they pretty much all falsies?"

"Yeah, but some of them are really cheap. You can see these nasty ripples and ridges when they move. That's beside the point, anyway. The point is that I don't get jealous."

"Hey, don't be so defensive," he chuckled, reaching around her and tickling her sides until she laughed. "It's nothing to be embarrassed about. I think it's kind of precious. Nobody's ever been jealous over me, even if it's just the TV."

"How is that possible?"

"What do you mean?"

"Ethan…you're painfully beautiful. Any woman who sees you must want you. How could someone not have gotten jealous over you before?"

"You're forgetting there was only Rachel. She liked the attention I got because having an attractive boyfriend reflected well on her. She cared less about me than what I brought her. So believe me when I say that it's a refreshing change to have someone care."

"Well, it's not like I'm going to shank the first girl who looks at you or anything. I'd just feel funny watching you ogle someone else."

"If it makes you feel any better, I'd like to beat the shit out of Bo Duke right now. And Jemaine Clement is next."

"But that's silly! They're just—okay, I see what you mean."

"You can't help how you feel. This is all new to me too. I've never been jealous in my life. I never needed to be." He turned sideways to face her. "You make me feel so many things, Lily. It really is like I'm alive for the first time in my life. Even sitting here with you like this… I've never cuddled with anyone before you. It's all just so…amazing."

"You amaze me, too, Ethan. Every day I'm with you is amazing."

"Then why don't you come back over here and we'll do some more of that cuddling? I liked that. Let's watch *Top Chef* and guess who gets voted off this round."

"I suppose," she smiled.

"And just for the record, you're the only brunette in shorty shorts I'm interested in ogling," he said, squeezing her bare thigh.

"Thank you," she giggled, kissing him quickly. "And I'd take you over a threesome with Bo and Jemaine any day."

"Well, that's comforting," he chuckled.

Ethan leaned back against the arm of the couch, pulling her down with him. After she got comfortable curled up against him with her head on his chest, he slowly began stroking her hair and humming softly to himself.

It felt so soothing that Lily's eyelids were growing heavy. The only thing keeping her awake was her struggle to remember where she had heard the tune he was humming. Eventually she lost the fight, her body giving over to sleep.

In her very last moment of consciousness, listening to the lovely song as it reverberated through his chest against her ear, the memory came to her.

He was humming their waltz.

9

"Since when do you have a new boyfriend?" Becky blurted out the next morning after hearing Lily making plans for lunch on her cellphone.

"What makes you think that was my boyfriend?"

"Because you don't blush like that when your dad calls you."

"That still doesn't make it a boyfriend," Lily hedged.

"Are we really going to play this game?" Becky huffed.

"What game?"

"The Jason-and-Natalie game, where everything you do is glaringly obvious to everyone around you, but we all have to pretend like nothing's going on." It was no secret that Lily's boss, Dr. Natalie Wilde, was sleeping with the newest, youngest doctor in the practice.

"I don't know what you're—" She stopped mid-sentence when Becky arched an eyebrow at her, letting her know in no uncertain terms that she was not going to believe any line of bullshit Lily might deliver. "Dammit, Becky. Not the eyebrow."

Becky simply crossed her arms and stared at her. "Spill it, bitch."

Lily sighed, turning her chair to face Becky more directly. "It's just that things are so new. It feels weird talking about it."

"New? I'll say it's new! Weren't you single on Friday? I didn't even know you were talking to anybody since Scott."

"Well…we sort of…ran into each other again on Friday night." Lily blushed again, thinking of how much things had changed since then.

"Wow, that must have been *some* weekend."

"It really was, and not in the way you're implying, either."

Although Lily would have liked that very much.

"I don't care how little happened—I just want some damn details! Who is the guy? How do you know him? Is he local?" Becky's barrage of questions was interrupted by Kim on the intercom, alerting her that Jason had a red chart waiting to be seen. She stood up and pushed in her chair, turning back to look at Lily. "Don't think you're off the hook yet, my dear. I'll get it all out of you somehow." With that she walked away, shooting Lily a look over her shoulder that said she meant business.

Almost three hours later, Ethan walked into the tastefully decorated clinic, glancing around uncomfortably at all of the pregnant women in the waiting room. When he reached the front desk, he noticed a vaguely familiar face in the pudgy blonde receptionist at the counter, but she was so engrossed in staring at her monitor that he couldn't quite place her.

"Can I help you, sir?" she asked in an irritated tone, never once looking up from her game of solitaire.

"I'm waiting for someone. I was wondering if you might know how long she'll be."

"What's her name and appointment time?" she huffed loudly.

"No, she works here. Her name is Lily Blake."

That got her attention, causing the girl's eyes to practically bug out of her head when she finally looked up at him. "Oh my God, *Ethan?*"

"Uh...yeah?" Apparently his face was less vague to her.

"It's me, Kim!" she smiled excitedly. He was willing to bet this was the most animated she'd been about anything all day.

"Kim…?"

"Sanders, silly! We went to high school together. I sat near you in English senior year."

"Oh…yeah, okay. How have you been?" He really couldn't have cared less, but he didn't want to be impolite to one of Lily's coworkers. He *did* remember her once she said her name—and his memories of her made him cringe inside.

She used to strut around the school like she was hot shit, hanging on the arm of any guy she thought might be worth something to her. All she would have to do was shove her big tits in their faces and giggle like the airhead she was, and they gladly ate it up. She'd even tried batting her overly-mascaraed lashes at him a few times, but he had no interest in pretending to care about her vapid conversation.

"Oh, I'm good. *Real* good," she purred. From the looks of her now, she had put on a good sixty pounds and hated her job. He could also tell from her bare ring finger and the way she was batting her lashes again that she was still sitting around on her widening ass, waiting for Prince Charming to appear and fix all of her problems.

It wasn't that Ethan cared what a woman weighed; he appreciated curves in all the right places and always had. He'd painted countless women through the years with many different body types and had always found the beauty he was looking for. There was just something depressing about an aging prom queen living in denial.

"So…Lily?" he asked, trying to make her focus on the here and now. "Any idea how soon she'll be ready for lunch?"

"Oh," she pouted, her face falling visibly when she finally realized that he had no desire to reminisce about the good old days. "Let me look." She clicked a few buttons on her keyboard, her eyes looking up at him every few seconds. "So, you and Lily, huh?" she probed nosily as she searched the screen. "When did that happen?"

"Recently," was the only answer he gave.

"All right," Kim sighed when he refused to say any more. "Well, it looks like she already took back her last patient for the morning. I'll leave her a message that you're here. She should be done soon if you want to have a seat."

"Thank you," he nodded curtly, walked over to the only section of empty chairs, and sat down, rifling through the maternity magazines as he glanced at his watch. He could feel the stares of the other women in the room burning holes into his flesh, giving a new meaning to the phrase "no man's land." He felt like the enemy, and before even two minutes had passed he was ready to apologize to them for every man in the world who'd ever gotten a woman pregnant. After five minutes, he was ready to apologize for even having a penis. When Lily finally found him a few minutes later, the sigh of relief he gave as he stood up could be heard throughout the room.

"Thank God!" he gasped the moment they had stepped outside toward his car.

"What's wrong?" she asked, barely containing a giggle.

"That was the most awkward I've felt in years. I swear they were just about to attack me when you came out."

"Who?"

"Those women!"

She couldn't hold it any longer after that, openly laughing at the expression of horror on his face. "What on Earth are you talking about?"

"It felt like every pair of eyes in that room was on me, like I wasn't supposed to be there," he tried to explain as he opened the passenger door for her.

"Ethan, there were a few other men there. They were all sitting with their wives, didn't you see them?"

"No, all I saw were pregnant women everywhere. *Angry* pregnant women, looking for justice." He closed the door on her laughter, still able to hear it through the windows as he walked around to get in the other side.

"That's ridiculous!" she choked out through her giggling fit once he was seated next to her.

"Then why did I feel like everyone was staring at me?"

After she wiped a tear from her eye, she took a deep breath and looked at him. "Baby, they were probably just wondering why you were there alone. *And* where you'd been all their lives."

"Oh, stop it," he said, throwing the car in reverse and backing out of his parking space.

"I'm serious. Do you have any idea how horny some pregnant women get? Having you dangled in front of their eyes for that long is actually pretty cruel. I'm not surprised you felt their eyes all over you."

"Oh man, that's even worse! Now I can never visit you there again. I'll always have to worry about mother-to-be gang rape!"

"Would you stop being so silly?" Placing her hand on his arm as he was getting ready to turn out of the lot, she waited until he was looking at her before she continued. "You're just feeling awkward visiting me at work." Lily could sympathize. The entire office was peeking through the door to the waiting area to get a glimpse of the new man in her life. "For what it's worth, seeing you there waiting for me has been the best part of my day. Now, can I have a kiss?"

Shoving his hands through his hair quickly, Ethan exhaled loudly before finally laughing with her. "You're right, I'm being an idiot." He leaned over and kissed her gently, smiling against her lips when she tugged him closer, refusing to let him back away without deepening the kiss. "Mmm…hello there."

"Now that's the hello I was looking for," she smiled. "Can we go eat now?"

"Oh, I suppose. How long do you have? Should we grab something quick or sit down?"

"I've got about an hour. Something quicker might be a better idea. I think the diner gets pretty packed this time of day, and something sit down takes too long."

"How about a burger at Tastee-Freez?"

"Perfect! We can eat in the car if we want to."

"Oh really?" he smirked, turning onto 3rd Street. "Have something in mind, do you?"

"Well, no," she blushed. "I just thought it might be nice to eat and talk wherever we wanted since it's such a pretty day, that's all."

"Sounds good to me."

He pulled into a spot at the old ice cream stand and they went up to the window, ordering two burgers and fries and two shakes, all to go. Lily rolled her eyes as the young girl behind the register giggled and flirted shamelessly with Ethan, reminding herself that it was simply something she was going to have to get used to if she wanted to continue dating someone so gorgeous. She knew the important thing was that he never flirted back—even if she did want to dump her chocolate shake over the dimwit girl's head.

"My God," Ethan moaned to himself behind her as they walked back to the car.

"What?" she very nearly snapped as she turned around, defensive about her newfound jealousy issues and fully expecting him to tease her about it again.

"I just…forgot how fucking sexy you look in your scrubs, that's all." He ducked his head as his cheeks tinted pink. When he looked back up and their eyes locked again, Lily almost forgot how to breathe. They both knew without saying that they were each remembering a heated sponge bath between a nurse and her very dirty patient.

Trying to ignore the sudden rush of heat through her body, Lily grabbed his shake and turned back toward the car. "Uh…let's get going before these melt."

"Any particular place you'd like to park?" The heavy-lidded gaze he gave her as he climbed into the car was enough to make her need to wipe her chin.

"Somewhere…private?" was all she could squeak out.

He said nothing in return, only inhaling sharply once before tearing off in the direction of the woods. They reached their special clearing in record time and ate their lunch even faster, although it was rather distracting for both of them. They tried to talk about their day as they ate, but Ethan found himself staring as she dunked her fries in her shake and brought them to her mouth, moaning softly as she chewed and licked her lips, and Lily couldn't keep her eyes off of his Adam's apple as it bobbed up and down when he swallowed.

"Okay, I'm just going to say it," she finally declared after a few more longing glances at each other. "This is really…" She tried to think of a word that wasn't *hard*. "Difficult."

"I know," he sighed, nodding his head in agreement. "It's taking all I've got to keep myself from attacking you right now."

"May I ask why you brought me all the way out here when you don't want us to do anything yet?"

"Well, you said you wanted privacy. This was the first place that popped into my head. Besides, I never said we couldn't do *anything*." He waggled his eyebrows at her playfully, which only caused her to moan louder. "What's wrong?"

"Would you please stop making such adorable faces?" Lily whined. "Why?"

"Because the cuter your face gets, the more I want to sit on it!"

"*Fuck!*" he hissed through his teeth, lunging across the console at her and sending their bag of trash flying in the process.

His lips crashed into hers with an almost painful force, his tongue probing her mouth hungrily as he pulled her to him. Once Lily realized what was happening she responded eagerly, wrapping her arms around his shoulders and sliding her hands up the back of his neck until she was anchoring his head against her, kissing him with everything she had.

"You just…can't…*say* shit like that, Lily!" he groaned into her mouth, punctuating his words with flicks of his tongue around hers, sucking her bottom lip between his teeth for emphasis.

"Why?" she gasped, her lips already swollen from his kisses. "It's the truth."

"Because my control is so weak right now, it could snap at any second! Here, feel." He grabbed her hand and ran it down his abdomen, bringing it to rest on the prominent bulge in the front of his jeans. "Feel what you fucking do to me!"

"Oh, God," she moaned, closing her fingers around it, cupping him firmly. "Then do something about it! Fuck me and put us both out of our misery!" She began to tighten her grip, rubbing and squeezing him through his jeans until his eyes were rolling back in his head.

"Lily," he whimpered, forcing himself to look at her again. "Please… just a little more time."

"But how *much* time? That's what's killing me! This is just torture!"

"Soon," he panted, leaning over to place open-mouthed kisses down her neck. Greg had called that very morning to let Ethan know he had a promising meeting scheduled for that afternoon. Ethan had told Greg to inform him the second he had an answer. "I'm supposed to find out today. As soon as I know when, you'll know when. I swear." He lapped at a bead of sweat that had collected on her collarbone before shifting and starting back up the other side of her throat. When he reached her earlobe he sucked it between his teeth, nibbling lightly and pulling back to whisper in her ear. "If I have my way, it will be as soon as humanly possible."

His hand began to wander up her side, stopping to close over her breast, the firm peak of her nipple poking into his palm. She arched into him more fully and cried out, her head reeling from an overload of sensation.

"Ethan…please…I need…"

"What do you need, beautiful girl?" he said in the most delicious, husky whisper against her skin, his tongue and lips making her forget her own name. "Tell me. Let me help you."

She could barely think, her head was so foggy with lust, so she let her body take over for her. Giving his erection a final squeeze before letting go and loving the hiss it caused him to make against her mouth as they kissed, she slid her hand back between their bodies until she could slip it inside the waistband of her pants, and then down farther, inside her panties. She was met with an embarrassing amount of wetness, her outer lips slick and swollen with desire. Sweeping two fingers across her heated sex, she pulled her fingers back out and held them up in front of his face.

He stopped everything he was doing, transfixed at the sight of her fingers coated and dripping with her moisture. A primal shudder ran through him, making his cock grow impossibly harder. Before he could gather his wits enough to say anything, Lily shoved them between his lips.

At the first taste of her fluids on his tongue, a loud growl ripped loose from his chest and echoed in the car. Ethan began sucking on her fingers furiously, worried that he might pass out from the absolute heaven of finally tasting her again. Only when he had lapped up every drop could he pull away long enough to snarl two words at her.

"Back. Seat."

She didn't need to be told twice, scrambling out of the car and running to the back. By the time she had shut the door, he was already next to her, pulling and yanking at her pants and underwear as he kissed her frantically. Once he'd gotten them down over the swell of her hips and toward her knees, he started inhaling in choppy, ragged breaths between his kisses.

"*Fuck*...I can fucking smell you already," he grunted, leaning back on his knees long enough to rip one of her shoes off and toss it in the front. "I need to see you, baby. I missed this delicious, beautiful pussy...so much."

Lily could hardly speak. She simply tried to keep from hyper-ventilating as she panted and kicked her legs to help him pull her pants the rest of the way off. By the time they had one leg free, they both decided it was enough without saying a word, letting the rest of the fabric bunch up around the shoe on her other foot as it dangled over the floor mat.

"Oh my God," he gasped, unable to look her in the eye once his gaze had locked onto her dripping sex. "You're so fucking wet for me, baby." He ripped his T-shirt off over his head and pulled up on her hips. "Here, lift up." When she was up high enough, he slid his shirt underneath her, putting a barrier between her and the upholstery. Slowly he slid his hands between her thighs, pulling her legs wider until her free leg was resting with her foot on the back window ledge.

"Oh fuck," he whimpered. "I thought I remembered how perfect you were...how gorgeous this was." When he finally glanced up at her, he looked almost apologetic. "No memory can compare."

And with that, he promptly buried his face between her legs.

The sounds that emanated from that car would have terrified any unsuspecting hiker who might have happened by after that. Ethan's groans and Lily's cries of pleasure blended together to make some sort of raw, primal soundtrack to their stolen afternoon.

He licked and sucked at her wet, swollen flesh, quickly feeling drunk on her lust. Swirling his tongue around and around her clitoris, he would leave just long enough to dip it inside her opening a few times before flattening it out once more and making long, broad swipes back up to her tightened bundle of nerves. When he eventually felt her hands clamp down on his head and hold him in place as she started to grind herself into his face, he growled over and over against her wet flesh, emitting noises she thought were merely animalistic grunts, but in truth was his possessive mantra: *Mine, mine, mine, mine!*

Ethan was so hard he was throbbing painfully, unconsciously shifting his hips against the seat beneath him to relieve some of the pressure as he devoured her. When he slid two long, slender fingers deep inside her and began massaging her from the inside while she bucked against him, he knew that it wasn't going to be much longer before she found her release. And when he curled those same fingers upwards and pressed in just the right spot, causing her inner muscles to clamp down and grip him tightly while she screamed his name and flooded his fingers with her fluids, he knew it wasn't going to be much longer before he found *his* release.

Lily's hands gripped and pulled at his hair as she rode out her explosive climax, nearly passing out from the pleasure. As she crashed back down to reality, she was surprised to feel a huge tremor pass through Ethan's body, a guttural moan escaping his throat before he collapsed with his head on her stomach. She stroked his hair lovingly, realizing that she had missed this intimacy with him even more than she had thought.

"That was so fucking amazing," she panted. When he didn't reply after a moment, she looked down to find that his face was buried in her stomach. "Is something wrong, baby? I didn't forget about you, you know. I just needed a second to recoup," she laughed lightly. "You almost knocked me out there."

"Um…I don't really think you need to do anything right now," he mumbled, still averting his eyes.

"But I want to! I miss you, too. We should have enough time if we hurry," she said, starting to sit up.

"Uh, no, that's okay," he replied, pushing her back down. "Just rest here for a minute before we have to go back. That took a lot out of both of us."

"Is something wrong?" She was beginning to get concerned at how distant he was acting. "Why won't you let me help you, too?" She propped herself on her elbows and forced his chin up until he was looking at her.

"Because I don't exactly need any help anymore," he muttered, his face turning beet red.

"Oh!" It finally dawned on her what he was trying to say. "You mean you…already?"

"*Yes!*" he snapped.

"Well, that's okay," she smiled. "Why are you so upset? Didn't you pretty much do the same thing yesterday on the pool table?"

"That was different, it was intentional. This wasn't."

"Why does that matter? I mean, I'm bummed that I can't repay the favor until later, but what's the big deal?"

"The big deal is that I haven't blown my load like a teenager since I fucking *was* a teenager. I got so goddamn turned on going down on you that I couldn't hold it once you started coming."

"Well, that's no reason to be embarrassed. I'm actually flattered."

"*Flattered?!*"

"Yeah," she smiled. "Now that I think about it, it's kinda hot."

"How can you possibly find that hot?"

"Okay, pretend for a second our roles were reversed. Look how turned on you get just knowing that I'm wet for you. How hot would it be if I just got so excited while sucking you off that I couldn't stop myself from coming without even touching myself?"

"Well…when you put it like *that*," he laughed.

"Exactly. It would drive you crazy, don't even try to say it wouldn't. It's the same for me. I'm actually going to have a very hard time concentrating at work this afternoon, just thinking of you so turned on for me."

"Speaking of work, we better get you back before you're late."

"Oh crap," she sighed, glancing at her watch. "Yeah, we should get going."

Lily shimmied back into her pants awkwardly, grabbing her shoe from the front seat and shoving her foot in it. When Ethan sat up and lifted his shirt to put it back on, she gasped loudly.

"Good Lord! Please don't tell me you're thinking about wearing that again."

"What? Why not?" He held it up and turned it back and forth, showcasing the enormous wet spot that had soaked through both sides of the material. "I don't see anything wrong here," he chuckled. "It's just a little love stain."

"Well, there's a whole lotta love on that shirt!" she laughed.

"No kidding, I think I might frame this thing. I mean, it's like a personal best. I sort of feel accomplished right now."

"No fair! If you get to frame that, then I get to scrapbook those jeans you're wearing."

He looked her in the eye and winked. "Touché."

Getting out of the car, Ethan walked to the back and popped the trunk. After a minute of listening to him rustle around, Lily grew tired of trying to guess what he was doing and stepped out to follow him.

The sight that greeted her nearly made her heart stop.

Ethan was standing in the bright sunshine, completely nude, rifling through a few boxes in his trunk.

Once she finally regained her composure enough to speak, she cleared her throat dramatically. When he stopped what he was doing long enough to look at her, she couldn't help but laugh. "Uh…baby, what the hell are you doing?"

"I have a box of old clothes in here with some of my art supplies," he explained as he shoved a few more things around. "I was thinking of maybe doing some sketching or painting out here later, and I always keep spare clothes around in case I get splattered on."

"You got splattered on, all right," she teased.

"You can say that again," he mumbled to himself as he tore open another box. "Ha! There they are."

Lily watched as he climbed into another pair of ungodly sexy jeans that rode low on his hips, accentuating the fact that he was going commando. She would have been perfectly fine to stand there slack-jawed and staring for the rest of the day, but when he pulled an old black T-shirt over his head and turned around, she almost squealed when she saw *I'M OLD GREGG* on the front of it in large, white letters.

"Oh my God! Where did you get that?"

"Over in England a few years back. Why do you look so surprised? I told you I was a Boosh fan."

"I don't know…I guess I just…" Lily had no idea how to articulate the fact that seeing him in a goofy, old, novelty shirt struck such a chord with her. It was like she was looking at a mixture of her soul mate and her wildest dream come to life. Smiling up at him bashfully, she blushed. "I guess I just really like it."

"Come here." Ethan held his hand out to her, pulling her close the moment his fingers closed over her own. "I guess I just really like *you*," he whispered, leaning down to capture her lips in a soft, gentle kiss. No one had ever looked at him like that before, as if he were the answer to all of their prayers, and seeing that expression coming from her made him a bit lightheaded.

When Lily broke the kiss a moment later, she leaned her head on his shoulder and sighed loudly. "I hate to say it, but I really do have to get going."

Ethan chuckled lightly to himself. "I know, beautiful. Let's get out of here."

They jumped back in the car and took off toward town, getting her back to work only three minutes late, which was better than either of them expected. She thanked him for lunch—and other things—agreeing to talk on the phone again later that night after she got off work.

When Lily made it back to her desk to clock in, Becky took one look at her and started laughing.

"What's up, Nooner?" she cackled.

"Shut up!" Lily hissed under her breath. "I have no idea what you're talking about."

"Oh whatever, bitch! Nobody, and I repeat, *nobody*, goes to lunch with Ethan fucking Foster and comes back looking that satisfied without having just been screwed six ways from Sunday."

"We did not have sex!" she gritted through her teeth, brushing through her hair quickly with her fingers and checking her reflection in the small hand mirror she kept in her desk.

"Okay, Bill Clinton," Becky smirked. "Whatever you want to call it."

"Don't you have a patient up?" Lily muttered, glancing around for eavesdroppers.

"Nope," she grinned widely. "My first one is a no-show and yours is still updating her insurance, so spill it."

"What do you want to know?" she moaned, knowing that Becky would keep asking until someone eventually overheard her.

"For starters, how the hell do you know Ethan Foster, and how long has this been going on?"

"How did you even know it was Ethan?"

"Please. Kim had the entire office on red alert the second you walked out the door. Now she's got a whole new reason to be bitchy to you."

"Why? They didn't date, did they?" Lily gasped, trying not to throw up a little in her mouth.

"No! But if she'd had it her way, they would have. Hell, we *all* would have!" Becky sighed wistfully. "Don't get me wrong, I love Jared, but Ethan was the unattainable perfection that we all fantasized about getting our hands on back in high school." That comment did not particularly help Lily with her jealousy issues. "But he never talked to any of us. Anyway, stop changing the subject. I want details!"

Lily finally caved, immediately feeling better about having someone she talked to on a daily basis up to speed with her life. She went on to explain that Maggie Foster had been trying to set them up a few months ago, but thanks to her unhappy engagement and his traumatic breakup, it wasn't the right time for either of them. However, she hinted that the sparks had still flown between them, and when they bumped back into each other over the weekend it had been a whole different story.

It wasn't the whole truth, but it wasn't a lie. She wanted to share as much as she could while still maintaining a modicum of privacy. The last thing she needed was to inadvertently give away their biggest secret to even more people. It was bad enough that Ethan's whole family knew they'd been sleeping together while she was still engaged.

She didn't need that little tidbit getting around her work, too.

"Have you told your father?" Becky gave her a knowing look.

"No," Lily groaned, not even wanting to think about that yet. "It's all so new. You're really the first person I've talked to about it other than Ethan's sister, Emma."

"How do you think he's going to take it? I mean, won't everyone else in the world pale in comparison to *Scott the Golden Boy*?" Becky had been open about her dislike of Scott for years, hating the way he seemed to expect Lily to drop everything to be at his beck and call. Her respect for Lily's father had dwindled for the same reason.

"Oh, I don't think it will be *that* bad, whenever I do decide to tell him. He's starting to accept that Scott and I were never meant to be, and I know he'd never admit it, but I think he's proud of me for starting over on my own."

"Well...good luck with that." Becky didn't bother masking the doubtful tone in her voice.

"It'll be fine," Lily replied with more conviction than she felt.

As long as Ethan sticks around long enough to actually meet my dad this time.

They both got back to work, each of them helping their respective patients for the rest of the afternoon. Whenever they would bump into each other again, Becky would ask another question, trying to get to the bottom of the Ethan mystery. By the end of their shift, Lily had promised to ask Ethan about possibly going out on a double date soon, which tickled Becky to no end.

Driving home in her massive boat of a car, Lily let her mind wander back through the day's events. She had been officially "outed" at work, fielding questions left and right after bigmouth Sanders blabbed to all who would listen that Lily was dating someone new. She also took it as a personal accomplishment that she'd managed to make everyone with a pulse completely jealous when her "someone new" turned out to be a certain Mr. Ethan Foster. The same Ethan Foster, in fact, who had treated her to a delicious lunch followed by an even more delicious orgasm.

All in all, it hadn't been too bad of a day.

As she turned into her parking lot, trying to think of what she might throw together for dinner, her phone beeped in her pocket; it was a text from Ethan. Swiping the screen excitedly, she felt her heart begin to pound in her rib cage when she read the two little words on the display screen.

Next weekend

Finally! They had a deadline for their frustration. She let out an enormous sigh, surprised at how much better she felt just knowing that in a little over a week they would once again be able to share themselves completely with each other. Hell, she might even be able to make it that long without sexually assaulting him in the process.

Had she thought this day hadn't been too bad? Scratch that.

This day had been perfect.

10

Ethan was gone for the next two days, only giving Lily the cryptic explanation that he needed to "finalize" a few things in Chicago before their big night in just over a week. She pouted when he wouldn't give her any more clues, but gave up gracefully when he assured her that being away from her for that long was going to be pure torture and promised to call her every night before bed.

When Ethan arrived in Chicago, Greg introduced him to Joan, the owner of a trendy new gallery that was gaining a lot of notoriety in the local art scene for its bold and ballsy collections. They spent the better part of an afternoon going over Ethan's demands and Joan's ideas, trying to meet somewhere in the middle. When they finally reached a compromise, they agreed to meet the following day to go over the final details of the plans that Joan would finish drawing up that night.

Not quite sure what to do with himself for the rest of the evening, Ethan took a deep breath and called his sister, shocking the hell out of her when he asked if she and Brandon wanted to grab some dinner.

A few hours later, he sat in their lavishly decorated guest bedroom and dialed Lily's number.

"I was beginning to think you were never going to call," Lily teased as she answered the phone.

"Sorry 'bout that, baby. I went out with Emma and Brandon. We just got back."

"Oh, you did?" she smiled. "That sounds fun!"

"It really was," he said, unable to hide the surprise in his voice. "That Brandon's a funny fucker once he finally starts talking."

"I know," she agreed. "I can't tell who's funnier, him or Eric. They both crack me up. Did Eric and Maggie go, too?"

"No, he's out of town until next week and apparently Maggie has been glued to her computer lately working on a new story."

Lily perked up like a curious puppy. "New story? What new story?"

"I don't know, fangirl," he laughed. "You'll have to ask her yourself. Whatever it is, I'm sure it will have lots of smut in it."

Lily sighed loudly. "Oh, I hope so! She does it the best."

"Really? I always thought we did it the best," he smirked.

"Well, when it comes to practical application, sure, but in the written form it's all her." They both laughed lightly, enjoying their easy banter.

"I missed you so much today," he whispered after a brief lull had settled over the conversation. "I know it's only been a few days, but I need to have you close to me. I want to be near you all the time, and it's worse now than it ever was before."

"How do you mean, 'worse than before?'"

"Well, before, I couldn't get you out of my head. I was always wondering if my beautiful goddess was going to visit me. But now that you're mine, my beautiful Lily, I just can't be close enough to you. I can't get enough of you in my life. I'm happy for the first time in years, and the only thing I'm high on is you."

A loud sniffle could be heard on the other end of the phone. "I love you, Ethan," she eventually managed to choke out. "I love you so much."

Every time she said it, his heart skipped a beat. "God, I love you, too, baby. So fucking much. I don't really know how to handle it, it's so overwhelming."

"Yeah, me neither," she chuckled, wiping her eyes.

"What are you thinking?" he asked after she was silent again.

"That I really wish you were here right now…and that we didn't have to wait any longer."

"Soon, Lily. So soon. And I can't wait to be back home so I can hold you again."

"You know, I don't think I've ever heard you refer to Aledo as your home, even though you grew up here. You always acted like you were just passing through."

"Home is wherever you are. I know that now."

"God dammit!" she sobbed, shedding fresh tears. "Stop doing that!"

"Doing what?"

"Saying things like that! I don't know how to take them, and they only make me miss you more."

"Just take them as the truth."

"I do. I believe you, it's just…I'm not used to hearing things like that."

Ethan smiled. "Well, you better start getting used to it. Apparently you've tapped into my inner cheeseball."

"Then can't you mix it in with something naughty? Give me a chance to adjust to the little girl you've become?" They both laughed at that.

"How's this? Lily, I love you more than anything and can't wait until I get to slide myself inside your tight little body again and fuck you senseless."

"Ooh, yes…that's more like it!" she giggled.

"It's true, you know," he said, his voice growing more husky and heated.

"Hey, don't start with that voice unless you plan on a repeat phone performance."

That reminded Ethan where he was, and he shut his eyes in frustration. "Shit! Good point. I'd love nothing else right now, but I'm at Emma's place for the night. I don't think I want them to hear us."

"I thought you were going to stay at a hotel."

"I was, but when Emma heard that she insisted I cancel my reservation and stay here."

Lily sighed again, rolling her eyes. "Damn that little shit, always interfering! Oh well, it's a big deal to her, you know, having her brother stay over. I bet you made her day by calling her up like that. I'm glad you did. She misses you more than you realize."

"I think I missed her more than I realized, too." They chatted for a few more minutes and then said their good-nights, each of them refusing to hang up first, feeling like blushing fourteen-year-olds with butterflies in their stomachs.

The next morning, some ungodly caterwauling in the kitchen woke Ethan. It turned out to be a pop song Emma was blasting about yelling timber or something like that. When he walked in covering his ears and scowling, she stopped mixing the pancake batter and turned down the speakers.

"Sorry! Did I wake you?" When he merely grumbled out the word "coffee" and trudged off in the direction she pointed to pour himself a cup, Emma went back to her mixing. After pouring out four large scoops of batter onto the sizzling griddle, she set down the ladle and turned around to face him. "I hope pancakes are okay. I wanted to make you something, but I haven't been to the store yet this week. So, it's either this or Grape-Nuts, and if I remember correctly, you won't eat those."

"*Blech*!" he shuddered, making a face as he walked around the island and sat on a stool across from where she had gone back to scraping and flipping. "How can you eat that nasty shit?" His voice was hoarse from sleep, and he hovered over his steaming cup as if it were the answer to all of his prayers.

"It's not so bad if you heat it up and sprinkle a little sweetener on it."

"And thus change everything about it in order to tolerate it. No thanks."

"I guess that's fair. I'm like that with Brandon and his grits. No way. I won't even make them. He has to wait and get them whenever we go out for breakfast."

"Where is he, anyway?" Ethan asked as he sipped his coffee.

"He had to go into the office. There was a meeting he couldn't get out of. I canceled my morning, though."

"You didn't have to do that, Em. Or make the pancakes."

"I wanted to. For both."

"Then thank you very much. For both."

They were quiet for a few minutes as she dished up two plates, placing one down in front of Ethan and walking around the counter to hop onto the stool next to him. Taking turns drowning their breakfast in maple syrup, they both chewed and swallowed huge mouthfuls in silence, with only an occasional grunt or sigh to prove that they were enjoying the meal.

"So," Emma said around a mouthful of food, "how are things with Lily?"

"Mmph," he grunted, nodding until he swallowed. "Good. Better than good, actually."

"Oh, I'm so happy for you two!" she dropped her fork and clapped enthusiastically. "Have you guys dropped the L-bomb yet?" At the telltale coloring of her brother's cheeks, she laughed loudly and bounced up and down. "Ooh! You did! You did! Who said it first? Tell me, tell me, tell me!"

"Jesus, Emma, what are you, twelve?"

"Oh, shut it! Can't I be excited? You're my brother, and I've never seen you so happy."

"That's because I haven't been. Being with her is just... God, Emma, I don't even know how to describe it."

"Like you found the other half of you?"

"You, too?" he asked, remembering his discussion with Eric about the same topic.

"Story of my life, brother dear."

"Is it always so...intense?"

"Yes. At least it is for me. But you get used to it after a while. You learn to adapt."

"Man, I hope so. This shit is seriously consuming me. And you know what scares me the most? The fact that it doesn't feel weird. I am seriously way too attached to this girl, way too fast, and rather than being bothered by that, I just feel...*right*. Does that make any sense?"

"Of course it does, Ethan. You're preaching to the choir, here. The first night I met Brandon, I asked him what his last name was. When he asked me why, I told him it was so I could find out what my new name was going to be. Any other guy in the world would have run screaming to the hills, but he just smiled and kissed me. And it just felt right."

"Jesus... I always thought stories like that were bullshit. Now I'm in the middle of one."

"Well I, for one, am thrilled that you're not fighting it anymore," she said, picking up the empty plates and tossing them in the dishwasher. "It's like you're a different person since you came back...or more like the real Ethan we all know and love decided to come back to us." She turned to him again, her face growing serious. "No matter what happens, I'll always love Lily for that."

"For what?"

"For giving me my brother back." She absently wiped at a tear as she spoke, and before he had time to think about it, Ethan had crossed the room and pulled her to him in a fierce hug.

"Hey," he whispered, rocking her back and forth. "I'm the lucky one. I have my whole family back and a woman I'm crazy about. I feel like I won the karma lottery or something."

After they had both cleaned up, they decided to take a walk down to the market since Emma still needed some groceries and Ethan's meeting wasn't for a few hours. He'd been evasive over dinner the night before when they asked him why he was in town, but Emma refused to let it go a second time. When he finally relented and told her what he was planning, she threw down the cucumber she was holding and started jumping up and down, insisting that he tell her every single detail.

Once Emma had been updated and sworn to secrecy, Ethan paid for her groceries as a thank-you for the room and the pancakes, and he even carried them home for her. Noticing that it was getting close to his meeting time, he grabbed his things and kissed his sister good-bye.

"Aren't you staying another night?" she called after him on his way to the door.

"Depends how late this all goes. I'd really like to get back earlier if I can."

"Good luck!"

His meeting with Joan and Greg ran longer than he'd hoped it would, both of them wanting to tweak a few more details with the final arrangements, and by the time they were done it was well after dinnertime. As soon as they wrapped things up, he tried to make a break for it, but Greg took him aside and reminded him that they were going to treat Joan to dinner as a thank-you for expediting everything with such short notice. When he started to complain, Greg told him that it was the least they could do for her, and that he and Rachel had done it many times for different gallery owners who hadn't put in half as much effort in twice as much time.

Huffing loudly, Ethan drove himself separately, hoping to leave town as soon as possible. After he parked at the restaurant he grabbed his phone, shooting off a quick text to Lily on the way inside.

> May not be able to call, stuck in late dinner meeting.
> Miss you.

He set his phone to vibrate and joined the others inside. A few minutes later, he felt his pocket buzzing. Not wanting to appear any ruder than he already had, he took it out quietly and peeked at her reply under the edge of the table.

> Jesus, meetings? What the hell are you planning? (Miss you, too)

He smiled to himself, eager for the following weekend so that he could show her just how much she meant to him. Glancing up and nodding in reply to make it appear as if he was actually listening to whatever Greg and Joan were babbling about that couldn't have interested him less, he quickly typed out another message.

> Shh! It's a secret. And I'm not telling.

She replied immediately.

> All right, fine. But then I'm not telling you what I'm wearing right now.

"Everything okay, Ethan?" Greg asked him after he broke into a coughing fit trying to cover his groan.

"Uh, yeah. I'm fine, sorry. Think I inhaled some parmesan cheese or something." When they finally slipped back into their conversation, he sent back another.

Very cruel, baby. I gotta go for now. Love you.

Deciding that he should at least try to pay attention for the rest of the meal, Ethan worked himself back into the discussion they were having, and before long he was surprised to find that he was actually enjoying himself. Joan had a lot of fun, fresh ideas for her gallery's future, and Ethan meant it when he told her he hoped his name might help her draw even more business.

"Oh, I can't imagine that it won't," she smiled. "But even if it didn't, I wouldn't care. I've been a huge fan of your work for years, and it's an honor to help you now."

It wasn't until after dessert and coffee that they finally said their good-byes, and when Ethan checked his watch again it was after ten o'clock.

"Dammit!" he swore to himself as he climbed in his car. Reaching for his phone to call Emma, pissed that he had to stay another night, he was surprised to see that he'd missed another text from Lily about twenty minutes before that.

Sorry we couldn't talk tonight. I'm calling it a night & heading to bed. Miss you and love you!

Ethan's mind flashed to an image of her curled up in her bed, thinking of him as she drifted off to sleep. Before he knew what he was doing, he had turned his car toward the interstate and finished dialing Emma's number.

"Hey, there," she answered on the second ring. "You heading back over for the night?"

"No, I'm driving back now. Just wanted to let you know I wouldn't be back."

"It's a three-hour drive! You'll fall asleep," she warned, the worried tone in her voice easy to pick up.

The image of Lily sleeping in their room flashed before his eyes again, and suddenly there was no other place in the world that existed. He glanced at the keys dangling from his ignition, the light reflecting off of one that was old and brass and had seen better days.

"I'll be fine. I'm going home."

11

Sometime after five in the morning, Lily opened her eyes begrudgingly, not wanting to ruin the best dream she'd had in months. Not knowing what woke her since she still had another hour before her alarm clock would go off, she closed her eyes again tightly, trying to will herself back to sleep, hoping that just once she would be able to pick up where she had left off in her dream. In it, Ethan had come to her, sliding into bed next to her in the darkness, wrapping her up in the warmth of his arms. It wasn't the content of the dream that was so wonderful—she'd certainly had more erotic dreams recently—but it was the fact that it felt more real than any other dream she'd had in her entire life.

Concentrating so hard on the heat of his body that she could swear she somehow still felt it, Lily was startled when the bed shifted behind her and a large hand with long, slender fingers slid under her tank top and settled on the bare flesh of her stomach. Choking back a loud squeak, she shifted her body enough so that she could roll over and face her dream visitor.

"Mmm...stop wiggling," a deep voice slurred next to her in the darkness, sounding heavy with sleep.

When her eyes finally adjusted to the lighting, Lily was treated to the sight of Ethan curled against her, his face peaceful with rest. Boober was rolled up in a fuzzy ball behind the back of his knees, effectively trapping him under the covers, and Wembley was stretched out on the pillow beside him, slowly tapping the tip of his tail against

Ethan's forehead. It was so cute that she hated to ruin it, but she knew firsthand what it was like to wake up to an eyeful of cat ass.

"Get!" she whispered, shooing Wembley away with a few gentle nudges until he relocated himself next to his brother. He took his sweet time moving, and the look he shot her as he padded across the mattress told her exactly what he thought of her at that moment.

Once Ethan was free of his cat bandana, Lily snuggled against him, wrapping her arm around his side and resting her hand on the firm muscles of his back. Kissing him softly on the lips, she pulled back just far enough so that she could look at him without her eyes crossing.

"I thought I dreamt you," she whispered, so close to him that her warm breath fluttered against his skin.

"Mmm," he mumbled, pulling her more firmly against him without opening his eyes. "Sleep."

Too excited to relax, she pressed him further. "I thought you were going to stay over another night."

"Missed you," he finally replied on the tail end of a loud yawn, distorting his words as he exhaled. "Couldn't wait."

"Aww," she cooed. "So adorable." She burrowed her head into the nook between his jaw and his shoulder, breathing him in deeply. Just as she was about to drift back off to sleep, another thought occurred to her. "Hey, how did you get in here?"

"Still have my key. Couldn't get rid of it…gave the landlady a copy. Was really happy you didn't change the lock."

"Never," she said with a catch in her voice, turning her head to kiss the angular curve of his jawbone. "I could never lock you out of our place." And then in an even smaller voice, "I kept hoping you would walk through that door."

That woke him up further. He reached up behind her and smoothed her hair back, cradling her head gently against him. "I've never told you how much it meant to me that you kept this place. When I learned that you were living here now, I just knew. I knew we had a chance."

Lily tilted her face up to meet his now serious gaze. "I couldn't let you go. It was all I had left of you."

"I'll be thankful for that for the rest of my life."

Their lips met in a tender kiss that slowly burned hotter. When he felt the wet tip of her tongue flicking against him, searching for entrance, he opened to it gladly. As the kiss deepened and they swallowed each other's moans, Ethan began to feel himself stirring in his boxer briefs, so he tried to pull his hips back from her a bit to keep from poking her in the stomach.

Lily, however, had other plans. As soon as she felt him trying to scoot away from her, she slid her hand down to his ass and gripped him firmly, pulling him back until his hardness was rubbing against her inner thigh. Moaning loudly against his mouth, Lily wrapped her leg around his hip, sending the grouchy cats sleeping behind him running for the other room. Before he could stop himself, Ethan cupped her bottom and thrust his hips, grinding his erection more directly against her moist heat.

"God, baby…we have to stop," he gasped as he pulled himself away from trailing wet kisses down the column of her neck.

"You stop," she panted, getting up on her knees and shoving him until he was lying flat on his back. "I'm doing no such thing." Kneeling at his side, Lily threw back the covers, exposing him to her hungry gaze. As soon as she saw the dark gray cotton of his underwear tented up with a telltale wet spot growing at the tip, she let out the most animalistic grunt that he'd ever heard her make before pulling and yanking the elastic down over his hips.

"What…what are you doing?" he somehow managed to ask, mesmerized by the look of determination on her face.

"Relax," she huffed, not looking at him until his boxers were down past his knees. "I'm not going to attack you—even though it's the least you deserve for showing up in my bed half-naked like this," she smirked. "I mean, a girl can only take so much teasing before she snaps."

She reached out and gently touched her fingertip to the underside of his erection, trailing it slowly up the length of him as it strained back toward his abdomen. When she reached the swollen tip, she swirled her finger around the collecting moisture she found there, causing Ethan to hiss loudly through his teeth. It wasn't until he looked back up and met her stare that she wrapped her fingers around his shaft and squeezed.

"Oh fuck!"

"No, not quite," she said, giggling to herself. "Someone won't let me yet. But don't think for one second that I forgot it's my turn to return the favor." With that, she leaned over and sucked him deeply into her mouth, not stopping until he hit the back of her throat.

"Jesus Christ!" he groaned, instinctively bringing his hand to the back of her head to guide her movements. Lily worked him viciously, bobbing her mouth up and down his length, swirling her tongue around him on the upstroke. His grunts and moans were steadily growing louder, accentuated by the thrusting of his hips. "Fuck, baby... it's been so long since I've felt you there...your goddam perfect fucking mouth." He sounded like he might cry from the pleasure, and there were more than a few times he had to stop himself from just grabbing her hair and pounding into her until she choked.

Lily moaned around him as she moved, growing more and more aroused at how primal his noises were becoming. She began to sway a bit on her knees, seeking out the friction between her thighs that she was starting to need more than oxygen. Before long, she felt Ethan's hand slide down from the back of her head to the back of her thigh, moving swiftly between her legs and pulling her panties to the side. One very long, talented finger slipped inside her aching heat, and after she moaned so loudly that it vibrated down the entire length of him to settle in his balls, he added a second.

"That's it, baby. Ride my fingers." He plunged them into her deeper and deeper, loving the way that she worked herself on him, bucking and grinding her hips while her inner muscles squeezed him tightly. "God…you're so fucking wet!" he whimpered when he felt her juices starting to drip down his hand. She could only moan and nod, unwilling to stop feasting on him for even a second.

Ethan slowly pulled his fingers free and sucked them into his mouth, her hypnotic flavor making his eyes roll back. With a possessive snarl, he reached over with both hands and started pulling at her panties, tugging them down over her bottom as he jerked her hips closer to his face.

"Get these fucking things off or I'm going to rip them," he growled. She lifted her knees, allowing him enough clearance to slide them down past her calves until she could kick them the rest of the way off. As soon as she was freed, he was pulling at her hips again. "Get the hell over here right now."

When she was close enough, he grabbed her, lifting her up so that she could swing one leg over his head. He settled her over his mouth, lapping at her swollen folds as she writhed around, squirming from the overload of sensation. Never once did she let up on her own task, sucking him deeper still and loving the feeling of his grunts and snarls against her wet flesh.

Lily bucked and swiveled her hips, grinding herself against his eager tongue, and when he slid two fingers back inside her from behind, she thought she might actually die from the intense pleasure. Knowing that she was going to be absolutely useless from the strength of her impending orgasm, she decided to try something new in the hopes of getting him there faster. Leaning forward, Lily sucked him as deep as possible. Only this time when he bumped the back of her throat, she swallowed.

It took her a couple of tries to relax her muscles enough for it to work, but when she felt the broad tip of him pushing into her throat she imagined that she was a porn star and Wonder Woman rolled into one. When Ethan let out a guttural moan against her and involuntarily jerked his hips, she felt damn near smug.

Eat your heart out, Jenna Jameson.

Lily could tell from the tenseness in Ethan's thighs that he was about to come, and the fact that he had begun working her even harder meant that it was going to be a race to the finish. His long fingers slid deeper and deeper, curling at just the right spot while he sucked on her clit, his own moaning making the most sensational vibrations. By the time Lily reached down to cup and massage his scrotum, it was all over.

The feeling of him swelling unbelievably harder in her throat sent her careening over the edge, and the feeling of her screams around his cock and the tightness of her inner muscles clamping down on him made Ethan come so hard that his ears began ringing. There was a moment when they became one enormous shaking orgasm before Lily fell to his side. She had barely enough energy to drag herself up next to him and collapse on his chest. No words were spoken between them, both out of exhaustion and awe at what they had just shared.

Before long, they were both asleep.

"Have I ever told you how much I love this little patch of freckles on the back of your shoulder?" Soft lips pressed to the area in question as Ethan wrapped his arms around Lily from behind, looking up at her over her shoulder in the mirror.

"I didn't even know I had a patch of freckles there," she laughed, leaning forward to finish applying her makeup.

"Well, you do. And it's adorable. I can't tell you how many nights I would lie awake, thinking of it."

Lily stopped and looked at his reflection again, her lip-gloss applicator suspended in midair. "You thought about my freckles?"

"Of course I did," he smiled, kissing her shoulder again. "You have tons of little treasures all over your body. Like this tiny chicken pox scar here, on your hip. Drives me crazy!" He leaned over and pulled the elastic of her pink cotton boy shorts down a few inches, smacking his lips loudly against a spot on her skin that she'd never even noticed before.

"Oh, you're crazy, all right," she giggled, a blush spreading over her exposed flesh at the thought of him paying such close attention to her. "I guess I'm not one to talk, though. You have a mole on the back of your neck that makes me want to do naughty, naughty things."

"Where?" he asked in disbelief, standing up and turning, trying to angle his head so that he could see himself in the mirror.

"Right here." Lily touched the small brown spot just below his hairline, and the gentle glide of her fingertips across his skin sent a shiver through his body.

"Stop that, you're giving me goose bumps."

"Gee, maybe that's because you're still standing here in a towel with wet hair. Now, would you please go and get dressed already? I'm trying to get ready for work and having you here looking like that and kissing on me is not helping!"

"All right, I'm going," he sighed, raising his hands in mock surrender as he backed out of the bathroom. "But only because you're going to lick my neck mole if I don't."

"Don't you forget it!" she called after him, rolling her eyes at how playful he was being and secretly loving every minute of it.

By the time Lily had thrown on her scrubs and tossed her hair up in a messy pile on top of her head, Ethan was already dressed and waiting for her by the door, munching on a warm s'mores Pop Tart. As she grabbed her purse and joined him to leave, he held out the pastry's twin to her, causing her to stop in her tracks.

"Here, I thought we could split a package since you're running late." When she didn't say anything for a moment and continued to stare at the item in his hand, he began to worry. "Oh, hey, I hope that's okay. I mean…I hope you don't mind that I helped myself. Shit, I should have asked, huh?"

After another second she reached out and took it, slowly shaking her head. "No, no…that's fine."

"Then what's wrong?" he asked as she walked past him in a daze, heading for the stairs.

"Nothing," she called back absentmindedly, leaving him to lock up as she nibbled her breakfast on the way to her car.

Ethan hurried after her, grabbing her by the elbow once he caught her in the parking lot. "Here, why don't you let me drive you today? I can pick you back up later and we can hang out here tonight, how does that sound?"

"You don't have to do that," she said quietly, averting her eyes from his.

"Who said anything about 'have to'? I *want* to. Besides…I don't feel right letting you drive off like this. You're starting to worry me." With that she finally looked up, and Ethan could see the tears collecting in the corners of her eyes. "Lily, please tell me what's wrong! I won't know how I fucked up if you don't tell me. *Communication*, remember?"

"You didn't do anything wrong, I swear. I'm just being stupid." When she tried to look away again he reached out and grabbed her chin, forcing her to look at him.

"Hey, I'm serious. Tell me what's going on."

"It's just that…nobody takes care of me. It's usually the other way around."

"Lily, it was just a Pop Tart."

"I know," she sniffed. "I know. But it was just a sweet, considerate thing to do. I guess I was just overwhelmed for a minute."

"Overwhelmed by what?"

She tried to look away again but he wouldn't let her move. "By how much I love you," she whispered.

Ethan tried to ignore how much his heart soared at her words, focusing instead on whatever had her upset. "You say that like it's a bad thing. I'm constantly overwhelmed by my feelings for you, by how strong they are, and I love it."

"It doesn't scare you?"

"No, honestly. It makes me feel alive." He leaned down and kissed her gently. "I've never felt as alive as I do when I'm with you. Why are you scared?"

She took a deep breath and decided that it was now or never. She had to be honest with him or else the stress of worrying all the time would eat her up inside. "Because…I won't be able to take it this time if you leave again. I already need you too much as it is."

"Okay, give me this shit." He grabbed the cooling Pop Tart and her purse and set them on the roof of his car before grabbing her face with both hands. "Look at me. Are you listening?" At her silent nod, he continued. "You have every right to feel that way after how I left before, but I need you to know that it's never going to happen again. *Ever*. Do you understand me?"

"But what if—"

"*No*. No 'what ifs'. I tried to fool myself into thinking that I didn't need whatever this is between us, that I could live without it, and it nearly ruined me. I kept telling myself that I didn't do anything wrong because I never promised you anything, but that was a lie."

"What are you talking about? I was the liar. I was the one who was engaged to another man. You didn't owe me anything."

"That's where you're wrong. From the first moment these hands touched your skin, I promised you my heart. I belonged to you from our very first kiss, and every kiss after that only bound me to you even more. When I left, I turned my back on that promise. I should have stuck it out and told you how I felt, but I ran away with my tail between my legs."

"We're both guilty of that," Lily sighed. "I should have ended my engagement the day I met you. I knew after that very first night that I would never feel that way again with any other man…even attempting to would have been pointless."

Ethan smiled down at her, sliding his fingers across her cheek to tuck a loose strand of hair behind her ear. "This connection between us is too powerful to fight, I know that now. I have no interest in even trying to exist in a world without you. Can we just…I don't know…start over?"

"I thought that's what we were doing."

"Yes, but we need to have faith in each other. I'm with you now, and I'm not going anywhere. I need you to believe that, or else you're always going to doubt me."

"I don't doubt that you love me, Ethan. I can feel it every time you look at me. I can hear it every time you say my name. I'm just…

apprehensive, I guess. I'm worried that it could all disappear again. I'm scared that I'll get too attached and you'll just be able to let it all go." Lily could feel the hot tears flowing freely down her cheeks.

"That's what I'm talking about. I need you to stop holding me at arm's length."

"What do you mean? I love you and I want this to work. I don't want to be without you."

"I know that, but if we're going to have any real chance of starting over, you're going to have to give me the benefit of the doubt. I am head over heels in love with you. Hell, my entire family is head over heels in love with you, and I'm pretty sure they'd choose you over me if I ever fucked up again."

"Oh, stop," she blushed, trying to look away again as she wiped at her eyes.

"No, it's true and you know it. I've opened up my life and my heart to you more than anyone else in my past, and that includes a relationship that lasted ten fucking years. I'm ready to give this everything I have, but you haven't even told your father about me yet, have you?"

Lily blinked a few times, shocked by his question. "Well…no. Not yet."

"Why not? Are you ashamed of me?" he asked, his words tainted with the slightest hint of insecurity.

"Of course not! How can you ask that?"

"Well, like I said, you've already met everyone in my family. They all played a part in getting us back together and know all the messy details of how we first met. Now, I'm not saying he needs to hear all of that, but I think it's a bit messed up that he doesn't even know I exist."

Lily immediately felt ashamed that she'd never considered his feelings on the matter. She'd been happy to let Ethan court her and invite her into his life, but when it came to returning the favor, her actions had been sorely lacking. She hadn't trusted him enough to let him into the rest of her life the way he had for her.

Leaning in, she pulled him to her in a fierce hug. "I'm sorry," she said against the fabric of his shirt. She could feel his hand close over the back of her neck, stroking her skin lovingly. "I never thought about it that way. I really did intend to introduce you…I guess I was waiting to make sure this was going to work out first."

"I understand," he said quietly, kissing the top of her head. "I made you a little gun shy. I get it. I just want the chance to make it up to you, and if you won't let me in I'm worried that will never happen."

"You're right," she sighed.

It wasn't fair to stand back and watch him jump off the cliff alone. It was time for her to hold his hand and take the leap together.

Lily pulled back and looked up into his patient jade eyes. "Ethan… would you come to breakfast this Sunday? I'd love for you to meet my father." She didn't think it was possible for his eyes to be any more beautiful, but the way they glowed as he gave her a blinding smile made her feel weak in the knees.

"I'd love to."

12

Ethan had never been quite so nervous in his entire life.

As much as he wanted to share every part of Lily's life with her, he was floundering in completely foreign territory, having never once met a girlfriend's father before. Rachel had never been close with her parents and she couldn't have cared less if he ever met them.

Ethan knew he had technically met Mr. Blake before, but it had barely been a passing nod in a diner and was hardly the same thing as announcing that he was the new guy giving it to his daughter. It didn't even matter that they hadn't officially had sex since they'd been dating—it was still understood that they eventually would, and that was already enough ammo for her father to hate him. He shuddered to think of what her father would do if he ever caught wind of what he had already done to her.

Ethan steered his rental car into Lily's lot, panicking slightly at the imposing sight of the car that was already parked in his usual spot. Pulling in beside it, he turned off the engine and checked his reflection once more in the rearview mirror anxiously, as if he were being graded on his appearance. His entire walk across the alley and up the stairs to her apartment was set to a soundtrack in his head, a never-ending loop of worried ramblings.

Calm down, calm down! He'll see how much I love her. Even if he still doesn't like me, Lily won't let that come between us. Right?

Lily met him at the door with a tight smile, her own nerves clearly visible in her eyes. He could hear the sounds of *Sports Center* blaring in the background as she stuck her hand through the opening, grabbing his arm in a quick squeeze as she mouthed the words "*I love you.*" For some reason, that little affirmation was all he needed to steady his own heartbeat. This was a first for both of them, but knowing that they would get through it together helped more than any pep talk he could give himself.

Smiling his first genuine smile of the morning, Ethan nodded to her quickly, letting her know he felt the same and was ready for whatever she had in store for him. He could see some of the tension melting away from her features as her own smile brightened and she opened the door wider.

"Good morning!" she said loudly, signaling to her father behind her that their guest had arrived. Ethan noticed that the volume on the television was lowered in the background, but it wasn't turned off. "Thanks for coming." She leaned in and kissed his cheek quickly, stepping aside to let him through.

"Thanks for inviting me." He stopped in the doorway and held out a half-gallon carton of orange juice awkwardly. "Uh…here. I don't like to go places I've been invited empty-handed. I usually bring wine for dinner, but since this is breakfast…juice?"

"Aw, thank you. I actually only thought to buy coffee, so this is great." Lily took the carton from his hand, desperately trying to control the flip-flopping of her heart at the adorable face he was making. "Why don't you come in?" She motioned to the man who was sitting on the loveseat and currently pretending that he was watching TV rather than listening to every word they said. "Dad, this is Ethan Foster. Ethan, this is my father, George."

"Ethan," he nodded gruffly. Lily glared at him until he finally stood up, knocking the sleeping cats off his lap.

"I'm pleased to finally meet you, Mr. Blake," Ethan returned, holding his hand out in greeting. He didn't care what Lily said, there was no way in hell that he was calling this man George to his face yet.

"I'd say likewise, but since I only heard about you two *days* ago," he stressed, shooting Lily a stern look as he shook Ethan's hand, "it would probably be more fitting for me to simply say that it's nice to meet you."

"*Dad*," Lily warned, giving him a look that clearly said she wasn't about to have that discussion again for the eight-hundredth time.

"Actually, we've already met," Ethan interrupted, hoping to switch the topic of conversation.

"You have?" Lily squeaked, looking back and forth between them.

"Only once, a few months back. I was with my brother Eric at the time." He watched as George's face lit up with recognition.

"Oh yeah, at the diner, right? How is your brother?"

"Very well, thank you."

"He's a good kid. Bit of a troublemaker back in the day, but always had a good attitude."

"Well, excuse me, gentlemen, but I'm going to go finish up in the kitchen. It should only be a few more minutes," Lily said, turning toward the other room.

"Do you need any help?" Ethan asked as she walked away.

"No, but thank you. I just have to get it all together. Stay and talk." She winked at him quickly before continuing on her way.

"Absolutely, Ethan, have a seat," George motioned to the open space next to where he'd just been sitting. Once they were both settled in front of the television and the volume had been turned back up, he steered the topic into more familiar waters. "So what does that brother of yours think about the Bears this year?"

"Uh…well, to be honest, I don't follow sports as closely as he does, but I know he said that they're looking pretty good right now. They'll start training again before too long and I know he's excited to be in one place for a while."

Lily peeked through the doorway of the kitchen as she scooped scrambled eggs into a large serving bowl. As she looked back and forth between the two most important men in her life, it was as if she could feel something click into place—and she just knew.

This was right.

It might be awkward until they worked out all the kinks and everyone got used to each other, but it seemed that George was the final piece of the puzzle. Her life felt complete in a way it never had before.

"All right, breakfast is served," she called out a moment later, her hands full with platters of food.

"Here, let me help you," Ethan smiled, jumping up and holding his hand out.

"Oh no, I've got this, but there are a few more on the counter in the kitchen if you'd like to grab some and carry them here to the table."

"Sure thing." He walked into the kitchen expecting to find one or two more platters of food, only to be bombarded with an entire buffet. "Holy shit," he said to himself.

"I know," Lily chuckled behind him, causing him to spin around and look at her. "I tend to overcook when I'm nervous. I hope you brought your appetite."

"I'm always starving when I'm with you," he whispered, leaning down to kiss the side of her neck.

"Hey now, none of that," she scolded lightly, unable to hide the purr of contentment that bubbled up as he kissed her. "Let's get this out there before it all gets cold." As she walked back into the front room, she yelled, "Dad, turn that TV off please."

George grumbled something under his breath as he stood up and made his way across the room. When he joined them at the table his eyes nearly bugged out of his head. "Jeez, Lil, ya think we've got enough food here?"

"Oh be quiet. I didn't know what everyone would be in the mood for, so I thought I'd cover my bases."

"Well, I think it all looks delicious," Ethan smiled.

For the next twenty minutes the conversation was fairly light as they ate, covering simple subjects like work schedules and the best places to hunt in the area. Hearing the word hunt made Lily shudder, which led her to ask Ethan if his family might have any use for a freezer full of deer meat since George was running out of room at his house and she refused to take any. After the previous hunting season was spent frying one deer steak after another, Lily was sick to death of the sight of it.

It wasn't until they had all finished a second plate of food and were sitting back to let their stomachs settle that George decided it was time to play Dad again. Leaning forward on his elbows and directing his gaze toward Ethan, he let the first question fly.

"So, Lily tells me that you're recently single after a very long relationship. Don't you think it's a little soon to be so serious about someone else again?"

"*Dad!*" Lily shot straight up in disbelief.

"No, he has every right to be concerned." Ethan waved her back into her seat, having expected something like this. "I probably would be, too. It doesn't look very good on paper." He smiled at her softly before turning back to George. "Yes, sir, that's correct. However, I can't say that I've ever been this serious about anyone before, so this isn't exactly happening *again* for me. It's the first time."

"Yet you were with her for *how* long? Almost ten years, I think Lily said," George goaded.

"Dad!"

"Yes, I was. And I was also very young and impulsive and immature." He looked to Lily, reaching out and holding her hand in a gesture of comfort. "I want to do things right this time around."

"Do you have any children?" he pushed.

"No, sir. Thankfully we didn't have to involve any children in our mistakes."

George flinched at his words, obviously thinking of his disastrous marriage, and glanced quickly at Lily before continuing. "Do you want any in the future?"

"Dad, this isn't an interview. He's my boyfriend and he already got the job."

"It's all right, Lily," Ethan soothed. "He's simply curious and direct." He thought for a moment before looking back up at George. "Well, before? I never thought I wanted any. But there's something about finding the perfect person that tends to change a person's outlook. Now? I think I might like that a lot. Someday."

"You do know how ass-kissy that all sounds, don't you?" George laughed.

"Yeah, I know. But it doesn't mean it's not true."

"Good point," he sighed. "Well, Ethan, all I care about at the end of the day is that you treat my daughter right. She's something pretty special, you know."

"I figured that out the first time we met, sir."

"Which doesn't sound like it was all that long ago," George arched his eyebrow, looking back and forth between the two of them. "But that's none of my business. As long as you are both happy and it works, then that's all that matters."

And just as fast as it started, the inquisition was over.

A few minutes later George moaned loudly, patting his stomach.

"Well, I should probably get going, hon."

"So soon?" Lily said, standing up to give him a hug good-bye.

"Yeah. I still have to go home and get changed before heading out to meet the guys. We're going bow hunting this time. Thank you for the enormous breakfast, honey. It was great." He looked at Ethan and held out his hand, smiling when he shook it this time. "Ethan, it was nice to meet you. We'll have to do this again sometime."

"I'd like that, sir."

"Just call me George," he added with a smile, petting both of the cats one more time before he walked to the door and let himself out.

Lily sat back down with a thud as the door closed, her mouth hanging wide open.

"What's wrong?" Ethan asked her, taking another bite of sausage because he felt like he needed to do something with his hands.

"This is…" she swallowed, looking back up at him. "This is really *real* now, isn't it?"

"I'm afraid so, baby," he smiled, leaning over and kissing her cheek. "I've been Daddy-approved. There's no getting rid of me now."

13

The rest of the week flew by faster than expected. Most nights Ethan would end up back at the apartment for dinner, followed by movie-watching with Lily cuddled up next to him on the loveseat. "Watching" was a loose definition, though, since by the end of the night neither of them could ever remember what they'd seen.

On Wednesday night, Ethan agreed to join Lily for drinks with Becky and Jared. He was thrilled to be seen around town with his beautiful new girlfriend on his arm, and Lily couldn't get over how nice it felt to actually be able to do things with her friends again without pissing her boyfriend off. They all had a great time, and Ethan found it particularly hard to leave for his own home that night when he was reminded that a tipsy Lily was a handsy Lily.

Before long it was Friday, and Lily was trying to pack her bag for the weekend. The only thing Ethan would tell her was that he was taking her to Chicago and they were leaving in the morning. Staring down at her empty luggage, she huffed loudly and grabbed her phone.

"Change your mind already?" Ethan laughed as he answered the phone. "I can be there in ten minutes, you know."

"No way! If you expect me to get any sleep tonight and be up early in the morning to leave on time, then your sweet ass better not be anywhere near me tonight. You are much too big of a distraction."

"All right," he sighed. "Then what did you need?"

"You have to give me a better idea of what to pack. I have no clue what to bring, and I don't feel like lugging my entire closet for a two-day trip."

"Well, if I had my way, you would be naked for the next two days, but I suppose you will need a few things here and there."

"Seriously, Ethan. If this is just some naughty sex romp at a hotel—don't get me wrong, I'm all in—but then I need to know so that I can pack every scrap of lingerie I own and nothing else. If you actually expect to take me out in public when we're there, then I need to know what else to bring."

"Okay, I suppose you're right. Make sure you have something casual and comfortable to wear for the ride there and the ride back. Other than that…just the lingerie."

"Ooh, so it *is* a sexy hotel romp!" she squealed.

"No. Well, hopefully later, but not the whole time."

"Argh! Then what am I supposed to pack for Saturday night? Formal? Casual? Help!"

"I told you, just the lingerie." He paused for a moment before adding, "Unless you want all new lingerie for tomorrow…then don't bring anything. I'm going to drop you off at Emma's when we first arrive in town. She's going to take you shopping for something new while I finish a few last minute details."

"Jesus, you're frustrating when you're secretive!"

"But you love me," he teased.

"I do…*dammit*," Lily huffed. "See you in the morning." She ended the call and tossed the phone down by her empty bag. Deciding to take him at his word, she stuffed the sexiest lingerie she owned into it as well as a few functional pieces. When she finished, she made herself go to bed early, only to lay awake half the night with butterflies circling in her stomach.

The next morning Ethan picked her up at 8:00 a.m., wanting to get on the road early so they would make it to Chicago before noon. Lily packed a thermos of coffee and some donuts for the road, and the two of them set off together on their very first road trip. They had a great time, playing silly old car games like I spy and the alphabet game, and they each took turns playing DJ with their iPods.

About halfway there, Ethan pointed out his side window and called out, "Horse!"

Without even thinking, Lily immediately responded with "Damn!" in her best New Zealand accent. Once she realized what they had just said, she turned to him slowly, a brilliant smile lighting up her features. "Oh my God, did you actually just quote *Eagle vs. Shark?*"

"Well, yeah. And you quoted back. I thought you were playing along." He noticed the astounded look on her face and turned toward her. "What? I thought that was one of your favorite movies?"

"It is. I just didn't realize you were actually paying attention when I had it on the other night. Anyone I've ever tried to show it to just looks at me like I'm crazy and asks me to put something else on."

"What are you talking about? I was laughing through the whole thing with you; it was hilarious. It's one of the few movies I really remember seeing this week," he smirked at her, waggling his eyebrows suggestively. "Great soundtrack, too. I recognized a lot of those songs from your Kiwi playlist."

"You remember that?" she gasped.

Ethan reached over and grabbed her hand, glancing away from the road momentarily so that he could look her in the eye when he kissed the back of her fingers. "I remember everything, Lily. Everything."

After that, neither one of them cared much about playing car games anymore. Lily scooted as close to him as possible, putting her head on his shoulder, each of them listening to the music without saying a word.

When they reached Emma's condo, Ethan parked long enough to walk Lily upstairs and deposit her and her luggage in the middle of the living room. He promised Lily that he would be back for her no later than six thirty to take her to dinner, kissed his sister on the cheek after whispering something conspiratorially in her ear, then disappeared out the door like a phantom.

"Well, so much for our weekend away together," Lily pouted.

"Hey, none of that!" Emma chimed, grabbing Lily's bag off the floor and carrying it to the guest room. "He's just got a lot of things to get done before tonight, and so do we!"

"What do you mean? I thought we were just going shopping for a little bit."

"Please, sweetie, this isn't amateur hour. We've got to find you the perfect dress and shoes for tonight before our salon appointment at four. Now, Maggie is going to meet us at the department store by noon, so we need to get a move on if you don't want to face her wrath."

They hurried across town, beating Maggie by a few minutes and teasing her mercilessly for it. As soon as they were all together, Emma barked out orders like a general, sending them each in different directions to cover more ground at once. When they reconvened about forty minutes later in the dressing rooms, there were nearly two full racks of outfits for Lily to try on: sixteen versions of the little black dress.

After a marathon changing session, they found the perfect one. It was simple and elegant, yet made Lily appear very sexy and sophisticated. A quick trip through the shoe department merited a sinful new pair of high heels, and their final stop before leaving ended with Lily agreeing to pick out a new set of lingerie after all.

The girls insisted she model a few different choices for them, and when she came out in the black satin corset and garter set with the delicate blue ribbon trim, both of them applauded loudly.

"Are you sure this is the one?" Lily called out, turning a deep shade of red as she ducked behind the changing room door to avoid any extra onlookers getting a peep.

Maggie merely cackled in response. "Girl, that's it! If you're giving *me* a lady boner already, I can't imagine what that thing is going to do to my pent-up brother."

"I agree," Emma giggled. "I sort of want to smack your ass a bit now. You've been hiding the goods, girlie."

"I don't know," Lily bit her lip in concern, joining them once she had gotten dressed. "Is this sending the wrong message, though?"

"What do you mean?" Maggie asked. She pointed at the item in question. "That sends out the message that you want to get fucked until you're cross-eyed. That's the truth, isn't it?"

"Well...yeah," she fought back another blush as she spoke, still adjusting to being so open about her private life with other people. "But I get the impression that he wants this to be deep and meaningful tonight. How deep and meaningful can it be if he's got me bent over the end of the sofa in five seconds flat?"

"Damn, now you're talking my language!" Maggie laughed.

"Lily, sweetie," Emma explained, "these kinds of things are romantic because of who we do them with, not what we do. Brandon and I go away on romantic trips all the time, but I would rarely call the nasty things we do to each other romantic. It's about sharing the passion together as much as the love."

"Exactly," Maggie nodded. "There are so many ways to have sex. Sometimes it's rough and dirty; sometimes it's gentle and tender. As long as you love your partner, it's all meaningful."

"I get it, I really do. It's just that...I don't want Ethan to think I'm trying to derail his special night by tempting him too much. Does that make sense?"

"Lily, from what you've told me about your little agreement and how he's been acting lately, it sounds like he's lost in his own sappiness. If you ask me, it sounds like that boy could use a good old dose of temptation to remind him that he's not a twelve-year-old girl and you're not some delicate flower." Maggie looked pointedly at the lingerie in her hand before arching her eyebrow in challenge. "Am I right?"

Lily took a deep breath and smiled. "Ring it up."

After shopping, the girls took her to their favorite salon for a bit of pampering, and when they got there, she was surprised to find that all three of them had appointments at the same time. Emma simply shrugged off her questioning gaze, saying that it was all about feminine solidarity, to which Lily rolled her eyes and told her to remember that when it came time for the bikini wax.

By 6:00 p.m., Lily was standing in front of the full-length mirror in Emma's bedroom, trying to recognize the sexy, confident woman looking back at her through the smoky eye makeup. Her hair was piled loosely on her head in some form of constructed chaos that looked effortless but had taken nearly an hour to style, and she still had no idea how there weren't streaks of burgundy lipstick on her teeth when she smiled.

Lily couldn't believe that she actually looked like a grown up. She glanced down at the large amount of cleavage that her corset created and giggled to herself. Perhaps she was a slightly slutty grown up.

"Hey, guys?" she called out to the other room, still looking at the stranger in the mirror. "Are you sure this isn't going overboard? I don't think I put this much effort into prom."

"Isn't Ethan worth a little effort?" Emma smiled as she walked through the door, handing her a glass of champagne.

"What's this for?"

"Celebration."

"What are we celebrating?" Lily asked, holding out her glass to clink it against Emma's.

"The fact that you're finally getting some tonight!" Maggie laughed, coming through the door with her own glass raised. "Perhaps we can all go back to our normal lives now that balance will be returned to the sexual force."

"Oh ha-ha, Obi-Wan. Very cute." Lily tried to shoot her a menacing glare, but it was ruined when her laughter broke through. She sipped at her drink for a moment as she looked at her two dear friends, slowly realizing that they were dressed just as formally as she was. "Hey, I thought I was the one trying to sexy it up tonight. You both look gorgeous! What's up? Are you coming to dinner, too?"

"Uh, well—" Emma looked caught off guard for a second until Maggie jumped in.

"Hell no! We've got no interest in watching you two moon over each other all night, do we?" She looked at Emma pointedly until she shook her head in reply. "Besides, we are much too hot tonight to waste all this sexiness on you. We plan on grabbing our menfolk the second they walk in the door and taking them out on the town."

"Yeah, Brandon and Eric won't know what hit them," Emma added, rubbing her hands together as if she were an evil mastermind.

"Well, whatever amazing things you do tonight, it's not half of what you deserve." Lily stepped closer and hugged them both to her, all of them trying to avoid spilling their drinks. "I can't thank you enough for everything."

"Please," Emma sighed. "Like we need a reason to shop!"

"Not just the shopping. Everything. You two have been there for me so much lately. I can't imagine what the last few months of my life would have been like without you."

"Ugh, bitch…stop it before you make me cry and ruin my makeup!"

Maggie huffed, wiping at the corner of her eye.

Just then there was a light knocking at the front door. Emma excused herself to answer it, only to call out from the hallway in a singsong voice less than a minute later. "Oh, Lily…I do believe your date has arrived."

Swallowing down the butterflies that threatened to fly right out of her mouth, Lily took one last look in the mirror and steeled herself for her night of mystery with the man of her dreams.

Or so she thought she had, but she was still blown away when she got a good look at him in his midnight-blue Gucci suit. He was absolutely breathtaking to behold, like some sort of majestic, fantastical creature.

As she slowly walked toward him, Lily started to worry that when she was finally standing next to him she might look like some sort of troll who crawled out from under a bridge for the night. However, once she saw the shock and desire on his face as he stared back at her, she realized that there might actually be a chance that she could hold her own.

Without a word, Ethan grabbed her hand and pulled it to his lips. The heat in his gaze as he looked up at her over her knuckles was enough to make small beads of sweat stand out on her forehead.

"Stunning," he whispered, kissing her fingers again lightly before letting them go. "My beautiful girl, you are nothing short of stunning tonight."

"I was just thinking the same thing about you."

"Nonsense," he scoffed, sliding his hand to the small of her back and leading her toward the door. "I pale in comparison to this goddess on my arm."

Lily was flattered by what she thought were only pretty words, but Ethan meant every one of them.

After a scorching round of eyefuckery in the elevator that Ethan clearly won, he led her across the parking garage to his waiting car. He was smiling as he held open the door for her, and his beautiful face distracted Lily so much that she nearly didn't notice that something was different.

"Wait a minute," she said, one foot already inside the car. "Where's your rental?"

"What are you talking about?" he smiled again playfully.

"We arrived here in a blue Nissan. This is a black Audi."

"Hmm…well, that's odd, isn't it?" He motioned for her to sit down and he closed the door quickly, jumping in the driver's seat and revving the engine.

"It's also the same model Audi that you were renting a few months ago," she continued as they drove across town.

"Imagine the coincidence," he smirked.

"Did you exchange your rental?"

"Nope."

"Then what? How did you get this particular car?"

"I bought it."

"You *bought* it?" she gasped.

"Mmhmm," he replied nonchalantly as he looked out the side window, as if it were nothing more than buying a cup of coffee.

"But…why?"

Ethan pulled into the lot of an elegant seafood restaurant and parked the car. When he turned to look at her again, his face had become very serious. "Because I've never owned my own car. I've gotten by on rentals and taxis and even on foot, but I never wanted any ties to anything before… I didn't want any attachments. Just like I've always stayed in hotels or rented space to paint. I always wanted to be able to pack up and take off at a moment's notice without worrying about making arrangements."

"And now?" she whispered.

"And now…I think I could use a few attachments in my life."

"So you bought your very first car?" She looked around the interior before smiling hugely. "Then, congratulations!" Leaning over, she kissed him loudly on the cheek. "I'm proud of you. But why this exact same car when you could have your pick of anything?"

He slowly reached up to cup her face. "Do you really need to ask?" Lowering his head, he covered her mouth with his own, telling her with the slightest pressure of his lips how important their shared memories were to him. As he pulled away, he left a trail of gentle kisses on her face, over her cheeks and nose, ending with soft pecks to the fragile skin of her eyelids when they fluttered closed. "Come on, beautiful," he said against her flesh. "Let's get you inside before I have second thoughts and drive straight to the hotel."

"Fine by me," she exhaled, feeling lightheaded at how closely he hovered over her.

"Don't tempt me," he laughed lightly, his sweet breath tickling her. Planting one more kiss on the center of her forehead, he sat back and shoved a hand through his hair. "Seriously, you don't know how close I am to throwing all of my plans out the window. All it took was one look at you in that dress."

"Well, in that case," she smiled tauntingly, "I wouldn't dare waste the opportunity to make you squirm all night. Let's eat. I want to enjoy sitting across from you, knowing that the entire time you're eating, you're really imagining how quickly you could have me undressed."

"Who says I would bother undressing you first? I bet that skirt flips up fairly easily."

"That's very true. But then you wouldn't get to see what I have on underneath, now would you?" She laughed playfully, climbing out of the car and strutting toward the restaurant. One look at the seductive sway of her hips as she walked told Ethan that he was in for a very long night.

Their dinner was perfect. They ordered different items from the menu, sharing bites of their meal with each other. The evening was full of laughter and lighthearted conversation, and when it came time for dessert they split a decadent slice of cheesecake. Lily allowed him to feed her large forkfuls, taking particular care to wrap her lips and tongue slowly around the delicious treat.

"You're not playing fair," he gritted through his teeth, his eyes never leaving her luscious mouth.

"Who said I was playing?" she returned quickly, her tongue flicking against the tines of the fork before she closed her eyes and moaned at the taste.

"Check, please!" Ethan called out, forcing himself to break her gaze. He knew he needed to get moving if he was going to get her to the gallery on time, and sitting around staring at her while she ate was only serving as a distraction.

A few minutes later he was pulling out of the parking lot and heading toward Halsted, the center of the arts district in the city.

"So where are you taking me now?" Lily asked as she fastened her seat belt, watching the Chicago skyline streak by through her window.

"You'll see." He turned his head long enough to smile at her, winking quickly before returning his attention to the road. When they reached a crowded street he pulled abruptly into a narrow alley, parking in a private lot hidden behind the corner building. As they walked around to the front entrance, Lily noticed a large group of people waiting to get in.

"Are we going dancing?" she asked, assuming it was the line for a popular nightclub.

"No."

"Then where are we?" She glanced around at the unfamiliar faces as they walked directly to the front of the line. Some of them were giving her dirty looks in return, while others were ignoring her completely and staring openly at Ethan. One woman even went so far as to tap her husband on the shoulder excitedly and point at him.

Rather than answer her, Ethan guided her to the bored-looking bouncer at the door. When he saw who approached, he stood up straighter and cleared his throat.

"Good evening, Mr. Foster," he said nervously, reaching quickly for the door handle.

"Good evening, Douglas," he nodded. "Big turnout, huh?"

"Yes, sir. We're almost at max capacity. I'm only allowed to go off the list when more people inside leave."

"Well, at least it's a nice night to be outside," Ethan smiled, placing his hand at the small of Lily's back again and leading her through the open door.

"Is this…some sort of art exhibit?" she asked, looking around at the large crowds of people huddled around various oil paintings.

"What gave it away?"

"I'm sorry, that was a stupid question," she giggled. "I've just never been to one."

"Don't be sorry, I was only teasing you. Yes, it's an art exhibit. Opening night, in fact. That's why it's so crowded."

"Do you know the artist? Is it a friend of yours?"

"As a matter of fact," he chuckled, "I've known him my entire life."

The way he was speaking made her feel as if she weren't quite catching on to some important detail. She looked around the large room more carefully, her head snapping back when she finally noticed the large lettering that had been stenciled high on the blank wall above the first section of paintings:

"Lily of the Valley"
A New Collection by Ethan Foster

Lily gasped loudly when all the pieces finally tumbled into place. *This* was her surprise. "You did all of this...for me?"

"Everything, Lily." He gestured back and forth with his hand in large sweeping motions, indicating the crowd as well as the paintings. "Everything you see here is all for you."

The largest painting was the only one that she could see from across the room, but in it she recognized the rear view of a woman's bare shoulder and neck, her dark brown hair spilling in waves over her pillow as she slept. The focal point of the piece wasn't the woman herself, but a smattering of light brown freckles on her shoulder.

It was Lily.

And suddenly she knew, without even looking at any of the other paintings, that they were all of her.

"But...why? *How?*" she choked out, already feeling the tears welling in her eyes. "When did you paint all of these?" The walls were covered—there had to be at least sixty paintings stretched out as far as the eye could see.

"While I was gone," he whispered gruffly. When she looked up, her eyes met intense, smoldering jade. He reached up slowly and brushed a tear away from her cheek with his thumb. "You were all I could think of, all I could see. I thought that I had given you up so that you could have a better life without me. This was my way of keeping you in my heart."

"What...what made you decide to show them like this? To display them for the world to see? You were so private about us before." She heard the waver in her voice and wondered if he could tell how close she was to bawling her eyes out.

"Because…" he took a deep breath before continuing. "I wanted you and everybody else in the whole wide world to know that I can't fucking live without you." He blinked a few times, and she noticed that his eyes were tearing up, too. Ethan cupped her face with both hands, leaning down to brush his lips gently against hers. "I love you."

With that, he pulled her into a crushing embrace, moving back only far enough to kiss her repeatedly. This time, when Lily tasted the salt of tears on her lips, she wasn't foolish enough to think that they only belonged to one of them.

14

They held each other closely and kissed for longer than was appropriate in a crowded room, only breaking apart when someone cleared their voice softly and tapped Ethan on the shoulder. Her cheeks coloring brightly, Lily shyly looked over and was surprised to see the face of a trendy-looking woman with spiky red hair and funky glasses smiling back at the both of them.

"I'm very sorry to interrupt, Ethan, but I just wanted to thank you once again for thinking of us. This is by far the most successful opening I've ever seen here."

"Don't be silly," he smiled warmly. "You were the one who did me the favor of setting this up with such short notice. Nobody else would touch it. I should be the one thanking you."

"Well, their loss is my gain," she laughed. "I don't like to be bound as tightly as some of the stuffier galleries around here. As soon as I heard that your name was attached I was all in." She smiled at the beautiful brunette on Ethan's arm, but right as she was holding her hand out to introduce herself, something that looked like a flicker of recognition flashed across her face. "Oh my God…you're *her*, aren't you?"

Lily blinked a few times, not knowing what to make of the animated woman. "Her?"

"Yes! *Her*." She swept her hand out, gesturing around the room at the many different canvases on the walls. "I would know those beautiful eyes anywhere."

Lily felt her face coloring a deeper shade of pink under the mystery woman's scrutiny. She followed the direction that her hand currently pointed and saw another large painting, this one showing nothing but a close up of her own eyes staring back at her in what could only be described as a very heated gaze.

"I'm sorry, where are my manners?" Ethan cut in. "Lily, this is Joan. She owns this lovely gallery and is the sole reason that I was able to put this together for you so quickly. And Joan," he smiled proudly, pulling Lily to his side. "This is my Lily."

"Her name is really Lily?" Joan gasped.

"Of course. That's how I thought of the title for the show," Ethan chuckled. He leaned over and whispered into Lily's ear. "I wanted to work your name into it without it being obvious to those who don't know you."

"Well Lily, may I just say that you are every bit as lovely as his paintings led me to believe," Joan smiled, finally shaking her hand. "Some artists' renderings glorify and glamorize the subject so much that I can barely see the real person anymore, but not so with Ethan. There is so much truth and love in these images, I had no trouble seeing it, and these aren't even full portraits of you!"

"Thank you," she smiled. "Your gallery is truly lovely. I haven't really been to anything other than museums, but I like how cozy and warm it feels here."

"I told you so, darling!" an extremely tall, regal looking woman said excitedly as she came up behind Joan and draped her arm around her shoulder, leaning over to plant a quick kiss on her cheek. "Didn't I tell you the very same thing?" She looked at Lily and smiled brightly. "This place feels comfortable, not like those cold galleries down the street."

It was Joan's turn to blush at the loving praise. "Ethan, Lily, I'd like you to meet my wife, Andrea."

"A pleasure, Andrea," Ethan said as he shook her hand.

"No, the pleasure is all mine, believe me. We've been such fans of your work for years. There is so much raw emotion in some of your pieces. I can't tell you how overwhelming it feels to stand in front of so many of them at once."

"Thank you. That's a lovely compliment." He absentmindedly pulled Lily a little closer to his side, as if simply being near her would give him the strength to face the long night of questions and opinions ahead of him.

"Have you two had the chance to look around yet?"

"Not exactly," Lily laughed lightly. "We were sort of…distracted at first. But I can't wait to see everything."

"Well, don't let me interrupt you any longer. I simply wanted to tell Joan that we have reached capacity."

"*Already?*" Joan gasped.

"Calm down, love. I just thought you might want to go over some more details with Doug before the line gets any longer outside."

"I'm so sorry," Joan apologized. "Ethan, Lily? Would you please excuse us?"

"Of course," Ethan nodded. "I've been dying to give this one a proper tour, anyway." Lily could feel his fingertips squeezing her hip possessively as he spoke.

"By all means, show the poor girl around. Let her see all of these amazing paintings she inspired!" Joan reached out and hugged them both quickly. "Ethan, I'll find you later if there are any questions or problems. Be sure to stop by the refreshment table for wine and cheese later. If they haven't eaten it all by then, of course," she frowned.

Lily smiled after them as both women scurried away to speak with the doorman. "Wow, they seem…elegantly frazzled."

"Yeah, I don't think they were expecting such a big turnout so early."

He paused for a moment to look down at her, his eyes lingering over her strategically accentuated curves as they roved over her body openly. When his gaze finally landed on her eyes it was full of heat. "I can't get over how amazing you look tonight." He exhaled loudly, shoving his hand through his hair. "How about we have that tour?"

"I'd like that." Lily was up for anything that kept her from jumping him in public.

They slowly made the rounds, sipping on champagne as they walked, Lily refusing to skip over one single piece. There were so many touching images she lost count of how many times she began to tear up. Many were like the two she'd already seen, small pieces of her that he had come to memorize, while others were more symbolic. She saw a few with a large sleigh bed in the background, mixed in with other reminders of days gone by, like the candle and chocolates from their Valentine's Day picnic.

Ethan was quiet as she looked, watching for her reactions. He was always right behind her if she wanted to ask him something about one of the pieces or if she simply needed him to hold her and reassure her of his presence. None of the images were graphic or overly revealing, but there were more than a few times that she buried her face in his chest to hide her blush, overcome by the sensuality of the memory he'd captured.

One painting in particular caused her to stop in her tracks, covering her mouth to hide her gasp. Ethan closed the distance between them and slowly wrapped his hands around her middle, pulling her back against his chest as he leaned down to whisper in her ear.

"Do you remember that night, Lily?" She felt his warm breath tickle her neck, and the sensation mixed with the seductive purr of his voice caused her flesh to tingle and her nipples to harden.

"*Yes*," she breathed, almost no sound to her voice. The painting showed the silhouette of two lovers dancing, locked in a heated embrace as the male figure dipped the female over a bed. "Our dance."

"I knew I loved you, even then," he said against her skin as he softly kissed below her ear. "I wish I'd had the courage to just tell you."

"I could say the exact same thing," she said without taking her eyes off the canvas.

"Do you remember how our bodies moved together that night?" He continued to assault her senses, kissing and blowing along the length of her neck as he spoke. "I felt your soul. Being with you is like a religious experience."

"Of course I remember," she panted, nearly swooning from the effects of the champagne and his proximity. "I remember everything."

"Good." He kissed the top of her shoulder, sending ripples of pleasure down her body until moisture was pooling between her thighs. "I can't wait to start making a lifetime of new memories with you."

"Starting tonight?" she whispered, unable to hide the hope in her voice. Ethan pulled her back into him more tightly, slowly thrusting his hips forward until she felt his hardness rubbing against her lower back.

"Starting tonight," he growled.

Lily turned and looked up at him hungrily, the words *let's get the hell out of here* on the tip of her tongue, when a familiar voice rang out behind them.

"There you are!"

Ethan winced, already knowing who the voice belonged to, and who exactly he would see if he were to turn around. He took a deep breath and counted to ten, willing his body to calm down. Mouthing the words "*soon, I promise*" to Lily, he planted a strained smile on his face and turned around to greet his entire family.

Emma had been the one to call out, and when Lily saw that she was surrounded by Ethan's family, she finally lost her battle with her tears. As they streamed down her face, she ran forward and hugged both Emma and Maggie, scolding them for keeping her in the dark about such an important event.

"Hey, don't blame us, we were sworn to secrecy!" Emma replied. "Our job was to get you ready for your date and keep you distracted. If we let it slip, Ethan wasn't going to let us in."

"Yeah, it was hard enough getting in as it was," Brandon laughed over Emma's shoulder. "Even having our name on the list and being related to the artist wasn't enough to get through the front door any faster."

"Sorry about that, guys." Ethan rubbed the back of his neck in frustration. "I guess they're at capacity, and Joan can only let in so many people as the others leave. I should have been watching for you... Maybe there's something I could have done."

"Don't be silly!" Barbara piped up, previously hidden behind Eric and Richard as they each glanced around at different paintings. She walked forward and put her hands on Ethan's shoulders, staring up into his worried eyes. "I was happy to wait. I am so proud that my talented son has so many people excited to see his work," she said. "And darling," she sighed, "you've outdone yourself. These are breathtaking."

"Really?" He had shown his work in galleries around the world, never once feeling awkward or seeking approval, but the moment his parents stood before him, Ethan felt like a six-year-old child holding up a doodle he hoped they might display on the refrigerator.

"Absolutely," Richard nodded, joining his wife in congratulating him. "Son, you know I've followed your progress through the years. I will gladly admit that I'm more than a bit biased, but these are simply amazing. It's your best work yet."

Ethan nodded sharply, swallowing past the painful lump in his throat. "Thank you," he uttered with a wavering voice. "That really means a lot to me."

"Just as finally being here for you really means a lot to us. Thank you for letting us share this with you." Richard glanced between his wife and his son, leaning forward to speak more softly. "It's obvious how much you love her, Ethan. I don't know what I'm more proud of right now."

Before Ethan could offer another choked-up reply, he was saved by his brother's interruption. "Dude, these paintings are fucking *hot*," Eric laughed, clapping him on the back roughly.

"Eric! Language!" Barbara scolded. "I know you're a grown man, but could you at least try to keep your voice down when you speak like that?"

"Sorry, Mom," he chuckled, leaning over and kissing her on the cheek loudly. "Why don't you two finish walking around? I know you haven't looked at everything yet. Emma and Maggie just stole Lily to ask her embarrassing questions about these paintings; I'm sure you could catch up to them."

"No, no. Let them have their privacy. Come on, darling," she sighed, grabbing onto Richard's arm. "Let's finish appreciating our son's gift."

Eric waited until they had walked far enough away to be out of earshot before speaking again. "So? Spill it. Did your grand gesture work?"

"Apparently so," Ethan whispered. "She hasn't slapped me yet, and she seems to be moved by many of the pieces."

"I told you she would love it."

"Yes, I know. I was just worried that this might be too much to take in at once, you know? Not everyone would be able to handle seeing so many intimate details of their private life displayed all over like this."

"True, but these are really tasteful. I'm just glad you took my advice and pulled those other two."

"Eric, I never intended on showing those; they were just for me. You would have never seen them either if you hadn't knocked me unconscious and gone snooping that day."

"I wasn't snooping… They were sitting out." He watched as his brother arched an eyebrow at him in disbelief. "Dude, whatever. I'm just happy that her nips aren't up here for any old perv to stare at. That might have been too much for her, and then I would've had to kick your ass again."

"You really do care about her, don't you?"

"I told you before, she's like a sister to me now. Not just me—all of us."

"I'm really glad. She's never had siblings before, and I know how much you all mean to her."

"Well, it's definitely mutual. So take good care of her."

15

Across the room, Lily was undergoing a similar line of questioning from Maggie and Emma.

"You sure you're okay with all of this? I mean, it's so romantic, but I'm sure it's probably a bit overwhelming, too."

"Emma, I'm good. No need to worry. Yes, it's overwhelming, but mostly because I just want to be alone with him right now and I can't be."

"That's my girl!" Maggie said proudly, squeezing her on the shoulder. "I knew you would be fine with all of this. And I must say, these paintings are so *erotic*! I never knew Mr. Stick-in-the-Mud had it in him."

"So he's got the Maggie Foster smut seal of approval?" Lily teased.

"Most definitely! Now, my dear…tell me more about this waltz painting," Maggie grabbed her arm and led her back to where they had started. "I am *more* than intrigued."

It took over an hour for Ethan to finally break free of the curious onlookers who set upon him after his conversation with Eric. Three different reporters spoke with him, taking his picture in front of some of the larger paintings. It had all been a giant blur to him, though, and his only concern was Lily and making sure that she was all right. No matter whom he was speaking with, he always managed to find her in the crowd. And as if she could feel his eyes on her, she would always look up and smile, letting him know that she would be there for him when he was done.

After their heated exchange in front of the painting earlier, he couldn't be done fast enough.

He needed her with such intensity that it was becoming painful. Not only for his insistent erection that would resurface every time he thought of her, but for the ache in his chest that had been growing ever since she had walked away with his sisters.

Just knowing that they were finally going to consummate their official relationship had him feeling possessive and needy. Lily had been very patient, allowing him to show her in his own way how much he loved her. Now that they were finally ready to take things to the next level, he was extremely antsy.

When he spotted Lily speaking with Joan and Andrea again, he made his move. Coming up behind her and wrapping his hand tightly around her waist, he smiled at the two women before turning his attention to Lily. "Can I tempt you to leave?" he asked quietly.

"Ethan, you are walking temptation," she whispered back, her sweet breath floating over his skin like a lover's caress. "All you have to do is say the word and I'm all yours."

"Ladies," he said, holding his hand out to Joan and Andrea. "It was a pleasure, but I'm afraid we must be going."

"Yes, I can see that," Andrea giggled.

"Thank you for everything tonight, Joan. I look forward to working with you again in the future."

"Likewise. I'll contact Greg after the weekend with the final sales figures."

With one last nod good-bye, Ethan steered Lily toward the exit. The moment they stepped outside his phone was in his hand and he was pressing a number on his speed dial. "Yes, this is Ethan Foster. I expect to arrive in less than twenty minutes." He listened briefly as they walked back to the car. "Yes, that's correct. All the arrangements have been made with the manager." He hung up abruptly, clearly in demanding business mode, and Lily hated to admit to herself how much it turned her on.

When they reached the car in the back parking lot, he pressed the remote to unlock the door for her, but as soon as she tried to open it he pinned her roughly up against the side of the car, effectively slamming the door shut again.

"I need you, Lily," he growled in her ear, pressing his hardened body into her back again. "I've never needed you so badly."

"Oh, God, me neither!" she gasped, leaning her head back on his shoulder. "I'm almost in pain."

Ethan's hand slid around the front of her dress, reaching up to cup her breast through the fabric. He bent down and nipped at the exposed flesh of her neck before licking his way up to her earlobe. After sucking it between his teeth and biting lightly, he released her long enough to whisper in her ear. "I wanted our first time together again to be sweet and loving, but I don't think I'm going to manage that tonight. I'm hurting for you, Lily. Can you forgive my weakness?"

She pushed him back enough so that she could turn around and face him. "Ethan, it's not weakness. It's still going to be loving. I love you and you love me." Her voice dropped lower until it became husky. "Now get me to the fucking hotel and lovingly fuck my brains out!"

He didn't need to be told twice. Without another word he opened the door for her, closing it quickly behind her and jumping in, speeding off into the night. Unwilling to let any distance intrude as they drove, Lily scooted closer and put her hand on his thigh. She could feel by how tightly the muscles contracted under her fingers that he was barely staying in control.

"You're playing with fire, little girl," he snarled through his teeth without taking his eyes off the road.

"Good," she replied, taking her hand back and slowly lifting her dress to the top of her hips. "Because I've got something over here that's rather heated as well."

Ethan glanced over long enough to catch a glimpse of black garter straps attached to the sexiest pair of thigh-high stockings he'd ever seen. There were tiny blue bows at the end of each strap, and when he looked closer he could see that she also wore a black satin G-string with a matching blue bow.

Looking back just in time to see that he was about to run a red light, Ethan screeched to a stop. "*Shit*! Are you trying to get us killed?" he hissed, turning to stare openly at her display. "Christ, Lily...what the hell are you wearing?"

"A present."

He reached over and delicately brushed his fingertips against the straps on her thighs. "A present, huh? Who's it for?" He moved his fingers higher and inwards, sliding through the dampness that had collected at the top of her thighs until he was brushing against wet satin.

"*You*," she moaned. "Always you."

He breathed deeply for a moment, trying to collect himself. When he spoke again, it was with a shaking voice. "God Lily...you're fucking soaked."

She put her hand on his cheek, directing him to meet her heavy-lidded gaze. "You, Ethan. It's always for you."

Just then a loud horn blared behind them, alerting them that the light had changed.

"All right," he gulped, crossing through the intersection. "I'm driving again. Maybe you should cover back up so I can concentrate."

"Is that what you really want?" she asked playfully.

"No."

"That's what I thought," she giggled. "I think you'd much rather see something like this." Lily lifted her right foot until her new sexy high heel was resting on the dashboard, opening her legs up more widely. He groaned loudly and went to reach for her, but she slapped his hand away. "No, sir. Hands on the steering wheel."

Once she saw his hand return to the wheel, she slid her fingers inside the tiny scrap of fabric masquerading as underwear and began to touch herself slowly. Her slick folds were swollen with need, but when she began to stroke small circles around her throbbing clitoris it only made her feel more hollow inside.

"God...baby...I need you inside here so badly," she nearly whined, her actions sending tremors through her legs and making them shake visibly.

"*Fuck!*" he gritted through his teeth, clenching his jaw tighter as he floored the accelerator. He would only allow himself furtive glances at one of the most erotic things he'd ever witnessed, knowing that if he actually turned his head to stare he would end up crashing. "Soon, baby. I promise. We're almost there. There's nowhere else safe to stop on the way or I would already be pounding into you."

"Hurry!" she cried, her inner walls beginning to clamp down on the single finger that she had slipped inside herself.

"Christ, you're too sexy for your own good," he ground out, wiping away a sudden sheen of sweat from his brow. "Come for me, baby. Just let go and I'll make you feel even better in just a few minutes. Come all over those pretty little fingers and let me taste it."

His words were her undoing, and his dirty talk sent sparks straight to where she was touching herself until she was crying out so loudly that it echoed through the car. Her body spasmed, flooding her fingers with a fresh coating of moisture. Sitting up quickly, she leaned over and shoved two glistening fingertips into his eager mouth.

Grunting around her digits as he sucked them clean, Ethan silently prayed that he would be able to get her upstairs to the room without embarrassing himself in his expensive new suit. The sign for the Four Seasons appeared as he turned the corner, and the sigh of relief he let loose was almost comical.

"Oh, thank fuck! We're here, baby. Come on, cover back up before we reach the valet and we'll be in the room before you know it."

After he pulled up to the curb to let her out, Lily stood for a moment on wobbly legs before she made her way slowly to the front door. Ethan noticed the valet watching her appreciatively as she walked away, causing him to shoot him a stern look of warning before surrendering his car. As soon as he opened the door and sat down in Ethan's place, the very distinct smell of delicious, aroused Lily wafted out into the night. The valet's eyes nearly crossed and he was unable to hide a quiet grunt.

"*Fuck*, dude. Good for you." And with that he shut the door and drove off.

Ethan wanted to be angry and offended, but he just couldn't find the energy. Lily was waiting for him. He ran after her, catching her just inside the front lobby.

"What about our luggage?" she asked, almost in a daze.

"Don't worry, it's already upstairs. I checked us in earlier this afternoon." He guided her into the elevator, keeping an eye out for any sudden extra passengers. The moment the doors closed, Lily was all over him.

"God…I want you," she panted against his neck, flicking her tongue over his skin before nipping and biting at his Adam's apple. She ran her hands down the front of his body and rubbed his erection through his pants, smiling at the feel of the vibrations under her lips when he threw his head back and moaned. When he tried to speak again, it was punctuated with tiny whimpers.

"Lily…baby…fuck!" He grabbed her shoulders, trying halfheartedly to push her away. "Baby, you have to stop for a minute."

"Why?"

"Because I'm going to come all over you if you don't." He took a deep breath to collect himself before continuing. "Now, as fun as that might sound if we were in bed and completely naked, I'd rather not explore that fully dressed in a public elevator."

"I'm sorry," she said, pulling farther back.

"Don't be sorry; just try to save it for the room. I'm wound so tightly after what you just did in the car, the littlest thing could set me off."

"So you liked it?" She smiled up at him shyly, biting her bottom lip.

"Like is an understatement." He bent down and kissed her quickly. When he pulled away, the ding sounded to alert them that they had arrived at their floor. As soon as the doors opened, Ethan breathed a sigh of relief, grabbing Lily's hand and running down the hall.

They kissed awkwardly and frantically the entire time he unlocked and opened the door, refusing to stop even as they walked inside. It wasn't until the door slammed shut behind them that they broke apart, and that was only long enough for Lily to shove him back against it. She kissed him furiously, pulling and tugging at the button on his pants before slowly lowering to her knees in front of him.

"Whoa, what are you doing?"

"Isn't it obvious?" she smirked up at him, unzipping his fly. "I'm relieving a little bit of tension." With that, she pulled him free and immediately sucked him deep into her mouth.

"Oh God!" he cried out, the wet heat of her lips and tongue surrounding him more than he was ready for. Shoving his hands into her hair, Ethan could no longer hold back how badly he needed her. "God, yes! You look so fucking good like that, baby, with your lips wrapped around my cock."

Hearing his words only made her moan around him loudly, sending vibrations through his body as she bobbed her head up and down his shaft. After barely thirty seconds, Ethan knew that he was done for.

"Oh God...baby, I'm gonna...oh *fuck*!" He clenched his jaw tightly and pounded his head into the door, feeling the warm rush of pleasure beginning to flood through him much too quickly. Finally he surrendered to it, gripping the back of her head and thrusting once, twice, until he felt himself explode with blinding pleasure.

Lily swallowed his release happily, thrilled that she could affect him so quickly. She knew it could be a blow to a guy's ego when he finished too fast, but sometimes it made her feel sexy and powerful. Especially with oral—it let her know that she was doing a good job.

It was Ethan's turn to stand on wobbly legs as he tucked himself away and helped her back to her feet. "What was that for?" he panted.

"Well, you said that you were going to go at any second. I thought I'd just help you along so we could focus on each other again as soon as possible. Now, why don't you help *me* get out of this dress?" She turned her back to him, presenting him with a long zipper.

Knowing that more delicious secrets lay hidden underneath her dress, Ethan happily pulled on the cool metal tab, watching as the teeth separated one by one. They were both holding their breath in anticipation, and the sound of the zipper opening seemed deafening in the room. When it was fully open they both let the dress drop to the floor and Lily stepped out of it, slowly turning around to face him.

And that's right about the same time that Ethan thought he might swallow his own tongue.

"*Jesus*..." he gasped, unable to think of anything more coherent. She was stunning: a sinful vision in black satin with light blue trim.

"You like?" she smiled timidly.

"Turn around," he growled. "Slowly."

He watched with hungry eyes as she spun around for him, showing off her amazing curves that were accentuated even more by the items she was wearing. Her ass had never looked better, framed perfectly by the garter straps, corset, and stockings. He was amazed to feel himself already stirring in his boxers, and every new angle she presented him with only made his fingers itch to touch her more.

When she finished her rotation, it was to find him staring at her, slack-jawed. Without saying a word he stalked toward her, scooping her up into his arms and carrying her into the bedroom. When they crossed the threshold she gasped loudly, taking in everything that he had prepared.

Candles were everywhere, lighting the entire room with a golden glow. Rose petals had been scattered over the floor and the bed and there was champagne chilling on a small table in the corner.

It was so romantic that she was afraid she might start crying again.

Setting her down gently at the foot of the bed, Ethan stepped back far enough to look down at her. He continued to stare, never moving his gaze from hers as he silently removed his suit piece by piece and draped it over the back of the nearest chair. He pulled off his tie, then slowly unbuttoned his shirt—his own version of a striptease. It was difficult for Lily to maintain eye contact as more and more of his amazing body was put on display, like the world's most delicious gift unwrapping itself for her.

When he was finally down to nothing but his boxer briefs he dropped to his knees, positioning himself between her thighs. Reaching out, he slowly began unsnapping the garters from her stockings.

"Did you want me to take all this off?" she whispered. He was being so quiet, it made her not want to raise her voice.

He only shook his head in response, reaching up to grab the thin straps of her tiny panties. When he began to tug on them, she leaned back on her elbows and lifted off the mattress, allowing him to pull them the rest of the way down. After tossing them over his shoulder, he quickly reattached the straps to her stockings.

Sliding his hands between and underneath her thighs until he was gripping her by the hips, he dragged her to the edge of the bed, spreading her legs wider around him as she was pulled closer. He stared down at her for a moment, her slick folds open before him, framed once again by her straps and stockings.

"That is the sexiest fucking thing I've ever seen in my entire life." His voice was little more than a low growl. Without another word, he buried his face between her legs, lapping at her wet flesh greedily.

She barely had time to process what was happening—it was a full-on assault to her senses. The smell of him filled the room, the feeling of his tongue flicking and stroking drove her to the brink of insanity, the grunts and snarls he was making echoed through her head like the most animalistic soundtrack she had ever heard. And the sight of him? Only one look down to see him lost in the pleasure of feasting on her was all it took to send her careening over the edge violently.

As she began to shake and scream her release, Ethan pulled her into his mouth more roughly, grinding her against the flat of his tongue before sucking at her swollen bundle of nerves. When she had finally stopped shaking he pulled away and stood up, looking down at her ravenously.

She watched as he slowly removed his last remaining article of clothing, groaning to herself when she saw that he was fully aroused again, his glorious erection straining back toward his stomach.

"I need you so badly," she whimpered, unable to pull her eyes away from his arousal. She could swear that she saw it twitch when she spoke.

"Like what you see?" He reached down and grabbed himself, pumping once, twice. She watched as the swollen tip turned a beautiful shade of violet with each movement of his hand.

"God...that's so damn hot," she gasped. "Please come here. Please?"

"Scoot back," he commanded, his voice rough and gravelly.

Lily did as she was told, inching herself farther up the mattress to make room for him. When she lifted her feet to the bed for more leverage, she realized that she still had her high heels on. "Oh, I guess I should take these off, huh?"

"*No!*" he barked sharply. "You're not removing one fucking thing until I say so, got it?" She only nodded, unable to speak, too turned on to form any words.

Ethan crawled onto the bed, sitting up on his knees between her legs. He grabbed her by the hips again and pulled her toward him, sliding her up over his bent knees until she was resting on his thighs. He looked down and saw that his erection was resting right above her glistening sex.

"I was wrong," he whispered. "*That* is the sexiest fucking thing I've ever seen in my life." He grabbed his painfully hard shaft and rubbed the tip against her slick flesh, watching as her fluids coated him. He swirled it around her clit a few times, loving the sounds it elicited from her, before lining himself up with her entrance. "Lily?" The tone of his voice made her open her eyes and look up at him.

"Yes?"

"I want you to know that I love you."

She smiled brightly, reaching up quickly to squeeze his free hand. "I love you, too."

"But I'm going to fuck you now...and it's not going to be gentle."

"Thank God! Don't worry, we can do gentle another time."

"My thoughts exactly." With that, he shifted his hips and pushed inside her, slowly at first, savoring the feel of her tight walls stretching to accommodate him. "Oh…God!" he cried out, clenching his eyes shut and throwing his head back. When he looked back down at her, he had such a pained expression on his face that she worried something was wrong. "I thought I remembered how good you felt…I was so fucking wrong."

He began thrusting harder then, grabbing onto her hips as he pounded himself inside her. Lily wanted to talk to him, to tell him that it felt better than any of her memories, too, but the angle at which he was grinding into her made words impossible. So she moaned. And she grunted. And it felt so fucking good that she would have sold her soul to Satan himself if he had offered to never let it end.

Ethan was hypnotized, watching their bodies join, watching his now glistening shaft sliding in and out of her as her inner muscles gripped him tightly. He moved one hand over until he was touching where they were connected, circling his thumb over her clit to add to the friction.

"Oh God!" she screamed loudly. That got the response he wanted. He felt her clamp down on him tightly, a warm rush of wetness coating him.

"That's it," he snarled through clenched teeth. "Come on me." He began pounding even harder, thrusting through her moans and cries. "Come all over my cock. It's been so fucking long since I've felt you."

When her shaking subsided he grabbed her by the arms and pulled her up, dragging her like a limp ragdoll until she was sitting up on his thighs. Once she felt her strength return she wrapped her arms around his shoulders for balance, looking into his glowing eyes. He looked feral, and frantic, and sexy as hell.

Sliding one hand between their bodies, Ethan pulled at her corset until her left breast was exposed, the tight pink nipple inviting him to feast. Growling low in his throat, he bent forward and captured it between his lips, sucking and biting as he continued to thrust so deep inside her that he wondered if he'd ever be free of her body, knowing deep in his soul that he never wanted to be.

After a few more violent thrusts, he knew that he wasn't going to make it any longer. It was all too much; the way she looked, the way she felt—even the scent of her sweet pussy and the sweat on their bodies was driving him insane.

"Oh God," he moaned against her skin. "Do you think you can go again? I can't hold it any longer."

She nodded quickly, answering him through broken pants and sobs. "I'm so close…you feel so good!"

He shifted his hips, grinding his pelvic bone into her more roughly, hoping it would provide the friction she needed but unable to focus any more than that with his own impending release.

"Oh God…that's it!" she screamed, her body clamping down on him tightly. "Oh! Ethan…God, I love you!"

And he was gone. His orgasm shot through him like a rocket, sending his body up in flames in its wake.

"I love you!" he cried out, thrusting his hips frantically as he pumped his seed deep inside her. "*Mine!*" he growled possessively, giving one final thrust before he collapsed on his side, taking her with him.

They lay there together gasping for air, a tangled heap of sweaty limbs.

"That was…God, Ethan, that was so…"

"Perfect."

"Perfect," she sighed, kissing him gently on the lips.

Their breathing began to even out as they rested, and right as Ethan was about to drift off to a light sleep, Lily's hushed voice broke through the silence.

"You know, I *am* yours. And you're mine. For as long as you'll have me."

He reached out for her without opening his eyes, pulling her tighter into his side. When he felt her there he kissed her forehead reassuringly and began to fall back asleep.

"Forever," he whispered.

16

When Lily began to stir over an hour later, it was to the faint sound of scratching in the distance. It had a rhythmic quality to it, the repetitive *scrape, scrape, shuffle, shuffle* almost lulling her back to sleep. Once she finally committed to searching out the source of the noise, she opened her eyes slowly, allowing them to adjust to the bright glow of the still-burning candles.

"Don't move," a rough whisper called out. "I'm almost done."

Slowly turning her eyes toward the sexy voice that had haunted her for months, Lily could just make out the shape of Ethan in her peripheral vision. The scratching noise continued, and she could see his arm moving over something he held in his lap. "What are you doing?"

"I'm sketching you."

"Oh," she replied awkwardly, not sure what else to say. "Can I turn my head? I can't see you." She didn't mind that he was sketching her, but she had never posed for anything in her life and she had no idea how still he needed her to be.

"Yes, I'm done with that part. Just don't move your legs."

When she turned her head more fully, she found him sitting in a chair to the side of the bed, his boxer briefs back in place and one long leg tucked underneath him. A sketchbook sat in his lap, and he kept looking back and forth between her and the opened page as his hand flew across the surface, applying the charcoal with measured strokes. Upon closer inspection she could see that his fingertips were covered in black powder, and that he must have absently wiped his face a few times because there were random smudges on his cheek and brow. Also, the more he concentrated, the more the tip of his tongue would poke out of the corner of his mouth and flick at his lip.

He was adorable.

As much as Lily would have loved to lay there for hours and watch him work without moving a muscle, she began to feel a familiar pressure building in her bladder. "Um…baby? Are you close to finishing?"

"Yeah, why?" he asked without looking up from the page as he shaded another area.

"I'm sorry, but I really have to pee." She could feel her face heat with embarrassment, but any longer and she was about to start squirming.

"Oh! Of course, I'm sorry," he apologized, looking up at her sheepishly. "I wasn't even thinking. I tend to lose track of things when I'm working. Yes, I have enough of what I need to finish here, go ahead."

Lily scurried into the large bathroom that was attached to the bedroom. After she had finished and tidied herself up a bit, she returned to find him still hunched over the sketchbook.

"So, is this something I'm going to have to get used to?" she smiled, draping herself across the bed sideways on her stomach so that she could watch him.

"What's that?" He didn't look up again, lost in his art.

"You know, waking up to find you sketching or painting at all hours of the night."

"Sadly, yes. I really do lose track of time when I'm at it, but it's not so bad when I don't start this late. I couldn't resist…you looked so deliciously wild and rumpled. I just had to get it down."

"Can I see?"

"Actually…yes," he said with a final flourish of his hand as he signed the sketch. "All done." He turned the book around and laid it down in front of her on the bed. "What do you think?"

"Oh wow!" she gasped. "Ethan…it's beautiful! I can't believe you did all of this just now."

"Well, I didn't put a ton of detail in it. I just wanted to capture the moment. I could've spent hours on it, making every little thing perfect, but this feels more…"

"Intimate?"

"Exactly," he smiled. "So you like it?"

"I love it! It's very sensual," she blushed, looking at the sketch of a disheveled woman who had clearly just been ravished beyond comprehension. Her stockings were twisted and her corset was askew, leaving one perky breast exposed to the world. Her legs were bent so that nothing truly indecent was showing, and the messy pile of sheets around her helped to hide everything else. Because it had been drawn from the side and she had been turned away, her face wasn't totally visible, but Lily could make out just enough of her profile to know it was her. "I can't believe that's me. I don't think I've ever looked so sexy."

Ethan grabbed the sketchbook and placed it on the table behind him before kneeling down in front of her to look her in the eye. "Believe me, this pales in comparison to the real thing."

"So, is this the artist's equivalent of taking dirty pictures of his girlfriend?" Lily teased.

Now it was his turn to blush. "Kind of," he replied with a low chuckle. "I try to capture the beauty in anything I see…but with you, the beautiful and the erotic go hand in hand. Don't worry; this one is going in my private collection."

"You have a private collection?"

"Of course. I have a number of pieces I've done through the years that I just couldn't bear to part with. They're all in storage right now, waiting for the day I finally settle down in one place and can put them up in my studio or something."

"Are there any of me in there?"

Ethan's blush deepened. "There are two."

"Really?" she smiled. "So what made those two different from the walls of paintings you showed me tonight? Those all seemed fairly personal to me."

"Every painting is personal to an artist; each one is like a child you've nurtured and watched grow before your eyes. But if you want to actually make any money doing what you love, you have to learn to detach yourself as soon as possible so you can sell them. I have everything photographed and cataloged so that I can look at them whenever I want, but every once in a while one of them is just too hard to let go—or it was never intended for anyone else's eyes but mine."

Lily nodded with understanding. "And the two of me fall into the latter category."

"Yes. When I did all of those paintings, it was like I couldn't stop until every memory I had of you was documented in some way. And as many of the paintings in the gallery showed you, a lot of my memories were sexual. I tried to keep them tasteful, but there were two of them that I couldn't handle showing anyone…and I didn't think you would be comfortable having anyone else see them, either."

"I appreciate that," she sighed in relief. "What were they of?"

"They involved a bit more nudity. Nothing shocking for the art world of course, but more than I thought was appropriate without your permission. I tried to record the perfection of your breasts in one of them, but I can see now that I didn't do them justice." He leered at her cleavage, reaching out a long, slender finger to trace the edge of one brownish-pink areola that had begun to sneak out above the top of her corset.

"And the other one?"

"Hm?" He looked up at her as if breaking out of a trance. "The other one? Ah yes…well, let's just say that the other involved…lube."

"No! Please tell me you didn't show that!"

"No, Lily, nothing so graphic. But the symbolism was there, and I knew what it meant. I couldn't stand for someone else to buy that memory…and I wasn't about to explain anything about it to people viewing it."

"Thank goodness for that!" she laughed. "So…will I ever get to see these paintings?"

"Perhaps…one day," he said absently, already lost in the valley between her breasts again. He continued stroking lazy patterns across her skin with his finger, watching as her flesh dipped and changed color under the pressure. When he finally dragged his gaze up to meet hers it was with great difficulty, and his eyes were dilated with lust. "It all depends."

It was hard to concentrate on everything he was saying between the touch of his fingers and the heat in his eyes, but she could tell from his tone that he was being playful. "On what?" she smirked.

He did nothing but look at her for a moment, allowing the tension to build between them. When he finally spoke again it was with a gruff voice. "On how fast you can get up on all fours and show me that delectable ass."

Without another word, Lily scrambled to her knees. Turning around abruptly and bending over to brace herself with her palms, she arched her back dramatically and flipped her hair back to look at him over her shoulder. "Fast enough for you?"

"Fuck," he growled, standing up quickly behind her. "Spread your knees," he commanded. Looking down at the sinful display in front of him, he had to swallow down the saliva that flooded his mouth. "I swear to Christ, Lily…I know I keep saying it, but you are the sexiest thing I've ever fucking seen."

"I feel the same…about you," she panted, her breath becoming choppy with anticipation.

Ethan stepped out of his boxer briefs, gripping his erection firmly before brushing the broad tip against her swollen sex. He watched as he swirled her moisture up and down the length of her silken folds, rubbing it more firmly over the hardened nub of her clitoris a few times before dragging it back up to her entrance.

"I can't get enough of you," he whimpered, gripping her hips tightly. He met her eyes briefly as she looked back at him, and his expression was almost panicked before he pulled his gaze back down to watch as he slowly pushed himself inside her. "I don't know what's wrong with me, but I just—I just *can't*."

She groaned loudly at his intrusion. "Good! I don't want you to ever get enough." With that, she flexed her hips and forced herself back onto him more roughly, thus ending any further conversation that didn't consist of grunts and moans.

Ethan continued to thrust inside her, eventually pulling her up flush against his chest so that he could grab her chin and kiss her hungrily. Yanking the front of her corset down, he gripped and squeezed Lily's breasts until she was sure they would bruise, but she was unable to care at all. The only thing that mattered was the heavy drag and pull of him inside her.

Feeling herself getting closer to the edge of oblivion, she fell forward onto her hands again, needing the support. Looking back over her shoulder until their eyes locked, she felt any remaining hesitation and shyness disintegrate.

He would always give her anything she needed, and would never judge her for it.

And she finally knew: *This* was true honesty.

Not strangers in a dirty apartment, hiding away from the real world, but two people who knew one another's flaws as well as their perfections, and loved each other even more for it.

Two people who didn't have to hide behind their anonymity to have the courage to ask for the things they truly desired.

"Ethan," she panted, "grab my hair!"

He could only manage a loud snarl in response, fisting her hair tightly at the base of her skull and pulling until she had arched back as far as she could go. He pounded into her faster, causing her to bounce back and forth with the frantic rhythm.

"God, yes!" she cried, her voice shaking from the force of his thrusts. "Baby…baby, I need you to smack my ass…oh, God, please, baby."

"Fuck!" Ethan gritted through his teeth, the veins in his neck standing out sharply with his effort to hold on. Letting go of his death grip on her hip, he raised his other hand and brought it back down with a light slap on the swell of her ass.

"Harder!" she begged. "God, baby, please harder! I'm not going to break."

Raising his arm higher, he brought it down with a resounding crack.

"Yes! That's it! Oh, God, don't stop…I'm so fucking close!"

Ethan kept up the spanking in time with his thrusts, not stopping through her cries of pleasure until he felt her body begin to seize up, gripping him tightly in an attempt to milk his own release from him. Letting go of her hair, he quickly grabbed her hips again for leverage, slamming and pounding into her so forcefully that the entire bed shook underneath them until he threw his head back and cried out his blinding ecstasy.

After collapsing again in a tangled heap, they lay together for a few minutes catching their breath. "Fuck, I love you so much," he exhaled loudly, rolling onto his back and pulling her with him. Brushing her sweaty hair out of her eyes, Ethan rose up and kissed her sweetly, an action that seemed so tame compared to his passion moments before.

"Likewise," Lily whispered, her voice now hoarse.

Stroking her shoulder lovingly, Ethan felt his heart stop when he saw a dark mark on her skin. Sitting up quickly, he pulled her up to inspect her, terrified that he had hurt her with his roughness. Once she was facing him, he saw that she was absolutely covered in the marks. They were all over her breasts, her shoulders, and her arms, and when he made her turn around he could see the outline of his fingertips on her hips where he'd held her, as well as a few random ones across her ass.

"Oh God, are these bruises?" he gasped, feeling his stomach start to turn in disgust.

"Huh?" she asked, a puzzled look on her face.

"Look at you, you're covered!"

"Ethan, calm down!" She laughed, grabbing his hands and holding them up in front of his eyes. When he finally stopped panicking and looked closely at them, he noticed that they were covered in black smudges. "You never washed the charcoal off your fingers. I'm fine."

"Oh God!" he laughed nervously, dropping his head to his hands in relief. "Jesus, that really scared me." He looked back up to see Lily brushing at a dark smudge on the slope of her breast. The more she tried, the more it smeared over her skin.

"Man, it looks like I was dusted for fingerprints," she giggled. "I don't think you could defend yourself against this evidence, Mr. Foster."

"What? No way. You're dreaming." He looked down at her black smudged skin. "I barely touched you."

"Barely touched me? I look like a cheetah!"

"I think that's a gross over-exaggeration," he said with a dead-pan expression. They both broke into sleepy laughter, and when they stopped, Lily couldn't resist a loud yawn.

"All right, beautiful," Ethan said, "let's get you cleaned up. How about a soak in the tub?"

"That sounds amazing," she sighed, her heavy eyelids slowly blinking.

"Okay, you stay here and rest. I'll be right back. I'm going to draw us a bath."

Ethan disappeared from the room, and before long Lily had drifted off into a light slumber. When she awoke a little while later, it was to the gentle tugging of Ethan's fingers on the laces of her corset. She slowly realized that he had already removed her shoes and her stockings while she slept and was lovingly unwrapping her like she was a priceless gift.

Once her corset had been removed as well, he scooped her up into his arms and tucked her against his chest. "Come on, Sleeping Beauty," he whispered as he carried her into the large bathroom.

"Oh wow!" she gasped, holding her head up and looking around as they entered the room. "Ethan, did you just do this? It's so beautiful!" He had moved and re-lit most of the candles so that the bathroom had a bright golden glow, and he had placed the untouched bucket of champagne on the marble countertop.

"I thought it might be more relaxing than the harsh lights in here. I want you to be able to just soak and relax. It's been a very long day."

"Mmm...with lots of physical exertion," she purred.

"Very true," he smirked, setting her down by the edge of the tub. "Now, go ahead and climb in."

Lily stepped carefully into the huge tub, sitting down with a loud sigh in the warm water, laughing as the thick layer of bubbles rose up and tickled her chin before settling down lower around her chest.

"God, this feels amazing," she moaned, laying her head back against the edge.

"I'm happy you like it, baby," Ethan smiled, grabbing the bottle of champagne. A loud *pop* could be heard as he sent the cork flying into the other room, and he quickly filled two crystal flutes with the bubbly drink. Sitting them on the large rim of the tub, he tapped lightly on Lily's shoulder. "Scoot forward for me."

Lily allowed him enough room to slip in behind her, sighing again as he pulled her back to rest against his chest. Handing her one of the glasses over her shoulder, he leaned down to kiss her neck.

"I think I've died and gone to heaven," she whispered.

"Well, you certainly feel heavenly," his gravelly voice vibrated on her back as he spoke. "But I don't think it's heaven."

"Why's that?"

"Because if it were heaven, at least my form of heaven, I wouldn't need any time for my body to recoup. Feeling your silky wet skin slide against me like this is more like torture when I can't do anything about it."

"Well, you're the one who climbed in here to relax. How can you relax if it's torture?"

"It's the best kind of torture," he whispered against her wet shoulder. "And it is relaxing. I just need to shift my focus a little—which is hard to do when you wiggle your ass like that."

"Sorry," she blushed. "I was just trying to get more comfortable."

"No worries, I'm only teasing you." He paused to grab his own glass and raise it out in front of her. "Now let's have a toast, shall we?"

"A bathtub toast?"

"Of course! Bathtub toasts are the most sincere, didn't you know that?"

"No, can't say I did. I'm starting to think you're making a lot of this stuff up as you go along."

"Yes, isn't it wonderful?" he chuckled. The vibrations his warm laughter caused against her back were instantly her new favorite sensation. "We can make it all up as we go along now. There are no rules or boundaries, just a clean slate."

"Or a blank canvas," she smiled.

"Even better!" He held his glass closer to hers. "To blank canvases."

"To blank canvases," Lily sighed.

The clink of their glasses echoed lightly through the room. After sipping quietly for a moment, Ethan could see that her eyes were starting to droop again. "Okay, give me that." He took her glass before she could drop it, then sat up a little higher in the tub and reached for a sponge. "Let's get you cleaned up before you pass out on me."

He dipped the sponge down into the bubble bath, bringing it up to squeeze the warm suds over Lily's shoulders. Scrubbing lightly at the charcoal smudges, he watched as her porcelain skin became clear again. At one point she accused him of paying extra special attention to the marks on her breasts, which he wholeheartedly denied, only to continue doing.

After everything was scrubbed properly multiple times, they both rinsed off and dried each other with enormous towels. Ethan sent her to bed while he blew out the candles and drained the tub, and when he slipped in next to her she was already fast asleep.

Pulling her to him in the dark, he wrapped his arms around her possessively and kissed the top of her head. Looking back on the day they had shared, Ethan wondered if it could have possibly been any more perfect.

Sleep claimed him moments later, and it was the most peaceful he'd had in years.

17

When Lily woke the next morning, it was to the sound of something being wheeled into the room. She opened her eyes to see Ethan looking groggy and disheveled, his already wild hair sticking up in different directions as he pushed a food cart toward the small table near the bed. He was wearing one of the hotel robes, and it had parted enough that she could make out a decent amount of bronze chest hair.

He looked positively delicious.

"Morning, sleepyhead." He smiled down at her when he saw that she was awake. "I hope you don't mind, but I ordered us some breakfast. I didn't really feel like going out just yet."

"Why would I mind?" she said around a yawn before sitting up to stretch her arms. "This way we can stay buried in our cozy sex cocoon until it's time to check out."

"I see we think alike," he laughed. "Did you want to eat in bed or sit here at the table?"

"Table's fine with me. I'm just going to run to the bathroom first."

When Lily was finished she splashed some water on her face, trying to rid herself of the last remnants of sleep that made her eyelids feel puffy and heavy. Finding a matching robe hanging on the back of the door, she threw it on quickly and joined Ethan at the small breakfast table he'd arranged.

"You better watch out," she teased. "I could get used to all of this spoiling." She lifted the cover off her plate to find a large pile of eggs, bacon, sausage, and toast. "Mmm...yes, I could definitely get used to this."

"Good," he mumbled around a large forkful of food. When he'd swallowed, he reached over and grabbed her hand. "You need a little spoiling. I'm looking forward to spoiling you for the rest of my life."

Lily ate in silence for a while, the only sign that she'd heard him showing in the pink hue of her cheeks. In reality, she couldn't stop her heart from pounding in her chest at his words. She knew how she felt about him; there hadn't been any doubt in her mind that she had found the one for her. But to hear her own thoughts of forever spoken back to her so easily—she thought her heart might explode right through her chest from the happiness.

The look she saw in his eyes when they finally met across the table mirrored her own. They didn't speak any further about it after that, switching the topic to less important things. It was silently understood between them that they would be speaking of it again in the future, because they both knew that their futures now belonged to each other.

And in the same way, she knew without asking that he wouldn't be returning to his family's home when they went back to Aledo. His home was with her now.

When they finished breakfast, they decided it would be a wonderful timesaver to shower together. Ethan told her to think of all the water they would be saving as well, and Lily was fully on board to do her part for the environment.

That is, until they began soaping each other up under the hot spray.

For some reason, they lost track of the time they were supposed to be saving, and ended up wasting twice as much water than if they'd showered separately.

Ethan pulled her closer to him, allowing his hands to slip and slide along her flesh as he washed her. He scrubbed her hair as she did the same to him, and when he asked her to lower her head so that he could apply the conditioner, she dropped to her knees in front of him.

"Go ahead," she purred, looking up at him from beneath her lashes. As soon as his hands began to spread the thick fluid through her hair, she took him deep into her mouth, bobbing up and down on his shaft, moaning loudly around him. He did his best to concentrate on the task at hand, nearly falling over more than once as she made him weak in the knees, and before long he was pulling her back to her feet frantically.

Positioning her under the spray, he told her to tip her head back so that she could rinse her hair. The moment she closed her eyes and leaned back, his hot mouth was everywhere. He began loudly slurping water from her slippery breasts, sucking each nipple between his teeth and biting lightly before dropping down and throwing one of her legs over his shoulder, sinking his tongue between her folds to lap at her moisture.

It was Lily's turn to nearly fall over, reaching out to grab onto the tile for balance. Within what felt like seconds, she was teetering on the edge and wanting nothing more than to fall over the cliff together with him.

"Please," she begged, dropping her leg to the side and tugging on his shoulders.

"Do you want me?" he whispered in her ear once he had slid his way back up her body. As he spoke, he was grabbing onto her waist and moving her, pushing her back against the sidewall of the shower.

"Yes," she groaned, loving the feeling of him pinning her there with his body. She could feel the heat of his erection rubbing against her, so very close to where she needed him most.

"Tell me," he said through choppy breaths as he bit her earlobe. "Tell me that you want me."

"I more than want you," she gasped, feeling him sliding against her more fully. "I *need* you. I need you more than oxygen. I need you inside of me *now*."

With that, he gripped her hips and lifted her legs around him, slipping inside her body.

They both cried out at the contact, words lost to them. He began to slowly move in and out of her, wrapping her legs around him tightly between his thrusts. Lily held him to her for dear life, loving the feel of his muscles rippling under her hands as he moved.

They were lost in each other for what felt like an eternity, and yet it didn't last long enough before they were both careening into the abyss. Lily felt herself shattering into a million pieces around him, and through her euphoria she heard him groan his release, pumping his seed inside her as he thrust his hips rapidly.

They stood there for a moment after he slowly released her, gasping for air, staring into each other's eyes as the now-cold water rained down around them.

"I need you, too," he panted. "Always." He kissed her roughly, sucking at the water dripping from her lips. "I never want to face a life without you again."

"Never again, Ethan," she whispered against his lips. Reaching up to brush the soaking hair out of his eyes, she kissed him tenderly before pulling back to look deeply into pools of jade framed by long, wet lashes. "We'll never be apart again."

Epilogue

18 Months Later

"'… And as the familiar strains of their waltz began, Evan pulled Lacey onto the floor for their first dance together as man and wife. He knew then, as he twirled her around the room before the eyes of God and his entire family, that their heated embrace on that long night so many months ago hadn't been their last dance after all. It was only the first of many.' The end."

Maggie Foster looked up at the large crowd gathered in the bookstore in Chicago and smiled her most dazzling smile. "Thank you so much for coming to my reading of excerpts from my new release, *Our First Dance*. Before I get to the signing, does anyone have any questions?"

A large sea of hands flew up in the air, all fans wanting the chance to speak to their favorite romance author. However, in the back of the room, standing against a shelf of books with their arms crossed, were two people in a mild state of shock. Ethan Foster had a large scowl on his face, and his new wife Lily was shaking her head in disbelief, her mouth hanging wide open.

"Did you know?" he whispered loudly to her, trying to be heard over the many fans laughing excitedly over something Maggie had said in reply to a question.

"Of course not!" she gasped. "Don't you think I would have said something? I've been asking her for months if I could read her manuscript, and she kept telling me it wasn't ready yet."

"Well, I think it's safe to say that's bullshit, since it has to have been with the publisher for months. Looks like I'm going to have to do some ass-kicking."

"Now, now," she patted his arm, trying to make him calm down. "It's not like it was *exactly* the same. She just sort of took how we met...and a few other details here and there."

"A *few?*"

"Yes, only a few. They were an important few, but still only a few. Besides, how did you not know anything about this? She used your waltz painting as the cover!"

"She asked me after she bought it if she could use it for her next cover. I never told you because I thought it would be a nice surprise, but I had no idea about all of this!"

"Well, that makes two of us, then," Lily sighed.

"What a welcome home," he grumbled.

The newlyweds had recently taken an extended honeymoon to New Zealand, renting out a flat in Wellington for a month. Ethan even secretly worked in a stopover in Australia as a surprise to his new bride. He had managed to complete a few new paintings (one in particular was headed to his private collection), and Lily had managed to do the sightseeing she had always dreamed of with her husband by her side.

They hadn't even returned to their new home in Aledo yet, having flown straight into Chicago so that they could make it in time for Maggie's reading. Despite buying a house, they hadn't given up the tiny apartment where their relationship first began. They kept it for Ethan to use as a studio, at least until he finally got around to renovating the empty space above their new garage. Neither one of them could bear to part with it just yet.

Now, all of their bags were sitting unpacked in their hotel room. They'd been late, and, not wanting to disrupt the reading, had hid in the back until they had a chance to move closer.

"I'm sorry, but that's going to have to be the last question for now," Maggie said to the many people with their hands still in the air. "I'm going to take a short break before the signing so that I can feed my little one before my boobs explode," she laughed, gesturing to Eric, who stood behind her next to Emma and Brandon, bouncing a tiny girl in his arms with huge raven curls and even huger dimples. The crowd laughed at her candor and applauded loudly as she left the podium.

"That's our cue," Ethan said, watching as Maggie took the baby from Eric and disappeared into a private break room. He grabbed Lily's hand, weaving through the large crowd of women forming a line at the side of the store.

Emma was the first to see them approaching. "Oh my God!" she yelled, running over to hug them both. "I was worried that you didn't make it back in time!"

"It was quite a rush to get here," Lily sighed.

"Well, at least you made it," Emma said with a smile. "I didn't even see you!"

"We were just hiding back there." Ethan pointed toward the wall of books. His expression turned grim. "But we did make it in time for most of the reading."

"Yeah…uh, about that," she blushed. "I swear I didn't know until it had already been sent to the publisher."

"Don't you think she should have asked us, Emma?" Ethan frowned. "Or at least *told* us?"

"Dude, you're here five minutes and you're already whining?" Eric interrupted, standing on their other side next to Brandon.

"Whining? Eric, that's our life. Our *private* life. Don't you think we should have been warned? Don't you think she should have asked someone?"

"She did ask someone," he answered, his tone becoming serious. "She asked me."

"What do you mean?" Ethan was thrown off by Eric's protective stance.

"She told me a long time ago that she thought how you two met was the stuff of romantic legends. She wanted so badly to use that as a beginning to one of her stories, but she was afraid if she asked, you would shoot it down before even hearing her out. Now, I know that you're shocked right now, but if you take the time to read it over, you will see that there are really not that many similarities. I told her if she felt like she had to write it, then to go ahead and do it and stop worrying what you might think." He sighed, scratching his hands through his short hair in a frustrated gesture. "It's some of the best writing she's ever done, and you two were her inspiration. Be proud of that."

"But—but what about—" Ethan was floundering, the wind taken out of his sails.

"Dude, have you even opened the book yet?"

"Well...no. We just got here."

"Here," he huffed, grabbing a copy off the large display next to him and thrusting it at Ethan's chest. "Just do me a favor and look in the damn thing before you jump her ass, okay? Now if you'll excuse me, I'm going to go check on my wife and daughter. Nice to see you again, Lily." He smiled and nodded at her curtly before stomping off to the break room.

"Wow, I don't think I've ever seen him so angry," Lily whispered.

"He's not angry," Ethan explained, opening up the book. "He's just standing up for her. Believe me, I've seen him angry." He looked down at the opening page, his brow rising in surprise. "Well…shit."

"What?" Lily scooted closer, looking at the page over his shoulder.

To Lily, the best nurse and friend a girl could ask for
And to Ethan, the very best brother

"Oh my God!" she gasped, tears instantly springing to her eyes.

Ethan sighed next to her, wrapping his arm around her shoulder. "All right, I'm an asshole. Let's go find her."

They walked toward the break room, only to see Maggie and Eric making their way back out. As soon as Maggie saw them coming toward her, a worried look crept over her face and her cheeks flamed bright red.

"Here, babe, would you take her for a sec?" she whispered, handing over the baby. Taking a deep breath to steel her nerves, she turned to face the two people she had been dreading talking to. "Okay, guys. Let's have it. How bad do you hate me right now?"

Lily couldn't even speak; she simply grabbed her and gave her the fiercest hug imaginable. "I could never hate you!" she finally sobbed.

Maggie looked over Lily's shoulder in question at Ethan and he merely shrugged. "She just read your dedication."

"Ah. So you're not mad?" she asked, still speaking over the sobbing Lily.

"I was pissed, I'll admit it. But after thinking about it and reading what you wrote, I'm also very flattered. Thank you." He looked behind Maggie to where Eric was standing, a bright smile on his face once again.

"Wow, really?" she said in disbelief.

"Really."

"God, *I* might just cry," she sighed before redirecting her attention to Lily. "Okay, little miss weepy, tell me about New Zealand! Was it great? Did you get a lot of pictures? Did you meet Jemaine Clement?"

Lily laughed before answering, "Let me see…yes…yes…and I wish! But enough about us for now, we have years to bore you with pictures of our honeymoon. Give me that baby!" She ran to Eric, eagerly pulling the little one from his arms. "Oh, little Eden, Aunt Lily missed you so much!" She began showering her little cheeks with kisses, smiling when the baby chortled loudly.

"Looks like she missed you, too," Maggie smiled. They both watched as Eden looked between them and suddenly held her hands out, fussing until Ethan moved closer. "Oh jeez, she still has her Uncle Ethan crush." Maggie rolled her eyes, watching as Ethan scooped her up. "And here I'd hoped that a month away from you would do the trick."

"Never!" he laughed. "Not my little princess. My goodness you've gotten big!"

"So how have you been feeling?" Lily asked Maggie, already in nurse mode again.

"Oh, stop worrying about me, I'm fine. Eden is almost eight months old now, and I'm clearly in the pink."

When Maggie was seven months into her pregnancy, she had begun lightly spotting again, and Dr. Wilde had put her on immediate bed rest until her due date. Knowing that she and Lily were practically family, Natalie arranged for Lily to drop her hours down to part-time so Maggie could hire her as her own private nurse. Between Lily and Barbara, they had her covered around the clock at the house in Aledo. Lily checked her blood pressure and her vitals, and basically kept her from wanting to pull her hair out from boredom.

It had been a difficult delivery, leading to an emergency C-section that took a long time to heal. Because of that, Lily had stayed on even longer to help her take care of baby Eden. When it came time for her to go back to work and for Maggie to return to Chicago, they had both been moved to tears.

"How soon are you guys all coming back to Aledo?" Lily asked, always eager to spend time with the happy family.

"Soon, actually. Richard and Barbara's anniversary is coming up. I thought we'd make a trip out of it and stay a few days."

"Excellent!"

"Now, enough about me. Look at your husband wooing my daughter." They watched as Ethan bounced Eden playfully in the air, blowing raspberries on her cheeks and tickling her sides. "Good Lord, she's going to be a sucker for the bad boys, isn't she?"

"Like mother, like daughter," Lily laughed.

"Damn. Got me there."

"What are you two talking about over here?" Ethan asked, moving closer to hear them better, the baby nestled into his side.

"Oh nothing," Maggie smirked, knowing just how to get under his skin. "I was just appreciating how good you look holding a baby. Doesn't he, Lily? He's such a natural."

"Definitely," she giggled.

He blanched, looking back and forth between them. "Dammit, Maggie, the ink on our marriage license is barely dry. Don't go filling her head with that stuff yet."

"I don't know…Eden is going to need a cousin or two to play with before long."

"Then why don't you go throw your baby vibes over there," he huffed, pointing toward where Emma and Brandon stood talking quietly.

"Oh, don't worry, I will. Why do you think I said a cousin or *two*?" At Ethan's obvious squirming, she couldn't hold back her laughter anymore. "Oh, for God's sake, stop getting your panties in a twist! I'm only fucking with you."

"Thank God," he sighed, chuckling nervously. He made his way next to Lily, pulling her into his side possessively. They both lost track of the conversation after that, becoming engrossed with keeping baby Eden entertained.

"*Although*…" Maggie paused, whispering to herself as she watched the two of them play with her daughter. "I am getting some wonderful ideas for a sequel."

4 Years Later

"Why am I lying naked on the floor while you're still fully dressed?" Lily asked as she watched Ethan pacing around the barely furnished, small apartment. It was *their* old apartment, where they had lived together before getting married and buying their current home. Ethan had kept it as an art studio through the years, which was, incidentally, what he had originally rented it for. He'd been meaning to renovate the space above their garage into a studio for years, but every time he thought about letting the apartment go, he just couldn't do it.

Now, Ethan was busy collecting supplies in his arms and muttering to himself as he went through his mental checklist, and he didn't hear Lily's question until she asked him again.

"I told you," he answered distractedly as he set various items down next to her. "There's something I want to try."

"Care to be more specific?" she asked, sitting up and crossing her arms over her breasts as he kneeled down beside her.

"I want to paint you." He leaned in and gave her a quick peck on the lips, pulling back before it could turn into anything more.

"You paint me all the time," Lily replied with a pout, wishing the kiss had gone on longer. "Why do I have to be on the floor today? And why the hell is this drop cloth so damn scratchy?" She gestured to the stiff material they were both sitting on.

"Because it's not a drop cloth; it's canvas. I want to try something different this time," he explained. "Do you remember when I painted those colors all over your body?"

"Mm," she moaned lightly, smiling at the memory. "My very first art lesson. If I remember correctly, that turned into a very hands-on demonstration."

"Yes it did," he chuckled. "Anyway, I was thinking about how passionate that was, which inspired me to try this."

"What is it, exactly, that you are trying?"

"I want to capture that passion. Last time was so sexy and amazing, but it was all just washed away down the drain when we showered that afternoon. This time I want to keep it."

Lily's eyes lit with understanding. "So when you said that you wanted to paint me, you meant paint *me*, literally."

"Yes. Is that all right?"

Lily laid back against the sheet of canvas on the ground, spreading her arms out wide. "Go on, Picasso, do your worst."

"Pfft, Picasso?" Ethan scoffed as he set up his palette. "Please. You know I hate Cubism."

"Forgive me, Master Foster. I forgot that no one could possibly compete with your artistic mastery."

"Hey, I'm not that arrogant," he said, dipping a large brush into a glob of paint that he had just mixed to a light shade of blue.

"Yes, you are," she laughed. "Ooh, that tickles." She wiggled at the feeling of the rough bristles dragging across her rib cage, leaving bright streaks of color in their wake.

"Stop moving," he commanded. "And, darling, I think you're confusing arrogance with confidence."

"You have both in spades."

"All right, I'll grant you that." He smirked at her as he grabbed another brush, smearing bright flares of red over her sensitive nipples.

"Is there any method to your color scheme here?" she asked, laughing when a bright bloom of yellow appeared down her thigh.

"I'm trying to tap into the emotion of colors," he explained seriously, his eyes never leaving her body as he worked. Lily watched as he lovingly traced her C-section scar with swirls of purple. "I want to capture your passion."

"Then come over here," she purred seductively.

"Not yet," he scolded. "I'm trying to concentrate."

And on it went for almost an hour, Ethan smearing and streaking her from head to toe in a wild array of colors and Lily hinting at and pouting for more contact from him. Every brush stroke was like a lover's kiss against her heated flesh, and it drove her crazy that he was so focused on his art.

"There," he said at last, placing his brush down emphatically. "Now turn over slowly." He helped her move the way he wanted, pushing down on her body in some places and adjusting her on each side until she began to feel like a giant paint roller. Just as she was about to call an end to the entire thing, he stopped and helped her sit up to look at the results.

"Oh, Ethan…it's beautiful." She was surprised to find that it truly was: brilliant shots of color spread across the canvas in different directions, creating a vibrant, captivating effect.

When she looked up at him she was surprised to find him frowning. "No. Something's missing."

"What could possibly be missing?" Lily asked. "I thought you were crazy when you first started, but this is lovely."

"I don't know how to explain it," he grumbled, tugging his hands through his hair in frustration. He kneeled down next to her again, sighing loudly. "It's pretty. I don't want pretty. I want primal. I see whimsy and joy and love here, but I want passion." His shoulders slumped in defeat before he finally met her questioning gaze. "I wanted so badly to recreate the passion that you bring to my life."

"Baby, don't you see?" Lily reached up and held his face, ignoring the bright smear of green she left on his chin. "You were never going to find that this way."

"What do you mean?"

"You're just rolling me around in paint here. It's much too one-sided. I meant it earlier when I told you to join me. This passion between us is something that we generate together; it's nothing either of us can create on our own. Ethan, you're my passion. Without you it just doesn't work. I mean, look at me." She waved her hand across her body. "It's all so deliberate and staged. Passion isn't like that."

He blinked a few times as he let her words sink in. "Passion is messy," he finally whispered.

"Yes."

"And out of control."

"Exactly."

Leaning forward, he rested his forehead against hers. "Have I ever told you how much I love you?"

"You might have mentioned it a time or two," she smiled, pulling him closer so that their lips could meet in a searing kiss. But when her hands went to lift his shirt up over his head he stopped her.

"Wait a second." He stood up quickly and went to his iPod, changing the playlist from the current, tamer songs to his tried and true "Fuck Songs" list. As soon as a sexy blues riff started to fill the room he turned back around and yanked his shirt off over his head, throwing such a heated look at his wife as he stalked back toward her that she feared she might melt right there on the spot.

"Oh, God," Lily moaned. "That's what I'm talking about."

Ethan stood in front of her, slowly unbuttoning his jeans and pulling them down over his hips. Once he had kicked them off he joined her again, kneeling in front of her like an offering. Without saying a word, he reached over and picked up the palette, setting it gently in her hands.

"What do you want me to do?" she asked in confusion when he looked at her expectantly.

"It's your turn."

"Oh!" She slowly ran her eyes down his sculpted torso, lingering on all the places that she loved to touch. Picking up the brush that laid between the different selections of paint, she barely glanced at it before tossing it across the room. Licking her lips excitedly, Lily dipped her finger into the blue paint and began to make bright streaks across his solid chest.

When she stopped for a moment and smiled at what she had done, Ethan looked down and found that she had spelled out the word *MINE* on his skin. Unable to keep his hands off her after that, he reached out and grabbed her around the waist, pulling her into him tightly. As their mouths collided frantically, their bodies began to slip and slide against each other, smearing all of Ethan's hard work from earlier into brand new colors that covered them both.

Lily pulled back long enough to find the palette that she had dropped, quickly slapping both of her hands down into different colors before returning to her husband with fire in her eyes. She reached for him, dragging him closer as she ran her hands over him possessively, leaving bright streaks down his arms and around to his back. Two definite handprints appeared on his ass when she pulled his hips to hers, moaning loudly into his mouth when she felt his erection prodding between her legs.

"So beautiful," he muttered between kisses, nipping at her lips with his teeth. "My beautiful girl."

"I want you so badly," Lily gasped. "You've been driving me crazy since we got here." She couldn't stop touching him, her hands leaving bright streaks and fingerprints all over his skin.

"Me? You don't know how hard it was to keep my hands off of you earlier, just lying there like an offering for me."

"Then why the hell didn't you take me?" she asked, biting his earlobe lightly at the feel of his hands squeezing her breasts, swirling the paint on her nipples even more with his fingers. "God knows I wanted you to."

"I was trying to stay in control," he panted, reaching around her quickly and grabbing her ass, grinding himself harder between her legs.

"Fuck control!"

"Damn straight," he groaned, pulling her down to the paint-splattered canvas. They kissed and groped like desperate teenagers, unable to get enough of each other. "I need to taste you. Fuck, it's been too long!"

"It's only been a week," Lily giggled as he kneeled between her legs.

"Feels like a year! That damn kid needs to sleep in his own room from now on." Their young son, Mason, who was quickly turning into a little replica of his father, was still having trouble committing to his new toddler bed down the hall.

"Oh, look who's talking, Mr. Softie."

"I don't think that name is very appropriate for me right now, baby," he chuckled, nodding down toward the rather prominent erection that bobbed between them.

"You know what I mean. You're the biggest pushover whenever he starts begging. You have only yourself to blame for the shortage of bedroom sports lately."

"I'll take that into consideration, but I've got more pressing matters at the moment." He shot her a wink before placing his hands on her inner thighs and spreading them wide, leaving rainbow fingerprints on her pale skin as he exposed her wet flesh to his hungry eyes. "God damn, that's fucking gorgeous. I wish I could use my fingers, too, but somehow I've kept you paint free here and it should probably stay that way. Oh well," he sighed.

Without another word he buried his face between her legs, lapping at her silken folds until she was writhing beneath him. Lily shoved her fingers in his hair, grabbing huge handfuls, making it stick up in multi-colored spikes as she pushed and pulled him where she needed him most. After four years of marriage, they had absolutely no qualms about letting each other know exactly what they needed, although they each knew the other's body so well by now that it was rarely necessary.

"Oh, God, right there!" she cried, clamping her thighs against his head when he started sucking on her clitoris. With a loud shriek and a spasm that ran the entire length of her body, Lily shattered into what felt like a million tiny pieces. But when Ethan tried to keep going in order to coax another orgasm out of her, she yanked on his hair hard enough to make him stop.

"What, no encore?" he asked, licking and sucking on his swollen lips. He had paint streaks all over his face from her death-grip leg lock and his hair was sticking straight up, but he had never looked sexier to her.

This was primal.

This was passion.

"No," she nearly growled. "You. I need you. Now!"

Ethan took one look into her eyes and felt his control snap. There was no time for thought or planning; they were both driven by a pure need for each other that caused a lust-induced haze to fog their brains. When looking back on the evening, both of them would only recall small snippets here and there: streaks of color, slippery paint, and a feeling of absolute bliss.

In reality, Ethan had fallen on her hungrily, lining himself up at her entrance with practiced ease before sinking inside her to the hilt. They both cried out at their joining, thrusting and slamming their bodies together frantically, as if they feared that they would never be able to get close enough. At one point Lily growled and shoved him over, rolling on top of him and pinning him down with her hands on his shoulders. He groaned at the feeling of her riding him roughly, unable to tell her in words just how much he craved her physical possession of his body. All he could do was grab onto her hips and guide her to another explosive release as he thrust up into her repeatedly.

At some point after that, Ethan regained control of her shaking body, kneeling between her legs again as he threw her feet over his shoulders, lifting her hips off the floor high enough to balance on his thighs. He leaned forward so that he could kiss her lips as he moved, bending her body backward—which caused such an amazing friction when he ground himself inside her that Lily could only feel the insane pleasure of him filling her over and over again until they finally collapsed together in a heap of paint-smeared limbs on the floor.

They lay there together for so long that they lost track of time, kissing and cuddling and simply existing in their own little private world for as long as they could. But eventually they began sticking to each other uncomfortably as the paint dried and became tacky, so they slowly made their way to the little bathroom to shower, leaving multi-colored footprints behind them.

"You still have blue and purple streaks in your hair," Lily laughed as she applied more shampoo to Ethan's head.

"And you have a lovely red-yellow combination going on," he chuckled. "It might stain for a while, baby. At least a few shampoos."

"That's all right; I'll just wash it a few more times before I go back to work on Monday." She looked at him thoughtfully in the steam-filled shower. "I kind of like it on you, though. It's like a punk-rock reminder of our wonderful afternoon."

"Yeah, but if Mason sees it he's going to want blue hair, too."

"God, you're right," she sighed. "I hadn't thought of that. Bummer," she pouted, imagining the epic tantrum that their toddler would throw.

"No worries. I'll just wear my baseball hat around him until it's gone. But at night," he wagged his eyebrows suggestively, "I can punk rock your world."

"Ooh, I like the sound of that," Lily laughed. "But as you mentioned earlier, we're rarely alone at night anymore."

"I know, I know," he sighed. "I need to put my foot down and make him sleep in his own room. I just…sometimes it just amazes me that all of this is really mine, you know? When you both pile in around me in the bed like that, I feel surrounded by everything that matters, and I just…I just feel so fucking lucky, baby." He fought through a sudden lump in his throat to continue. "Having you and him has completely changed my life. I have no idea where I would be if I didn't have you. Sometimes it scares me shitless when I think about it."

"Hey, look at me." Lily reached out and held his face in her hands. "I understand how you feel. I think about it sometimes, too. I try to picture how my life would have turned out and I just can't do it. You and Mason are the only future I can ever see. You're stuck with us and we're not going anywhere, so we might as well find a way to sleep more comfortably at night." She smiled and stretched on her toes, angling up to kiss him sweetly as the water rained down over their heads.

"Have I ever told you how much I love you?" he asked when she pulled away.

"You might have mentioned it a time or two."

When they were finally as clean as they could manage, they dried off and got dressed again, returning to the front room to survey the damage.

"Holy shit," Ethan said with a laugh, noting all the smears and streaks of paint that covered the floorboards and even parts of the wall. "I don't think we stayed in the lines."

"Your poor studio!" Lily cried. "Should we try to clean it up now before it gets any worse and dries?"

"Hell no," he answered without blinking. "I love it. I'll always have a reminder of today whenever I'm here working." They walked over and looked down at the large sheet of canvas on the floor. "Well, what do you know?"

"Oh my God!" she gasped, covering her mouth in shock.

"I think I'd call this a success," he said with a chuckle, taking in all the handprints and different shapes and streaks created by their flailing limbs. "That's definitely passionate. I suppose this should go in my private collection, huh?"

"Ethan Foster, don't you dare!"

"What?"

"I forbid you to hide this away like those naughty little distractions you paint. You don't have to sell it, but you really should show it."

"You don't think it's too personal?"

"Of course it's personal, but it's abstract enough to be comfortable with. That is one of the most beautiful things that you've ever made. I thought it was going to end up a big muddy mess, but all of those amazing colors! Can you believe we did that?"

"Of course I can," he whispered as he smiled down at her. "Our love makes amazing things happen."

Two months later, they stood together in front of the same canvas, now stretched carefully around a frame and mounted on the wall of the art gallery showcasing Ethan's latest collection. It was large, at least eight feet wide and just as tall, and it was definitely the show-stopper of the evening.

Critics and fans alike had swarmed around it, unable to tear their eyes away from the primal electricity the piece conveyed. It was evocative; whether they loved it or hated it, nobody could deny that it made them *feel*. The crowd around it had been so huge that Ethan and Lily hadn't even bothered going near it until the party was over and they could grab a few moments in front of it alone.

Once the coast was clear, Lily leaned into Ethan's side and rested her head on his shoulder, sighing fondly as they took in the canvas again. She read the title card next to it on the wall and smiled to herself.

"Spread Your Love"
A Study in Passion

"Wasn't that the song that was playing that night?" she asked.

"Good memory," he said with a nod, leaning down to kiss the top of her head. "I'm sure other songs played later, but that was the only one I could remember for certain. It seems to fit, don't you think?"

"Perfectly."

"It still blows my mind when I look at it. I mean, that night couldn't have been more perfect, and now there's this amazing reminder of it that we'll always have."

Lily smiled more broadly, deciding that there would never be a better time to tell him. "You know…that's not the only thing we made that night."

"What do you mean, the mess in the apartment? I told you not to worry about that. I love it! It's actually rather inspirational," he added with a wink.

"No, sweetheart." She grabbed his hand and placed it over her still-flat belly. "I'm telling you that we made something else. Another amazing reminder."

Ethan cocked his head to one side before his eyes went wide with disbelief. "Bullshit!"

Lily threw her head back and laughed, loving that he'd had the exact same reaction the last time she told him they were expecting.

"You're serious?!" he cried.

She only had time to nod before he whooped loudly and picked her up, twirling her around in circles.

"You aren't upset, are you?" she asked when he finally set her down.

"Woman, are you crazy? Was that the reaction of someone who's upset?"

"Well, no, but I know you've mentioned to your family that Mason is such a handful, and we're barely managing with one. I wasn't trying, I swear. I was still getting my shot. I don't know how, but it just… happened."

"Hey, what did I say to you that night?" he asked, grabbing her chin in his hand and tilting her face up to meet his eyes.

"'Our love makes amazing things happen,'" she answered softly as she swallowed past a lump in her throat.

"It sure as hell does." Ethan leaned down and kissed her gently before pulling her into another fierce hug.

They decided later that night as they whispered together in bed that they would never sell that painting, regardless of all the offers Ethan had received that evening. But they did agree that one day they might leave it to their unborn child as a keepsake of the night he was made. Whether they would actually *tell* him about it was another story.

6 Months After That...

"Mason!"

A loud yowling could be heard down the hall, followed by the clumsy thuds of a toddler running across the floorboards.

"Mason George Foster! Get back here!"

Lily couldn't help smiling to herself in her bedroom mirror as she applied a light coating of lipstick and listened to Ethan's voice bellowing from the front room. Two minutes later she was nearly knocked over by a fuzzy orange streak as Wembley shot under the bed—his new favorite hiding place—followed closely by her two-year-old son.

Her two-year-old son who was currently wearing nothing more than a *Yo Gabba Gabba!* T-shirt and one sock.

"Wembee!" he yelled, getting down on his hands and knees to peek under the bed. "Wembee, come outta there!"

"What seems to be the problem there, bud?" Lily asked, trying very hard not to laugh as she turned to face his bare bottom sticking up in the air.

"Mommy, Wembee won't play wif me!" his muffled voice carried back to her.

"Well, what do you expect, sweetie? We've told you and told you that the cats don't like to be played with so roughly. If you keep scaring them they might get mad and bite you. I don't want that to happen, do you?"

He turned around and looked up at her with huge jade eyes. "No, Mommy."

"Good," she smiled, holding out her hand to pull him up until he was standing in front of her. "Because I've already had their claws taken out. I can't take their teeth out, too." She heard louder footsteps approaching behind her and turned to find Ethan standing in the doorway holding a pair of pull-ups, jeans, and the other sock, a familiar frazzled expression on his face. "Where's Boober?" she asked knowingly.

"Hiding on top of the fridge," he grumbled, coming forward to sit on the edge of the bed. "I can't get him to come down."

"Don't worry," she chuckled, watching as Ethan lifted their son onto the bed and began fighting his kicking legs to finish getting him dressed. "He'll come down when we leave."

"Mason, would you stop fussing, please?" Ethan scolded. "We told Grandma that we would have you there by now. Don't you want to go play?"

"Is Edie there?" he asked hopefully, always enjoying when his older cousin Eden came to stay.

"No, sweetie," Ethan frowned. "I told you earlier; Edie is with Uncle Eric and Aunt Maggie on her book tour. They won't be visiting until next month."

"Then I don't wanna go!" he yelled, kicking his newly donned sock off his toes before Ethan could pull it over his foot. Lily grabbed it and handed it back to Ethan, asking with her eyes if he needed help. He shook his head quickly before turning his attention back to Mason.

"What are you talking about? You love Grandma Barbara. She's been looking forward to this all week."

"I wanna go fishing with Bampa George!" Mason cried, gearing up for a Grade-A hissy fit.

Ethan took a deep breath and sighed, deciding that it would be pointless to remind his son that he had whined and cried out of sheer boredom the only time George had taken him out fishing. Mason had recently decided that no matter what he was supposed to be doing, it was nowhere near as fun as anything else he could think of.

"Bampa George is hunting with friends today," Lily chimed in over her shoulder as she finished brushing out her hair in the mirror. "We're gonna see him on Sunday."

"No, *now!*" he whined, kicking his leg again and nearly hitting Ethan in the jaw as he pulled the tiny jeans into place.

Lily paused for a moment, as if she were considering it. "Well, I can call him if you want…but Grandma might be sad. She'll have to throw *all* those cookies away."

"Cookies?" His tiny voice was suddenly very serious.

"Yeah. She said you are such a good helper in the kitchen, she couldn't wait to make tons and tons of cookies today. But now they'll have to go in the garbage because she won't have her helper."

"I help?" His wide eyes looked back and forth between his parents.

"Of course, silly!" Ethan laughed, leaning over to blow a raspberry on Mason's stomach. "You help her *eat* them."

After letting out a loud peal of giggles, Mason sat up and looked at him. He nodded his head once decisively before declaring, "You're right, Daddy. Gramma needs me."

"She certainly does. I'm proud of you for making the right decision, son." It took every ounce of strength Ethan had to keep from laughing at his somber expression.

"All right, you two," Lily called out, grabbing a duffel bag full of Mason's clothes and toys that was sitting in the bedside chair. "Let's get a move on."

Ethan jumped up and reached for the bag. "Let me carry that, baby."

"No, don't be silly; this is nothing. If you wanna grab something, grab him." She pointed at their son, who was trying to do somersaults on the mattress, causing his thick brown hair to stand up in tufts all over his head.

"C'mon, mister, you heard the lady." Ethan grabbed Mason around the middle, lifting him up sideways and carrying him like a football down the hall, Lily following closely behind them.

When they had made their noisy way to the car, Mason watched his mother from his car seat as she awkwardly tried to fasten her seat belt. "Mommy, why does your tummy look like a basketball?"

"Because there's a little baby sleeping in there, remember?" She looked back between the seats and smiled at him.

His face brightened with recognition. "Oh yeah! Daddy said he put it in there."

"Oh he *did*, did he?" She shot a sideways glance at Ethan, who simply shrugged before returning his attention to the road.

"Yeah, he said that he made a teeny tiny baby seed, and he needed to plant it somewhere for it to grow bigger, so he buried it in your tummy."

"Well, that's…disturbingly accurate," Lily smiled uncomfortably.

"When will it wake up?"

"A little over a month from now."

"On my *birthday*?" Mason's eyes got wide and he sat up excitedly. He had become obsessed with the thought of his birthday ever since he had been to his cousin Noah's first birthday party the month before in Chicago. Emma had thrown a ridiculously large event for her son that had been nowhere close to age-appropriate, and Mason had become convinced that *everyone's* birthday meant cowboys and jugglers and balloon animals. He also still didn't understand why his own birthday didn't happen every week, and it had been a dark, dark day in the Foster house when Ethan finally sat him down with a calendar and made him count the months until October.

He still didn't quite grasp the concept of months, but he definitely understood *not for a long time*. Of course, that only meant that he now asked about his birthday every *other* week.

"No, sweetie. It will probably be the middle of August. But that's good, because that gives the baby time to go shopping for your birthday present."

"I'm gonna be *this* many!" Mason suddenly yelled out, holding up three pudgy little fingers, the topic of newborn siblings quickly forgotten.

"That's right, buddy," Ethan chuckled, glancing at him in the rearview mirror. As he turned off the highway onto the long drive that led to his family's house, he was suddenly struck with a familiar ache in his chest and a lump in his throat. It happened more and more lately, usually when he was playing with Mason or watching him do little mundane things with Lily, when he would be absolutely blindsided with emotion. It was almost a panicky feeling, as if his mind just couldn't wrap itself around the fact that he was sublimely happy for the first time in his life.

Ethan had thought that love and happiness weren't in the cards for him, that he was destined to be an outsider…an observer. If anyone had told him six years ago that he would be married with one child and another on the way, he would have laughed in their face and said that he didn't believe in happy endings. But now, looking between his son and wife and the growing lump in her belly, he had a *reason* to believe…and sometimes it simply scared the shit out of him. They were his entire world, and he often found himself getting choked up at the thought of losing them.

Noticing the tight set of her husband's jaw, Lily reached over and grabbed his hand, smiling sweetly when he looked at her. She knew. Somehow, Lily always knew when he was feeling overwhelmed. With a slight squeeze of his fingers and the stroke of her thumb across his knuckles, she was able to tell him with no words *exactly* what he needed to hear.

We love you, too. We'll always love you…and we aren't going anywhere.

And that was all it took. He felt the heaviness lift from his chest, replaced by a feeling of peace. Pulling her hand up to his mouth, he leaned over and quickly kissed the back of her fingers in a silent thank-you.

The heat generated in the long look they shared had Ethan stepping on the accelerator, desperate to get on with their day.

They pulled into the drive to find Barbara waiting at the front door, and made quick work of dropping off Mason for the day. They begged her not to let him eat *all* the cookies again, and promised to be back before his bedtime to pick him up.

"Don't rush," his mother smiled. "He can always lie down in the spare room." Ethan couldn't resist rolling his eyes; the "spare room" Barbara was talking about was an enormous suite that she had remodeled last year, knocking down a wall and making two rooms into one gigantic play land for her three grandchildren. They had all tried to explain to her that such a large room wasn't necessary since they were rarely all together at the same time except for the holidays, but her mind had been made up.

"Thanks again, Mom," Ethan smiled, leaning down to give her a quick peck on the cheek.

"Nothing to thank me for, darling. I love having him here." She and Mason stood on the top step and waved good-bye as Ethan and Lily drove away, watching in the mirrors as they became two little dots in the background.

When they were officially on their own, Ethan smirked at Lily in the way that he knew made her weak in the knees. "You're mine now.

For the next eight hours at least, you're all mine. Are you sure you're up to the challenge?"

Lily took a deep breath to settle the butterflies in her stomach before she arched an eyebrow at him. "I think I can handle anything you give me," she teased playfully.

"Ooh, you better watch that sassy tone, young lady, or else I'll give you something to *handle* right now."

She sighed in mock boredom. "Just keep your lame comments to yourself and drive the car. I don't know how I let you talk me into *this* again."

"I don't exactly remember twisting your arm. I think you like it. Matter of fact, I think just the thought of it turns you on...almost as much as it turns *me* on."

Lily smiled wickedly and leaned over the console, biting his earlobe quickly. "You *know* it turns me on."

"Good," he said abruptly, stomping on the gas and steering the car in a direction so familiar he could drive it with his eyes closed. He glanced down at her swollen belly and felt the tightness beginning in his chest again. "Because I really need this today."

Her soft voice whispered against his cheek, her gentle breath fanning over his skin. "Me, too."

An hour later, Lily was sprawled out naked along a chaise lounge in their old apartment.

Sexy music filled the room, and the only words spoken were Ethan's gruff commands: "Yeah baby...just like that. Arch your back for me a little...fuck *yes*, that's hot."

Lily was getting into it herself, her breath coming in shorter pants with each new instruction he gave her. She found it incredibly erotic when he was so carried away and intense, but she also found it terribly frustrating.

He hadn't laid one finger on her yet.

"Stay right there—I'm just going to adjust the lighting a bit more." She held her position and watched him as he walked away from his easel to a lamp that was positioned at the foot of the chaise. While he tilted and shifted the shade to cast just the right angle of lighting on her skin, Lily couldn't resist drinking him in with her eyes.

He had discarded his shirt quickly, not wanting any more paint stains than necessary and enjoying the freedom of movement it gave him. His jeans were slung low on his hips, so low that she could see he had gone without underwear. Whether it had been laziness on his part or a conscious decision to slowly drive her insane with lust was yet to be seen; but if she had to guess, she would always err on the side of lust when Ethan was concerned.

As her eyes traveled back up his beautiful torso, stopping briefly on the flat copper nipples and light dusting of sandy hair that made her mouth water, her gaze finally met his…and he threw her another smirk and a wink.

Oh, yes—it was all intentional. He knew exactly what he was doing to her.

Picking up his brush again, Ethan did his best to ignore his growing arousal and focus on Lily's. He didn't simply want to pant her nude; he had done that plenty of times. He had also painted her pregnant many times before with Mason; his *Mother & Child* series had sold out in record time. But those had all been more heartfelt works; they were filled with his excitement at becoming a father and the beauty of how sacred he'd found her pregnancy to be.

Her clothes had stayed on for those.

This painting, though…this was for him. Through the years, he periodically did pieces for his private collection, all starring Lily, all meant for their eyes only. Many of them were painted from his vivid memories, but on a few special occasions she had sat for him. This was just such an occasion, and Ethan had big plans for this piece.

Now, rather than focusing on the ethereal beauty of her pregnancy, he wanted to tap into the primal, wanton sexiness of it. He made no secret of the fact that he somehow found her even *more* irresistible when she was carrying his child, and it had only gotten worse the second time around. With Mason, they had both been so nervous at first that he was almost afraid to touch her, not wanting to cause any harm. That had lasted until her hormones kicked into overdrive, leaving them both exhausted almost every night until right up to her ninth month. Now that Lily was pregnant for the second time, none of the uneasiness was there. They had already been through it and knew what to expect, so this time had been a wild ride from the beginning.

And now, Ethan knew exactly what he was doing. He had denied Lily sex when they first arrived at the apartment, stating that he needed to get straight to work and "perhaps they might find time later." He was walking around in nothing but his jeans—a quick way to stoke the fires in his wife; she had told him repeatedly how much she went crazy for his bare chest. He wanted to get her good and worked up, hoping to capture the erotic vision that haunted him every night in his bed: his gorgeous wife, full with his child, a look of pure need in her eyes. That was the epitome of sexiness to him. Lily became lust personified…his own personal sex goddess.

Ethan swept his brush across the canvas, filling in the larger areas of color before starting in on the finer details. The more vigorously he worked, the more entranced he became. After another hour, his body was covered in various streaks of color. There were even patches in his hair from whenever he would absentmindedly shove his fingers through his wild locks.

He kept throwing out commands and encouraging words, wanting to make Lily comfortable, but also hoping to coax out her darker side. When he noticed her breathing becoming choppy, he knew he was close.

"*Ethan*," she whined, "when will we take a break?"

"You just went to the bathroom less than five minutes ago."

"Not that kind of a break. When will *we* take a break?" She jutted her lower lip out in an exaggerated pout, making it very hard for him to concentrate. She was testing his willpower, and every ounce of him wanted to go to her. He was sorely tempted to stop for a half hour and relieve some tension, but he needed to capture her hunger, not her gloating satisfaction.

"Soon, baby. I promise. I have enough done that I'll be able to finish most of this on my own later, but there are a few more details that I really need to get while you're here like this. Fuck...you look incredible."

"Incredible...or *edible*?" she teased, licking her lips suggestively.

"Both," he gritted through his teeth, her words making him instantly harder with the images they evoked of him kneeling before her and feasting on her body. He shook his head quickly, trying to clear it so that he could focus. "Now stop talking. I'm doing your mouth."

"Mmm...I know another way you could do my mouth," she purred.

"Dammit, Lily!" he scolded, reaching down to adjust his now painful erection. Her eyes followed his hand to the prominent bulge she could see from across the room and her throat went dry. She whimpered loudly, and the sound made him squeeze himself more firmly through his jeans. In that moment, he finally saw the changes in her appearance he had been waiting for. He watched as her nipples puckered up tightly, rising and falling with her quickening breaths. When he looked into her eyes, he saw that they were nearly black, completely dilated with lust.

"Oh God...don't fucking move," he growled, dipping his brush quickly back on the palette to collect more black paint, wanting to catch her eyes in that exact state of arousal.

"You're doing my eyes now, aren't you?" She could tell by the way he barely broke eye contact, only casting quick glances at the canvas as his brush moved over it.

He didn't speak; he merely grunted with a slight nod. He had become completely consumed by her...and Lily understood the feeling. Keeping her eyes locked with his, she slowly moved one of her hands from its designated position, sliding it over one of her swollen breasts carefully to softly pinch her nipple. They had become quite tender recently, almost bordering on painful, but she found that it was a good kind of pain if she didn't linger too long.

She slid her hand even farther down, over her rounded stomach and her little protruding belly button, until she was lightly cupping her dripping sex. Ethan's eyes had never left hers, but she knew he could tell what she was doing when a soft groan passed his lips.

"*Fuck!*" Lily gasped as she slipped two fingers between her slick folds. "I'm so wet for you..." It came out in a loud moan that might have embarrassed her any other time, but she didn't care how desperate she sounded. She *was* desperate—desperate for her husband, who had yet to look away from either her eyes or the canvas. She could, however, see distinct beads of sweat breaking out on Ethan's forehead as he worked, so she knew he was starting to crack.

From that point on, it was a race to see who would finish first. Lily started touching herself in earnest, moaning and writhing, using every tool in her arsenal to break him down and make him touch her. Ethan, on the other hand, started painting frantically, trying to capture the most important details of the moment before they were lost forever. It was becoming increasingly difficult to resist her efforts, though, and he knew damn well that if she climaxed before he was finished, he would *never* finish.

He locked his eyes with hers and did everything in his power to block out what she was doing, but it was impossible. He could see her hand moving in his peripheral vision, he could hear her panting moans, and before long he could hear the wet sucking noises as her fingers moved inside her body at an increasing speed. She never looked away from him, though, and her eyes had become liquid fire. It was the most intense look they had ever shared, and it made Ethan want to cry out in agony.

Before long, her noises were almost drowned out by the roaring of blood in his ears. It pounded to the same rhythm of the pulsing in his dick, which hurt so badly that he whimpered. When Ethan saw her body beginning to tremble, he didn't know if he would make it. He was so fucking close to finishing, but apparently so was she. With one hand still rapidly painting, he used his other to pop open the buttons on his jeans without even looking, gripping himself roughly to relieve some of the pressure.

Lily tried to maintain their eye contact, but she couldn't stop herself from sneaking glances at his fist as it worked his engorged flesh. It was hypnotic, watching the way his broad tip turned almost purple on the upstroke, and the grunts and growls coming from him were driving her to the brink of insanity.

It was suddenly too much for her. She needed him too badly, and seeing him like that was all it took to hurtle her over the edge. She began trembling violently, throwing her head back and closing her eyes to the ecstasy as a litany of curses and moans broke through her lips. Somewhere in the distance she heard a loud growl, followed by thunderous footsteps.

When Lily opened her eyes seconds later, Ethan was towering over her at her side. The ravenous look on his face as he stared down at her was almost scary in its intensity, but it only turned her on more. He was a man possessed. She noticed that he had kicked his jeans off completely, and his cock stood straight up, almost curving back toward his stomach.

With a deep groan, Lily reached out and grabbed his hips, pulling him closer to her mouth. She looked up at him one last time before gripping his erection firmly by the base and swirling her tongue around the tip, sliding her lips over him quickly and sucking him to the back of her throat. Ethan snarled violently, far past words, and thrust his hips forward, pulling back slowly at first only to thrust back in faster the next time. Lily moaned around him as he moved in her mouth, and Ethan reached down and took up where her hand had left off, slipping inside her silken folds to circle her clitoris with two fingers. She moaned again loudly, her body shaking around him, and it became too much. He didn't want to finish in her mouth, and if he didn't stop, that was exactly what was going to happen.

Moving quickly, he knelt at the foot of the chaise, spreading her thighs roughly before burying his face between them. Ethan lapped at her juices, using broad strokes with the flat of his tongue, knowing just how she liked it when they were being fast and dirty. Her cries rang out through the room, heaven to his ears, and in less than a minute he felt her fingers gripping his hair painfully, holding him in place as she ground herself against his hungry mouth.

Knowing that she was seconds away from another powerful orgasm, he leaned back on his knees, quickly positioning himself at her entrance. He knew that he wasn't going to last very long, he was just too fucking excited, but this way he might still be able to feel her coming around him when he was inside her. There was absolutely nothing in the world that felt as good as Lily's pussy when she clamped down on him mid-climax, milking him dry.

He paused for a moment, looking down at his cock against her wet flesh. Gripping himself, he rubbed the swollen tip back and forth against her clit a few times as she lifted her hips, seeking out more pressure. When their eyes met this time over her outstretched body, her gaze was full of such heat that he was afraid he might actually come before ever getting inside her.

"Do you want this?" he grunted, holding himself back with every ounce of his energy. It was her turn to be out of words, driven half-insane with need; the only thing she could do was nod vigorously. Ethan let himself go long enough to grab her ankles and lift them up to rest on his shoulders before guiding his cock to her entrance once again, sliding all the way to the hilt in one thrust.

"*Fuck!*" he snarled through clenched teeth, holding still for a moment, willing his body to calm down.

"Oh *God*, Ethan…don't stop now!" Lily cried out in frustration.

"I'm not stopping," he panted. "I'm just…getting my bearings here."

"Your *bearings*? Let me help you out. You're balls deep inside me. Now get moving!"

"Yes, dear," he smirked, trying not to laugh. Lily didn't seem to suffer too many mood swings, except when she was denied sex. There had been numerous occasions lately when he had needed to fast-track Mason's bedtime stories and resort to bribery with Happy Meals to get him to go to sleep on time and keep Lily from getting grouchy.

Luckily her little diversion had pulled Ethan back from the edge and he was ready to continue. He held onto her shins and watched as he slowly moved inside her. He could see her juices coating him, making his erection glisten as he slid in and out of her welcoming heat. The feeling was indescribably amazing, and watching as it happened only intensified it that much more.

"So…fucking…beautiful," he panted, thrusting his hips faster.

Lily was thinking the exact same thing, but she was staring up at her glorious husband. He looked powerful, the muscles shifting under his skin as he flexed his hips, pounding into her more roughly. His masculine beauty never failed to take her breath away, and he was never more divine than when he was inside her.

"Touch yourself for me, baby," he begged. "I'm so close. I want to watch you." She complied immediately, slipping her fingers between her folds to rub at her tightened bundle of nerves.

"Oh, *God*," she moaned, already feeling the tremors beginning in her thighs. He changed his angle slightly, grinding into her as he moved. "Oh Ethan…*yes!*" Her inner walls began to grip him tightly, and they both came unglued.

"*Fuck!*" he cried out, throwing his head back as he rode out his release, exploding violently inside her with thick spurts of fluid. As they both came down from their high, Ethan slowly set her legs on the chaise and slid in behind her, pulling her back to rest against his chest.

"That was…"

"*Amazing*," Lily finished.

"Exactly," he sighed, kissing the top of her head tenderly. He slid his hand around her waist, holding her baby bump possessively. "God, I love you. I just don't know what I would do without you."

Lily covered his hand with her own, their fingers entwined together over their unborn child. "You'll never have to find out."

At that moment, the baby chose to give a strong kick right underneath their hands. "Well," Ethan laughed, "it looks as if someone agrees with you."

"I think so. Unless someone is feeling left out."

Ethan slid out from behind her quickly, running across the room to the small worktable set up beside his easel. When he grabbed his palette and brush, Lily groaned.

"You're not already painting again, are you? Can't we have even five minutes to hold each other?"

"No, I'm not." He came forward again, kneeling down in front of her.

"Then what are you doing with that?"

"Well, just in case you're right, and someone *is* feeling left out, I want to take care of that right now." He dragged his brush through the small pile of soft blue that he had mixed to match the shade of the chaise and brought it to her stomach, allowing the bristles to glide smoothly over the rounded flesh. "There!" he smiled, setting down his palette and leaning back to appreciate his handiwork.

Lily looked down to see his elegant script stretched across her skin: *Layne.*

Ethan leaned over her belly and kissed it softly. "I can't wait to meet you, baby boy." He laid his head down and looked up at his wife. "Do you think he'll like me?"

"Are you kidding me?" Lily laughed, running her fingers through his hair. "Children of all ages adore you. What makes you think he will be any different?"

"Because I already adore him and he isn't even born yet. How will our kids ever respect me when I'm wrapped around their fingers?"

"Maybe you should ask Richard how he handled it with you three. Or my dad. I'm pretty sure they will all tell you they felt the same way. You've done pretty well so far."

Ethan considered this quietly while Lily continued to stroke his hair. After a few minutes he sighed loudly. "Thank you for today, baby."

"Which one of us are you talking to?"

"Both of you." He kissed her stomach again before standing up and holding out his hand to her. "Now let's get you cleaned up so we can go pick up our son."

"All right, but only if you join me in the shower…and promise to scrub my back."

"Why Mrs. Foster—are you trying to seduce me?"

Lily looked at him with a wicked smile. "Always."

Over an hour later, after showering for *much* longer than they had intended, Ethan and Lily were finally ready to leave. On their way out the door, Lily caught sight of something in the corner of her eye, making her stop abruptly in her tracks.

"What's wrong?" Ethan asked, following her gaze across the room, trying to figure out what she was looking at.

"I totally forgot about the painting," she whispered, her eyes glued to the back of the canvas sitting on the easel across the room. Suddenly feeling ashamed that she had stopped him from doing the only thing he had begged to do that day, Lily couldn't help but apologize. "I'm so sorry, baby."

"What the hell for?" he asked, looking at her as if she had just sprouted a second head.

"For being selfish and keeping you from something that you have wanted to do for months. No matter how badly I wanted you today, I can have you any time. We could have been together later tonight, or after you were finished."

"Are you seriously apologizing for the insanely hot afternoon we just had?"

"Well…yeah, I guess. Between my job and your mother's, it's not so easy to set up a good time for her to take Mason all day so that I can pose for you. Now you didn't finish and it's all my fault."

"What, are you having seducer's guilt or something?" he teased.

"Yeah," she pouted, causing Ethan to laugh loudly before wrapping her in his arms for a tight hug.

"Come here," he said, pulling her across the room. When they were standing in front of the canvas, he forced her to turn and look at it. "There. Does that look like I didn't finish?

"Oh my God!" she gasped loudly.

Ethan continued talking as he looked at it, not realizing that Lily had gone completely still next to him. "I might tweak some of the shading tomorrow, but overall, I'd say I made pretty good time. What do you think?" When she failed to answer him, he finally turned toward her. "Hello? Earth to Lily!" He waved his hand in front of her face, wondering why she looked so shocked.

"Is that…is that supposed to be *me*?" she whispered, slowly holding out her hand to point at the stranger on the canvas.

"Of course it is."

"But it doesn't look anything like me."

"I beg your pardon?" he said, pretending to be insulted. "How does that not look like you?"

"I mean, it *resembles* me, but I don't normally look so…so lustful… and seductive…and voluptuous."

"Yes you do."

"No I don't! I'm as big as a house right now and about as sensual as a buffalo!"

"Look at me," he commanded, grabbing her chin firmly, forcing her eyes up to his. His gaze was hard and serious, and when he finally spoke, his tone left no room for argument. "First of all, I know you feel awkward and enormous right now, but I have never once lied to you when I say that I find you *ungodly* sexy like this. I always do, every single day. But this woman here," he gestured to the painting, "she fucking *haunts* me. This is the woman I see whenever you let go and decide that you need me no matter where we are or what we're doing. I didn't make this up, Lily; that's *your* face. That is the exact expression you make when you surrender to your need."

"Really?"

"Why the hell do you think I was so desperate to keep painting earlier? Any other time, I would have jumped you in a second and gone back to painting later, but that specific look was what I was trying to capture today." He broke into a smile before continuing. "I'm actually really proud that I lasted as long as I did. That look is fucking lethal." He leaned down and kissed her softly, flicking her lips with the tip of his tongue before pulling away, knowing that if he allowed it to grow more heated they would never leave. "Now, let's go pick up Mason," he smiled.

"Okay," she mumbled, feeling dazed and lightheaded by his teasing kisses. They walked back to the door, their locked hands swaying between them. "So what are you going to call this one?" she asked when she finally had her wits about her.

"Oh, I dunno," he sighed. "It's always best to keep the title simple and true. I was thinking something along the lines of *Portrait of a Sex Goddess*."

"Well that's certainly…subtle."

"That's me, baby. I'm the king of subtle." He winked at her and swatted her backside playfully as they entered the hall, pulling the door closed behind them as they left, heading out into the night to pick up a sleeping boy with a belly full of cookies.

About the Author

Amanda Black was born and raised in the Midwest, where she still lives with her husband and spoiled-rotten dogs. She earned a bachelor's degree in Studio Art before deciding that she actually needed to pay some bills, which is when she took a position as an ophthalmic technician.

For the past few years she's been a closet romance writer in her spare time and would love nothing more than to make it a full-time career. When she's not writing her next steamy love scene, her interests include reading, sketching, and annihilating her friends and family in movie trivia.

Visit Amanda on her website,
amandablackauthor.blogspot.com

CPSIA information can be obtained
at www.ICGtesting.com
Printed in the USA
LVHW092246210420
654253LV00001B/1